JUDGE FEAR'S BIG DAY OUT

AND OTHER STORIES

An Abaddon Books™ Publication
www.abaddonbooks.com
abaddon@rebellion.co.uk

This anthology first published
in 2020 by Abaddon Books™,
Rebellion Intellectual Property Limited,
Riverside House, Osney Mead,
Oxford, OX2 0ES, UK.

10 9 8 7 6 5 4 3 2 1

Creative Director and CEO: Jason Kingsley
Chief Technical Officer: Chris Kingsley
Head of Books and Comics Publishing: Beth Lewis
Editors: David Thomas Moore,
Michael Rowley and Kate Coe
Cover Art: Greg Staples
Design: Sam Gretton, Oz Osborne
and Gemma Sheldrake
Marketing and PR: Hanna Waigh

Judge Dredd created by John Wagner and Carlos Ezquerra.

ISBN: 978-1-78108-853-1

Printed in Denmark

JUDGE FEAR'S BIG DAY OUT

AND OTHER STORIES

EDITED BY MICHAEL CARROLL

ABADDON
BOOKS

WWW.ABADDONBOOKS.COM

CONTENTS

INTRODUCTION

MICHAEL CARROLL

AT A CONVENTION in Chicago in 2013 I was helping out at the *2000 AD* booth in the dealers' room when a youngish potential customer stopped to examine our wares. "Oh," she said. "There are Judge Dredd *comics* now!"

A brief chat extracted the fact that she had been unaware of the then-recent Karl Urban movie, and only knew the character from the 1995 Sylvester Stallone adaptation, which she described as, "Mostly all right, mostly." She liked the bits with the robot.

Yes, the spectre of that Stallone movie still lingers, even though there are now Dredd fans whose *parents* were too young to watch it in the cinema.

The potential customer left the booth that day with no graphic novels (I did my best!) but she did have a much greater understanding of the character. She knew that, indeed, there *are* comics featuring Judge Dredd. And t-shirts and board games and video games and toys (I mean, collectibles).

And ever since "Tales of Dwedd" in the 1980 edition of the *2000 AD Annual*, the character has appeared in prose form, too.

From a story-telling viewpoint, comics and prose are very different. Comics are almost exclusively a third-person medium: even if the tale follows one character throughout, and it's peppered with narrative captions in that character's voice (or, rarely used these days, thought balloons), we're still looking at them on the page. No one wants to read a Judge Dredd story where we're looking out through his bionic eyes and past his visor and seeing only what he sees. Not least because unless he's regularly passing in front of mirrors or walking past the TV store *à la* the opening of the TV series *Peep Show*, Dredd wouldn't appear on the page.

With a prose tale we can easily carry the reader around inside Dredd's head, or any other characters', seeing what they see and reading their thoughts. You'll encounter some of that in the stories in this anthology, almost all of them culled from the pages of the monthly *Judge Dredd Megazine* (launched in 1990 and still going strong!).

Not only does the prose format allow for deeper tales, it's flexible enough for *stranger* stories, too, some of which just wouldn't work as a comic-strip. We've got the lot here, folks. This collection of adventures—crafted by established Dredd writers as well as newcomers—delivers a very generous portion of your recommended daily allowance of science fiction, horror, and fantasy, with plenty of action, a considerable amount of gore, some very dark humour, a good bucketful of pathos, and—at times—just the slightest touch of normality. We've got one-offs, sequels to established Dredd tales, competition winners, one that was commissioned for a limited-edition anthology and thus has almost never been seen before, and even a couple that are magically squeezed right into the *middle* of established stories.

That very flexibility of the short-story format means that this is a mixed bag, of course. Not every one of these tales is going to be regarded as a stone-cold classic. But they are all memorable, and some are downright unforgettable. The sort of story that gets its teeth into you and just won't let go. Ever. (I'm looking at *you*, Alan Grant, and your stories "The Pack" and "Paranoia." Well, I say "stories," but a more accurate description would be "bloody nightmare fuel!")

So dip in at random, or read them in order if you're the law-abiding type and prefer things neat and tidy, but do be sure to consume them all. Trust me, these stories will take you to places you didn't know you wanted to go. And a few places you very much did know you *didn't* want to go... Enjoy the ride!

Michael Carroll
Dublin, August 2019

A NATIVITY TALE

GORDON RENNIE

'HEADS UP, MEGA-CITY! *Christmas Eve in the Big Meg, and not a creature was stirring, not even a mouse. Well, one mouse, and maybe the estimated 80 to 120 million of you who are out on the skeds and megways tonight. So, whether you're visiting friends and family, delivering presents to loved ones, going home for the holidays or just trying to get the hell away from all this Christmas stomm, this is Drivetime Sam giving you the lowdown and high-five on all the latest travel news...*

'Item! Our local, friendly Justice Department informs us that there's a heavy-duty rad-storm blowing out of the Cursed Earth. If you're travelling in any sectors along the northern circuit of the West Wall, and especially along the Link, then check your vehicle's rad-seals are intact and keep your dashboard Geiger counters on active. Our friendly Justice Department advises that citizens in those sectors affected by the storm should only travel if

their journeys are strictly necessary—but, hey, this is the Big Meg, and since when the hell have we ever paid any attention to what the Judges say?

'Item! Talking of Christmas Eve, and creatures stirring, those helpful folks at Justice Central have also seen fit to inform us that an Iso-Block transport went down this evening in the rad-ruins between Sector 502 and real, proper Big Meg civilisation. Catch units are in operation, but many hardened and dangerous perps remain unaccounted for. Drivers travelling to and from the Pit are warned not to pick up any suspicious hitch-hikers en route—although Drivetime Sam says that, frankly, if you're dumb enough to stop to pick up any hitch-hikers on the Link then, buddy, you deserve everything you're gonna get. So keep those unlicensed handguns handy in the glove compartment, right where you can reach 'em in a hurry, Pit-cits. Remember, it may be the season of peace and goodwill to all men, but we're still all living in Mega-City One, so take Drivetime Sam's self-defence advice and aim high, keep a steady grip and group your shots tightly in the target's central body mass.

'Item! This one just for our friends living in Sectors 501 to 505. Lethal rad-storms? Dangerous escaped perps on the loose? A crime-rate which makes Cuidad Barranquilla sound like a easy-going vacation destination? What are you, INSANE? Move out of the Pit, people! Move back to the rest of the Big Meg, and find out what real, proper 22nd century civilisation is supposed to be all about! Borrow some money from rich relatives, commit armed robbery... do ANYTHING to get the hell out of that craphole!

'This is Drivetime Sam, giving you the lowdown and the high-five on everything that's happening travel-wise tonight in the Big M, with maybe some biting social commentary thrown in for free. And now here's a few words from the schmucks dumb enough to actually sponsor this show...'

'SWITCH IT OFF, honey,' groaned Therese from the cramped back seat of the stalled car. 'I hate that creep.'

She was sprawled on the back seat of the small vehicle. The Christmas presents they'd put back there—not much, really, but all they could afford under the circumstances—had been unceremoniously dumped out onto the road outside. Therese groaned in pain again, feeling the sudden shock of the contractions, and tried to make herself more comfortable. It wasn't easy. Nine months ago, she had thought of herself as being on the right side of slim; now, when she looked in a mirror, all she saw staring back at her was the twin sister of Two-Ton Tony Tubbs.

'Everyone hates him, honey, that's why everyone listens to him,' answered her husband Howie, leaning in to switch off the radio. He was standing at the open door on the driver's side, wrapped in a cheap anti-rad coverall and staring out disconsolately into the swirling grey murk of the rad-storm.

The DJ's words had stung them both, him especially. He was the husband, so it was his fault that all they could afford when they got married was some scuzzy apartment in the Pit. They'd moved there in the aftermath of Chief

Judge Hershey's big Pit reclamation project—'good opportunities for good citizens', the campaign publicity had promised—but, of course, it had never quite worked out that way. The work opportunities had dried up, just as they had started putting some serious bedtime effort into the idea of starting a family.

Which was why they were out here on Christmas Eve, stranded out on the Link in the middle of a rad-storm. Therese's parents lived in Sector 178, on the right side of the nuked-out Apocalypse War ruins which separated the Pit from the rest of the city. The baby wasn't due for a couple of weeks, and they were going to stay at her parents' apartment until then. It went unsaid that it would be better if Therese had the baby in Sector 178, rather than one of the run-down, dismal places which passed for a med-unit in the Pit. Howie, swallowing his pride, just wanting the best for his unborn child, took his relatives' charity, knowing that everything else tonight was still his fault.

His fault that they couldn't afford the strat-bat fare, especially with the extra seasonal hike the airlines added on to the price at this time of year...

His fault that all they could afford was a second-hand Mavverland economy roadster, which was probably past its best back when all this was still a real part of Mega City instead of nuked-out rad-ruins...

His fault that it had broken down here, in the most desolate part of the most dangerous megway in the city, on a night when they hadn't seen any other passing traffic in more than an hour...

His fault that his cheap, crappy cell-com couldn't pick up a signal out here. Yeah, Drivetime Sam was coming in loud and clear through the rad-interference, but could they get a call through to the Justice Department rescue line?

With a curse, he threw the cell-com into the swirling murk of the rad-storm, the sheets of falling, flaky ash material quickly swallowing up the useless device, smothering the sound of its impact on the grey rockcrete surface of the road.

A groan of pain from the back seat of the vehicle behind him reminded him sickly of the biggest problem of all.

Yeah, and breaking down on the Link on Christmas Eve, with your pregnant wife going into early labour—whose fault was that? And who was going to pay the price for it?

'Don't worry, honey. Someone will come along soon, I just know they will,' he called out to the figure in the back of the car, trying to sound a lot more confident than he actually felt. 'They'll stop and give us a ride, and maybe we'll be able to call for a med-wagon too.'

He turned back to the empty road ahead of him. The blank, grey face of the storm stared back at him, mocking his hopeful lies. Maybe if he started walking he would come to one of those Justice Department emergency contact vid-phone booths which were dotted all along the Link. Maybe—

'Lights, honey! I can see headlights!'

The shout escaped from his lips before he had even properly registered the flickering glimmer of powerful high-beams coming towards them from out of the churning gloom, and then he was running towards them, shouting and waving his hands, slipping on the powdery blanket of fallen ash and falling clumsily to the ground, still shouting and waving.

Blinding light washed over him. He heard the sound of a powerful engine, revving down to a slow, growling idleness. Booted footsteps, heavy and serious, crunched towards him across the ash surface. He looked up, squinting, and saw a tall silhouette padded out with bulky but familiar armour.

'What's the problem, citizen?'

That voice. Howie had heard it maybe a thousand times since he had been a juve, on the vid-news and Justice Department info-casts. Always gruff, always terse, and with an edge of barely-restrained impatience. Never saying much, but always speaking volumes about the power and natural authority behind it. Usually it scared him, like maybe it was supposed to, but it was strangely reassuring too.

The Apocalypse War. Necropolis. Judgement Day. The Second Robot War. Howie remembered them all, and their aftermaths, and he remembered that the owner of that voice had always been there to set things right again, to let people know that, no matter how bad things seemed, they were about to get better again.

'It's my wife, Judge Dredd,' he managed to stammer out, pointing back towards the car. 'She's going to have a baby!'

* * *

'So whatya think?' growled Vocko, the weird modulation of his throat implant giving his voice that distinctive feral buzz. A Lawgiver's bullet had torn out his larynx years ago. The implant the Med-Judges had given him was programmed to speak something that pretty much resembled a normal human voice. Vocko had had other ideas about that—and had made a few alterations, preferring the menacing electronic growl this gave him instead.

Hakka thought that Vocko was nuts, of course, but was careful to keep that opinion to himself. He had seen what Vocko had done to that chump back in the cubes who had nicknamed Vocko 'Davrax', after that robo-guy in that dumb juve vid-show.

Hakka lowered the binoculars, which were still stained with the blood of the Judge-warden he had taken them from. The same warden's scattergun was slung over his shoulder. Ditto with the rad-cloak which hung from his shoulders and the pouch belt buckled round his waist.

'Still can't see much through this sludge, even with these things, but I see lights, and I see transport, so that means a way outta here, and more rad-pills.'

He looked at the others. Vocko growled in agreement. Pushkin—who, absolutely and without question, really was completely nuts—giggled and licked the dried blood off the home-made shiv he had already fashioned for himself. They were stone lifers, like Hakka himself. Elpees, as they called them in cube-ling. Lifelong Perpetrators; write-off cases whom the Judges were quite happy to lock up and forget about.

Hakka spared a contemptuous glance towards the other perps, shivering and frightened, huddling in the ruins below his vantage point. They were cube-fodder, the kind of raw meat the city's justice system chewed up and spat out again without a moment's thought. They had their place in the great scheme of things—Hakka had been happy to let enough of them buy the farm instead of him, in the massed scramble for escape after the transport they were all on had crash-landed here in the rad-ruins... and Hakka would be happy enough to let them do the same again. They stared back at him, frightened and confused. Most of them were armed with makeshift weapons from the crash site or scavenged from somewhere amongst the rubble during their journey towards the Link. A couple of them shivered and mumbled incoherently to themselves, showing the first signs of rad-sickness. Hakka silently earmarked these chumps as cannon-fodder, to be happily expended in the opening rush attack on the vehicles down there.

They needed more rad-protection, all of them, if they were going to make it out of these ruins. Hakka didn't know what kind of stuff the chumps down there on the megway might have, but he doubted there would be enough to go around amongst him and his merry band, so some natural wastage was pretty much in everyone's interests then, wasn't it?

DREDD TOOK IN the situation in the roadster's rear compartment with a single glance. His voice-activated helmet mike crackled into life.

'Control—Dredd. Med-wagon pick-up required urgently, my locale on the Link, 60 kilometres north of Checkpoint Chico.'

There was a pause of several seconds, and Howie wondered if even the Justice Department's more powerful radios could penetrate through the static veil of the rad-storm. Then came the reply, faint but audible.

'No can do, Dredd. Busy night for med-emergencies, what with the storm and all the usual Christmas Eve mayhem. Estimate we can't get anything out to you in anything less than 90 minutes. That going to be a problem?'

Dredd paused for a moment, thinking. Ninety minutes wasn't going to cut it in time. He could maybe take the woman on the back of his Lawmaster, getting her to the med-unit at Chico—but that would mean exposing her to the rad-fall, and she was better protected right where she was in the back of the vehicle. It would also mean leaving the husband here on his own. On a night like this, that was maybe as good as a death sentence.

Quickly, he came to the only logical decision. 'Control, find Med-Judge Kaminski, and patch me through to her straight away. She's at Central Med 18. Her civilian medicine speciality is obstetrics.'

'Obstetrics?' said the voice on the radio, unable to disguise its disbelief. 'You mean *childbirth*, Dredd?'

'Copy, Control. Tell her I need expert radio-assist on how to deliver a baby.'

*　　*　　*

HAKKA CREPT FORWARD through the slow, steady rain of falling ash, pausing once or twice to check the scene ahead with his binoculars. They were a lot closer now, moving down through the rubble, climbing up the side of a support stanchion and up onto the megway itself, and he could see the details of the scene with much greater clarity.

One vehicle, some kind of beaten up old roadster, maybe crashed or stalled, with a Lawmaster nearby.

That meant a Judge. Some of the cube-fodder weren't too happy about going up against a Judge, seeing as how they were supposed to be on the run from the Judges, but that was just too bad. Hakka and Vocko and Pushkin, and especially Pushkin's ability with that shiv of his, had persuaded them otherwise, though. And if that meant that they were already one piece of cube-fodder less than they had been, well, that was just too bad too, wasn't it?

Hakka wasn't afraid of street Judges. He'd gone up against them before, and won, and he had the blood of two Judges—even if they were just the dumber Judge Warden type—on his hands already tonight. So he didn't figure that one lone Judge, on his own and without backup, was going to give them too much of a problem. Judges had rad-pills, lots of 'em, especially the ones who did patrol circuits on the Link, and that was all Hakka was really interested in.

And besides, he reminded himself with a grin, it's not like he'd be putting himself directly into the firing line anyway, not when he had all the rest of the cube-fodder to use up.

Beside him, Pushkin giggled to himself, his keen madman's eyes staring into the gloom ahead, his gaze fixed on the stalled roadster. They were close enough to hear noises now. Cries of pain, it sounded like. Probably someone injured in the crash, Hakka figured, which meant one less chump to worry about, and suited Hakka just fine.

It sounded like a woman, though, and that was enough to get Pushkin all hot and excited. Hakka knew what Pushkin had done to earn that life sentence. Hakka could never have been described as squeamish—his Justice Department perp sheet was one long catalogue of brutality and atrocity—but that kind of stuff didn't float his boat. Pushkin had his uses, as the cut-up, bloodied heap cooling under a blanket of rad-ash in the ruins behind them could testify, but if he turned into too much of a liability then Hakka wasn't afraid to do what was necessary, not when he had a fully loaded scatter gun in his hands.

Pushkin wouldn't be the first unreliable partner Hakka had had to divest himself of, and Hakka doubted he would be the last.

Silently, stealthily, the group crept forward towards the vehicle and the sounds emanating from it.

DREDD HAD ALMOST single-handedly won dozens of block wars. He'd faced the Dark Judges, and won. He'd been shot, stabbed, blown up, beaten up, crucified and tortured. He'd rather be doing any of those things again, all of them together—a dozen times over, maybe—than what he was doing now.

'Dilation's about ten centimetres, I guess,' he dutifully reported to the voice on the other end of the radio link.

'Okay,' answered the calm, reassuring voice of Med-Judge Kaminski. 'That's about right. Look down—can you see the baby's head yet? Maybe just the start of the crown?'

'Check.' Dredd's reply, terse, and giving absolutely nothing away.

'Okay, we're ready to deliver a baby now,' said the voice on his helmet radio. 'Don't worry, Dredd, you're doing fine. A few words of comfort and reassurance to our patient wouldn't go amiss, though.'

'Try and remain calm, citizen,' Dredd told the sweating, groaning woman. 'Everything's going according to plan. Hopefully we'll be finished up here soon.'

Kaminski, listening on the other end of the radio link mentally sighed to herself. Dredd's bedside manner didn't really have much in the way of the calm and reassurance she'd been looking for, but she guessed that this was going to be the best she was going to get from him.

Also crammed into the rear of the vehicle, crouching at the open door on the other side from Dredd, Howie did what he could to comfort and reassure his wife.

'See? Everything's gonna be okay, honey. You're doing great, and the Judge says it's all gonna be over soon...'

He mopped his wife's face with a piece of damp sterilising gauze. The fresh, cool water from Dredd's canteen supply and the contents of the med-kit carried in his bike's stowage compartment—pain-killers, coagulant spray, sterilising tabs, anti-rad pills and a few simple medical tools—had been a real Grudsend, and might well already have made the difference between someone's life or death tonight. For the first time since the roadster had shuddered to a halt in the middle of the rad-storm, that feeling of sickening dread inside him was starting to go away.

Dredd's next words would quickly bring it all back again.

'You know how to handle a weapon, citizen?'

Howie looked at the lawman in blank incomprehension. 'A little, I guess. I was in my local Citi-Def unit for a couple of months, but it wasn't for me. Why?'

'Good,' said Dredd, not lifting his attention from the delivery process. 'Then I need you to do something important. You've still got the smartkey I gave you to access the bike stowage. Go to the bike, open up the stowage again and get the ammo for the scattergun. Then use the smartkey to unlock the scattergun from its holster. Bring it back here with the ammo and get ready to use them both.'

'Why? What's happening?' Howie almost shouted, panic rising up within him.

Dredd looked up at him, sparing him a glance from the business of the delivery. 'Keep calm, citizen. Panic won't help the situation. You hear that beeping sound?'

Howie paused, listening, and then nodded, dumbly. Now that Dredd mentioned it, there was a faint but constant electronic beeping coming from the Lawmaster, an echo of it sounding quietly over Dredd's helmet radio.

'Bike computer, giving an alert that it's picking up multiple PIDD signals from nearby.' Dredd caught the look of incomprehension on Howie's face. 'PIDDs. Perp ID Devices, transmitter chips hidden inside standard issue iso-cube clothing. We use 'em to track escaped perps. That's what I was doing out here, when I found you. Too much interference from the rad-storm to pick up the signal at anything other than extreme close range.'

Howie was already on his feet and scrambling towards the bike, even before he heard Dredd's warning. 'Better get moving, citizen. They're probably no more than a hundred metres away, and closing on us.'

He was back in moments, desperately trying to remember his Citi-Def training as he fumbled open the scattergun's loading mechanism and locked a full magazine of shells into place. He presented the loaded weapon to Dredd, who just stared back at him.

'Not really what I had in mind, citizen. I'm the only one here with any med training. You're the one who's going to have to do the shooting. Lucky we've got some other extra firepower those creeps might be aware of, though...'

IT WAS HARD to measure distances through the sheets of falling ash, but Hakka figured they were maybe only about 50 metres from the target. Yeah, almost home and dry, he thought, beginning to wonder if it really was going to be as simple as this. An easy fight meant no casualties, and no casualties meant too many live bodies sharing too few rad-pills, so Hakka was just starting to figure out what he was going to do to solve that problem, when the shattering sound of heavy cannon fire ripped through the solitude of the storm, shredding apart the two pieces of the most expendable cube-fodder which he'd placed up ahead on point.

Hakka dived for cover, eating rad-ash, as more shots sprayed out into the darkness. There was a gurgling scream to his right, and the sound of a body hitting the ground. Hakka looked round, seeing Vocko hugging cover nearby. The two of them locked stares, thinking the same thing.

Bike cannons. Judge has got his bike on automatic, letting it stand sentry for him. With its target acquisition systems and IR scanner, the drokking thing would have this whole citybound side of the meg-way scoped out.

A couple of the cube-fodder lucky enough to have guns opened fire on the bike's presumed position, but Hakka knew it was a pretty pointless exercise. Even if they hit the thing—and none of these chumps were exactly expert Mob assassin snipers—those fancy Judge rides were armoured up the wazoo, and all you'd get for your trouble would be to draw the bike's cannon fire back on yourself.

As if to prove Hakka's point, there was another burst of fire, followed by the sound of another falling body. Still, at least it gave Hakka the opportunity he was looking for. 'C'mon, we'll flank 'em,' he ordered, getting to his feet, and signalling for Vocko and Pushkin to follow him as he crouch-ran towards the divider wall between the two different citybound and Pitbound sides of the meg-way.

As he ran and vaulted over the wall, he heard the staccato bracket of more bike cannon fire from behind him. More gunfire and more screams meant more casualties and left-over goodies for the survivors.

And Hakka was nothing else if not a natural born survivor.

HOWIE TRIED DESPERATELY to remember what little Citi-Def training he had actually managed to take onboard. Dredd had warned him that the bike cannons' ammo supply was limited. After that ran out, he would be their next line of defence. The cannons had come to a stuttering half a minute ago. The 30 seconds which had followed had so far been the longest of Howie's life.

Several figures had come running, shrieking and yelling, out of the falling ash. 'Don't be afraid about not getting a clean hit on what you're aiming at,' Dredd had told him. 'It's not called a scattergun for nothing.'

It had been good advice. The weapon's report had been shockingly loud, a roaring boom, designed by the Justice Department's gunsmiths to clear open spaces and quell unruly mobs partly by sheer sonic shock value alone. It had a fearsome kick to it also, and Howie was almost knocked off his feet by the weapon's recoil. He had let rip with most of the mag, just as Dredd had told him to, and, when he looked to see the results, he saw three of the figures lying on the ash-covered surface of the road. One of them was groaning and making feeble movements, futilely trying to get up, but the other two did not look as if they would ever be getting up again.

The other figures were melting away, retreating in panic back into the concealing shelter of the rad-storm grey-out. Howie was just starting to relax, just starting to think that the worst of it was over, when he saw the other three figures off to his right and climbing over the divider between the two roadways.

He raised his scattergun to fire, and saw one of the figures do likewise. Almost stupidly, he noticed that he and the mirror image figure was both carrying the same kind of weapon. The mirror image illusion was shattered when the figure fired first. Howie felt the chill air around him almost sizzle as hot fragments of scattergun shot flew past him, and then he felt a series of lightning-fast blows punch into him, knocking him off his feet.

The next thing he knew he was lying a couple of metres away in the ash. The weapon which he had been holding up to a few seconds ago was a long-forgotten memory. Now he knew three things about scatterguns. They were loud, they were powerful and being shot by one of them didn't hurt as much as you'd expect.

He stared up at the sky. That ash stuff must be falling storm must be falling even heavier now, he thought to himself as delayed shock took effect, because now everything was starting to fade to a grey blur, right there before his eyes.

The last thing he heard before he passed out was the crying of a newborn baby from somewhere close by, but also impossibly far away.

'SOUNDS LIKE YOU'RE almost there, Dredd. Tell her to bear down and give it one last big push.'

'One last push, citizen, then we're all done here.'

Dredd heard the footsteps crunching towards them across the roadway. Three of them, he estimated. They'd be on him in a few seconds. Seconds which he probably didn't have.

The woman screamed, whether from fear or pain, Dredd didn't know. Scattergun fire hit the side of the car. Dredd threw himself forward, using himself as a human shield against the fragments of glass and scattergun shot which flew the air inside the cramped interior of the car.

Protecting the woman. Protecting the tiny, red, squalling thing which lay there on the seat in front of him.

He picked the child up, shielding it with the bulk of his body. It was still attached to its mother by its umbilicus. Dredd was already reaching for his boot holster.

HAKKA, VOCKO AND Pushkin were running hard now, bearing down fast on the vehicle. They could see the Judge now, crouched with his back to them in the back seat. Hakka didn't know what was wrong with the chump— why he wasn't doing anything to stop them, like maybe he was injured, or something—but he figured that wasn't really his problem.

He ran on, pumping another round up into the scattergun. He was just about to fire when the Judge spun round. Hakka noticed three things at once, one of them weird, two of them just plain bad news.

Weird: the Judge had what looked like a red-streaked doll cradled on one arm. The doll was crying, and moving its tiny little toy limbs.

Bad: the Judge had a Lawgiver in his other hand.

Very bad: the name on his badge. *Dredd*.

The punchy, rapid-fire sound of Lawgiver shots drowned out the expletive on Hakka's lips.

Dredd's first three shots hit Pushkin square in the chest, blowing him off his feet and instantly cutting short the psycho's whoops of bloodthirsty excitement.

Second time around for Vocko, as Dredd's next shot took him through the throat. The Med-Judges wouldn't be fitting him with a replacement voicebox this time; instead, the workers down at Resyk would be picking the pieces of the implant out of the mangled ruin of his throat, just before they fed his body onto the conveyor belt.

Hakka took one in the stomach, two in the chest and, for extra good measure, one in the brainpan. The natural born survivor, the King of the Iso-Cubes, hit the ash in a red heap.

'MOTHER AND BABY are doing great, according to the Med-Judge on the scene. What about the husband?' asked Kaminski, still on the radio link.

It was an hour later. The storm was clearing, and a med-wagon had arrived minutes ago. Dredd watched as the injured citizen and his wife and newborn child—a boy, the Med-Judge had told Dredd, as if Dredd might have been interested—were loaded aboard.

'Gunshot wounds, but nothing too serious. They'll all spend a few days in the med-unit at Checkpoint Chico.'

'You did a good job tonight, Dredd,' ventured the voice on the radio link.

'Maybe,' said Dredd, looking at the carnage spread out across the megway, where more than a dozen corpses lay waiting for meat-wagon collection. 'Got all the escaped perps from that transport crash accounted for now, especially the Three Wise Creeps.'

Dredd's gaze shifted to the three nearest shapes buried under their red-stained shrouds of softly falling ash. Victor 'Hakka' Hicks, Ronald 'Vocko' Sauckel and Dmitri Pushkin. For tonight at least, Mega-City One would be a slightly safer place now that those three were out of circulation.

'I meant you did a good job protecting those people, Dredd,' Kaminski persisted. 'What's going to happen to them now?'

'What's your point, Kaminski?' asked Dredd, impatiently, sensing the Med-Judge was leading him towards something.

'If what you told me is true, Dredd, then that kid showed some real guts tonight. Hershey's starting this new cit-relations scheme, a Citizens' Bravery award. A citation like that might help that kid get a better apartment for his family, might even help him get a job. All it takes to be nominated is the recommendation of a senior Judge.'

The unspoken question hung in the air for a moment. 'I'll see what I can do, Kaminski,' Dredd answered finally.

In her quarters at Central Med 18, Kaminski smiled to herself at the seemingly grudging tone in Dredd's voice, both of them knowing that one word from Mega-City

One's most famous lawman was usually enough to move mountains.

'Thanks, Dredd. Call it your obligatory good deed for Christmas.'

'Then thank Grud it only comes once a year,' came Dredd's parting shot, as he climbed onto his Lawmaster and moved off to finish the rest of his patrol shift.

EVERYTHING MUST GO

DAVID BISHOP

BIG BERTHA BLOOMINGDALE stirred, halfway to being awake. The silk sheet felt smooth and luxurious beneath her massive body. A hint of lavender and cinnamon wafted in the air, like a country meadow. She loved the last lingering moments of a good night's rest, before the cares of the day began to weigh her down. Already a delicious dream about some leather-bound hunk indulging all her most secret, sordid desires was fading away. She kept her eyes firmly closed, hoping to keep some last vestiges of the fantasy alive.

Somebody moved beside her on the bed, startling Bertha. *Maybe it hadn't been a dream after all*, she thought. Maybe she had enjoyed a night of guilty pleasure. Her body certainly felt like it had seen some action. Every muscle ached and her head was pounding. Bertha tried to reach a hand up to her face but found her arm held back by something heavy. The characteristic tug of a metal

ring biting into her wrist could mean only one thing—
she was handcuffed to the other person on the bed. Not
daring to take a peek, Bertha reached over and touched
the nearby body. It was hard and taut, rippled with sinew
and muscle. Best of all, it was clad in leather—just like in
her dream. Could it have all been true? She hoped against
hope. A voice rasped in her ear, the sound of granite and
flint grinding together.

'Touch me again and I'll break that arm.'

Bertha's eyes snapped open involuntarily. Lying beside
her was the one person she had hoped never to see again:
Judge Dredd. He had been stripped of his equipment—
no Lawgiver, no utility belt, no boot knife—but the
scowling mouth visible beneath his helmet was instantly
recognisable.

'Where am I? What happened? How? Why?' Bertha
spluttered. She tried to jump off the bed but the handcuffs
linking her to the lawman jerked her back.

'Shut up and stay still,' Dredd snarled. He was trying to
pick the lock on the handcuffs with a bent paperclip. 'The
sooner I get this undone, the sooner we get out of here.'

'Out of where?' Bertha looked around. She and Dredd
were lying in the middle of a massive, heart-shaped bed
on a raised platform. It was surrounded by dozens of
similar platforms, each with a different bed atop it. Pools
of light bathed them from concealed lights in the ceiling.
As Bertha sat up a soothing melody swelled from speakers
set into the floor. 'What is this place?'

'Your guess is as good as mine, punk. No sign of our
captors—yet.'

'Captors? How do you know—'

'Why else would they drug us and bring us here?' Dredd pointed at the empty holster in his boot. 'Why take my weapons? Or snap off my helmet mic?'

Bertha looked at her metal-ringed wrist. 'Why did they cuff us together?'

Dredd sneered at her. 'I did that. You weren't getting away from me, Bloomingdale—not again.'

The clouds in Bertha's memory finally parted. It all came flooding back.

BERTHA HAD BEEN hiding in the Sector 66 'dust zone with her brother Byron. They were grifters from Brit-Cit who came to Mega-City One as part of a complicated sting selling fake 20th century antiques to gullible punters. It was amazing how many people were taken in by dodgy reproductions. Bertha was selling copies of Princess Diana's final, hand-written diary faster than Byron could write them. But the Judges had heard about the scheme and Dredd turned up uninvited at a meeting with an eager client. Bertha and her brother escaped the lawman, but only by abandoning everything they had earned.

Forced into hiding until a way out of the Big Meg could be found, they took refuge in the abandoned industrial zone. As a home away from home it was decidedly unpleasant. Pools of acid littered the landscape and pickings from persuading passing pedestrians to part with their possessions proved thin. Only the brave and the foolish ventured into the 'dust zone, an area notorious for a spate of missing persons cases and rumours of organ legging.

Bertha and Byron had just snared their first victim for a week, a balding transvestite, when the shot rang out. 'That was a warning. Drop the citizen or I drop you.' Bertha had only been in Mega-City One a few weeks but she still recognised the harsh voice. 'Not him again!' She dived behind the cover of a crumbling wall, a task not easily achieved when you weighed so much. Byron was too slow and three bullets punctured his chest. Bertha watched her brother bleed to death as Dredd rode closer on his Lawmaster.

'Citizen, step away from the corpse!' The terrified transvestite came tottering towards Dredd on three-inch heels, black mascara tears running down his cheeks. 'What are you doing here? The Justice Department issued warnings against using this zone as a short-cut!'

'I—I was on my way to see a f-friend,' the citizen stammered.

'Name?'

'King. Cosmo King.'

'Dredd to Control. Any previous on a Cosmo King?'

'One count of solicitation. Suspended sentence of a month in the cubes, given a warning about future conduct.'

'Some creeps never learn. Dredd out.'

Bertha used this exchange to crawl away from her brother's corpse.

'Hmm. Looks like you've been out touting for business again,' Dredd sneered at the transvestite. 'Three months for suspected solicitation, another three for ignoring safety advice. Turn yourself in to the nearest sector house.'

'Y-yes, Judge Dredd. T-thank you.' King staggered off, his heels clip-clopping away into the distance. Bertha kept crawling but a voice from behind brought her to an abrupt halt.

'Stay where you are, Bloomingdale! You can crawl but you can't hide. Especially with an ass that fat.' Dredd strode towards her, Lawgiver aimed at her head, a finger poised on the trigger. 'Now, get up—slowly.'

Bertha pulled herself into a standing position, puffing and panting. 'You killed my brother.'

'He tried to run. Presumption of guilt.'

'He didn't even have a weapon! We don't use weapons!'

'Then I'm amazed you lasted this long, Brit.' Dredd pulled a pair of handcuffs from his utility belt and clamped them tightly to one of Bertha's wrists. But she was no longer paying attention. Behind Dredd half-a-dozen hooded figures had emerged from the shadows. They advanced on the Judge, each holding a black staff in front of them. The ends of each pole crackled with electrical sparks of blue and white.

'D-Dredd—b-behind you,' Bertha stammered.

'Spare me the subterfuge, punk. You're—'

Dredd's words were cut short as the hooded figures plunged their weapons into his back. The Judge screamed in agony as electricity engulfed him, his spine arching, his limbs spasming. The hooded figures drew back and Dredd slumped to the ground, still twitching.

'W-What do you want?' Bertha asked.

The figures moved forwards again, surrounding her. Dredd reached up a hand from the ground and grabbed the unused end of the handcuffs hanging from her wrist.

'You don't get away from me again,' he gasped, closing the handcuff around his own wrist. Dredd's other hand pulled a tiny key from inside one of the pockets on his utility belt. With a final effort, he tossed the key into a nearby acid pool. The metal sunk into the stagnant liquid, melting into nothing. Then the Judge's head fell forward and he moved no more.

The figures closed in on Bertha, staffs raised...

'WELCOME, SHOPPERS! WELCOME to the new, improved Mega-Mall of America!' A grating, metallic voice snapped Bertha back to the present. The words rose up from the floor speakers, replacing the muzak melodies. 'We've got bargains galore but only for those who are willing to shop 'til you drop! So get ready for the biggest sale in the history of history itself! Thank you!'

Dredd was already up off the bed and dragging Bertha across the silk sheets towards him. 'Move it, punk!'

Bertha scrambled the rest of the way across the bed and got to her feet. 'Will you stop pulling me? That hurts my wrist!'

'I don't care if it breaks your wrist.' Dredd was looking around them, searching for something. 'I need to find a way of getting these cuffs off.' He marched off through the many beds, pulling Bertha after him. 'They'll be coming for us. The sooner we get out of here, the better.'

'Alright, alright—no need to run!' the obese woman complained, trotting to keep up with him. 'How did you find us, Dredd?'

'Find who?'

'Byron and me.'

'I wasn't looking for you,' he replied, still striding briskly towards the nearest exit. 'I was investigating missing persons cases in the 'dust zone. Finding you two was just coincidence.'

'Byron never had much luck,' Bertha said. They had reached a doorway. Dredd leaned round the corner to get a look outside. 'We should never have come to Mega-City One, but he persuaded me it would all work out fine.'

'He was wrong.' Dredd gestured through the doorway. Beyond it Bertha's brother was tied to an X-shaped cross. His corpse was tinged with blue, a vivid red slash cut into one arm. His abdomen had been split open and the internal organs gouged out. A signed was hung round his neck, two words printed on it: *UNHAPPY SHOPPER*. Bertha turned away to vomit.

'WHY WOULD ANYONE do that to Byron? He was already dead, there was no need to cut him open like that.' Bertha had recovered enough from the shock to be led past her brother's mutilated corpse by Dredd. Now they were walking down a long corridor, each side lined with shops. Their footsteps echoed around them, hollow and empty like the surroundings.

'Organ leggers,' Dredd replied. 'Strip the body of anything with a resale value. Normally they prefer to take from those still alive, but a fresh corpse is almost as good.'

'That's my brother you're talking about!' Bertha could hold back her anger no longer. She flailed at Dredd with big, fleshy arms, her pudgy fingers balled into fists. 'You murdered him and now he's been gutted like a fish!'

Dredd grabbed her wrists and clamped them firmly together with one hand. With his other hand he slapped her across the face, the sound of his gauntlet smacking against her cheek like a hand-clap. 'The same thing will happen to us unless you pull yourself together! There's something else going on here—more than just organ legging. All the blood was drained from his body too. Normal organ leggers don't bother with the blood.'

'What are you saying—whoever did this are vampires?'

Dredd shrugged before gesturing around himself. 'We're in some kind of shoppera—but look at the stock. Everything is old, like it's been here for a hundred years or more.'

Bertha pulled her hands away from Dredd and wiped the tears from her eyes to see what he was pointing at. Each store running off the corridor was filled with items for sale, all covered in a thick layer of dust. 'So?'

'Shopperas in the Meg are busy, filled with people round the clock. This place is deserted. My guess is we're down in the Undercity.' Bertha's puzzled features prompted further explanation from Dredd. 'When Mega-City One was being planned, architects decided it was easier to concrete over the old cities and started again, building on top. Some people choose to remain down here.'

'Who would live down here for a hundred years?'

'Fugitives. The homeless, the desperate. Creatures that don't like the light. Criminals, bloodsuckers—even werewolves.'

Bertha snorted in disbelief, but Dredd's face remained grim and impassive as ever. 'You're telling me the truth?' she asked.

'I've been down here before. I've seen what lives here. The sooner we get back to the surface, the better.' Dredd started marching again, dragging Bertha along behind him. They were approaching a right-angled corner. A sign on the wall ahead offered hope: *ROOF GARDEN THIS WAY.* 'Come on!' Dredd urged, quickening his pace.

The pair ran round the corner to find the space filled with hooded figures, each pointing an electrified staff at them. As one the figures reached up and pulled back their hoods. This revealed masks of metal and plastic, features sculpted in a grotesque, smiling parody of the human face.

'Droids? They're droids?' Bertha gasped breathlessly. The menacing mechanoids advanced on the duo, electricity arcing from the ends of each staff. The nearest robot had fresh blood splashed across its robe.

'It's worse than that,' Dredd muttered. 'They're killers.'

THE TWO CAPTIVES were herded back the way they had come and then onwards, deeper into the complex. Finally, when Bertha felt her legs were ready to collapse beneath her, they reached a large hexagonal chamber decorated with plastic plants and a simulated waterfall. A mall lined with stores fed out from each wall of the hexagon.

Dredd and Bertha walked into the chamber but the droids did not follow. Looking up, Bertha could see a succession of balconies, one above the other. 'This place is enormous! It must have at least seven levels!' She gagged at the smell of rotting flesh, intermingled with lavender and cinnamon. 'What's that stench? I've never smelled anything like it.'

Dredd pointed at the edges of the balconies. Human corpses in various states of decomposition hung from the railings. Some were little more than skeletons, ragged remains of clothing clinging to the bones. Others were still putrefying, skin coloured by blotches of blue and purple, maggots moving in the open wounds. Just a few feet above them was a fresh corpse—Cosmo King, the terrified transvestite Dredd had encountered earlier above ground. 'They must have grabbed him too,' the Judge observed. 'He should have gone to the nearest sector house, like I said. He'd still be alive.'

'Welcome to the Mega-Mall!' A metallic voice boomed around the chamber, full of squeaks and harsh static. It has hard to know if the speaker was male or female. It certainly wasn't human. 'You are welcome here for the ultimate shopping experience! This shrine to consumerism has stood the test of time, outlasting governments, market trends and competitive outlets. At the Mega-Mall of America, our motto is simple: Live to Shop—Shop to Live!'

'I don't like the sound of that,' Bertha hissed to Dredd. He put a finger up to his lips, motioning her to silence.

The tinny tannoy continued its address.

'Customers, you have the chance to be our Star Shoppers. You will be given everything your heart desires, be able to pick and choose from the millions of items available to buy in this unparalleled cathedral to capitalism—all for free. But to ensure you are worthy of this bewildering bounty, the Mega-Mall of America asks to first undertake a small challenge. Do you agree?'

'What if we say no?' Dredd glared around him, fists resting on his hips.

'That would be... unfortunate,' the voice replied.

'How unfortunate?'

The barrel of a machine-gun emerged through the simulated waterfall and began firing at the captives. Bertha cowered in terror but Dredd remained still, watching the floor around his feet be shot to pieces. After thirty seconds of rapid firing, the machine gun clattered to a halt and quietly withdrew again.

'Most unfortunate. The galleries above you are decorated with the remains of those who refused—or failed. Do you accept the challenge?'

'We need a moment to consider your... generous offer.' Dredd turned to Bertha, who was still cowering in terror behind him. 'This whole place is running on automatic. Unless we accept, the security system will cut us down before we move five paces. If we stick together, we might survive long enough to find a way of disabling whatever is controlling all of this—agreed?'

Bertha nodded, her hands shaking in terror. 'I don't have much choice, thanks to these handcuffs.'

'True. I hadn't expected to face this.' Dredd turned round again and shouted into the air. 'We accept the challenge! We will be Star Shoppers!'

'Congratulations! Stay where you are and one of the Mega-Mall's helpful staff of robotic personal shopping assistants will come to your aid. But be warned—the Mega-Mall's management does not look kindly upon those who are unable to pay for their purchases. You may have observed previous shoppers who failed in this way. Their internal organs were surgically removed to offset their final bills. That is all.' The tannoy clicked off, its final words still bouncing around the glasseen walls.

Dredd's upper lip curled sourly. 'That explains all the missing persons cases. When the mall stopped getting customers, it sent droids out to abduct new ones and bring them here.'

Bertha looked up at the display of previous customers. 'Poor sods.'

A single droid emerged from one of the corridors and marched towards Dredd and Bertha. 'Welcome to the Mega-Mall. My name is XL66 and I am your personal shopping assistant for today's challenge. How can I be of help?'

'What is the challenge?' Dredd asked tersely.

'I'm glad you requested that information from me. I have assisted many previous visitors as they attempted the challenge. Alas, none have been successful to date, but I hope and believe you will surpass my expectations.' XL66 bowed to them, its metallic hands clasped together.

Bertha stood up impatiently. 'Cut the crap and tell us about the challenge, chrome-dome!'

'Now, Miss—I may call you Miss?—there is no need to get abusive. Customers who breach the Mega-Mall's guidelines about etiquette and civility may be subject to an instant fine.'

'What's that?'

'Let's just say you'll find strolling the boulevards of this wonderful world of shopping a little more difficult without your feet. Do I make myself clear?'

Bertha smiled weakly. 'Yes. Thank you. Sorry.'

'See? It doesn't hurt to be civil, but rudeness can lead to agony.'

'You were going to tell us about the challenge,' Dredd interjected.

'Yes, indeed!' XL66 nodded several times, as if in a state of ecstasy. 'All you have to do is buy fifty-five items in under sixty seconds.'

'That's all?'

'Yes. Buy fifty-five items from any of the thousands of stores around you.'

Bertha was bemused. 'Sounds simple enough. What's the catch?'

'Catch?'

'How come nobody else has succeeded in meeting this challenge?'

XL66 held up one finger. 'Ahh, well—you see, you must

have the correct change. Incorrect change equals a failure to meet the challenge and then...'

'Slice and dice time,' Dredd muttered.

'Exactly! Well, your sixty seconds begins... now!' XL66 stood aside and looked at the two humans. 'I'd advise you to hurry along.'

Dredd and Bertha started running.

THE DUO PELTED into the nearest store, a children's clothing emporium. 'How may I be of assistance?' a droid asked as they entered.

'Ignore it! Just grab two handfuls!' Dredd commanded. He was already ripping items from the shelves. Bertha quickly followed his example and then they ran to the nearest checkout. Bertha counted the items as Dredd piled them up before the serving droid. 'We'd like to buy these.'

'How many do you have?'

'Fifty-three, fifty-four, fifty-five!' Bertha finished counting and Dredd stopped adding to the pile. 'Could you make it snappy, please? We're in quite a hurry,' she added with a smile.

'Now, madam, you can't hurry good service. It's the little touches that ensure the customer's happiness. That is our paramount objective.' The serving droid began laboriously scanning the barcodes on the items, individually packing each one before moving on to the next. XL66 entered the store and approached the checkout.

'Your time is nearly up. Have you completed the challenge?' it enquired.

'Your serving droid is taking too long!' Bertha hissed back nervously. 'We would have done it otherwise!'

XL66 tutted to itself. 'Another failure, it seems. What a disappointment. And I had such high hopes for you two.' Behind the droid a group of ceiling panels slid out of sight and a dozen machine-guns dropped down into view. Each engaged an auto-targeting system, locking aim on Dredd and Bertha. XL66 shook its head sadly. 'It seems you'll be joining the ranks of the other unhappy shoppers. Your sixty seconds is—'

'Wait!' Dredd shouted. He picked up one of the items still waiting to be scanned, a child's top that had one sleeve torn off. 'This merchandise is defective. What kind of establishment are you running here?'

'Defective? I don't think that can be possible!' XL66 leaned forward to examine the cloth more closely.

Bertha stared at Dredd in bewilderment—what the hell was he up to?

'I'm not happy about this,' the Judge continued. 'Surely you believe in the maxim that the customer is always right?'

'Certainly, sir.' XL66 straightened up again. 'I'm afraid to say you're correct—this item is defective. Most distressing.'

'It's not good enough,' Dredd announced gruffly. 'We demand to see the manager—this minute!'

'Well, I'm not sure we can do that, sir—'

'If you believe the customer is always right, then you must agree to my request to see the manager—immediately!' Dredd folded his arms, glaring at the two droids. Bertha smiled. Despite herself, she had to admit the lawman might just have saved their lives. But would the droids' own dogma save them?

XL66 made a series of internal clicking, whirring noises. 'First I must consult with Head Office, to see whether your request has been approved.' The droid fell silent, its head tilted to one side. Bertha took this opportunity to sidle nearer Dredd and whispered to him.

'How did you know that would work?'

'I didn't. But if droids have one weakness, it's their reliance on internal logic. Exploit that and we might get out of here alive.'

XL66 jerked back into life. 'I will take you to see—the manager!'

DREDD AND BERTHA were led back into the centre of the complex and then into a concealed elevator behind the simulated waterfall. This dropped downwards quickly before gliding to a halt. The doors opened and XL66 ushered them out into a long, narrow corridor. At the far end was a single, solid door with the word *MANAGER* emblazoned on it.

As the duo walked towards the office, Bertha wondered what they would find inside. Another droid? Some crazed inhabitant of this Undercity? Whatever happened, she would let Dredd do all the talking. While they remained cuffed together, he was better off keeping her alive. As a corpse her vast bulk would make escape impossible for him.

Dredd knocked on the manager's door. 'Come in,' a faint voice wheezed. Dredd opened the door and stepping inside, Bertha following close behind.

The office was a spartan room without windows or other doors. It had no desk, chairs or storage units. Instead the space was dominated by a hospital bed, surrounded by life support machines and security monitors. On the bed lay a wizened husk of a man, his ancient body pale and emaciated. Surgical scars criss-crossed his waxen frame, evidence of dozens of operations. A cluster of wires and tubes connected the patient to the machines around him, draining different fluids from his body and replacing them with fresh supplies. A droid hovered nearby, monitoring the old man's vital signs. One of its arms had been replaced with a surgical drill. The old man beckoned Dredd and Bertha closer with a weak gesture. They approached him warily.

'You... you have done well,' the old man said.

'Who are you?' Dredd demanded.

'I am the manager—and have been for more than a hundred and thirty years,' the patient replied. 'I wanted to retire but they wouldn't let me.'

'Who? Who wouldn't let you?' Bertha asked.

'The staff... the droids. They said protocol demanded a human remain in charge of the robot workforce. They kept me alive all these years...'

'How?'

Dredd pointed at the manager's body. 'Any way they could from the looks of him. Organ transplants, blood transfusions. Beyond his skin and skeleton, there probably isn't much of the original manager left.'

The old man nodded. 'They did terrible things... terrible.' He turned to the droid. 'Leave us. I wish to rest.'

'But I—'

'Leave us!'

The droid complied, closing the door as it left the office. The old man pulled himself up into a sitting position and pointed at the security monitors. 'I saw how you tricked them. Very clever. You have what it takes, young man...'

'To do what?'

'Succeed me. I want to die, I want this agony to end. Kill me and you become the manager. All of this will be yours.'

'I don't kill in cold blood,' Dredd replied.

'Hundreds have been murdered by the droids to keep me alive. Ultimately, I am responsible for those crimes. Pass sentence on me, Judge.'

Dredd nodded. He reached towards the life support machines and began switching them off. Alarms filled the air but by the time the droid returned, the manager was already dead. 'What happened?' it enquired.

'Hostile takeover,' Bertha replied. She pointed at Dredd. 'He did it.'

The droid advanced on Dredd, its surgical drill whirring into life. 'Is this true? Did you murder the old manager?'

'Yes.' Dredd pushed Bertha behind himself, preparing to attack the droid.

The mechanoid paused and then bowed to the Judge, its surgical drill switched off again. 'Congratulations, sir! You are now the new manager of the Mega-Mall of America! What is your first directive?'

Dredd stroked his chin thoughtfully. 'It's time for a

closing down sale. Gather all the droids in the centre of the complex. I need to address them all.'

'Certainly, sir! I will spread the word.' The droid departed, leaving just Dredd and Bertha beside the old manager's body.

'What are you going to do, Dredd?' Bertha asked.

'There's enough merchandise to feed and clothe an entire sector,' the Judge said. 'The droids can carry it up to the surface and distribute it to the needy. Then the Mega-Mall of America is going out of business.'

'And what about me?'

'By rights I should deport you back to Brit-Cit immediately—I'm sure the New Old Bailey has several outstanding arrest warrants with your name on them. But I'll give you another option. Help with the closure of the mall and I'll put in a good word for you with the authorities in Brit-Cit.'

Bertha sighed. 'So I'm still being sent back home either way?'

Dredd almost smiled. 'The Mega-Mall of America is under new management and everything must go— even you. Now move it, fat ass!'

RAT TOWN

JONATHAN CLEMENTS

Judge Hotchkiss

I WAS FIRST on the scene of the Code Four. Yeah, here come the Judge! Seventeen minutes with a Full Eagle, and I was already doing it! You wait 15 years for that power and that authority, and then you're like, Grud above, I can't control these people! What am I gonna do? Yeah, I'll wait for the Judges, they'll sort it out. But, like—man, I *am* the Judges now! This is my problem.

Citizens ran across the street, away from the bank. A muzzle-flash flickered among the Greek columns at the top of the steps, and I heard a second salvo of bullets. But no ricochet on the sidewalk... no broken glass from the facing buildings. Whoever they were inside, they were firing into the air. Maybe they didn't want to hurt anyone.

The citizens didn't know that. How could they? So they were running for their lives, a rictus of terror on their faces.

Now me, I'm dressed for action. It's not just a uniform. I've got the gear. I've got the bike. I've got armour and back-up. But these people, they were dressed to impress, which ain't quite the same thing.

Girls teetered on heels that must have looked great on a catwalk. Now they were a liability. I saw one fall, and none of the men stopped to help. One kinda thought about it, but he just half-heartedly yelled 'You okay?' behind him as he ran.

A bunch of them were going a little slower, banking on the fattie behind them shielding them from any bullets. But he was in trouble. His belly-wheel spun out from under him. He went over like... like a great big fat guy falling over. His gut only had about a foot to go before it reached the ground and cushioned the rest of him. There was no way he was getting up without a crane. I guess someone else worked that out, because one of the other guys ran over to him to 'help'.

Yeah, right. He crouched down low to check on the fattie. Then a little lower. His head craned up, peering towards the front of the building. As another, shorter salvo of rounds burped from the unseen gunman on the steps, the good Samaritan hit the deck, using the fattie for cover. Nice.

The radio crackled in my ear: another Judge with an ETA. Oh yeah, I'm like supposed to be doing something about this. I couldn't seem to move. I told myself this wasn't real. I told myself this was just some kind of advanced drill, on one of the Rat Town beats where it was all just a test. I pulled my Lawgiver and fired three APs at the front of the bank. Glass broke, and there was a final *pwang!* as the last round bounced off a marble column. And I thought to myself, what do I think I'm doing?

'Come out... ahem... Come out with your hands up!' I yelled, my voice cracking. I tried to clear my throat, but the hailer was still on. You could hear me cough three blocks away.

For a moment, it was real quiet. I mean, real quiet. Far off, I could hear sirens, and that made me feel good, 'cos they were on my side.

Then two guns opened up on me from the bank, and I was ducking behind my bike like it was my personal fattie. And then a lucky shot got me in the head.

The Perp

ROBINSON SAID 'BULLSEYE!' And then him and Enus are high-fiving it, and doin' that dumb dance thing they do, waving their guns around. And I'm up from behind the counter, 'cos I know if something was getting them that happy, it's not gonna be good news.

'What did you do?!' I shout. They just giggle for a moment.

'Top score on the slitch!' says Robinson.

'Right in the head!'

I nearly lose it right there, but I try to keep my cool. I kinda fail.

'You shot a Judge! You drokkin' moron! They'll nuke this bank before they let us out alive. What were you thinking?'

The guys are all placating, shushing me and pointing at the people on the bank floor.

'She's okay!' says Enus. 'She had a helmet on! Calm down, man.'

'Easy now,' whispers Robinson. 'You don't wanna scare the hostages.'

They're pretty scared already. There's lots of sobbing and moaning and the guys givin' me the hard stare—like, you know. You and me, pal. Without the gun, you and me. Put the gun down and let me kick the drokk out of you in front of Lucy from Account Services, so she knows who the hero really is.

I know Lucy's name 'cos it's on her little badge. And she's been my teller of choice all week, when I came in with the creds to change, and the foreign currency, and all the other excuses we had for casing the joint. And I'd always stand in her line, no matter how short the other queues were. I think she kinda saw that, and thought I had a crush on her. I've got her carrying the bags of money up from the safe, because she's too skinny to fight back. She's only a little thing, too. Mascara's all ruined now, and she's got this little sniff thing going because her nose is starting to run, but she's bringing the money up like a good girl. And we got most of the bags in the centre now, and there's just the minor problem of getting the drokk out of here.

'Listen, honey!' I shout down the steps at the lady Judge. 'Sorry about the bullet-in-the-head thing. No hard feelings, okay?'

And she gets to her feet and gives me the silent treatment. And I think, this is really bad. Because when my girl would... Never mind. I just know it's bad. So I try to keep her talking and I say:

'I mean, we don't wanna hurt anyone, and that includes Judges, okay! We thought you were ninety-nined just now, and we're real sorry about that.'

'Are you tryin' to get her phone number or something?' says Robinson, and he's psyched. He's loaded for bear and he's got this glint in his eye.

'She's just a kid,' I say. 'I don't think she knows what to do.'

'Boohoo,' he says, lifting his rifle and looking down his sights straight at her. 'Now you tell her we want a safe route outta here with the cash. Or we start shooting the hostages.'

The Judge Spotter

I SIMPLY COULD not believe my luck. Two weeks out of Brit-Cit, and thus far I have only had minor infractions. Really little more than a few Fives and a Six. I wanted to see a block war before I went home, or perhaps a murder. I was starting to think I might have to make something up, because the Judge Watching Club were going to have a baby if I came home empty handed. And then this one fell into my lap. Literally fell in my lap.

I didn't even have to move from my seat. I had a bottomless no-caf at a topless diner, and a window seat... and Grud love me, the window was smashed so I could hear everything. It was great enough watching the lady

Judge shooting at the perps (they call them perps) in the bank. But I couldn't wish for a better birthday present. I was really excited. Really, really excited. And the sirens were getting closer—I could hear them for real. At least a dozen Lawmasters all converging on my location... and an H-Wagon, a honest-to-Grud H-Wagon. Jovus, it was beautiful. Squat and powerful, hovering in the air like it belonged there, then coming down to land right by the diner with the wind belting out from beneath it, blowing the newspapers around the diner, with everyone except me ducking for cover. But I love it and the fact that it's buffeting me, and the noise so loud, and the jets with this smell like... like *tar*. And I remember thinking, I know how an H-Wagon smells! Losers! I know how a drokking X24 H-Wagon smells and you've never even left Brit-Cit!

Sorry, right. But it got better, it just kept getting better, because the door opens right in front of me and it's Dredd! It's Joe drokking Dredd! And that's it, I've beaten Eden's score, because he only ever saw Hershey once from a distance, and there I was in spitting range of Dredd himself. Not that I would spit, because that's like a Code Fourteen. Actually, Eden says it's a Code Thirteen, and we really have to clear that one up, because it interferes with the scoring. And the Judges open up for seven seconds. I counted. Seven seconds—it was covering fire, just like in the manual! It's true, covering fire, just enough for the lady Judge to make it over to Dredd, and they are right in front of me, and he says:

'Calling for back-up on your first day, Hotchkiss? You got an alien invasion or something?'

You know, he was joking. I don't think he meant anything by it. I think it's banter, you know. He's got a dry sense of humour. Don't believe what they say. But this child, Judge Hotchkiss, she was a wreck. An absolute wreck. And she's stammering, and clearing her throat, and she's not looking him in the eye, I suppose because she thinks she's in trouble.

And she gives him the sitrep, you know what that means? Right, okay, because some people, they don't know. Three robbers, a dozen hostages, and they intend to kill them off one at a time unless they get out of there with the loot.

But while she's talking, Dredd is sort of staring straight ahead. And I think, I know what he's thinking. He's thinking stumm gas. He's thinking snipers. And I am sweating with excitement. But he's actually staring at this other Judge, who's waiting behind Hotchkiss. And after a while, Hotchkiss kind of peters out, and she turns to look at this man as well, and because I'm right up close, too, I see that his badge is blank! His badge is actually blank! There's no name on it, no nothing.

And when he speaks, it's sort of muffled, because he's got his faceplate down with the rebreather, which hides even more of a Judge's face than usual. And he says: 'Judge Dredd, is this your situation?'

And Dredd says: 'Yes, it is.' And I look at Hotchkiss, and I see her wilt, because she was first on the scene.

And the Judge with no nameplate, he says: 'We must speak privately.'

Without a word, Dredd opens the hatch on the H-Wagon, and the two of them go inside. They slam the hatch shut, and that's the last I hear.

* * *

Judge X

DREDD GOT STRAIGHT to the point.

'Did anyone see you get here?' he barked.

'Hope not,' I said. 'I had to wait until there were more Judges around. Do you know who I am?'

'No,' said Dredd, impassively. 'Nobody knows who you are.'

'And we have to keep it that way,' I said. 'If they don't know know who I am, they can't pick me out.'

Dredd wasn't listening, he was checking the monitors, watching the blips of other Lawmasters heading for the scene.

'Why aren't you in Rat Town?' he said, his eyes watching the screens as his fingers tapped out a request on the keyboard. PSU footage of the earlier gunfight came up on the alpha screen, and he started nudging the images into clearer mugshots.

'You haven't been there for a while, have you Dredd?'

'No. I met you once, but you were someone else.'

Three years ago, if I read the reports right; there have been at least four Judge Xs since then. The X Dredd knew got shot by a double-agent. The one after that did his term and rotated back to regular duty. He got a new name, and a transfer. The one after that—well, here's irony for you. He left Rat Town. Said it was better for training to get the cadets used to the real world. He hung up the X uniform and got an ice-cream van. Undercover cadets looking to report or assign, they had to find him in the park. But he got shot by a perp who wanted his wallet.

'We have real crimes to deal with,' said Dredd. He got two full faces and a partial on the three robbers holed up in the bank. Not bad going.

'Where'd you be without the Wally Squad?' I heard my voice raising slightly, in spite of my plan to keep cool. 'You think they're second-rate? They've got all your training and more! They go right through the Academy, and then learn to act like they forgot it all. Do you know how difficult that is?'

Dredd eyed me in silence. If I wanted an argument, I was going to have it with myself.

'There are officers who've been in deep cover for years, Dredd. Years! And they can't even be seen talking to a Judge. Can you imagine what's that like? Not being able to talk to any of your buddies, ever! You've got buddies, right?'

Dredd continued to stare impassively. The pause stretched into an uneasy silence. I was beginning to think I'd lost him.

'I'm not a social animal,' he said, after an age. 'Get to the point.'

'We've got a problem,' I replied.

There was a flicker of realisation on Dredd's face. He swung back to look at the screen. '"We thought you were ninety-nined",' he said.

'Sorry?'

'Hotchkiss has one of the perps saying that,' said Dredd. He jabbed a finger at the partial image. 'This creep here, on the inside. What's a perp doing using the code for a Judge down?'

'I knew you were smart,' I said.

'He's an undercover Judge,' said Dredd. 'He's drokkin' Wally Squad! That's why there's no sheet on him. Who is he?'

'Judge Jones—Dayvee Jones,' I said.

I heard a tell-tale beep, and realised Dredd had something in his hand. He was holding a 75 series Birdie, and it just spiked.

'Lie detector says "no",' said Dredd.

'So sue me,' I said. 'I'm risking several people's lives, my own included. That's all you're getting.'

'What do you want me to do?' he asked.

'Let them go. Let them take the money, and let them go.'

'You're going to tell me that the mission this "Dayvee" is on is too important to jeopardise?' said Dredd.

'He's been in a gang for years, Dredd! You can't buy that kind of penetration. He's way up near the top.'

'Not my problem,' said Dredd. 'It's up to him to get free when my snipers start playing join-the-dots with his buddies as targets.'

'Actually, it's the buddies I want to talk about...' I said, uneasily.

Dredd took a deep breath, and spoke with exaggerated care, like he was trying to stop himself from from punching me in the neck. 'How many of your people are in that bank?'

Gingerly, I held up three fingers.

He wasn't happy.

*   *   *

The Fattie

THIS IS A life choice. I used to be old-school high-carbs—pasta and chanko. Then I switched to straight lard. Wasn't long before I moved to Flabbon, and then I've never looked back. Fact is, I haven't been able to look down either. That was a joke. Point is, I'm fat—okay, I accept that. I'm morbidly obese. But I'm not deaf.

And the guy hiding behind me is such a whiner! For Grud's sake, you're using me as a human shield, guy! Would it kill you to show some respect? We've kind of exhausted the conversation you can have with someone who's clinging to your ass in no-man's-land, sobbing while the bullets whistle overhead. He told me his name—I forgot already. He's got a wife and kids, apparently. I really couldn't care less, and I know I'm stuck here for the foreseeable. Which is why I kicked him in the head and told him to can it, because Dredd was back out of the big floating cop-truck thing, and that's not a sight you see every day. Like I said, I'm fat, but I ain't deaf. And when a celebrity like that is just a few feet away, you wanna eavesdrop. Am I wrong?

So Dredd comes out of that vehicle, with the other Judge—didn't get his name. And he's kinda ticked off.

'How can this happen?' he says to the other Judge.

'Dredd,' says the other guy. 'Let's fix the problem, not the blame—okay?'

Jovus, I thought Dredd was gonna punch him.

'It's your problem,' he said. 'It's your job to make sure this doesn't happen. Were they all egging each other on? All expecting a medal when the other two got rolled over? You go in there and tell them all it's been a big mistake.'

'Have you been listening to a word I said?' yelled the other Judge. 'These guys are from separate gangs. Each can't find out about the other two!'

'This is insane! You want me to let them g—'

A vein was pulsing in Dredd's neck. He turned to look at me. I guess he had been getting a little loud. I grinned feebly and gave him a little salute. He didn't smile back.

'Dredd, it's your call. You know my recommendation. If you've got any better suggestions, then feel free to make them known right now.'

Dredd's nostrils flared. He was mighty angry. He stood there face-to-face with the other Judge, and three breaths became four. And then he nodded and pulled his gun.

Lucy

I CARRIED ALL the money up, and I put the bags where they wanted me to, and I didn't know what to do next. I figured I should just stand there. They were ignoring me, though, so I sat back down next to the manager. He patted my arm gently.

'You did good, Lucy,' he said. 'Don't cry, you did what any of us would have done.'

One of the robbers heard him. It was the one who used to come to the bank every day, and smile at me in line.

'And *you!*' he yelled. 'You, just shut up!' The manager looked away, back down at the floor, and he took his hand off my arm, which made me want to cry again. I don't know why.

Outside there was a sudden feedback shriek, and a voice came over a loudhailer.

'You in the bank,' he said. 'This is Judge Dredd.' I smiled; how was anyone not going to know that? 'You have three minutes to make up your mind. Like you said before, nobody wants to get ninety-nined.'

The first guy with the rifle, Robinson. He was getting an up-close look at Dredd with his 'scope.

'I can take him out from here, no worries,' he said. 'Say, what's a ninety-nine?'

'Don't ask me, man, don't ask me how'mIsupposedto-knowthat,' said Enus. He was kinda jumpy.

'You know what he's talking about?' said Robinson to the Smiler—to the nice one who turned out to be a bad one, like all the others.

'What?' said Smiler.

'What's a ninety-nine?' said Robinson.

'I dunno,' said Smiler. 'Er... isn't it like slotting someone? Er... they say it all the time on that vid show.'

'What vid show?' said Enus.

'Er... that, er... that Judge show.'

'I wish you wouldn't use words you don't understand,' said Robinson, still staring down the gunsight.

'Two minutes,' said Dredd's voice. 'Then you're meeting my friend Harvie.'

That confused just about everybody. The manager

muttered that Dredd seemed to have lost it. But it was my turn to grab his arm.

'ARV ID Extraction,' I hissed. 'They're gonna fill this place with smoke, boss. Pull your jumper over your mouth and keep your eyes closed. Okay?'

'How do you know that?' he said.

'Saw it on a vid show,' I said. 'Now pass it on.'

'*Who the drokk is Harvie?!?*' Robinson was shouting.

'Whatever it is, man, we'd better get ready to run!' said Enus.

'Okay boys, one bag each,' said Smiler. 'We wait for the smoke, and we split. Okay? Every man for himself.'

'Cool with me,' said Robinson. 'I'll see you guys on the other side.'

'What makes you think they're gonna throw a smoke grenade?' said Enus.

'Who said it was gonna be a grenade?' said Robinson.

'I saw it on a vid show,' they said, all at once. There was a pregnant pause and then they high-fived each other and went for the bags, just as the windows shattered in three places and the canisters bounced across the floor.

SJS Judge Garcia

BUELL LEANED ACROSS his desk, trying to hide his interest.

'What did Dredd give him?' he asked.

'Who?'

'The Jimp. Judge X.'

'Ah.' I said. 'Impersonating a Judge with intent to

commit a felony, well, that's 20 years. And actually trying to enlist a Judge to help you commit a crime—wow!'

He laughed, too. We didn't even have a proper serial number for that one.

'So considering the nature of the offence, and the serious need to keep it quiet, Dredd split the difference and booked him on an additional Code 23. Gave him 25 years on Titan.'

'With all the other Judges!' Buell shook with laughter. 'That's... that's priceless.'

He tried to regain his composure, and nearly made it.

'All right, Garcia, case closed. Clean this up before people start asking questions.'

He didn't get up to show me to the door of his office. He was still snickering in his chair. But Hotchkiss was waiting for me out by the no-caf machine, helmet in hand, still fingering that dent from the bullet.

'You need to get that fixed,' I said.

'Judge Garcia, if I might have a moment—' she began. This wasn't gonna be easy.

'I'm a busy man, Hotchkiss,' I said, a little too sternly. But she didn't let up. I keep forgetting, she's a Judge after all.

'What about the three robbers?' she asked.

'What about them?' I said, evasively.

'They should be looking at 18 to life,' she said. 'And frankly, I wouldn't mind seeing someone throw in a Code Two for shooting at me... er... sir.'

'You weren't even scratched,' I said, picking up the pace for the door, but she kept up with me.

'If Judge X was an impersonator, then the three robbers can't have been in the Wally Squad!' she said. 'They were just perps with an accomplice who thought they'd found a great escape route. There was no need for an ARV extraction. No point in letting off the smoke and dragging 'em in. So I'm wondering, on my first day on the job, am I chalking up one arrest or four?'

'Hotchkiss,' I said, halting. 'I appreciate your fervour. But it's in hand. The robbers are in the interrogation cubes.'

'But, Judge Garcia, they won't let me see the—'

'Enough.'

But the kid wasn't letting go.

'How did Dredd know that Judge X was a phoney?'

I sighed.

'It was a smart plan, Hotchkiss, but they were very unlucky.'

'The only way he could,' she began, 'was if the *real* Judge X was somewhere on the scene.'

'Yes, Hotchkiss.'

'Unless—'

'Hotchkiss!' I barked.

'Unless they really *were* the Wally Squad and this was just your way of making them look like *bona fide* perps!'

'Hotchkiss...' I sighed.

'Is that what it was?' she breathed. 'Was this all some kind of Rat Town graduation ceremony? With a bonus game of "Shoot the Rookie"?'

'Judge Hotchkiss,' I said carefully.

'Are those perps even in the cubes?' she said. 'Or are

they already somewhere out there, bragging that they got away?'

'Let's drop it, Hotchkiss,' I said. 'Don't worry about it. In fact, I order you to stop thinking about this.'

'But... did I do the right thing? My record's gonna say I—'

'All the documentation in this case is gonna disappear by tomorrow afternoon.'

'How do you know?'

'Because, Hotchkiss, I'm ordering you to make it disappear. All the depositions and all the cube interview transcripts. Clear?'

She took a deep breath, then held open the door to my transport.

'Yessir, I understand,' she said. 'I *think*...'

As the door slammed behind me, I motioned for my driver to wait a moment.

'And Hotchkiss?' I said.

'Yessir?'

'Get a squad vehicle to take that bank teller home. Don't make her wait for a hoverbus like that. She's had a hard day.'

BERNARD

JONATHAN MORRIS

'SLICE IT! SLICE off your grandmother's face!' I yelped, hopping excitedly on the spot. I bounded across the living room and thumped myself down onto the sofa, my tail all-a-shiver. The scent of blood hung thickly in the air, and I salivated with sick delight.

The corpses of Mr and Mrs Wrench reclined in their armchairs, their arms slung across their bellies, their faces flickering in the weak television light. Their skin had a mannequin pallor, the fat bulging in folds from their cheeks and chins, their mouths agape. They stared ahead, enraptured by the soap opera even in death. The Traveller's Rest had a new landlady who was announcing that 'things would change around here.'

The living room was a mess. Blood daubed the floral wallpaper, the floral sofa, the floral pouffe. The coffee table had been overturned, spilling mugs and colour supplements across the floral carpet. Lamps had been smashed, pot plants unpotted and duck three had fallen off the wall.

The little girl kneeled by her grandmother's side, her Sunday-best skirt stretched over her knees, her dark-golden hair in tangled curls, a blood-wet kitchen knife gripped in her right hand. Some gristle had accumulated on the serrated edge, and she wiped it clean on her stripey blue jumper.

Humming a jolly tune, she lifted the knife again and levelled its edge against her gran's saggy cheek. Then she turned to me, her wide, innocent eyes glistening with uncertainty. She bit her lip and frowned. 'Shouldn't I? Isn't it bad to cut off Nana's face?'

'You should!' I said gleefully. 'You should make her messy, messy, so no-one need ever look at her nasty, horrid, spiteful, how-many-times-have-I-told-you-to-tidy-your-room face again!'

'But—' began the girl. 'But it feels like a doing-wrong thing.'

I bounced on the spot, my ears flapping impatiently. Some blood had congealed on my bright-blue fur, I could taste it as I licked myself clean. 'Would I lead you astray? Would I make you do something that wasn't for the good and the true and the very, very best?'

She considered. 'No. You're the bestest friend anyone could have in all the wide whole world.' She gave me an affectionate pat on the head, then returned her attention to the knife. She pressed the point it into a fold of jowl and increased the pressure until the flesh burst. The knife slipped through, and a thick glue leaked out.

I leaned in closer to get a detailed view, to allow the scent of death to fill my shivering nostrils.

The little girl lifted her elbow to improve her purchase on the knife, then tugged it down to the jaw, ripping away a flap of skin. Smiling wet teeth were revealed. Next, she cut along the upper lip as though carving away the Sunday roast.

Her work done, the girl repeated the process on her grandfather's corpse. I watched intently, my nose all a-twitch, my eyes able to make out every detail in the gloom. I eat a lot of carrots. I'm a rabbit, you see.

A giant bright blue rabbit that can talk.

She smiled and returned to her song. I looked at her, and my evil, cancer-black heart filled with delight. I loved that girl. I loved her with all of my being. I would do anything for her. I would give my life, my soul and my bushy-bushy-bob tail to protect her. I would help her, and listen to her, and keep all her secrets. We would share confidences and giggle at private jokes. We would laugh until we snorted. She would ask me what she should do, and I would tell her. Always the best advice. For her own good.

Her name is Annabelle. My name is Bernard. I'm her imaginary friend.

THE BROKEN GLASS scrunched under Dredd's boots. He strode down the aisle, stepping over the huddled bodies, his lawgiver rifle raised. He turned, his lips set in a sneer, and stepped into the spotlight. He did not flinch as he surveyed the horrific scene.

According to the infra-red, there was no-one left alive. Dozens upon dozens of corpses sat slouched in their seats. Their heads lolled, their eyes wide in panic.

Dry-ice drifted through the beams of coloured light. The stage was littered with used ammunition and discarded machine pistols. Behind the stage, at the centre of the glitter drapes, the club's logo: Longeur's.

Dredd kicked the smoking corpse that lay by the microphone stand. A corpse wearing a glittery suit. A corpse with half a face.

'Control,' breathed Dredd. 'Replay the call.'

Some hollow, tinny laughter roared out Dredd's radio. And a terrified male voice: 'Judges? Is that you? You've got to get down to Longeur's. It's Smarm Pimberly, the comedian. He's gone futsie.'

'No heckling!' There was a burst of hollow, tinny gunfire, followed by the lambasting of a comedian, 'For the love of Grud, I am trying to do comedy here! Will you drokking listen? Where was I?'

A voice shouted out, 'You were on the flight—'

'...I was on the flight on the way over, and the stewardesses were doing the routine, in the event of a crash, "the emergency exits and here, here and here, and the lifejackets are here". But they never tell you where they keep the parachutes!'

More nervous laughter.

'I mean, if the plane is going to crash, I'd quite like to get off before it hits the ground, thank you very much. "What's that—the wings have fallen off? I'm drokking off out of here!" The pilot, he's got a parachute, he's drokked off, the stewardesses, they know where the emergency exits are, they're "here, here and here," they've drokked off. But for the passengers, it's "after you've been crushed to death you can put on your lifejacket"!'

A light smattering of applause.

'Is that it? I spent six months on this routine! Laugh, you bastards! Laugh!'

A ferocious stutter of gunfire, followed by a roar of unenthusiastic laughter. Someone even whooped.

'Drokk,' muttered Dredd. 'Meat-head's dying on his backside—and he's taking the audience with him.'

The recording dissolved into static, and then Pimberley's voice yelled out:

'Alright! And now for some audience participation!'

Laughter turned to screams.

'Is there anyone here from Brit-Cit? Anyone? You couldn't give me a lift back—' The recording cut off with an electronic pop.

Dredd spoke into his radio. 'Control. Get a meat-wagon to Longeur's. Creep's had his last laugh.'

'That's a roj, Dredd.'

Dredd glowered at the glittery-suited corpse. It clutched a microphone in one hand. 'Comedian should've got himself a sense of humour.'

'Dredd, we've a suspected double homicide in Hyde-Pierce...'

Dredd was already moving. 'On my way.'

* * *

THE SUBWAY CARRIAGE juddered from side to side and the lights flickered. The windows looked out onto the ghosts of the passengers within, rocking with the motion of the train. There were a dozen of them; a mixture of ages and races. The young couple gazing into each other's besotted eyes. The clerk, rap-a-tap-tapping on his laptop. The disgruntled newspaper reader. The sullen-faced youths swinging from the ceiling bars.

And Annabelle, gazing at her reflection, absent-mindedly tugging her skirt over her knees. Her knife rested on the seat between us. I watched her, a smile on my lips.

'Where are we going, Bernard?' She turned to me with a smile, and ruffled my hair between my ears. My most ticklish spot. I giggled and snorted.

'We must run away,' I said. 'You and I. We must scamper and hide down a bunny-hole where no-one will ever find us.'

She stroked my chin as she considered. 'Together? You'll stay with me? Promise.'

'Always and always and always,' I whispered into her ear. 'And then for more always after that. We shall be as close together as tea and biscuits. Cross my heart and hope to have my bushy-bushy-bob tail pulled 'til it bleeds.'

'Why must we run away?'

'Because the big clompy Judges will be finding what-you-did-with-the-knife and will be wanting to stop me from ever seeing you again. Just like Grandma and Grandpa threatened—'

She seemed shocked. 'That mustn't happen! I couldn't bear to be without you, Bernard.' Her eyes filled with frightened tears. 'You're my bestest of best friends.' She swung her arms around me, nuzzled her nose into my fur and hugged. I patted her head with my paw.

As she nuzzled, I noticed that she had attracted the attention of the other passengers. The young couple stared with disbelief. The clerk halted his rap-a-tap-tapping. The newspaper reader stopped reading his newspaper. The youths no longer swung but gaped.

I could feel their suspicious eyes burning straight through me. Because I'm invisible, you see. Or rather, you don't! I'm not really here—remember, I'm a figment of Annabelle's imagination. Only she can perceive me. I'm only real for her, and for her alone.

As far as the other passengers were concerned, Annabelle was sitting next to an empty seat and was burying her face into thin air. How strange it must've looked! No wonder they were astonished. No wonder they gawked and pointed.

Annabelle looked up at me with streaked cheeks. Then she noticed she was the centre of attention. 'Why are they are all looking at me?' she frowned.

'They're not used to seeing little girls out on their own,' I told her. 'Remember, they can't see me.'

'Of course. But if only they could,' she giggled. 'What a surprise that would be!'

'A giant bright blue bunny rabbit surprise!' I laughed.

Annabelle studied one of the posters, mouthing the words aloud, then reached for her knife. 'Do you think they'll tell? They'll tell the big clompy Judges where to find us?'

'I think they definitely might. They would remember seeing a little girl. It would stick in their heads.'

'Should I stick the knife in their heads instead, then?' She lifted the blade and rotated it. It glistened with wicked glee. 'Just to be on the safe side?'

'Yes.' I nodded. 'I think that's probably best.'

'NAMES?'

'Patrick and Chlamydia Wrench,' Judge Parson picked her way through the wrecked, gloomy living room. Her boots stuck to the blood-soaked floral carpet and colour supplements. 'Seventy-two and seventy-seven respectively, of 101 Hyde-Pierce.'

The corpses' faces had been gouged open to reveal leering grins. The television news flickered in their wide, glassy eyes. The stench of death filled the air. According to procedure, Judges should take only shallow, mouth-only breaths in such circumstances to avoid nausea, but Judge Parson still could feel her stomach beginning to churn.

Dredd breathed deeply as he examined the wounds, the corpse's skulls reflecting in his visor. His expression remained unmoved. 'Multiple entry points on the lower torso,' he muttered. 'Wide blood-spread indicates live victim.'

Parson swallowed. Her forehead prickled with sweat. 'So they were stabbed to death?'

'Facial mutilation conducted after blood flow halted,' observed Dredd. He straightened up and placed his hands on his hip-belt. 'The creep killed 'em, and carved 'em!'

Parson nodded. She had to get out of this apartment before she threw up. 'Anything else?'

'Meds may get something.' Dredd surveyed the living room, the overturned coffee table, the smashed lamps, the grounded wall-duck. 'No signs of a struggle. Perp vandalised the place afterwards. Eldsters were murdered where they sat. Must've been quick.'

Parson stepped into the kitchen; a narrow room, the surfaces smeared and grubby, the sink overladen with pots, mugs and plates. 'What do you think, Dredd? Robbery?' She removed her helmet and shook her hair free. Her breathing was short and rapid and her throat tightened. She doubled up over the waste-disposal chute and vomited.

After she had finished, Dredd appeared behind her. He looked at her with no sympathy or understanding. His mouth remained set in a downturned sneer. 'Unlikely. The female is still wearing a necklace and two gold rings. No obvious motive.'

Parson activated the waste-disposal, but an orange light indicated it was blocked. It gurgled, sputtered and died.

'Witnesses?' said Dredd.

'Neighbour reported the disturbance after popping around to collect holiday funds.' Parson turned the tap, wetted her hands and then brought her cold palms to her cheeks. 'Apparently they go on sightseeing trips to the Cursed Earth—'

'No accounting for dumbness.' Dredd approached her, something held in his right hand. A framed photograph.

The photograph showed the two eldsters beaming beneath some Christmas decorations. Between them perched a young girl. The girl had golden, curly hair and a contented, innocent smile. All their eyes were flash-red.

Parson punched in a locate ID command on her wrist computer. It flashed up a pixelgram of the young girl. 'Annabelle Wrench. Age six. Parents killed in mopad-rage incident two years ago. Lives with grandparents—'

'We've got ourselves one potential witness.' Dredd switched on his radio. 'Dredd to Control.'

'Control receiving.'

Dredd led Parson back to the living room. He gazed out of the rain-spotted window, out into the skyscraper-lit night 'Inform patrols to keep a watch out for one juve, Annabelle Wrench, in vicinity of Hyde-Pierce. I want a full door-to-door and radius search.'

'That's a roj.'

'I also want a Psi to apartment 101. Find out what happened here.'

'You got it. Dredd, proceed to Lower Eighth subway station. Reported incident on subway carriage. Twelve fatalities. It ain't pretty, but whoever it was, they were pretty thorough—'

Dredd was already on his way.

IT WAS LATE evening and the mall had emptied of customers. Shopkeepers locked up for the night and pulled down the grilles over their windows. A single Clownburger bar remained open, its customers bathed in a clinical light.

Annabelle and I descended the escalator, hand in paw. After leaving the station, we'd made our way through the back alley-ways and underpasses. We had no idea where we were going, but we had to find somewhere to hide.

Annabelle looked up at me and smiled as though to reassure me. 'As long as we're together,' she said, 'the bad clompy Judges will never catch us.'

You're probably wondering why I was telling Annabelle to kill people. Of course, it was true that the passengers would've informed us to the bad clompy Judges. Of course, it was true that her grandparents were wicked and mean and deserved to have their faces sliced off.

But the main reason was I didn't want to lose her. She meant everything to me. I adored her, I helped her, I was her secret, bestest friend.

And, being imaginary, I was entirely reliant upon her for my existence. If she forgot about me, I wouldn't be around any more. If she decided she didn't want to know me, there wouldn't be any me to know.

But Annabelle was growing up. She was six, going on seven. I had been sneakily reading child psychology textbooks and I knew that soon she would grow out of me. I knew that I was just a phase that she was going through. Soon she would be interested in glass ponies, boy-bands and make-up.

But then I discovered there was a way. A way that Annabelle and I could remain together forever.

I would drive her insane.

If she was insane, she would never forget about me. We would be together, always and always and always, and then for more always after that. If she was insane, she would even forget that I was imaginary. She wouldn't know what was real and what was not. And then I would be safe.

I started slowly, of course. I began by telling Annabelle to do harmless, naughty things. Writing on the walls. Not eating up her custard. Not tidying away her toys. Poisoning the dog. Each time she would resist, but I would persist, I would dare her and double-dare her and call her a cluck-cluck. And then she would do as she was told.

Then I made her steal the kitchen knife. I taught her how to surprise people with it, how to leap up and frighten them when they least expected.

Oh, the fun we had.

And then the day came when I would push her over the edge. I told her to kill her grandparents.

She enjoyed it, I could tell. She wasn't sure at first, but I convinced her. Because she trusted me. She trusted me more than trust itself.

And now she was beyond help. Now she would never get better. Now she would always imagine there was a giant blue rabbit walking beside her.

'Bernard,' said Annabelle as she skipped off the escalator. 'I'm hungry.'

'Me too.' We approached the Clownburger restaurant. The greasy-sweet smells invited us in. I found that I was bouncing on the spot, my bushy-bushy bobtail all a-quiver.

'But we haven't got any money, Bernard,' she protested, tugging my arm. 'You need money, else it's stealing.'

'It's not stealing,' I explained, 'if there's no-one left alive to pay.'

*   *   *

DREDD APPEARED ON the subway platform and appraised the scene in one glance. The area had been taped off as a clean-up crew fumigated the interior of the carriage with RapiKleen—the Number One Gorebuster. Black bulging hygiene bags lined the platform, each I-D tagged and ready for Resyk; there were more bags than there had been casualties.

Judge Bell approached Dredd and gave a deferential nod. 'All the wounds followed the same pattern. Knife to the throat, then—'

'Closed-circuit?' muttered Dredd, straight to the point.

'Vandalised.' The station manager, a short, oily man, shrugged helplessly. His shirt was sodden with sweat. 'The juves, we've been trying to—'

'Security coverage on public transport is a legal obligation. Two years.'

'I'm merely a consultant, security initiatives are the responsibility of a delegated third party private contractor—'

'Then sue them.' Dredd's voice was like gravel. 'From your iso-cube.' He turned to Bell and indicated that they should leave. 'Anything else?'

'Some facial mutilation of the corpses—'

'Drokk,' muttered Dredd. 'It's the same perp!' He climbed the steps three at a time. 'We can't be more than thirty minutes behind. Get me all the CC footage of the station. I want an I-D.'

Bell jogged after him. 'The teks are on to it already.'

Dredd's helmet radio gave a crackle. 'Dredd, Judge Karena here, Psi-division. I'm at 101 Hyde-Pierce. It's strange. I'm getting a vivid mental image of the murder, it's like a tri-D movie. Very Technicolor, detailed—'

'Spare me the film critique.'

'POVs are not usually so graphic, Dredd. I can see a little girl, about seven, blonde. She's talking, but I'm getting the sense that she's alone. She's afraid. There doesn't seem—' A short gasp. 'Dredd. It was her!'

Dredd breathed another 'drokk' and clicked a setting on the radio. 'You get that, Control?'

'Roj.'

'She took out a whole carriage single-handedly?' said Bell as they emerged into the foyer. Dredd's Lawmaster was parked in the entrance. 'Quite the little girl.'

'Judges should approach suspect with caution,' Dredd told Control as he swung himself into his seat. 'Any incidents in the area?'

'Nothing significant—no, wait. A report of a blood-frenzied attack on a Clownburger joint, Lewinsky Plaza—'

Dredd throttled and was away.

AT THE SOUND of smashing glass, we ran. Discarding our ClownMeals, we bounded out of the restaurant as fast as our feet would carry us. We left the customers slouched over their tables and the workers face-down in their bubbling vats, a ClownCrispy coating forming over them.

An engine sputtered. One of the entrances to the mall had been forced open, and a Judge was driving through the debris on his Lawmaster He sat high in his seat, his jaw set in rigid contempt. In one hand he raised a ferocious-looking gun.

I squeezed Annabelle's hand and tugged her out of sight. 'We must scamper away,' I whispered. 'We must let our bunny-legs turn into whirling blurs and bound and leap and never-been-seen-again.'

She looked up at me fearfully, then ruffled my furry chin-chin. 'Hop onto my back,' I told her. 'Grab hold of my long, flippy-floppy ears and I'll bunny-back you away.'

I crouched and she climbed. Her knees rested on my shoulders and I gripped her ankles. Then I darted softly down the avenue of shops, my padded feet making no sound. The mall was in draped in near-darkness. I knew I would be safe—I am invisible—but feared for Annabelle.

The engine drone grew louder. A loudhailer announced: 'Halt. This is your only warning.'

I broke into a run. Annabelle clutched my ears tightly.

A shot rang out and something exploded behind us. The floor shook and I felt a whoosh of hot air. Some debris cut into my legs, but I kept on going.

DREDD SKIDDED HIS Lawmaster around the ornamental fountain and down the avenue past the Clownburger Bar. Ahead, the covered street disappeared into shadows. Dredd kicked down the accelerator and the bike thundered forward. He activated the forward lamp and a beam blazed through the blackness, its reflection glaring in the shop windows, revealing the floor tiles speeding towards him.

He glimpsed a shadowy figure ahead. It had a strange bobbing up-and-down motion. Range twenty metres.

'Dredd to Control,' he muttered into his radio. 'Suspect located. In pursuit.'

'That's a roj.'

'Heatseeker!' barked Dredd. His lawgiver gave an affirmative beep and switched to the new setting. He levelled and fired. The bullet swerved on the figure before crashing into a heating grill. Dredd drove straight through the crackling flames.

According to the reading, the figure was now range thirty metres. The bike was travelling at forty miles per hour; whatever it was, it was shifting at a superhuman speed.

Dredd gunned the bike up to sixty.

'Dredd,' came the muffled voice of Control. 'We've just been contacted from the clean-up crew at 101 Hyde-Pierce. They've found something in the waste disposal—'

The figure scampered up a stationary escalator. Its shadow grew into a giant as it was caught in the lamp beam.

'And we've got the footage from the Lower Eighth subway. The perp's ID—you're not going to believe this Dredd, but—'

Dredd increased the throttle and rode the Lawmaster up the stairway. 'I know,' said Dredd grimly. 'I can see it, and I don't believe it.'

'THE WRENCHES BROUGHT it back from the Cursed Earth,' explained the iso-cube geno-psychologist. 'A mutie in the form of a super-intelligent giant blue bunny rabbit. Name of Bernard. We presume it was meant as a gift for their daughter.'

Dredd stared into the iso-cube through the small, square plasti-glass window. The figure within squatted in the corner, shivering. A hunched-up shape with large ears, a bushy tail and long, padded feet.

'It killed them and fed the girl into the waste disposal. Odd thing, though. It seems to be suffering from a form of schizophrenic delusion. It believed that the girl was still alive, and was accompanying it throughout.'

'An hallucination?'

'In a way, but more than that,' said the psychologist. 'A transferral. The creature is convinced that it was the girl who committed the murders, acting under its instruction. It was that belief that psi-judge picked up, the belief that the acts were not perpetrated by itself, but by its... well, its imaginary friend.'

AND SO I ended up here. Locked up by the big, clompy judges in a dank, gloomy cell. I sat in the corner, hugged my knees and cried. I cried big, wet, splashy, dribbly tears, because my evil cancer-black heart was sick with pain and grief and fear.

'Don't worry,' said Annabelle, gently stroking my cheek. She nestled herself against my shoulder and looked up at me with wide, sympathetic eyes. 'I'm here with you. And I'll be with you always. Always and always. And then for more always after that.'

LAZARUS

GARY RUSSELL

SHE FELT THE subtle judder as Justice One dropped out of drive, and heard the even more subtle whine as it settled into orbit. She also knew what was coming next.

'What's going on, Karyn?'

That was good. She hadn't even heard the bridge door open. To her left, she saw the Engineer stiffen involuntarily. To her right, the Pilot took in a breath. And across the bridge, without even knowing, she knew the Nav would be hunching her shoulders, trying to look as small and insignificant as humanly possible.

If Judge Dredd knew he commanded this reaction just by walking into the area, he never showed it. To him, people were people. The just or the unjust. The perps or the victims. The crew of Justice One were even more insignificant, and Karyn knew Dredd was barely aware they existed.

'We're in orbit around Lazarus, sir. Waiting to see if we can pick up any signals.'

'Well?'

Karyn sighed. She allowed herself to do that. Working with Dredd as often as she had had given her that little bit of freedom. 'Well, what?'

Karyn smiled to herself—her insubordination would have been noticed by the others and they were probably tensing themselves for Dredd's reprimand. Of course, that's because they only knew Dredd by reputation, not in actuality. It was a reputation Dredd himself saw little reason to challenge, but for Karyn it was tiresome. It made her ability to do her job that bit more difficult.

Dredd was standing beside her, eyes fixed on the view outside. Dull grey clouds, obscuring a dull grey planetoid.

'Well,' he said quietly, 'can you pick anything up?'

'At this range? I'm a Psi-Judge, not a comms unit. The most I can pick up from here is the fact that everyone on board Justice One wishes you'd open an airlock and go for a walk. Suitless.'

'Good,' said Dredd. 'Then we all understand each other.' He turned to the Pilot, who blanched under Dredd's stare. 'Tarrant, tell your crew to prepare for a landing.'

Tarrant tried to reply but couldn't. Instead he just squirmed, shrugged and nodded. Finally he spoke, in a voice that was far less authoritative than a man in his position should have used. 'Umm, sir. Judge Dredd, sir. Telemetry's not in yet on the surface. I'm not quite sure where we can, umm, well, land. You know, I mean, the ground. Could be soggy. Or rock hard. Or, well, perhaps all molten. Umm, so is it all right if we, well, you know, check first?'

Dredd sighed. 'How long, Pilot?'

Karyn wasn't sure if Dredd's tone as he said 'Pilot' related to the question, or a sense of disbelief that such an inadequate could hold such a rank on Justice Department vessel.

'Ten, fifteen at most sir.'

'You've got five, Pilot.' Dredd walked out.

Karyn turned and winked at Tarrant, who smiled sheepishly back.

'He's not as bad as all that,' she said, hoping it would be encouraging.

'No, he's worse,' muttered the Engineer across the bridge.

Karyn got up, stretched and rubbed her left shoulder. Then, seemingly without taking a beat, she was in the Engineer's face, her nose almost touching his, lips drawn back in a snarl.

'That man,' she said, 'has saved your ass more times than your mother wiped it when you were a baby. That man deserves your obedience, your attention and above all, your respect. Is that understood?'

The Engineer didn't flinch. 'Respect is earned, Judge Karyn, not given.'

Karyn didn't breath, she didn't even blink. Instead, she moved away and headed towards the aft door, where Dredd had gone. As she reached it, she called back to the Pilot. 'Four, Tarrant. You've got just four minutes left.' And like Dredd before, she marched out.

*   *   *

DREDD WAS WAITING for her in the rest room.

'You took your time,' was all he said by way of a greeting.

'We have trouble.'

Dredd shrugged. 'Let me guess. The Engineer. Stavin.'

'How did you...?'

'I'm a Judge. It's what I do. Judge people.'

'You know?'

'Know what?'

'He's a droid.'

Karyn noticed with some degree of satisfaction that this idea didn't seem to have occurred to the Judge sat before her. Then again, he was never the easiest of people to be sure about, and she knew better than to try reading his mind. Grud alone knew what she might find inside his head.

'Interesting,' he said. 'You think maybe someone's up to something? Someone doesn't trust us?'

'Doesn't trust you,' she corrected.

Dredd just stared impassively ahead. 'Us,' he corrected. 'I requested you on this assignment. So perhaps we're both under scrutiny.'

Karyn was furious. Her integrity and professionalism were at question, simply by association with Dredd. She considered pointing out how unfair it was, but knew that Dredd's reaction would be utter disinterest, so she squashed her anger down.

He nodded. 'Use it, Karyn.'

'Use what?'

'Your anger. Use it to focus. Something on that planet needs reading. Needs you. That's why you were chosen. That's why I chose you.'

*   *   *

LAZARUS WAS, MUCH to Tarrant's relief, neither molten nor soggy. It was pretty Earth-like, really. Hard, dry ground, a few rocks, some copses and bushes and a dry heat in the air. As he disembarked, he glanced back at Justice One, gleaming, sleek and beautiful.

Home.

They'd left the Navigator aboard. Stavin stood beside him; to his left was the Weapons Officer, Greull—a strongman whose brutish features might have caused him to be screened for evidence of mutant genes somewhere in the family pool.

A few paces behind walked Dredd. Not speaking. Not reacting to anything. Just walking purposefully, always keeping exactly thirty paces behind Tarrant's group.

If it concerned the Pilot that Psi-Judge Karyn wasn't present, he chose not to question it.

After ten minutes' walk, Greull volunteered the first question.

'Why're we here anyway?'

Tarrant shook his head. 'Beats me. Dreary planet anyway.'

Stavin threw a look back at Dredd before responding. 'Lazarus is named after some guy who came back from the dead. It's a new thing—they've been running ads on the Euthanasia Channel, and in the grief-zines. Mega-City One has no established presence here, hence this survey. The outer colonies are using it as a cemetery, apparently.'

'A what?' asked Greull.

'A cemetery. Where they bury their dead,' muttered Tarrant.

'Why?' Greull was confused. A regular Mega-City Judge grunt didn't go in for such things.

'Dunno. P'raps they like it. It's probably just a passing fad.'

Dredd spoke at last. 'Some people believe that we come from "the planet". When you die, it's fitting you return to it.'

Tarrant thought this was daft. 'I mean,' he said, 'I can see that if they bury them on their homeworlds. But if they didn't come from Lazarus in the first place...'

'I don't like dead people,' piped up Greull. 'When I worked the graveyard shift, there was this Auxiliary in the mortuary. Used ta love the stiffs, he did. Kept sayin' that no matter what happened to 'em, he could always make a body look good again...'

Something had jogged Tarrant's memory. 'Not—Hoppy? Hoppy the Necro? I heard stories about him, back in Sector Seven. Hopper, his name was. That guy was a legend. And a bit scary. Some said he loved his corpses a bit too much, if you know what I mean—'

He stopped when a laser blast tore a mug-sized hole through his right calf. He barely had time to cry out before Dredd returned fire, joined by Stavin and Greull, raking Standard Round after Standard Round into the group of trees where the laser had been fired from.

Branches and trunks fell under the gunfire. Dredd signalled for them to stop.

Greull was immediately beside the injured Pilot, helping

him up. Tarrant was trying not to cry out in pain, but it was difficult. Dredd tapped his communicator.

'It's gone wrong, Karyn,' he said. 'Get out here now.'

Minutes later Karyn arrived, slightly breathless. 'My head's killing me,' she started, then saw Tarrant.

'Back-up plan's gone,' Dredd said simply. 'Greull, get the Pilot back aboard. Stay with him. I want him ready to lift off when I get back.'

Greull nodded.

'I should go,' said Stavin. 'Greull's more use to you than me.'

Dredd ignored him. Instead he pointed with his blaster. 'See if you can find the remains of who shot him in the trees.'

Stavin shrugged and wandered off.

'I'd feel happier with Greull, frankly,' said Karyn.

'Why? You can't read a meathead any more than you can a droid.' Dredd looked back at the departing Greull. 'Besides, he's too stupid to do what we have to do. Stavin's got to be more reliable.'

Karyn said nothing, knowing she could never persuade her Senior Judge otherwise.

'Did you get the job done?' Dredd asked after a moment's silence.

Karyn nodded.

'Good. Let's see if Stavin's found anything.'

GREULL WAS EFFORTLESSLY carrying the Pilot in his arms, like a baby. If Tarrant felt embarrassed by this, he didn't say anything. It was more comfortable than walking, anyway.

As Justice One came into view, so did a group of five or six humanoids.

They wore long white cloaks with a blue cross on the right shoulder. They smiled beatifically as the two soldiers got closer.

'Welcome, friends,' said a middle-aged woman. 'Welcome to Lazarus. Welcome home.'

'Not our home,' said Greull, gently setting Tarrant down, the Pilot leaning against him for support.

The woman still smiled. 'Lazarus is everyone's home,' she said.

Greull shrugged. 'Not,' he said simply.

Tarrant thought it was time to take charge. 'I am Judge-Pilot Ferdinand Tarrant. This is my Weapons Officer, Judge Greull. We are from Earth. Are you... expecting us?'

'Oh yes,' said the woman. 'Your plots are prepared.'

'Plots?'

'For your internment. For your burial.'

'But we're not dead,' Tarrant said. Then he felt Greull's hand on the top of his head. 'Greull?' was as much as he could say before the Weapons Officer twisted his head around 180 degrees, snapping his neck instantly.

The woman smiled at Greull, then looked towards Justice One. 'There is another aboard, I believe?'

Greull nodded mutely, then headed into the ship.

The group waited and watched, until a moment or two later, a splash of thick red liquid splashed across the interior of the bridge windows.

'Two down, two to go,' said a younger woman in the group. The leader nodded. 'Indeed, Sister. The Judges will be judged.'

KARYN COULD SEE that Stavin was sifting through ash and dust. He looked up as the Judges approached.

'Automated defences,' he said. 'Tarrant must've triggered something. Could've been any one of us, really. He just happened to be eighteen centimetres ahead of Greull and me.'

'How precise,' Karyn said coldly. 'But then, I suppose that's what droids are good at.'

If Stavin was surprised that she knew, he didn't show it.

'I think the burial grounds are this way,' he said simply, and walked further into the less-than-flourishing wooded area. 'If we trigger off any more defences, it won't hurt if I get hit.'

'Well, he's practical,' Karyn said to Dredd. 'If a bit dour.'

'He's doing his job,' Dredd replied. 'Better to lose a droid than a Judge.'

Karyn decided she couldn't really argue with that and followed them both, lagging a few steps behind, ready for trouble. It was getting dark now, and her head was still throbbing.

As if reading her mind (hey, that was her job!) Dredd called back: 'How's your head?'

'Still aching,' she replied. 'It was definitely a psychic attack. Whatever's down here wanted me out of action.'

'How long?' was his response.

'Until I'm up and ready? Not long. I could try a sweep now,' she added, hoping he wouldn't agree. With her head aching as it did, it'd hurt more than a little to try reading anything on this planet; and since she didn't have a specific area to focus on, a planet-wide scan took a lot of energy. Energy she felt she lacked right now.

'Do it,' was Dredd's emotionless response.

Great. Thanks, Dredd, she wanted to say. Instead, she closed her eyes, stood still and focused her mind. She pictured herself in the wooded area they were walking through; then imagined a vid-droid's view of the area, pulling away, further and further, revealing more of the locality. She saw the edge of the wood, Justice One stationed nearby. She saw fields and hills. She saw lakes and rivers. She saw vast areas until they were surrounded by water, islands. Countries. She saw two, three, four...

She could see the whole planet, mapped before her, flattened like a scan. And she concentrated, concentrated on picking up a mental signature. The signature that had tried to block her earlier.

Nothing.

There was no life on the planet except her. And Dredd. And Greull. And...

Where was Tarrant? Where was Gillespie, the Navigator? Why couldn't she read them?

'Because they are no longer alive,' said a soft voice in her head. *Well, obviously*, Karyn agreed. *Otherwise they'd—*

Hang on!

Who are you? thought Karyn.

'No need for you to use this much mental energy, my

dear,' replied the voice. 'I'm who you're looking for. Welcome to Lazarus. We've been waiting for you.'

Karyn opened her eyes.

She wasn't where she had been. Instead, she was in a flame-lit cavern. She knew instinctively she was underground—the air was slightly stale, the flambeaux didn't move in the wind and there was a small but regular *plip-plop* of dripping water somewhere off to the right. She was stood on a rocky ledge, above a carved out amphitheatre. Sat in this were dozens of robed figures of different ages, heights, sexes and races, even—the latter were aliens, not mutants. Somehow she knew that.

'Why am I here?'

The female voice behind her purred quietly. 'Not "Where am I?" Oh, that's good.'

Karyn shrugged. 'I'm a Psi-Judge. I'm well conversed in astral planes, dreamscapes and mind-jacks.'

Karyn felt, rather than saw, movement. Somehow she knew the owner of the voice was moving around, coming in front of her. Yet she was still surprised to discover that the speaker, whose voice suggested a woman in her fifties, was a small human girl of about five, with blonde pigtails, a blue polka-dot dress and holding a big red balloon. When the tot spoke, the voice was still that of an adult, adding a further disquieting aspect to this particular mind-jack.

'You are here,' said the little girl, 'to bear witness to the revenge of those on Lazarus. Those cast aside by their families and supposed loved ones.'

Karyn frowned. Or was aware that this astral representation of herself frowned. 'I thought that the bodies buried on Lazarus were here because they believed in such a tradition.'

'Did anyone ask them?'

Karyn suppressed a sneer. 'I imagine not. They were dead, after all.'

The girl smiled—a rather thin, cruel smile, Karyn noticed, on one so apparently young and innocent. 'Let's ask them.'

As one, all the robed figures in the amphitheatre turned and looked directly at Karyn and even at the distance she stood, Karyn could see their faces clearly. All were decomposed, putrid, some just skulls, others, rotting cadavers.

One broke ranks, standing in the fourth row. It let its cloak fall away, and Karyn could see a dull, grimy and torn uniform. It might have lost its sheen, but she knew a Mega-City One Judge's uniform anywhere.

The little girl raised her hand without taking her stare from Karyn. Over her shoulder, Karyn saw the spectral Judge raise into the air and take steady, sure steps towards them, walking through the air as if invisible stairs were carved into it.

After a moment, it hovered behind the girl, and Karyn could see the badge; recognise the wolfish features.

'Walker?' Karyn raised an eyebrow. 'Psi-Judge Walker, you ended up here?' She laughed quietly. 'Dredd would find that amusing.'

The little girl however answered. 'We're sure he would, Karyn. Do you recognise any of the other faces here?'

'None,' Karyn replied quickly.

'Oh, I think you need to think about your answers a little more carefully, my dear,' said the little girl. And she clicked her fingers, whereupon a large number of the other robed figures rose into the air and walked across nothingness to reach Karyn.

The Psi glanced at each face. Nothing. She recognised none of them.

The little girl tugged at her sleeve, causing Karyn to look down at her. The little girl tapped the side of her head with her finger and Karyn realised what she was implying.

'No way!' she cried, but it was too late. The suggestion triggered off an automatic instinctive reaction in Karyn's training and she tried reading the corpses.

And, once again, her head seemed to explode inside itself and she screamed in a pain greater than any she'd ever felt before...

DREDD AND STAVIN were crouched over one of the destroyed automated blasters when Karyn's scream reached them. Without speaking, they both launched themselves at full tilt back to where she had been standing.

She was lying on her back, her face contorted in pain, but frozen and now silent. Her hands, similarly now unmoving, were clasped to her head. It was as if she were a statue—but of flesh, not stone. Dredd knelt beside her, feeling for a pulse.

'She's alive,' he muttered after a few seconds.

'She's catatonic,' Stavin said, then looked up as something crashed towards them through the undergrowth.

Dredd's blaster was already drawn, but he let it lower as he realised it was Justice One's Weapons Officer. He glanced sideways at Stavin.

'Greull,' the droid whispered.

'Where's the Pilot, Greull?' asked Dredd. 'Where's Tarrant?'

Greull just stared at the two Judges, and at Karyn's stiffened body. Then, with a roar, he charged them.

Not much in life surprised Dredd. Frankly, not much could halt his reflexes, honed to an immediate response after all his years on the streets. But Greull's unexpected—and loud—attack had taken him by surprise. As a result, he barely aimed as he fired. The shot missed Greull only by an otherwise impressive half-inch, but it was enough of a delay for the big man.

Greull slammed into Dredd with the force of a speeding mopad hitting a griblig—and the Judge's body literally flew through the air, landing twenty feet away. Dredd heard as well as felt at least three ribs crack as he hit the ground, but it didn't slow him down. He'd dropped his Lawgiver gun, but he still had his boot-knife—which he threw with force, the blade whooshing through the air before embedding itself just beneath Greull's collar-bone.

Dredd thought it unlikely he'd killed Greull—but an injury like that should have slowed him down, no question. Greull just grunted, muscles tensing as he wrenched the knife from his body, gore blossoming on his uniform. He advanced on Dredd, shoulders hunched, the knife gripped purposefully in his hand. 'Drokk it!' muttered Dredd.

Suddenly Stavin was there, punching Greull in the back of the head with a sound like a whip cracking.

Greull was on his knees instantly, but still conscious. He growled at Dredd—then stopped.

Dredd watched as, almost in slow motion, accompanied by a louder whip-like noise, Greull's face became a scarlet blur, replaced in a split-second by a gloved fist that sent bits of bone, eye and brain in a variety of directions.

Finally the oversized body topped forward, headless and momentarily jerking onto the ground. Dredd didn't move an inch until Greull's body ceased convulsing.

Then, with a deep breath that hurt his ribs further, he got up, walked silently forward and scooped up his Lawgiver.

Stavin was wiping his gauntlet on the grass.

Without a word, Dredd walked past Greull's body, then turned and fired three shots into the man's still back.

'Not sure that doesn't qualify as Excessive Force, Dredd,' said Stavin.

Dredd glowered at him.

Stavin gently eased Karyn's body up. It was rigid. 'Every muscle in her body is locked,' the droid said. 'She'll be wrecked for a couple of days after she wakes up.' Then he shrugged. 'If she wakes up.'

'Oh, she'll wake up,' said Dredd. 'Someone went to a lot of trouble to draw our attention.' He nodded to both Karyn and then Greull. 'First her scream, then his attack. Greull could have killed me easily. Someone wants me damaged, but alive.'

'Why?'

'Because if I'm weakened, it makes me more susceptible.'

Stavin frowned. 'To what?'

'To this,' said Karyn suddenly, flicking out her hand and touching Dredd's forehead.

And Dredd, like Karyn before him, screamed in agony.

'IS THIS THE best you can do, Hoppy?'

The little girl was looking straight at Dredd.

Karyn was surprised that she wasn't surprised to see Dredd materialise beside her on the ledge overlooking the amphitheatre. She wasn't surprised that Dredd knew Hoppy. He would. Hopper had been Judge Walker's partner in some scam—using knowledge gained from the mortuary slab to extort money from families with undetected Psi-tendencies, she'd heard; fleecing families desperate to stop their children being forcibly inducted into the Academy. Dredd had helped expose Walker's corruption; shot him dead when he resisted arrest. But Hoppy hadn't been a little girl, had he?

'I'm not *really*,' said the little girl, clearly reading Karyn's thoughts. And instantly she changed into a thin, weaselly-looking man with a scar over one eye and a smile playing across his slim, colourless lips.

'Why the girl?' asked Karyn.

'If you'd seen me as me, you might've put two and two together too early, and not given me who I really wanted.' Hoppy flicked his head towards Dredd. 'Seeing Walker was enough to get you curious, but not enough to put your mental guard up.'

Dredd looked at the group of corpses surrounding

Hoppy and Walker. 'Thought I'd seen the last of these creeps,' he muttered.

Karyn just looked at him. 'You knew, didn't you? Before we came on this mission, you knew what we were going to find here.'

Dredd nodded. 'Calling this planet "Lazarus" was Hoppy's invitation. After Walker died, the trail went cold. But I knew Hoppy would want revenge eventually, so I waited. And waited.'

Karyn sighed. 'And "these guys". You know them?'

Dredd nodded. 'All punks I've killed over the last five or six years. Must have needed a good power source to keep this lot going.'

Karyn looked at Dredd. 'I'm lost.'

Hoppy just laughed. 'Go on, Dredd, fill her in. Or better yet, let her read your mind. She'll get the full story and a few truths she might not like. All suits me.'

'No thanks,' said Karyn. 'I can imagine what the inside of Dredd's mind is like, thanks all the same.'

'Can you, sweetheart?' asked Hoppy. 'Can you really? I doubt that very much. I don't believe anyone as gullible as you can have any idea of the depths he can go to, or the sacrifices he's willing to make.'

'You underestimated me, Hoppy,' said Dredd quietly. 'As always.'

Hoppy ignored him. 'Sacrifices, Karyn. You're always just Dredd's sacrifices. If it wasn't you, there'd have been another Psi, another flight crew ready to die for him.'

Karyn looked back at Dredd. 'The crew?'

'All dead.'

'You knew they'd die?'

Dredd nodded. 'Pretty much why I requested them all. Justice One needs a good crew—Tarrant's team weren't it.'

Karyn was appalled. 'You were willing to sacrifice their lives?'

'No good to anyone else, Karyn.'

Hoppy was delighted. 'You see, girly? Y'see? He's evil. A heart darker than a black sun. I've done the world, the whole galaxy a favour bringing him here!'

'Your man gave it away, Hoppy.'

'Which one?'

'Greull. Blabbed to the SJS that he knew you. Used to get bodies fresh into the mortuary, didn't you? Scan their brains for that last little fragment of brain activity, siphoned it off if you were quick enough. And Walker here used to be a Psi-Judge. He created the special network needed to keep them stored safely on their way here.'

'Why?' was Karyn's next question.

Hoppy clapped his hands. 'Revenge, girly. They all wanted revenge—and Walker and I were getting paid handsomely, both by the living and the recently dead, to take Dredd offworld and kill him. Even now, with his body dying on the planet and his mind trapped in this astral plane, millions of credits are flowing into my bank account.'

'After I took out Walker,' explained Dredd, 'all Hoppy needed to do was use the same resources he'd set up previously. And Hoppy didn't even need a Psi any more— Walker had done all the hard graft.'

'Why me?'

'Sorry, Karyn,' said Dredd. 'I knew that Hoppy would want to get me inside this electronic brain-circus of his, and I knew he'd need a Psi to do that. With Walker gone, he'd be unlikely to find another rogue Psi-Judge, so I needed a Judas goat.'

'*Me?*'

'You.'

Karyn looked around the amphitheatre. 'So, our bodies are on Lazarus, but our minds are inside some kind of computer?'

Hoppy clapped again. 'She catches on quick, Dredd. I can see why you like her. Perhaps I'll keep her here as a playmate for you.'

'I'm not going to die?'

Hoppy laughed. 'Grud, no! Where's the satisfaction in that? No, I've been paid well to kill your body—but your mind is here, in purgatory, for eternity. Poetic justice, I think they call it.'

Dredd shrugged. 'You overlooked one thing, Hoppy.'

'Oh? And what's that?'

'Where exactly is this computer that's got all our minds stored in it?'

Hoppy nodded at Walker. 'That was his idea. It's with you, Dredd. You brought it with you!'

'Stavin. The droid!' Karyn swore loudly. 'Of course.'

Dredd laughed cruelly. 'Right—Walker's idea. The one who got found out. The one who got himself killed. The one who, as he begged for his life, fingered you as his accomplice? That Walker?'

Hoppy smiled. 'What can I say? Who knows, if the positions were reversed, I'd probably have done the same. But forgive and forget, I say—I'm really terribly loyal.'

Dredd nodded. 'I can see that. Trouble is, loyalty is a strong bond. It works both ways. Some things are terribly loyal to Justice Department. And, as I said, Walker told us everything.'

For the first time, a look flashed between Hoppy and the reanimated spectre of Walker. It wasn't a happy look. 'What did you tell them, Walker?'

But instead of Walker, it was Dredd who answered. He grabbed Karyn's hands and pressed them against his head. 'Read me!' he commanded.

Karyn's instinct was to refuse, but she realised there was only a split-second to decide.

So she read his mind.

And the first thing she saw clearly was Stavin. She spoke his name.

KARYN WOKE UP with a start. She was lying in the grass, Dredd with his head in her lap. There were electrodes attached by plastic limpets to her forehead and Dredd's, connecting them both. She yanked them away as he stirred, and pushed himself up.

Then she saw a third, longer cable from the side of her head and going along the ground towards—

'Good work, Karyn,' said Dredd, breaking her concentration.

She didn't care for his gratitude. Instead she looked

across the grass, following the cable to its end, in fact to where Stavin stood, holding Hoppy in a tight grip. The human was trying to escape, but Stavin had him held tightly. The cable that had been attached at one end to Karyn went into a socket in Stavin's neck.

'You're the repository?' she asked.

Dredd answered. 'Stavin came to me eight months ago. He was originally a clean-up droid that Walker and Hoppy rebuilt to store their mindscape in. I had him rebuilt and reprogrammed to pose as an Engineer, and got him posted on attachment to Justice One, ready for when Hoppy here sent me the bait.' He looked at Hoppy. 'As I said, loyalty is a strong bond.'

Hoppy spat at Dredd. 'I suppose you're going to kill me?'

Dredd shook his head. 'No. You're going to an iso-cube in Mega-City One.'

Karyn pointed to Stavin. 'And the minds locked inside him? Inside Hoppy's psychic circus?'

Stavin answered her. 'When we get back to Earth, my hard drives will be completely dumped and erased. The "psychic circus", as you call it, will be gone forever.'

Karyn was appalled. 'That's murder,' she said.

Dredd shrugged. 'They were already dead. They can't die again, not in law.'

Karyn was livid. 'I'm not talking about Walker and the others. I'm talking about Stavin. You're going to erase him. His personality. Everything. That's murder!'

'No,' said Dredd, impassive. 'That's loyalty.'

JUDGE FEAR'S BIG DAY OUT

SIMON SPURRIER

AN OLD MAN sauntered along a gravel pathway.

If it were possible to personify an adjective; to somehow distil the essence of a personal characteristic to its utmost purity before pumping it, doughnut-style, into its unsuspecting host, then his name should, by rights, be 'Cheery.'

It was not. His name was Emmet McBarlot.

He was eighty-seven. He wore an ancient raincoat with more pockets than a novelty Shuggy table, a lurid sweater designed for the less tasteful class of acid-junkie, and a knitted hat that, upon closer inspection, said *World's Best Mom*. He radiated joviality. He oozed open-minded acceptance and honest, genuine interest in the world around him.

He was as blind as a brick, and today—like every other—he'd come to the park for his lunch. He ambled along the path with a smile, savouring the feel of smooth pebbles through the worn soles of his Oldfellas™ orthotics. So familiar was the route that he barely needed his lasercane; brandishing its telescopic tip only to avoid the more kamikaze breed of jogger. Given that such anaerobic futsies had thus far remained absent, Emmet was the very picture of serenity.

At irregular internals he paused to enjoy the sun on his wrinkled face, or to smile at the happy shrieks of distant juves at play. At large within the pleasant environs of the Norman Lamont memorial gardens, rarely was there a happier being in the whole of Mega-City One.

Oh, there had been misfortunes in Emmet's life, of course. Losing his eyes to a crew of overzealous organleggers; his Mary succumbing to the Black Rot after the Big Nec'; he'd even spent a spell in the cubes when the Dems organised a protest march right along his daily stroll-route—but not once had he complained. He went through it with a smile and a nod, and in the chaos of the Meg that was as rare a thing as an apologetic Judge.

At a certain point, halfway along the shingle path, near the tinkling fountain and the copse of *Real Actual Organic* trees, there stood a styrosteel bench. Today the tip of his lasercane tapped at an unexpected protrusion; buzzing angrily at its contact with something long and bony.

'*Ow,*' it said.

'Sorry,' Emmet grunted, shuffling further along the bench, 'didn't see you there.'

'*No...*' The stranger's voice owed less in its cadence to the usual *seen-it-all* Big Meg burr than to something scaly with a forked tongue. '*Nor anything else, it would seem...*'

'Heh,' Emmet grinned, 'you got that right.' Satisfied that the remainder of the seat was unoccupied, he lowered himself with a geriatric creak. 'Not fer a good few years, anyhow.'

'*That is... unfortunate...*'

'Ah, you get used to it. Name's Emmet, incidentally. Emmet McBarlot. Don't think I recognise your voice. First time in the park?'

'*Not entirely...*' The silence dangled, and Emmet had the distinct impression that the stranger was sighing—as silent as a shadow. '*I did some of my best work here, once...*'

'Once?'

'*I've only just got out of the cubes, Mister McBarlot.*'

Emmet considered this and waved it away with a shrug. 'City like this,' he said, 'everyone's been in trouble maybe once or twice. Coupla months inside ain't no sin in my book, friend. Don't exactly make you *evil* or nothing, does it?'

'*Evil is as evil does.*'

Emmet nodded amiably, not really listening. His concentration was instead applied to a search through his many pockets for a bag of crushed wheatymunce which, when finally extricated, he began to scatter at his feet.

'For the birds,' he explained.

Sure enough, the sound of frantic fluttering circled closer, mingled with the appreciative chattering of cheery avifauna. Emmet imagined their colourful bodies, sweeping down from the magnificent trees, and sighed happily.

His companion watched with interest as a squadron of obese radsparrows disentangled themselves from the fungus coated *faux*-furs and swooped clumsily, pecking and clawing each other aside. The old man, chuckling at their delighted squawks, remained blissfully unaware that their delight had proved a little *too* intense for mere wheatymunce, and that they were now engaged in a frenzied brawl to determine which of their number should be cannibalised first.

'Now, now,' Emmet smiled (as a disengaged sparrow leg spiralled past his ear), 'there's plenty to go around.' He leaned towards the stranger. 'They really love their wheatymunce.'

'*So I see...*'

The stranger shifted his weight. Bending down to admire the birds, Emmet supposed.

One by one the guzzling sparrows—now dripping with gore—glanced up at the tall figure, its dark shape blotting the sun.

Their eyes bulged.

'Ah,' Emmet nodded, noting the abrupt silence. 'They've settled down a bit.'

He rummaged in another pocket and produced a crumpled hamplant sandwich. 'You want to share, kid?'

'*Thank you, no,*' the reed-thin voice hissed. '*I require no sustenance...*'

'Fair enough,' Emmet shrugged, spraying crumbs. 'Dieting, huh?'

'*Something like that, Mister McBarlot...*'

'Call me Emmet, kid.'

*　　*　　*

ROOKIE JUDGE DELPHI was familiar with the idea of failure. He'd been expecting it ever since he could remember, and all the many times it had conspicuously failed to materialise hadn't dented his certainty of its eventual arrival.

He'd wanted a quiet existence. A Tek posting, maybe, or—*dare he dream?*—an administrative role in Accounting Division. Something bookish and out of the way, that was as high as *he'd* ever climb; he knew that. He'd *always* known it, and so he'd buried himself in the Academy's library, he'd shirked theory classes, was deliberately obtuse around tutors and had spent every combat lesson assiduously avoiding violence. His conviction that he would be incredibly bad at it all was overpowering, so why bother?

And then—drokk it all—he'd gone and passed each of his combat, ballistic and aggression examinations with top 2% grades. The examiner had called him a 'natural-born street Judge'. It simply wasn't fair.

He'd spent his whole life awaiting failure, and had somehow neglected to enjoy the successes he'd achieved in its place. He'd been aware of its spectre for the last nineteen years, hanging over him like a rusty Sword of Damocles.

It simply seemed particularly unfair that it was today— the most important of his life—that it had finally decided to acquaint itself with gravity.

'Eyes on the monitor, rookie,' a voice said, startling him. 'Quit daydreaming.'

It was a voice built of granite.

Therein lay the problem. Street assessment, his research had shown, would involve a fairly standard patrol:

breaking heads, keeping the peace, blasting creeps, blah blah *blah*. Smoothing out the city's kinks whilst some holier-than-thou senior Judge sat around and watched. He'd never been one for undue confidence—but, riding the crest of his apparent inability to do wrong, he felt that even *he* could handle such evils.

He hadn't expected to run into (so far) a mob of hungry muties, a futsie aeroball team, an out-of-control construction droid and an endless parade of sobbing children, screaming mothers, battered eldsters and a million-and-drokking-one other things that made the Academy look like a giggle.

And all under the watchful eye of His Majesty. Old Stoney Face.

Judge Joe Dredd.

Rookie Judge Delphi had drokked up so spectacularly since the examination began that he felt like he'd entered a meta-state of *antibrilliance*. It was like he'd saved up a lifetime of drokk-up just to spend it all at once.

'I have to tell you to pay attention one more time, rookie, there'll be trouble...'

Dredd's voice, like a tombstone in his ear.

He leaned over the viewing screen and tried to ignore the whine of the H-Wagon's engines. Hovering several thousand feet above the city was all very well, but getting travel-sick, he was pretty certain, was *not* something that happened to a street Judge.

Why did it have to be Dredd? His mere presence had been more than enough to throw Delphi's aim off, and just the thought of that iron countenance (the iceberg chin, the lips like a bow aimed at the sky, the eyes like... well, who the drokk knew?) staring at the back of his head was all it took to leave him floundering like a first-year cadet. This was a man who'd failed his own *clone*, Gruddammit! How was a slacker with a taste for literature like *Delphi* supposed to pass? It wasn't *fair*!

And it got worse.

Chump-dumping, chav-ganging, zziz-running, kerb-crawling: these were crimes Delphi could have handled. The escape, on the other hand, of an immortal alien supervillain—part of the infamous Dark Judge quartet which had plagued the city and massacred countless cits — went beyond merely 'unfair'.

Halfway through the installation, the Teks reported, of a high-energy ion zone around Judge Fear's glasseen prison, something had gone wrong. The bubble picked up the charged ions and overheated; the failsafes failed; the shutdown circuits shut-down themselves—and before suction traps could be deployed, Fear's spirit was oozing up the ventilation shafts like a particularly repugnant smell. A report from a sector 34 costume-shop attendant claiming that a 'ghost' had possessed her boss and vanished with half the GoffMob© stock came as little surprise.

In times of crisis, the city knew who to turn to. Someone dependable. Someone intractable. Someone who'd led it from danger time and time again.

Someone to whom Delphi was, currently, unavoidably attached.

Wherever Dredd went, *he* went. Rookie street assessment.

Hoo-drokking-ray.

His monitor *pinged* with inappropriate cheerfulness.

'We've got him,' he announced, fighting dread. 'PSU have a fix. Y-you, *ah...* you want it on screen, sir?'

Dredd was at his side in an instant: a blue and gold storm-cloud packed with rocks.

'You read the rap-sheet, Rookie?'

'O-of course, s—'

'Then you know the MO. You look into the face of Fear, you're munce. You want to die of terror, rookie?'

'E-even on *screen*, sir?'

'You want to find out?' A gauntleted hand waved the suggestion away. 'Where is the creep?'

Delphi eyed the PSU report nervously. 'In a public park, sir. Sector 108. Reports of fatalities.'

The H-Wagon dipped as it raced off, the pilot not waiting for a cue. Delphi resisted the urge to puke.

'What are his movements?' Dredd barked. 'Can we cut him off?'

Delphi frowned, wondering if someone was having a joke at his expense. 'The, ah... the perp appears to be sitting on a bench, sir.'

'What?'

'He's just... sitting there. Not doing anything.' Delphi's eyes hit upon a nugget of information. Enlightenment dawned. 'Ah! PSU think he may have a hostage!'

The revelation sank like a lead sponge.

'Hostage? *Bullstomm.* Death and his boys aren't big on negotiation...'

The PSU system dumped a series of flickering notes onto the screen, automated cameras supplying IDs and records.

'"Male citizen",' Delphi read aloud, 'name of "Emmet McBarlot" ...uh... "*citizen lacks sight following criminal theft in '04*" ...He's blind, sir.'

'That explains why he's still alive. Doesn't explain what he's doing there.'

Delphi squinted at the notes one last time, and swallowed.

'He... ah...'

'Yes?'

'He's eating a sandwich, sir.'

JUDGE FEAR SLOUCHED against the bench and relaxed necrotic shoulders. The bear-traps mounted there were heavy and hot; but the image was worth the discomfort.

To his great surprise and slight embarrassment, he was enjoying himself. He felt better than he had done for years, which—given his incarceration within a dollop of glasseen for much of the decade—was not a great feat. Still, the growing pile of dead joggers, strays and young lovers scattered at his feet was a pleasant addition to the already revolting scenery of the Lamont Memorial Gardens: the perfect place for introspection. During his colleagues' brief reign—the Necropolis, as they'd called it—he'd lost count of the cits he'd dispatched in this place. The addition of mock-spot sunlight bulbs, speakers that piped the sound of happy juves, and a fountain so sludge-clogged that even the used Bonkadoms floating on its surface provided welcome colour, could not absolve the smog of gloom that pervaded it.

Except, it seemed, to the blind.

Emmet, Fear had decided, was like a machine: indiscriminately shovelling out good intentions and advice. He poured forth his cheerful observations with breathless optimism, pausing only for recourse to his own mighty founts of experience.

'So,' the blind man asked, when his most recent anecdote—*How I Survived the Robot War and Got Hitched, All in One Day*—ended, 'what brings you to the park?'

'*Oh... you know. Just...*' Fear shrugged, on uncertain ground, '*...thinking.*'

'No better place for it,' Emmet waggled a finger, 'long as it leads to action. Unemployed, are you? Man can have too much thinking time.'

'*No... I have a job. I'm just...*' Fear fumbled for the right word, lamely settling for: '*Sick. Of it all, that is.*'

Emmet, still chewing on his leathery sandwich, considered this.

'Well...' he said, spraying hamplant, 'not really my place to say, but... hell! There's people'd *kill* for a job... and here's you saying you got one but don't like it?'

'*It's not that simple, Mister McBarlot. It's more a... a vocation, you might say. I just wonder whether I'm suited...*'

'What's it you do, son?'

Fear steepled his claws. 'The Annihilation of All Life, Everywhere' had always sounded so *pompous*.

'*Let us say... population relocation...*'

'Making sure there's enough habs to go round?'

'*And a healthy surplus eventually, we hope...*'

'We?'

'*My colleagues.*' Fear shuffled in his place, embarrassed despite himself. '*I'm sorry to say they are currently incarcerated also...*'

Emmet's noisy mastication paused and an edgy look flitted across him, as if this association with criminality stretched even his tolerance. A broad smile quickly dawned.

'*Ahhh...* Corporate tax evasion, right? *Meh*—like I said, we all been in trouble before. Can see how it might make things tricky, mind.'

'*Mm... Besides, I'm weary of... playing second fiddle...*'

'Don't get on with your boss?'

'*He's the life and soul, Mister McBarlot. I'd just appreciate a little more recognition...*'

'So you're feeling worthless. Understandable. But, hey—you're better off than most, right? One day you'll look back on this and laugh, you take it from me.'

Fear watched with quiet interest as a group of Judges sprinted between the nearby mould-vines, guns drawn. He'd been expecting them.

'*Laugh...*' he echoed, distant. '*Mm.*' He waited until the fools were close enough to draw a bead on the bench, glaring through rangefinders, before hinging open his visor.

The Judges collapsed, one by one.

'*You know, Mister McBarlot, I think you might be right.*'

''Course I am,' Emmet nodded, oblivious. 'It's never as bad as it seems.'

'*You have job experience?*'

'I'm eighty-seven, son. Not much in this town I haven't done.'

'Tell me... Did you ever start a task... a monumental task... only to realize that you will never... never... be finished?'

Emmet allowed this quandary to sink in.

'We-ell,' he ventured, squinting. 'There was one time I got this job up at the Alien Zoo. Mucking out, right? I tell you, some of them big critters don't do things by halves... Some days it sure felt like I'd never be done.'

'An interesting analogy,' Fear said, gloomy. *'Shovelling stomm and a lifetime's vocation.'*

To his infinite astonishment, Emmet reached out blindly and slapped him companionably on one spiny shoulder.

'Heh, well. Stomm happens, kid. Fact of life.'

Fear regarded the heap of bodies strewn around the bench. *'To some more than others, it seems...'*

'Right again. Thing is, you gotta keep going. You gotta go the distance, see, 'cos there's too many folks'll give up at the first sign of trouble—and then nothing ever gets done.'

If he'd had one, Fear would have chewed his lip. *'You make it sound easy, Mister McBarlot.'*

'Heh—it *is*!' The old man grinned. 'You just gotta *enthuse*, see? It's not the end of the world, is it?'

'Not yet...' Fear nodded, feeling far chirpier. *'Not yet...'*

STREET JUDGES HUNKERED close to the grimy walls of the park's perimeter, leaving a blue and red wall of cooling Lawmasters behind them. As with even the least impressive of spectacles, the city's bored masses, fed by the usual assortment of snackychow stalls and hotsprog wagons, had gathered within moments to gawp. Hov-cameras swarmed like sentient basketballs, guided by scoop-hungry journalists, and it was only when several were sentenced to obliteration (Code 53#Z: Getting in a Judge's Way, Drokk It) that the media effort cooled.

On Rufus Dogg Overped tactical command had been established aboard a dented HQ Platform, its steel hull rust-stained and its oily interior crammed to capacity. Unit Commander Klintyre, unwittingly the highest-ranking Judge, thus found himself presiding over veterans, Teks, Psis and a legion of others, each with the firm conviction that *their* opinion was correct and that everyone else was obliged to hear it. Klintyre's attempts to affect order had so far succeeded like a fattie's diet, and it was with an enormous sense of relief, and only a *little* overbearing awe, that *He* arrived.

The throng fell silent.

'Who's in charge?' Dredd said. Or maybe shouted. There was little distinction.

'Sir,' Klintyre saluted, face reddening.

Dredd looked him up and down. His expression put Klintyre in mind of a lion-tamer being confronted by a bedraggled kitten.

'What's on the cards, Klintyre?' Dredd barked. 'You got an escaped supercreep out there. Where's the cavalry?'

Oh Grud, Klintyre thought.

'Sir, early attempts to storm the park were... *ah*... w-we lost a few good Judges and—'

'Someone order them in?'

'N-no, they volunt—'

'Their own damn fault, then. What action since?'

'Well, obviously we've been discussing our options an—'

'Options?' Dredd spat the word. 'Only "option" is what kind of ammo to use.'

'Sir, it's not that simple. There's a civilian inv—'

'Civilian?' The lip curled further still, now in serious danger of turning inside out. 'Klintyre, you got munce for brains? That's *Judge Fear*! You'll lose more than one drokking cit if he goes AWOL! Get onto Arms-Div, get a flyer out there, *nuke* the creep! You blast him to stomm, you suck his spirit up. End of story.'

'B-but the civilian—'

Dredd almost roared. '—is *toast*! What's the matter with you all?' He scowled across the room like an angry teacher. 'You got problems with *acceptable casualties*?'

'Er...' said a voice. Something small and rotund waddled into the light. Dredd regarded it like he'd found it on the sole of his boot.

His name was Freel. He was the PSU delegate. Cowering beneath Dredd's visored gaze, there had never been a more wretched individual.

'T-there... ah... there may be a problem...' he said.

OUTSIDE, DELPHI REGARDED his reflection in the grimy flanks of the HQ Platform, listening at the door with as much discretion as he could. Dredd had told him to wait outside. He hadn't felt inclined to complain.

'Ultra Deep Cover,' the little PSU man was saying within. 'H-he's a sleeper—thinks that he really is Emmet McBarlot, respectable, care-in-the-community, all the works, sir. We, uh, we haul him in once a month and, f-flip the switches, as it were. When we put him back he forgets everything.'

Dredd's silence, Delphi reflected, did not bode well.

Still, it made sense. Some people were born to chat to, to confess to, to ask for advice. All the eavesdropping-in-bars in all the world couldn't hope to outdo a blind eldster in a park in the race to rake in dirty secrets.

Emmet McBarlot, the little man suggested, had the highest stoolie-rating anywhere in the city. The Wally Squad, the Council of Five, the Public Surveillance Unit—none of them were keen to lose their golden boy.

The pause stretched out after that, and when Dredd's gravelly tones announced a speechless 'Drokk' of irritation, Delphi found himself jerking involuntarily. He'd heard it all too often today—generally as a result of his own dismal performance.

He stared at himself in the reflection again and felt an ugly voice stir inside his mind. It chattered behind his eyes, already knowing it wouldn't like the answers to its questions.

What now? it whispered. *Wait 'til Old Stoney fails you? Wait for the lobotomy? Or, hey, maybe you'll get lucky—maybe they'll just kick you outta the city. It's not like they'll just turn you loose, hotshot. You're a liability. What now? Eh? What now?*

He realised with a tiny stab of surprise that he wasn't

nearly as accustomed to the idea of failure as he'd imagined, and a small tremble grew in his fingertips. Why, he wondered, did his mind wait until *now* to go and get *ambitious*?

Well, it was too damned late. Dredd had enough on his plate right now without some inept rookie trying to impress him, and he'd just have to live with that. He'd spent his whole life expecting to screw up. It was too late to change his mind.

He stared at himself... and stared... and stared... and slowly realised that what he was looking at wasn't his reflection, but the reflective surface itself.

A memory sagged into his brain like a bubble rising through oil; something plucked from one of the countless books he'd flickered through when he should have been training. One more wasted afternoon, at the time. One more moment, just marking time until he crashed out of the Academy.

The book had been called *Perseus and the Gorgon*.

'Drokking hell,' he said.

And then—astonishing everybody, though certainly nobody more than himself—he stepped into the HQ Platform and started shouting.

HAD HE POSSESSED a face, Judge Fear would have been smiling. Or, at least, *sneering*.

He was already feeling brighter. He felt as if he'd taken a cold shower after waking, and was looking at the world in a new light. He was feeling urges that slowly, reluctantly, had been ebbing away though all the long years of his imprisonment. They made him feel young and giddy, like an irrational teenager who'd discovered girls for the first time.

Fear had never felt like that about girls. His adolescent revelations had revolved around far less mundane concerns.

He wanted to kill and kill and kill and kill and kill and kill...

'I dunno, kid,' Emmet was saying, 'I guess I'm just too darned old for all these gizmos and optic-wotsits and whatnot. Not my thing, see? But—whaddabout you? No offence, but it sounds like you got a definite throat problem, there.'

'The nature of my task is such that certain... physical adjustments are necessary...'

'Work related injury? Maybe getting back into your job ain't such a good idea after all.'

'No, no... You were right before. You've convinced me. I've been hesitating too long. It was never like this in the good old days.'

'Hah! I hear that!'

'It's time I started pulling my weight again...'

'That's the spirit!'

'What's the saying?' Fear drummed his claws on the metal of his skull-like belt buckle. *'"No rest for the wicked."'*

'Hah, never a truer word, kid,' Emmet chuckled. 'Speaking of which—time I was off.'

Emmet unfolded in a series of awkward ratcheting movements, grunting all the way, wobbling arms reaching for his cane. Fear stood slowly beside him, cloak draping around him like a living bruise, bear traps sending toothy glints across the park. Pendulous chains unravelled from the rising form, dragging and twisting like slack, reluctant serpents.

The Dark Judge bent slowly at the waist, head drawing close to Emmet's.

'Well, it's been real pleasant, kid.'

'*Indeed, Mister McBarlot... It's been an education...*'

'And you remember what I said—you gotta keep *going*, remember?'

'*Oh, I intend to... I owe you my thanks, Mister McBarlot...*'

'Ah, no sweat, kid. Give 'em hell, you hear?'

Fear's hand curled backwards, razor-point claws straightening.

'*I shall, Mister McBarlot... I shall... Starting now...*'

And Fear's hand shot forwards faster than a bullet; talons shredding the air; a blur of knife-points snatching for Emmet's wrinkled brow—

—and bounced off something hard and flat.

Fear looked down at his crumpled limb, shredded knuckles dislodging shards of glass from the screen that had materialised before him. Adjacent to his crippled hand a fractured mirror image reflected his recoil of surprise. Bewildered, he glanced up in furious enquiry—and saw something entirely unexpected.

FIFTY FEET ABOVE, Rookie Judge Delphi struggled with the H-Wagon's winch controls, its precious cargo dangling on taut adamnstyn cable. The Sector 108 Mega-Mart droids had been more than a little surprised at the Judicial team that had burst in moments earlier to commandeer one of the twenty-foot mirrors reserved for the new ballet school in Patrick Swayze block. Delphi wondered how they might have felt had they known its purpose.

Of course, when Perseus killed Medusa he used the mirror himself, getting close enough to the freaky fem to hack off her head. Delphi had always wondered about that. Surely, he'd reasoned, if everything she looked at turned to stone, it was far easier to stand *behind* the mirror and let her ex *herself*.

Not mythic enough, maybe.

'You daydreaming, rookie?' Dredd growled, voice as emotionless as ever. If he was even remotely impressed by Delphi's plan, he didn't show it.

Delphi sighed, returning his eyes to the winch.

'Of course not, sir.'

JUDGE FEAR STARED into his own face for a fraction of a second. It was, put simply, the most horrific and soul-wrenchingly awful thing he had ever seen

His stolen body jolted as if electrified. Its heart detonated somewhere inside its ribcage, its blood boiled in its veins, its brain haemorrhaged so violently that its head all but exploded, and Judge Fear's immortal spirit was ejected, screaming, from the useless morsel that remained.

He coiled into the air like a tornado, a feral howl boiling across his contorted face, an ethereal cloak of shadow and evil spiralling around him—

—straight into the suction trap on the underbelly of the waiting H-Wagon. He was compressed into its metallic confines like a pulsating banshee, clutching at the air in a vain attempt to resist the pull.

Somewhere, on the edge of his hearing, from the guts of the hovering beast that had thwarted him, a gravelly voice said:

'Good work, Delphi. Just had a message from Control. Seems Grand Hall are setting up a new Division off the back of all this thing. Strictly experimental.'

'S-sir?'

'Literary Research Division, *Judge* Delphi.'

AND IN THE park, shielded from the inhuman shrieks of a newly-captive spirit by the delighted sounds of giggling juves and tinkling water fountains, Emmet McBarlot ambled along the path and whistled through his teeth.

'What a nice young chap,' he muttered, cane *tap-tap-tapping* at the gravel.

PASSIVE/AGGRESSIVE

JAMES SWALLOW

DREDD STRUCK OUT with his fist. It was textbook, right out of the manual, and it slammed into the soft, fleshy matter of the leering face in front of him. The impact brought a satisfying crunch of synthi-bone.

'*Izzat the best you got? You hit like a little girl!*'

He followed with an uppercut and another right. His target moaned and fell away from his coiled fists, sinking into the floor. The walls twitched and new shapes emerged from them. Some looked like ordinary citizens, others grotesque caricatures of famous celebrities. He had to rein himself in from striking something that bore a startling resemblance to *himself*. Dredd kicked the *faux*-Judge aside and fought his way up the spongy line of the corridor, ducking lazy haymakers from the droning doppelgangers.

'Yes!' It was almost a cheer, echoing through the air from the hidden public address speakers in the domed roof.

'That's the spirit! That's real aggression, not the diluted tizzies you simps think is angry! Get stroppy, Dredd!'

He dispatched more flesh-dummies and mock blood splattered from their squashed noses. Dredd's gritted teeth bared in a snarl, and he made a backhand strike that was plainly gratuitous; for a second, the Judge almost felt like he was enjoying this.

'You are your own worst enemy!' said the other voice, nasal and whiny. It was one of those voices that made you want to hit someone. Hard. 'Look at this barbarity! I ask you, is this really what we want for our children?'

The last figure doubled up from a crippling knee in the gonads and folded away. With a sigh, the fleximorph walls went quiet and returned to a neutral state.

'*Thank you for using the Punchateria and please come again! We hope you enjoy the rest of your hyper-violent day at the Aggro Dome!*'

Dredd emerged from the arcade and surveyed the theme park with a scowl, ignoring the automated pleasantries. 'Leary!' he snapped into his radio, 'How far now?'

'We're having trouble locking down the location—'

'I don't want excuses!' Dredd retorted. 'Where's the office, drokk it?'

He could hear the other Judge recoil over the link. 'Uh, go north past the Big Leap and the Wood Chopping stand... Then right through the Smash 'n' Bash...'

'On my way,' growled Dredd, striding forward. His hands flexed absently inside his dark green Department-issue gloves.

'I'm appalled,' the nasal voice whined from the PA.

'This is just horrid, it really is. I mean, can't we all just... get along?'

'Oi oi oi!' Dredd spun on the spot as a rough-looking Oi-Bot emerged from the shadows and menaced him. 'D'yoo wont saahm?'

His Lawgiver was in his hand faster than he could think; the pistol bucked and a bullet took the robo-thug's head from its shoulders. A sneer escaped Dredd's mouth. His fuse was getting pretty damn short.

He pressed on; faintly, he could still hear the moronic chanting of the protestors outside...

'DON'T GET MAD! Mad is bad! Don't get mad! Mad is bad!'

Judge Dredd's lip curled as he brought his Lawmaster to a halt in the plaza. 'Must have taken them weeks to think that one up,' he muttered, climbing off the bike and throwing a cursory nod to the site officer—a female Judge, watching the crowd from the lee of a parked H-Wagon. He glanced at her badge. 'Leary?'

'Dredd,' she returned the nod. 'Just routine crowd control, we've got it covered. What brings you here?'

He indicated the broad copper hemisphere of the Aggro Dome. 'Passing through. Thought I'd check it out.' The flat sides of the theme park were reflected in his visor. Huge blood-red letters and a massive mailed fist cresting the roof. 'Hard to believe this place is still doing business.'

'Not for long,' said Leary. 'As of five today, Houston Parks Incorporated are shutting it forever. The mayor caved in to these busybodies and ordered the closure.'

Dredd scanned the gathering with a practised eye. These weren't any angry cits on a job march, or wannabe block maniacs; they were, for want of a better word, *tame*. They carried placards that said things like 'Love not Hate', 'Peace On, Not Peace Off' and 'Cuddles = Wuv'. Most of them seemed to be New Nu-Agers and Happy Clappers, busy strumming lutes and plaiting each other's hair. 'They got a permit for those instruments?'

Leary nodded. 'Sadly, yes. Be glad you weren't here yesterday when they had the accordions.'

'Grud...' Movement among the demonstrators caught Dredd's eye, and he watched a figure in a smock drift through them, stepping up to address the crowd. 'Who's the simp with the teeth?' he asked, as the man smiled a perfect toothpaste ad smile.

'Cliffo Phabian, of the Campaign for a Kinder, Gentler Mega-City One. He's the head cheese of these peaceniks.'

'Cheese is right,' Dredd noted, as Phabian beamed.

When he spoke, Phabian's whiny voice carried across the plaza. 'My friends!' he began. 'We told the mayor to give peace a chance... and today we can bring peace to a— uh, a piece of our lovely city!' There was some clapping before he spoke again. 'For too long the Big Meg has had to tolerate this out-of-date eyesore!' He jabbed a finger at the dome. 'This monstrous carbuncle encourages violence and hate... and we all know that this is a metropolis of peaceful people!'

'Ten minutes on the Graveyard Shift would beat that idea right out of him,' muttered Dredd.

'Thanks to our diligence,' gushed Phabian, 'incidents of uncontrolled aggression inside and outside this horrid place were reported to the city council and the Aggro Dome was exposed as the bad influence it truly is!' The demonstrators chanted their approval. 'Today is the day the violence dies!'

Judge Leary eyed him. 'You don't look convinced, Dredd. I thought you'd be pleased to see this place shut— you tried to do that the day it opened, right?'

He nodded. 'Summer of '02. Hot that year, short tempers. Chief Judge sent me in to give it the once-over and things got out of hand. I recommended closure, but the owner cited "teething problems".'

'And it's been here ever since, letting drokked-off citizens beat up robots and break things for ten creds an hour, nine to five, seven days a week...'

Dredd grimaced. 'There's only one way to control citizen aggression,' he said, tapping his badge, 'and we're it.'

'Wait a second,' said Leary. 'Somebody's coming out.'

'Trouble?'

'Maybe...' The Judge spoke into her helmet mic. 'All units, look sharp.'

'I see her.' The voice of another Judge across the plaza sounded in Dredd's helmet speaker. 'It looks like the Tarbox woman. She's got two droids with her.'

'Betsy Tarbox. She's the senior staff at the dome.' Leary nodded. 'Disagreeable type, if you ask me.'

'A human employee?' Dredd was mildly surprised. With unemployment rife citywide, meeting a citizen with an actual job was a relative rarity.

'The only one. She's an anger manager, helps people get in touch with their inner rage, that sorta thing.'

Dredd began a slow approach. 'I don't like it,' he said. 'She looks too calm for someone about to lose their career. This place shuts, and her job is in the toilet.' He tapped his helmet mic. 'All Judges, be advised. Potential Future Shock Syndrome incident in progress.'

Leary's face soured; she had respect for the veteran Judge, but now he was walking in and taking over without so much as a by-your-leave. 'Dredd, just a Gruddamn minute—'

The crowd had made way for Tarbox, glowering at her and her robot 'hurt-me-mechanoids' from the Slap-a-Rama. 'Mister Phabian,' she said in a clear, even accent, 'I applaud your efforts, and just to show there are no hard feelings, I wondered if you'd like to officially shut the park down.' She held up a remote control unit. 'It's 16:59. I'd like *you* to press the button.'

Cliffo blinked owlishly and then let out another dazzling smile. 'What a lovely gesture! In the spirit of peace and harmony, I'd be happy to!' Phabian reached for the control.

'Hold it!' said Dredd, pushing his way through the protestors. 'No one is touching anything—'

His order came a moment too late.

It all happened in a flash. The remote—actually an electro-taser—discharged in Phabian's grip, and he fell into the arms of one of Tarbox's robots, twitching and frothing at the mouth. The other droids produced fans of spit-guns from hatches in their casings and started

firing into the crowds, scattering the screaming citizens.
Dredd reeled under the flood of people, trying to draw a
bead with his Lawgiver. Laughing wildly, Betsy fled back
into the dome with her robots and the insensate Cliffo,
dropping a safety hatch down behind her.

'Stomm!' spat Leary. 'So much for peace and love!'

A CYCLOPS LASER made quick work of the security door,
and Dredd was stepping through the hole even as Leary
called in meat wagons and ambulances. 'Might have
known this would kick off the moment he arrived,' she
said, under her breath.

If Dredd heard her, he ignored the comment. 'Got
a thermo-scan on that H-Wagon?' The female Judge
nodded. 'Tarbox and Phabian are the only warm bodies
still in the dome. Use the scanner and locate them, feed it
to my channel.'

'Dredd, this is a hostage situation now. There's no telling
what that woman has got in there.' Leary indicated the
theme park. 'What about backup?'

'Keep the perimeter secure,' he replied, 'and get me
those scans.'

Leary watched him vanish into the shadowy interior of
the Aggro Dome. 'This day just gets better and better...'

MOST OF THE attractions inside were still running, the
gaudy neon beckoning visitors to try their hands in the
Ultra-Violent Room or the Chainsaw Chop-Up. Dredd

watched for any sign of danger, the noise and lights of the park washing over him. A nerve in his jaw jumped and he felt himself tensing. Years of street duty had programmed him for instant awareness, but there was something about the park that set his teeth on edge. He frowned. He'd never liked the dome; corralling citizens in one place and giving them free rein to run riot... It was insanity, typical of the kooks Dredd was forced to stand warden over every day.

With a screeching feedback howl, the park's speaker system bubbled into life. An irritated Tarbox began a tirade against Phabian's demonstration, and in the background Dredd could hear the peacenik's whining. That was good; if they were still together, it would be easier to isolate them and bring things to a close much quicker.

'Listen to me, Mega-City One!' bellowed Tarbox, 'I'm doing this for your own good! You can't shut the Aggro Dome! We provide a vital safety valve for the frustrations of Big Meg life—'

'Untrue!' Phabian broke in, 'A diet of mock-tofu and a daily regimen of chanting and colonic irrigation is more than enough to bring inner peace—'

There was a muffled thud and Betsy snapped 'Peace this, jerk-o!' Dredd heard Phabian whimper. 'This place stays open or else I get my droids to give toothy here the full aggro treatment! You hear me, Judges? I'm not losing my job for this munce-brain!'

'Dredd,' Leary's voice was in his ear. 'She's broadcasting from the administration block, on the upper level. I'm trying to get you a fix.'

'How do I get up there?' he asked. Dredd felt the first glimmers of impatience. He wanted to end this and get back on the street where *real* crime was happening. 'Come on, speed it up.'

'Justice Central's given me the building plans, I'll guide you. Go right and cut through the Punchateria.'

Dredd cracked his knuckles and waded in.

'SEE? SEE?' TARBOX shouted at Phabian, shaking her fist at him. 'Dredd understands the art of angry!' She stabbed the replay control from the Punchateria's cameras and put it up on the vu-screens. 'Watch him go! Oooh!' She winced as the playback showed the Judge hammering down the punch-bag dummies. 'Now that's what I call aggression!'

'Just another example of the hostility being propagated in this city,' Cliffo replied though swollen lips. He struggled in the grip of one of Tarbox's droids. 'The Judges are the worst!'

She slapped him again. 'Shuddup! It's people like you that are turning Meggers into apathetic, indolent wimps! If you can't lose your temper now and then, what kind of person are you? Eh?' Tarbox menaced him with a glare.

'Shall I hit 'im again?' asked one of the robots.

'Not just yet—' A crash from the screen drew her attention back to Dredd. The Judge dodged his way through the Vape-a-Teacher firing range as schoolbots flicked at him with canes or threatened to give him lines. Dredd's Lawgiver barked, high-explosive bullets blasting the droids apart in bright flares. She clapped her hands.

'Overkill! An armour-piercing round would have been enough, but oh no! Joe goes for the big bang! Yeah!'

Phabian sniffed. 'You won't get away with this, you nasty woman!'

Tarbox ignored him; Dredd had vaulted over a wall and landed on the Road Rage Raceway.

PODCARS AND ROBOTRUCKS roared past him, cutting each other up and throwing out synthesised curses in between blaring horns. 'Geddout the way!' spat a trucker-bot, narrowly missing the Judge. Cars whizzed past him, catching Dredd in their slipstream. He snarled and spun in place as a slabcycle bore down on him. Dredd struck out and tore the robot rider from the saddle, sending the uncontrolled trike smashing into the median strip. The droid flailed in his grip and Dredd pummelled it with the butt of his gun. 'Eat this, roadhog!'

'Dredd, this is Leary.' The words took a moment to penetrate the angry red mist that had overcome the Judge.

He stamped the robot's head under his boot and roared into his mike. 'What the drokk do you want, Leary? I'm busy here!'

'Dredd, I've got Tarbox's location...'

'I don't give a stomm about—' His voice trailed off and Dredd stopped. He looked at his oil-smeared fists and took a long, deep breath. For a moment, he had actually been *relishing* the anger. Marshalling his iron self-control, Dredd pushed away the rage. 'What's going on in here?' he said aloud, instinctively looking up. In the gantry overhead, something metallic glinted, out of place among the dark steel framework.

'Dredd,' said Leary, 'I'm feeding a digi-map to you. Tarbox is in her office with Phabian, but she's got two mechanoids in there with her. You'll need to get the hostage away from them.'

'Copy,' he replied. 'She's got cameras all over the place. I need them dealt with.'

'Wilco. The Teks can cut her out of the circuit.'

'Do it,' he said, 'and one more thing. Pipe me into the intercom. I want to talk to the anger manager.'

'Spug-drokk-stomm!' spat Tarbox, smashing the screen. 'I've lost visual!'

'Your swearing is very unpleasant,' said Phabian. 'Try counting to ten instead.'

'Shut your hole, sneck-wit!' she retorted, 'Or I'll have my bots fill it for you!'

'I'm just trying to create an atmosphere of friendly discussion.'

Betsy's angry, foul-mouthed reply was cut short by a growl from the PA speakers. 'Tarbox. This is Dredd. Your hostage drama is over. Free him and it'll go easier for you.'

'No!' she shouted. 'This stinking spugger is just like all the rest of those mealy-mouthed wimpos! I have to make a stand for anger! I gotta maintain the rage!'

Dredd gave a hollow chuckle. 'Really? From where I stand, you're a poor example. I'd say you wouldn't even rate "irate" on my scale. More of a snit, I reckon.' With care, he made his way along the corridor, ducking low to avoid being seen. Tarbox's office was just a few metres ahead.

Betsy sputtered and snarled. 'Snit? I'll snit you, Dredd! I'm full-on fuming! I've got a mad-on! I'm drokking pissed off!'

'I don't think so,' the Judge's voice filled the air. 'If you're so peeved, why are you letting a robot slap Cliffo around instead of doing it yourself?'

'Oh yeah? Yeah? Watch this!' Tarbox pressed a control and the droids holding Phabian twitched and went inert. The protestor dropped from their grip into a cowering heap. 'Now I'll make it personal!'

Cliffo pointed over her shoulder. 'You can't hit me. Judge Dredd is right behind you.'

Betsy smacked her fist into her palm. 'You'll have to do better than that, twit!' She grabbed him by the collar and hauled back for a big windup, her face red with aggression.

Dredd crashed through the office window and landed in a roll; two AP shells spat from his gun, scoring direct hits in the brain-cases of the aggrobots. Tarbox struck out hard, slapping Phabian into a pot plant.

'Leg shot!' The Judge put a bullet into the anger manager's knee and she fell with a scream.

'Oh,' began Cliffo. 'Judge Dredd. You saved me from that awful lady. Thank you... but couldn't you have done it without resorting to violence?'

Tarbox hissed and spat as Dredd cuffed her, releasing a string of inventive and vicious swearwords. 'How can you come down on his side, Dredd?' she snapped. 'Getting angry, that's part of what makes the Big Meg great! If you didn't have aggression, you couldn't do your job!'

'There's such a thing as too much aggression,' Phabian sniffed archly.

'Yes, there is.' Dredd tossed an electronic device near Cliffo's feet. 'Recognise this?'

The protestor went pale. 'I've never seen that before in my life.'

The Judge didn't need to look at his Birdie to see the lie. 'Is that so?' Lightning fast, Dredd struck out and punched Phabian. He reeled backward.

'Yeah!' Tarbox cheered. 'Old school brutality! That's the stuff!'

Something small fell from Phabian's ear and Dredd caught it. 'Give that back!' Cliffo shouted abruptly.

The Judge held it up. 'A beta-block. These are illegal, citizen.'

'What is it?' said Tarbox.

'A brainwave modifier. Same technology as a sleep machine, induces a peaceable, blissful state of mind.' Dredd glanced at Phabian, who was rapidly turning purple with annoyance. 'Without it, you'd be as riled up as any normal cit. Guess that explains some things.' Cliffo pawed at the blocker, but Dredd shoved him away. 'Big mistake, Phabian. Using the same circuitry in this as you did in the anger inducers you planted.' He indicated the box-shaped device.

Tarbox struggled against her restraints. 'Anger inducers? You little snecker!'

'I had to do it!' Phabian exploded, 'I was sick of this place! They wanted to be angry, so we made them angry! Angry-er, I mean...'

Dredd grimaced. 'That's why people were flipping out in here. You turned up the dial on the aggro in the Aggro Dome and blamed it on them to get the park shut.' He snapped a cuff around Phabian's wrist. 'I'm taking you both in.'

'Ha!' Tarbox snapped, 'Not so touchy-feely now, are ya?'

'Bitch!' retorted Cliffo, clawing at her face. 'I'll smash your teeth in!'

'Dickweed!'

'Stomm-face!'

'Munce-breath!'

'Maniac!'

'*Enough*!' Dredd smacked their heads together. 'By order of the Justice Department, the Aggro Dome is officially closed. From now on, the only person who gets angry around here is *me*.'

'But... but what about peace?' whimpered Cliffo.

'You'll get all the peace you need in an Iso-cube, creep. Now move it. Unless you want me to lose my temper...'

DEAD MAN WALKING

JONATHAN CLEMENTS

'How's the eye?' says Dredd.

I just squint back at him through the bruises and say nothing, like he cares anyway. I look around for a distraction, someone I can suddenly have important business with, but I don't know any of these people. There's Sector Commanders who would never talk to Accounts. There's Holocaust Judges looking like they've just got out of bed, with battered armour and torn uniforms. And then there's me.

Judges bite it every day, it's not like it's a special occasion. I know the rules as well as Dredd. If it's one of the clone Judges, there's no ceremony. File the report, chalk another one down, and send up to the Academy for a replacement. If it's Wally Squad, they look after their own. No Judge presence allowed at funerals; keep them undercover even in death. Even if they tick the box for post-mortem disclosure, check with Special Judicial first. If SJS can trace relatives or fellow officers, then so can the creeps. Over-ride the instructions, save someone from a revenge killing.

If a Judge ain't a pal or a former squad mate or something like that, Accounts won't approve your attendance. I know it. You know if there's a Code Red and a Judge don't make it, he'd want to know that instead of wasting an hour watching him trundle down a conveyor to Resyk, his buddies were out there taking down a few more criminals in the name of justice.

But if you're actually on the scene when a fellow Judge kicks the bucket, you qualify for the send-off. Because Holocaust Judges always have the tough jobs, they tend to have a lot of people around when they choke. Their funerals are packed to the rafters, with people who were at the scene, people who were ninety-nined and waiting for Med, people who were *en route* when something blew up. The whole deal.

So me being an Acc-Judge, from Acquisitions, I feel out of place. Yeah, I'm a real Judge. You think anyone except another Judge can do Accounts? We've done time on the streets. We've fired Lawgivers and all that stuff. We just have different ways of contributing. Someone pays for all that hardware, you know. Someone has to order the bullets and keep up the maintenance on the sleep machines. But yeah, we're off the streets. That means no personal involvement in arrests. So we tend not to be around when Judges get ninety-nined, so we don't qualify for the funerals. I'd never done one before, but the boys said that there might be a buffet. So I went full bird, with the shoulder armour, which weighs a full-on bitch I can tell you. I polished the eagle (okay, I got Lloyd to do it), and I got one of the spare helmets, you know, to carry under my arm, for appearances.

It's the eulogy. *Blah blah blah*. Judge Volkoff. *Blah blah blah*, honoured service. *Blah blah blah*, ultimate sacrifice. I don't see no buffet, neither.

Big deal, he joined the Holocaust Judges. I see these drop-outs every drokking week, they're just upstairs from Accounts. I'm their Supplies Manager, and they still treat me like I'm the class geek. We have to put up with their music and their girlfriends and their parties. You know, they ain't that special. All Judges die in the line of duty. Duty is what we do. You take a bullet or you get radar love from a beam weapon, or you turn your back on it all and let the CE take care of it on a Long Walk. You go bad and ship out to Titan. Whatever, we've all got it coming. I don't see what the big deal is.

So Volkoff's Holocaust buddies are there, like the bad boys at the school reunion. Their eagles are beat up. Their uniforms are patched. They're big-time scarred. More eye-patches than a pirate parade. They don't give a drokk. They're dead men walking and they know it. But he knew what was coming to him, too. Volkoff signed up for that! He signed up!

For whatever deep-seated, psychosomatic loser reason, he said: *Hey, I ain't getting enough danger as a regular Judge, I think I'll join the suicide squad. I'll be the gimp they send in when a power plant's on meltdown. I will be the first to step forward when there's a zombie infestation. If I'm likely to die, then sign me right up.*

Okay guys, you got my attention, because that's all you really want, right? Yeah, yeah, you rock. You are so dangerous. Try asking one of them to get a cat out of a tree. He'll be, like, *Is it a very big and dangerous radioactive cat that is likely to eat me alive?* No, moron! It's a drokking kitten. Just climb the ladder and bring it down. But, oh no, that's *beneath* the Holocaust Judges. They want the danger, they want the rock-star lifestyle.

So we're standing to attention. Dredd is *right next to me*, straight as anything. He keeps the helmet on, he stays bolt upright. Just being next to him makes me wanna stand up straighter.

Then he sniffs. He doesn't seem to move a muscle, but he sniffs, and then he turns his head and sniffs again.

'You smell that?' he says to me.

I'm facing eyes-front, like you're supposed to, I'm not getting into this. But yeah, I know what nicotine smells like. And this is one, maybe two sticks, lit up and toking, and somewhere close. So I look back at him, and I kind of shrug, best I can with shoulder plate. *Dammit*, I think, *are we going to go through this again?*

Dredd breaks rank. The speeches are still going on, the guards are still at attention, but whose gonna miss one Judge? Actually, who's gonna miss me, too, since he's beckoning me over. Grud above, whose gonna miss the other two, the two Holocaust Judges who must have been there a few seconds ago, grinding out their nicotine cigarettes on the floor, leaving the empty, crumpled packet behind.

Dredd picks it up, folding it back open in front of me.

Debonairs, Low Tar, whatever that is supposed to mean. Off-world contraband.

Look. It's a blind eye thing, okay? It's a last meal for the condemned man. That kind of attitude. If you're an HJ, they cut you some slack. You can turn up a funeral in a beat-up uniform, what the hell. And while you are sitting in your Ready Room waiting for the call to go out and kill yourself in the line of duty, nobody's gonna complain if you bend the rules a little. I've had SJS guys walk right through the Holocaust Ready Room, coughing at the smoke, swearing they can't smell a thing. I've had six Holocaust Judges chasing me through Accounts, threatening to give me a wedgie because I didn't get them enough whisky that week.

Yes, whisky. Lager, vodka, wine. You name it, tobacco, fine. Crack? Coming right up. Tea, coffee, why the hell not? You'll probably die tomorrow, so knock yourself out. And whichever poor punk ends up as your Acquisitions Officer, he's gonna have to get it for you, because you're so drokkin' special. And even though he's breaking the drokking law, he's gonna have to find ways to get you cocaine at three in the drokking morning. And if you don't like what you're getting, you can do what the hell you like to him, because you're a Holocaust Judge. What are they gonna do, *punish* you? You've already got a death sentence! So turn Acc-Judge Barrs into your pusher, who's gonna care? Welcome to my world.

'Someone,' says Dredd. '*Someone* has been smoking nicotine at this funeral.'

'I guess so,' I say. I look over at the SJS Judges in the

honour guard. Yup, they're busy looking the other way. Who would have guessed?

Dredd glares at me like it's all my fault.

I guess, in a way, it is.

I saw it, okay. And—newsflash!—when something's deep cover, that means really *deep* cover. So nobody told me the Wallies were running a scam again. Cruising the Megway looking to round up the mobile dealers. If I'd have known, I would have stayed low, not got involved.

It was kinda high-profile, and that pissed enough of the brass off as it was. The dealers were running dope out of mo-pads, trading at 200. You wanna score cigarettes, or spirits, or something even harder, you call him up and dial in his wheel code. Your mo-pad'll drive you around the megway until you're close enough to bump dockers. And then it's like: *Hi, I'm your drug dealer this evening, here's the stuff, here's the cash.* Bang, you're both outta there, drugs to your door, as long as your door is on a vehicle doing a continuous circuit of the city.

So the Wallies got themselves a Q-truck and they went cruising, looking for trouble. They found it. They hit the mother lode. It was the biggest of big-rigs, a full double-articulated 100-wheeler, two levels. A giant dancing cow-waitress down the side and the words *MOVEABLE FEAST*.

She wasn't just a dope joint. She was a whole damn factory. There was space for a contraband warehouse, there was a distillery, everything. The Wallies got wise because their undercover health inspector couldn't get a table reservation. You figure, a restaurant as 'exclusive' as Moveable Feast claimed to be would have had a few reviews. But no, nobody had ever covered it.

Way I hear it, they called in a favour with Gimpy the Pimp, and he hooked them up with a guy, who had a quarter-brother, whose last slitch-but-one had a sugar habit. Operation Funky Mo-Pad dropped a dime to the West Side dealers, and they gave them the number. What do you know, it went straight to the Moveable Feast truck.

Dredd was on it before you could say 'I am the Law!' He had a bunch of Judges circling. When the Wally heading in for the deal gave the signal, they were ready. But so were the perps.

The gunfight broke out somewhere near the front of the truck. Nobody knows why. All the PSU footage shows was the infrared, which is so many heat sources sparking. The Wallies were down, the perps were fighting back. The Judges cut off their exit to the escape vehicles. It was a mess. The fight made it to the cab, where someone was trying to nudge the Moveable Feast over to a slow lane, ready for the clean-up.

I don't know what happened next. A lucky shot, a stun grenade shorting the control panel. Whatever, the Moveable Feast had one of those Megasoft drives running an OEM traffic negotiator that belonged in a hover car. It was the wrong software, it defaulted to its last entered destination. It decided to head for home. It turned the 100-wheeler into the only thing worse than a runaway truck—a runaway truck on a mission.

The Moveable Feast took the next Megway turn like

there weren't a thousand other cars there. Its proximity buffer was shorted out, so it rolled over the cars like they were bugs. Its altimeter was off, so it just went right off the Megway, dropping a hundred metres to the next road below.

It was one of those tough, overengineered Hondo models, designed for running radioactive terrain with hostiles. It kept on going, its axles screeching, spare wheels flying off and taking out unlucky roadside stores. It revved itself up and pushed its motors as far as they were go. It was built for hauling much bigger weights, so there was plenty of torque to go round. Its tachygraph maxed out at 300, but the news people placed it at least 20% above that.

The PSU footage was killer Tri-D. Giant wheels rolling through the middle of the department stores. Cars flying off the Megway and into unsuspecting bystanders. Thanks to the Moveable Feast changing lanes, roads and heights, it had already caused three Megway pile-ups. Now it was barrelling south on the Billie Piper Turnpike, heading straight for Babylon Bridge. The change in altitude was the killer—there was an APB at the level of the original bust, but a hundred metres below, nobody had thought it was their problem. Judges are assigned horizontally to their districts, not vertically. The trouble literally fell out of the sky on the people below.

I'd walked back in the Acc-Judge office, and I found the boys watching it. Oh yeah, the Q3 ammunition audit could wait. Lloyd had a bunch of requisition orders for Psi-Div, he figured they would understand if he put if off. Stan's radio was off. They were gathered around the biggest monitor like it was an Aeroball game, yelling abuse and encouragement.

'Guys,' I said. 'Has anyone seen where it's headed?'

Most of them ignored me, but Lloyd looked up out the window, and saw what I saw. The Moveable Feast truck was far in the distance, twinned with the close-up on our screen, heading our way, heading straight for the Halls of Justice.

'It'll go round, right?' said Lloyd. I turned to look at the sector map on the wall. Sure enough, the Piper Pike hung a slow left all the way around the Halls before it hooked up with the Eccleston Megway. Which was good.

'She's already taken a dive off one road,' I pointed out. 'She's heading straight for us!'

I guess we weren't the only guys who realised it. A body dropped past our window from the floor above. *Holy drokk*, I thought, *are they jumping?*

But it was a different kind of suicide. I heard the jetpack kick in a few floors down, and the jumper swung back into view. It was Judge Volkoff, flying straight for the oncoming truck.

I won't say we were friends. I won't say I even knew him that well. He was another jerk of a Holocaust Judge with issues, waiting for a time to die. I guess he figured today was the day.

Even with the real events happening outside our window, we preferred to watch it on the news. The angles were better; the voice of Enigma Smith told us what was going on and pretty much got it right most of the time. It was cool to be on Tri-D. It made it feel like the danger was happening to other people.

Even as the Moveable Feast smashed through the barrier on the curving Piper Pike, Volkoff was there like a bolt of bright fire, tearing at the access hatch. He was in there so fast that his exhaust was scorching up the upholstery, grabbing at the wheel even as his jets set fire to the cabin. They threw up a storm of loose paper in the cab, darting around him like fiery snow as he strained at the wheel. Tri-D had it bang-on—a full close-up, Volkoff in the inferno, already on fire himself, dragging the wheel right over.

The Moveable Feast truck hit the ground badly. But Volkoff helped it along. The front tyres juddered and skidded, and then it started to pitch. The second articulated area fishtailed and the rest of the truck went with it. She went right over and rolled right across the Justice Park. So much for the ice-cream van and quite a few ducks. I'm still dealing with the overtime paperwork from the landscapers. But she stopped. The truck skidded to a halt at the base of the Halls of Justice steps. We were safe.

Then she blew. The fuel cell in cab went critical and the whole front end erupted in a fireball. The noise took out all the windows on the north side of the Halls. The paperwork is a nightmare.

I was out there on the lawns as fast as I could. The back of the truck was smashed open, and there were cartons of cigarettes all over. The place was crawling with Judges, Meds pulling injured Wallies from the wreck, and regulars keeping back the crowds. I slipped in something that smelt like whisky, and realised that we were talking a lot more flammables than we'd previously thought, and the cab was already on fire.

Forget Volkoff, he was already munce. But the Debonairs, now they were gonna go up in smoke whatever happened. So I lifted a carton. I mean, let's be sensible here. Next week, Volkoff's buddies are gonna want more smokes, so why not use these? That's part of my job, after all, requisitioning contraband from the pound, registering it as 'Destroyed.' Hey, I ain't even lying, they are 'Destroyed,' right, they're just destroyed by a Holocaust Judge sucking them down to nothing.

'Hold it there,' said a deep voice. I've heard it a hundred times from a hundred different clones, but this is the original. No Tri-D duplicate here, it's Dredd. So I turn, with my box, all ready to explain myself.

And he punches me in the face.

Go ahead, laugh all you want, the Holocaust Judges sure did. It was just a misunderstanding, all cleaned up. SJS were ready to believe my side of it because, well, they know that the Holocaust Judges' little perks have to come from somewhere. And Dredd was assured that I wasn't stealing anything from the scene of the crime. He even apologised. Straight up, he said: *'I apologise for assuming you were committing a crime, and punching you with unnecessary force.'*

Whatever. Now I figure it's a story I can tell in the mess-room, and it pays if Dredd owes you a favour.

Except now we're here at Volkoff's funeral, and he's

staring at the empty pack of Debonairs. Dredd gets to his feet, looking at the pack.

'These are old,' he says. 'But they have the same log number as the crate you were lifting.'

'So?' I says.

'So they came from the same shipment,' says Dredd. I wipe my forehead because it feels kind of wet. It's hot in here, which is a surprise because, like, in Resyk, you expect they would keep it cool.

'Moveable Feast was heading back to the Halls for a reason,' says Dredd. 'The Halls were its last logged location.'

I stammer because I don't know what to say. It's on a loop of the city, so yeah, it's probably been all over. It was heading *through* the Halls, yeah, but nobody knows exactly where it was heading. The cab blew up, remember?

'What's the betting,' says Dredd, 'that back-up PSU is gonna show you in a car docking with the truck somewhere near the Halls? Maybe a half-hour before the bust went down.' Behind him, the honour guard are raising their rifles for Volkoff's salute. There's a double-dozen bang as they fire into the air, and again, and again.

'Dredd,' I whisper in the silence. 'We've been through this. The Holocaust Judges get some slack, know what I'm saying? They get to lift a few things from the impound... ear-marked for destruction...'

But he's not buying it. His fist crumples the pack again in front of my face.

'The dealers' truck,' he says slowly, 'was heading *away*

from Justice, because that's where you *sold* them the cigarettes.'

'Now, listen,' I say, hoping to buy some time.

'You listen,' says Dredd. 'You can bend a rule, or you can break it. And if you've been selling contraband back onto the streets, I can hear the snap.' He leans close. He's a big guy.

'You,' I say, 'You—you can't prove that.'

'I don't have to,' he says. 'You're not gonna be punished.'

'I'm not?'

'No,' says Dredd. 'You're getting a promotion.'

I smile. Dredd is the coolest.

'You're heading upstairs,' he says, resting his hand on my shoulder. And suddenly I feel cold.

'You mean—?'

'We've lost a Holocaust Judge,' says Dredd. 'I think it's great of you to volunteer to take his place on the team.'

'No,' I say. 'Wait a second. That's a death sentence!' I mean, I'm a desk jockey. I haven't fired a gun in how long. I can't run up two flights of stairs. You've gotta be peak physical for the Holocaust Judges. And you've gotta have a death wish.

'Let's see how you do,' says Dredd. He gestures back at the honour guard, and at Judge Ironwood, the HJ liaison.

'There he is,' says Dredd. 'Your new boss. No time like the present.'

'You want me to *volunteer*...?'

'It's a good way to go,' says Dredd. 'Let's see how long you last.'

He's serious. I've got no choice. This or the cubes? This or Titan? This is it. I try to fight back the tears, and I start towards Ironwood.

'Make way,' says Dredd to the crowd. 'Dead man walking.'

DOG FIGHT

CAVAN SCOTT

THE FULL MOON reflected in the sea of blood that poured from his belly.

Davy glanced down at his body, his mind struggling to break through the fog that was sweeping in from all corners of his consciousness. This wasn't right. Surely his insides should be, well, inside him, not splattered across a Mega-City One sidewalk. At least it had stop hurting now. In fact, he had no sensation at all. Except for the cold. He couldn't even feel the teeth of the rat that was gnawing his lower intestine. That should hurt, right? As the rodent met his eye, his lifeblood caked around its jaws, Davy realised that he couldn't remember how he had ended up like this. They were trying to capture something, weren't they? Something with talons that had gutted Davy like a fish. Or were they claws? Davy didn't care any more. He just wanted to close his eyes. Nothing mattered. Nothing at all.

The rat basked in the moonlight for a second before burying itself deeper into Davy's gut.

DREDD CUT THE engine of his Lawmaster. The pungent air of the block stung his nostrils, the night unseasonably cold. He'd heard other Judges moan and whinge that tonight seemed as if it would never end, and like toddlers they had bleated that they needed their sleep machines. Dredd's scowl grew grimmer. They didn't deserve to wear a Justice Department shield. Crime never slept in this city, so why should the Law? It was their duty. If they didn't like it, then they should never have put on the helmet.

Dismissing the thought as easily as he'd dismiss a lily-livered rookie, Dredd flicked his communicator.

'Dredd to Control. Have arrived at the corner of Talbot and Glendon. You got that apartment number for me yet?'

'That's a rog,' came Control's clipped response. 'Mrs Valerie Hull, apartment 5391. We've checked out her story and can confirm that no-one seems to have seen her husband since he left work four days ago.'

'Why wait so long to call it in?' asked Dredd rhetorically, boots crunching on the tarmac as he stalked towards the block entrance.

WILFRED WINCED AS his fingers traced the deep gash in his shoulder. When he brought his hand back into the light it was slick with blood. If he had anything left in his stomach he was sure that he would have disgorged it by now, but the only thing inside him was stabbing hunger.

He had no idea how long he'd been trapped inside the cage. It felt like days. It might have only been hours. It certainly hadn't been that long since that lout had swaggered into the cell, cracking the whip above his head like some kind of ring-master. Wilfred could still feel the searing heat of the leather on his back. He couldn't put up with this for much longer. Even if he could take the starvation or the regular beatings, he needed his medication. They had no idea what would happen if they refused to bring it. Why wouldn't they listen?

'P-please,' Wilfred stammered into the darkness. 'Please, can someone help me?'

As the tears came again, the only answer was ominous, cold silence.

'NOT WHILE I'M on duty, citizen.'

Mrs Hull's eyebrow wavered in curiosity.

'But it's only a cup of synthi-caf, Judge Dredd. Oh well, if you insist.' Valerie Hull placed the china cup back on the trolley. 'What do you need to know?'

'You claim that your husband disappeared on Monday on his way back from his place of employment.'

'At the Naughton Financial Institute, yes.'

'So how do you know that he vanished on his way home?'

'Oh, that's simple. He called me just after he left the

office. Always does, to let me know that he's on his way. My Wilfred is a man of routine.'

'And you're sure he'd already left his office?'

'Oh yes—I could see the skyline behind him on the screen. He was walking beneath the Lockhart tower.'

'What I don't understand,' Dredd rumbled, 'is why you chose to wait until tonight to contact the Justice Department. Why not make the report as soon as you realised that your husband was missing?'

Mrs Hull shifted uncomfortably in her seat. She'd hoped that the grumpy Judge wouldn't have noticed that.

'Well, I didn't want to waste your time, Judge. I know that you boys are so busy what with all the crime and what-have-you. I just though Wilfred would, well, show up.'

Swallowing hard, she prayed to Grud that Dredd couldn't hear her heart beating wildly in her chest. It felt like it was going to burst through her ribs. Why was he just staring at her like that? Shouldn't he be riding off on his Law-doodah by now? She'd given him all the facts.

'I don't think you've given me all the facts, citizen Hull,' sneered Dredd. 'Anything else you've "forgotten" to tell me?'

Mrs Hull's eyes fell to Dredd's fist, tapping the daystick by his side. Surely he wasn't thinking... No, of course not. There *were* stories, but Judge Dredd wouldn't go around beating 68-year-old women in their own homes, would he? Even if they weren't telling the truth. That would be inhuman.

As Dredd leaned in, Birdie lie detector hovering inches

from her nose, Valerie knew she'd made an error of judgement.

'Citizen Hull?'

'Y-yes, Judge?'

'Either you tell me the full story right now, or prepare to spend your retirement in a cube for obstructing justice.'

SPITTLE AND BLOOD dripped from Wilfred's mouth onto the sawdust below.

'Why are you doing this to me?' he whimpered, only drawing another kicking from the oaf who, only minutes before, had dumped his brutalised body in the middle of the ring. Out of the corner of his eye he could see figures in the gloom, eyes gleaming in anticipation, all trained on him. What did they expect him to do?

Through the pain Wilfred could hear snippets of conversation all around him.

'Are you sure he's one of them? Looks like the runt of the litter to me.'

''Course he is. He was on the list.'

'Well, I hope you're right, otherwise we're going to have a lot of angry punters on our hands—and I don't know what's more terrifying, one of those evil bastards in there, or a customer who thinks we're trying to sell them a lame dog.'

'Stop worrying. It's almost time anyway. Full moon rising.'

Full moon rising? He'd hoped and prayed that he'd been wrong, that in the confusion of the kidnapping he'd become disoriented and lost track of the days. If it was time, and he hadn't taken his medicine... They had no idea.

His heart racing, Wilfred peered up to the skylight, watching in horror as the clouds in the night sky parted to reveal... *No!* He would fight it, fight the agony that threatened to rip him apart. It was as if something, an excrescence from his very bowels, was clawing its way out of his body. If he let go, for even the merest second, no-one would be safe.

The pathetic yelp caused his head to snap up. No, that was impossible. They wouldn't do that. Surely not. At the back of his mind, something laughed. To think they called *him* the animal. At least he would never throw a helpless, young slip of a girl into the ring with a monster. Was this sport for them? Was this fun?

As he writhed on the floor, his hands tearing at the cheap fabric of his suit, the poor darling just stood there, staring at him with wide, terrified eyes. Even as he felt his spine shift, Wilfred realised that she could only be 12 years old if she were a day. A skinny little thing—but kinda sweet-looking, despite the fact that she'd just lost control of her bladder. Dark, shiny hair framed those expansive, petrified eyes, her lip trembling as he dragged his twisted body toward her. That was a pretty dress too. Looked like she'd been going to a party. Was probably looking forward to it. A bit of dancing, a few games and a spot of food...

Something to eat.

Grud, he was hungry. Gnawing, unappeasable hunger

snatching at his innards, driving him to the very edge of madness.

Darkening eyes stared hungrily at the girl's goose-bumped flesh. Pure. White. Delicious. Yes, he was hungry—and by the light of the moon he would feed.

Wilfred Hull threw back his head and, as his skull flattened and coarse hair erupted from every pore, bayed to the sound of the cheering crowd.

'DR PIERCE, YOU will open this door immediately or face the consequences.'

No answer. From beneath his helmet Dredd's eyes flicked to the name plate above the intercom.

Dr John Pierce. For all your clinical needs. No infection too small.

Dredd set his jaw. Bargain-basement quacks. Robodocs made 'em all redundant, unless the patient had something to hide.

The door shattered as Dredd's boot crashed into it. As he crossed the threshold, Dredd's nostrils flared involuntarily at the stink hanging heavy in the air of the surgery. The yellow, wet smell of stale death. If Dredd read the signs correctly, and he usually did, a broken door would be the last of Dr Pierce's worries.

The corpse was behind the desk, lying in a thick patina of dried gore. Dispassionately, Dredd flipped the body over onto its back with the toe of his boot. Unseeing eyes stared into his own. Pierce's limp face was covered in the juices which had flowed from the yawning slash running from one temple to the other. Well, at least that made the job a little easier. Sometimes, it was almost like these perps *wanted* to be captured. If you're going to commit homicide, why advertise your handiwork? Arrogance? A God complex, considering themselves invulnerable, somehow above the consequences of their actions?

'Dredd to Control.'

'Control here. What have you got, Dredd?'

'The late Dr Pierce. Someone obviously didn't like the diagnosis.'

'Murdered?'

Dredd glanced at the wound one more time.

'Looks like Pierce was held down while the attacker took a cleaver to his head.'

'A cleaver? Isn't that the signature of...?'

'Patrick Terksic, aka "The Lobotomist".'

'One of Jim Thorne's goons. And Pierce's computer?'

Dredd scrolled down the integrated screen, bolted into the doctor's fake-mahogany desk.

'Wiped clean. The log states that a list called "LOUP_ GAROU" was transferred to a memory dongle seconds before everything was deleted."

'French for "werewolf",' confirmed Control as Dredd leafed through Pierce's diary, ignoring the scarlet stains that washed over ancient synthi-caf rings. The pages were filled with appointments, countless names one after another, about one in twenty marked 'LG'.

'Send a forensic unit and a meat wagon,' Dredd ordered, 'and check for recent activity from Thorne's mob.'

'Accessing. Please stand by.'

As he waited Dredd continued to run his finger down the diary entries. So many of them. Perhaps Pierce had been a rich man after all.

'Dredd.' Control snapped him back out of his thoughts. 'Got something. Earlier today Judges Tovey and Ross broke up a ring of bodysnatchers at George Waggner block. Apparently they were fighting over the body of one Davy Dunne.'

'Don't know the name.'

'One of Thorne's gang. Strictly muscle, nothing more. But this is interesting: Tovey reported that the corpse had been completely eviscerated—as if, quote, "by a massive canine". Coincidence?'

'Nothing usually is.' Dredd snorted. 'Have there been any missing person reports filed in George Waggner over the last 24 hours?'

'Let's see now.' Control said, pausing as he checked the information before him. 'That's a rog. Megan Cleasby, aged 13. Snatched yesterday, around the time the meds believe Dunne died.'

'Cleasby?' In a flash, Dredd flicked back two pages of the blood-splashed diary. Where had he seen it? 24 October? No, here it was. 21 October, 3pm. Megan Cleasby. And by her name, in Pierce's spidery hand, two clear letters: 'LG'.

'Drokk,' exclaimed Dredd. 'She's one of them!'

THE CREATURE THAT had once been called Wilfred Hull crashed into the protective force-field, sending sparks crackling through the air like you'd see in a mad scientist's lab in some cheesy Tri-D movie. Thorne chuckled as its howl filled the warehouse. The stomm-heads had all backed Hull, not one betting a single cred on the Cleasby girl. When would they learn that appearances are definitely deceptive in this game? Yeah, so she's all sugar and spice most of the time, but shove a full moon over her and, well, their faces when she transformed had told the full story. Yup, looked like they had a new champion on their hands. She was making a dog's dinner of Hull. Good girl.

The hairs rising on Thorne's neck told him that someone had sidled up behind. A late punter. Too bad.

'Sorry, bucko,' he slurred, eyes still fixed on the fight, 'Too late to place bets once the carnage has begun.'

Later, Thorne would report how he nearly choked on the cigarette hanging from his fat, moist lips when he heard the voice in his ear.

'The only bet I'm making is how long it takes me to book and cuff you, punk.'

The sound of Dredd's Lawgiver echoed throughout the building. Even Cleasby, consumed with the need to excoriate Hull and feast on his fleshy tissue, glanced up before continuing her attack.

All around Thorne's mobsters reached for their pieces, wondering how Dredd had flushed them out.

'You're a dead man, Dredd,' yelled Thorne, pulling his own shooter from its holster.

'James Thorne, I am arresting you for the kidnapping in order to stage illegal werewolf fights.'

Hull swiped at Cleasby, sending a handful of fur and gristle into the air.

Thorne sneered. 'I don't think so, Dredd. Look around. Every man in the place has you in their sights. We'll feed you to Cleasby when she's done.'

Cleasby roared in triumph as her jaws closed around the scruff of Hull's neck.

'All I need is one shot,' droned Dredd, 'One shot to bring you all to justice.'

'Oh, yeah,' smirked Thorne. 'Go on, big man, do your worst.'

Dredd's arm swung up as he took aim. 'Hi-Ex!'

The forcefield generator hidden in the corner of the room erupted in flames as the barrier between the mobsters and werewolves instantly died. In the ring, both creatures spun around, stunned by the barrage of new scent in the room. Why should they slay each other when they could feed on human flesh?

Thorne was the first to realise the danger.

'Stomm! They're free. Everyone out. Run for your lives!'

Gangsters and punter alike took to their heels. One goon, slower than the rest, screamed in terror as he felt Hull's maw lock around his skull. Seconds later his headless carcass hit the dirt.

Thorne shoved Dredd roughly out of the way as he fled. Dredd let him go. The thirty Judges circling the warehouse would pick up all the escaping perps. Besides, he had a bigger problem to deal with. Looking up, Dredd found himself staring straight in the ferocious eyes of Cleasby, the foetid ichor of recently digested gangster handing from her fangs. Behind her the wounded hulk of Hull prepared to spring forward.

For what seemed like an eternity the trio of hunters eyeballed each other before Cleasby made the first move.

She leaped with a deafening war-cry, claws ready to slice and dice. Dredd twisted and issued a single, brusque command.

'Ricochet!'

The bullet ruptured Cleasby's brain, sending scarlet matter arcing in its wake. Hull spun on his haunches as the missile bounced from wall to wall before exploding through his chest cavity. As he fell back, a roar of surprise and agony escaping from his throat, the projectile burned inches from his heart.

Dredd stepped over the still form of Megan Cleasby and strode over to where Wilfred was gasping his last. The dying man gazed up at the Judge, shivering from the agony of both the sudden transformation back to a mere mortal and the metal lodged inside him.

'Silver bullet?' he asked, his voice weak and pathetic.

Dredd grunted. 'Standard cryptobiological issue.'

'And the girl?'

'Dead.' Dredd didn't even turn to look.

Wilfred's tear-drenched eyes scrunched shut.

'P-probably for the best.'

His body was beginning to chill as Dredd began intoning his sentence.

'Wilfred Hull, you are charged with being an unregistered lycanthrope.'

'But I controlled it, Judge. The drugs...'

'The Cassidium you received from Dr Pierce to stabilise your condition was also contraband. He was breaking the law when he dealt with you people. Once he'd diagnosed lycanthropy, he should have informed the Department without delay—'

'S-sure,' murmured Wilfred weakly. 'So the Department could've caged us up in a "special facility"—for our own good, yes?'

Dredd ignored him. 'The list of lycanthropes stolen from him by Thorpe led to the arrangement of these "dog fights".' Wilfred could almost taste the displeasure dripping from Dredd's words. 'If Pierce wasn't past caring, he'd be spending the rest of his days in a cube.'

'And w-what about me, Judge Dredd?' Wilfred stammered, black spots appearing in his vision. 'What am I facing?'

As Dredd's trigger finger tightened, Wilfred closed his eyes and allowed himself to enjoy the warmth of the moonlight on his face.

LUCKY FOR SOME

JONATHAN CLEMENTS

MORIKAWA DIDN'T KNOW how long he'd been out. Long enough to be thirsty, his lips black with charcoal residue; long enough to do an entire cycle in an infirmary healer, apparently. He knew this because he felt great. Happy pills.

He glanced down at his foot. Bandaged, yes, but still in one piece. He scratched his head. There was still sand in it.

'DNR,' said Dredd's voice.

'You have got to be kidding me! How'd you know?' someone said.

'Think again!' growled Dredd in reply. 'You think I was gonna sit here for eight hours and not do my job?'

'But Dredd,' said the voice. Morikawa remembered a half-heard whisper from the rescue evac ship—Med-Judge Fogerty. He tried to turn his head to look, but it made him feel dizzy. 'Dredd, you should rest.'

'I *borrowed* an SJS laptop,' said Dredd. 'From Judge Timo.' From somewhere down the aisle, a muffled complaint from a bandaged figure in traction implied that Judge Timo wasn't too happy about it. But Dredd was on a roll.

'I ran the sheets myself! That guy in Bed Three made it all the way from Texas City!'

'He *walked* it?!?'

'He *Long* Walked it!'

'That's impossible!'

'Trust me on this one,' rasped Dredd, without the slightest trace of irony, 'it's possible to survive longer in the CE than you think.'

Bed Three was just in front of him. Morikawa forced his rebellious eyes to focus, seeing the old man for the first time. LaBrune. Now he remembered.

FISHER HAD THE wheel.

'Pedal to the metal!' shouted Dredd, his breath hot on her neck.

'This is as fast as she'll go!' spat Fisher. 'Sir!' she added, a bead of sweat on her forehead, her eyes locked on the bolting jetcar ahead. The other rookies loved it, crammed in the rocking cockpit, the engine monitors redlining as the H-wagon strove to keep up.

'They're getting away!' yelled Dredd, willing the pilot to make the H-wagon go faster. The towers of Mega-City One shook and blurred on the rear-view monitors, steadily shrinking in the distance. Below Fisher's feet on the stabiliser pedals, there was nothing but the featureless grey roofs of the south sectors, strobing into one endless flicker of gunmetal grey.

'Drokk it!' shouted Dredd, and Fisher flinched.

'Not my fault, sir!' she yelled above the rattling engines. 'We're losing 'em!'

Dredd's grip tightened on the back of Fisher's seat. But not even Dredd could soup up an old H-wagon by willpower alone. The smugglers had a head start, and their hovercar was modded for rocket fuel.

'We're outta luck!' agreed Morikawa from the co-pilot's chair. 'And we're burning fuel.'

He tapped his condition monitors for emphasis, with the fuel gauge flashing in the warning area. A row of critical monitors bathed all the cockpit in a red light. Morikawa wondered if this was the time to point out that nobody would mind if they let the smugglers go. This was supposed to have been a training mission after all. Nobody had been expecting real perps.

'No!' shouted Dredd, shoving himself forward between Fisher and Morikawa, his bulky shoulder eagle scraping against Morikawa's head. Barely able to move in the cramped forward section, he grabbed at the targeting computer.

'Rookies!' he yelled, his fingers flicking off the missile limiters. 'What is the Law?'

The others looked at each other.

'We're speeding in a built-up area?' ventured a voice from the back.

'Right, Martin!' grunted Dredd. But they were chasing

perps. Speeding was fine as long as they didn't cause any damage through their actions. 'Anyone else?'

Fisher's glance darted nervously at the factory district below. The cross-hairs of the targeting computer flashed into existence on the forward windshield, locking dutifully into place on the white-hot signature of the fleeing smugglers.

'Urban area!' Fisher shouted. 'No discharge of missiles in an—'

But was it urban? she suddenly wondered. They were heading straight for the west, the sun low on the horizon in front of them, but the factory area was dark beneath them. The lights were off, nobody was home. This was a rad area. They were already outside habitable Mega-City limits. This was practically Cursed Earth.

Fisher didn't even wait for Dredd's order. She batted her hand down on the big red launch button.

'Fox One!' said Dredd, with what almost sounded like approval. The rocket sped ahead of them with a roar, the only physical effect of its launch the slight jolt as the graviters compensated for the change in mass.

The contrail whooshed ever closer to the bright light of the fleeing smuggler vehicle, and the knot of rookies watched intently. Except there was another contrail looping forward from the fugitives, turning inexorably back towards their H-wagon.

'Incoming...!' hissed Dredd, under his breath. 'Everybody—' But there was no more time, as the retaliatory missile slammed into the H-wagon.

Half a mile away, glowing red in the sunset, the smugglers'

ship took a dive towards the sands of the Cursed Earth. But nobody on the Judge craft was watching, they grabbed for something to hold on as the lateral spinners shorted out, the H-wagon lurching sideways with a scream of tortured engine, flames racing up along the side, molten droplets of fuel cascading behind it like fiery rain.

'Brace for impact!' shouted Dredd through the smoke. 'That means you two!' he yelled at Morikawa and Fisher, who were frantically and pointlessly trying to regain control. Full marks for effort, but they were all going down.

Dredd threw himself over the pilot and co-pilot seats, his armoured body slamming down on top of the two cadet pilots. But their muffled protestations were drowned out by the final, sputtering moments of the H-wagon, as it ploughed into the sands.

Up was down for a moment, then sideways, then nothing.

Dredd was up immediately, his Lawgiver out.

'Shield your eyes!' he yelled, not waiting for acknowledgement as he shot out the glass in front of the pilots. Before the deafening echoes of two Standard Execution rounds had died away, Dredd was dropping through the hole and onto the desert, shards of glass falling from his armour.

Fisher and Morikawa shared a moment, the weight of Dredd suddenly off them, the realisation that he had just saved their unarmoured lives by functioning as a human air bag.

'Move it!' shouted Dredd from outside. 'They could still get away!'

Morikawa began to chuckle, unsnapping his restraints, looking round in amazement as the other rookies woozily piled out. There really was no stopping Dredd. He was a shouting, shooting machine; that much was true of all the rumours they'd heard.

Morikawa dropped through the broken windshield, landing knee-deep in soft, damp sand. The long oblong gouges of Dredd's impatient footprints sloshed away towards the top of a sand dune.

This was more than just luck. This was blind, once-in-a-lifetime rookie luck, thought Morikawa. The H-wagon lay half on its side, half-buried in a dune, its crash turned into the softest of landings by tonne after tonne of damp, post-rainstorm sand. What were the odds, of hitting that dune, at that time, after that storm?

A series of loud gun reports was followed all too swiftly by answering fire. Slug rounds pinged around the dead hulk of the H-wagon, and Morikawa saw his fellow rookies flinging themselves to the sand.

'High-ex!' bellowed a familiar voice from further up the ridge, and Dredd's Lawgiver launched an explosive round with its distinctive *whump*. Morikawa couldn't resist a smile.

'Come on!' he shouted back at the others. 'Dredd's showing us up!' Again.

The smoking wreck of the smugglers' craft was only a few hundred yards away, across a scattering of sand and large rocks.

Lucky for us is also lucky for them, thought Morikawa with a snort. None of his fellow rookies were hurt, but every silver lining came with a cloud. The smugglers were just as alive, and just as pissed off.

Dredd was already advancing, not waiting for his cadet charges. He crouched behind each rock as he plotted his next move, lobbing Heatseekers over his head and darting for the next cover as the smugglers ducked and ran. Suddenly, there was a quiet, ominous click from his Lawgiver.

Morikawa didn't stop to think. He found himself leaping to his feet, his Lawgiver on full auto, charging down the ridge after Dredd. Somewhere under the stuttered roars of his gun was the sound of Morikawa calling for suppressing fire, but not even he could hear it over the noise. He just kept firing, pelting down the ridge towards Dredd, drawing the enemy fire while Dredd reloaded, diving behind a boulder of his own just as the smugglers wised up and started firing back.

Morikawa took two breaths, harsh ricochets ringing around him as his chosen rock protected him from the worst of the return fire. Damn, that must be what all that training was *for*! He was alive! He was alive and he was loving it! For the first time, Morikawa felt like a Judge. Like someone who would sacrifice his life for the Law... He hadn't even given any thought to himself, just to laying down cover for Dredd.

Some of the other rookies were taking the hint, running down the hill for cover themselves, leaving the smouldering H-wagon behind. Morikawa watched as Fisher threw herself prone ahead of a cascade of bullets. He saw Johnson take a laser in the leg and drop.

Unlucky, thought Morikawa, glancing back at the others, still clambering from the H-wagon.

The H-wagon erupted in a ball of flames, the innocuous smoke trails from its engines a sudden oven of inescapable fire. The screams went on for far too long. Morikawa tried not to think about it.

Unluckier, he thought. In pursuing the Law, in being like Dredd, he had put himself in the line of fire, but he had also saved his own life from the conflagration.

'Eyes front, Morikawa!' shouted Dredd, dropping down beside him. 'You look at what's *in front* of you.'

'But—!'

'But nothing! You look left, you look right, and you're missing what's right in your drokkin' face. Let Fisher cover her field, and you cover yours.'

Morikawa hadn't actually looked that closely at the Judge to his other side. But Dredd was right, it was the curvy form of Stacey Fisher, staring down her gunsight at the perps, whispering sweet nothings into her Lawgiver's mic.

'*Heatseeker...*' she breathed, jerking back on the trigger, not even blinking at the kick and loud report. '*High-ex...*' Her words barely audible, in sharp contrast to the boom of the gun. For a moment she was quiet, watching something move in the distance, her gunsight following it, leading ahead of it, until—

Fisher fired another, a Standard that didn't require verbal affirmation. Morikawa's eyes darted to follow; a running perp tensed in the distance, clutching at a wounded thigh as he fell. But Fisher wasn't looking, she was already shifting on her rock, her Judge's uniform tight on her long legs.

Morikawa grinned to himself and turned back to face the action. His left foot slipped on the soft sand and he hissed under his breath. The ground beneath his feet gave way again, slices of red-brown sand. But this time it didn't stop. Morikawa's foot kept sliding into a much bigger hole, he dropped knee-deep and stumbled.

'Drokk!' he said, more out of embarrassment than anything else. Nobody laughed, they had their minds on other things. They kept their heads focused, kept their Lawgivers trained, and kept firing.

Something stung at Morikawa's ankle. A distant childhood memory of nettles floated into mind, but the pain would not go away. Then Morikawa's leg sunk further, dragged further down...

'Uh-oh... !' he found himself saying. 'Something's—'

Dredd's hand slapped into Morikawa's face, shoving him backwards. As the protesting Morikawa crumpled to the sand, Dredd loosed three rounds into the dirt around Morikawa's feet. The muzzle blast deafened in such close quarters, the heat of the flash singeing Morikawa's uniform. There was a sensation like something stamping on his buried toe, and Morikawa realised Dredd had just shot him in the foot.

The knowledge hurt more than the SE round. Morikawa was too shocked to do anything more than call his leader a *drokker*, before the sand around him seemed to thrash.

As wolfworms went, it was a big one. Its trunk as far around as a burly man's chest, its crocodilian snout a metre of tapering toothy death, it thrashed through its sandy element, letting go its hold on Morikawa's leg.

Lucky, thought Morikawa, the chain of events starting to catch up with him; the chance spotting of the fleeing smugglers, the crash, the explosion, the ducking of the bullets and the evading of the wolfworm. He wasn't even a full-eagle Judge, and he was already wondering how many lives he would need to get through just one day on the job.

Morikawa felt faint. *Blood loss*, suggested a voice in his head. *Tiring day*, said something much more grandmotherly. *PTSD*, said a Dredd-like inner voice. Morikawa didn't care, he just wanted to lay down, here on the damp, cooling sand.

The ground around him erupted in not one, but an entire nest of wolfworms, the sand collapsing from their daytime lair as the mutant creatures sprang into action, sensing the two-legged prey that had wandered too close for safety. Dredd barked orders at the surviving rookies, ordering them off the sands. A wolfworm reared up behind Fisher and clamped its jaws on her head, dragging the pretty Judge away in unsettling silence. Two others coiled round Johnson, the burly Judge pleading for mercy to his dumb animal assailants, even as they crushed him. And then it was just Dredd, standing over Morikawa yelling at the wolfworms that he was gonna make it tough for them.

Morikawa didn't hear it, he just wished he could close his eyes for one last, long sleep. And then Morikawa was sure he was dreaming. Because *he* came out of the whirling dust like it was part of it. Tall, grizzled, a weatherbeaten face beneath a hat that had seen even better days, the tattered ruins of a Texas City Judge's uniform. A face baked in unbearable sun, across a thousand days of radiation hell. The dust of a million steps and stumbles. A man alone, out of the dust.

Morikawa didn't see LaBrune so much as he saw the damage he did. Wolfworm heads blown open, the liquid punch of rounds slapping into snake-like torsos, followed moments later by the eruptions that gave them away as High-ex. Warm wolfworm blood landed on Morikawa's face, and some woozy part of him remembered not to taste it, not to let the radioactive material anywhere near him. He dropped back to the sand as he tried to wipe it off, and the last of the attacking creatures coiled reluctantly back into the sands.

For a moment, there was nothing but the sound of the crackling fire from the crashed H-wagon. Then, Morikawa could make out the distant screams coming from the smugglers' ship. More wolfworms... and no rescuer so timely and so close.

Unlucky, thought Morikawa, wryly, the pain returning to his leg. He remembered he was hurt. But then he remembered that he was alive. Him and Dredd were the only ones who made it... and LaBrune.

'Where'd you come from?' growled Dredd, but the dusty figure was already walking off. LaBrune's legs gave way underneath him, but he regained his balance with some effort.

'Hey!' shouted Dredd at the retreating old-timer. 'I'm talking to you!'

He floundered through the knee-deep sands after the Texas Judge, grabbing for his arm.

'Where are you going?' asked Dredd. Morikawa heard the whine of sirens in the background. Help was on the way. They wouldn't be in the radlands for much longer. *Lucky*.

Labrune pointed vaguely to the north-west.

'Thataways, I guess,' he said, his voice the whisper of someone who no longer spoke habitually. But his legs buckled again, and the far-travelled Judge fell. Dredd tried to help him up, but had the sands were shifting, his grip was slippery, with blood... blood, from the holes in his arm, the toothmarks from a wolfworm he hadn't noticed... Delayed reaction to... to...

Dredd fell too. And Morikawa closed his eyes, listening with a smile to the welcome noise of the rescue landers. *Lucky. For some.*

MORIKAWA PREFERRED DAYLIGHT. He preferred the warm hum of the infirmary and the bright lights. It was very different from being out in the Radlands.

'No,' Dredd was saying in the next unit. 'I'm healed! I ain't missing a shift!' Morikawa shuffled to get a better view.

'You are *supposed* to be resting!' scowled Fogerty.

'Crime doesn't sleep, and neither do I!' said Dredd. 'If you want to know about Bed Three—I dug it up.' He spun the screen of the purloined computer to show Fogerty.

Fogerty shook his head in amazement.

'So, three years ago, he took the Long Walk out of Texas City,' breathed the doctor.

'Yes,' said Dredd. 'But, see here. There was a filing error.'

Fogerty took a moment to realise.

'He's listed under 'L' and 'B'...?' he said.

'Right,' said Dredd. 'Blame the Cajun surname. Our man's one of the most decorated officers in history.'

Fogerty chuckled.

'Wow,' he said. 'I wonder if he ever knew, what with all the medals filed in two different places!'

Morikawa looked back at LaBrune. His healer was dialled up to the max, with auxiliary drips, but he wasn't waking up. Ever.

'And he walked all the way from Texas to the outskirts of Mega-City One...' said Fogerty in awe.

'If we hadn't hauled him in,' said Dredd, 'he would have kept on going, too.'

Fogerty looked back over, past Morikawa at Bed Three, his smile fading when he saw the monitors.

'Listen,' added Fogerty as he turned to go. 'You know the deal, right?'

Dredd nodded.

'I'll do it,' he said.

Fogerty's back was already retreating down the hall, heading for another consultation.

'What does he mean?' asked Morikawa. Dredd ignored him, busily pulling away the monitors stuck to his chest. Morikawa realised that Dredd was still fully clothed, still wearing his helmet even. The docs never expected him to hang around for long, even in intensive care.

'Can you imagine?' said Dredd, easing himself out of his bed. 'How tough it would be to be the most decorated Judge ever.' He walked over to Bed Three, patting the top of the healer reverently.

Morikawa snatched up the computer where Dredd had let it drop.

'Yeah...' he said. 'Like, every perp in the world would want a piece of you.' He skimmed down through LaBrune's list of decorations. If anyone had known his full awards, he might never have lived long enough to make the Long Walk.

'Jovus,' said Morikawa. 'You seen how many partners he's been through? That's one lucky guy.'

'Not if you're his partner,' said Dredd.

Yeah, thought Morikawa. *Friendly fire. Collateral damage*. Better to be standing anywhere but beside the luckiest Judge in history.

'But lucky *us*, right,' said Morikawa. 'Lucky us for meeting him when we did.'

'Yeah,' said Dredd.

But Morikawa could see he was thinking of a dozen rookies who hadn't been lucky enough. Johnson... Martin... Bertram... *Fisher*... 'You can see the chart,' added Dredd. 'It's almost like he sucks the luck out of any situation.'

Suddenly, the medilab seemed quiet, and Morikawa was cold despite the cranked hospital heating.

'Psi?!? You think it's psi?' he breathed.

Dredd looked back at him, his emotions unreadable beneath the visor of the helmet.

'Forget it,' said Dredd. He tapped LaBrune's medical record. 'It's too late. He's in a coma.'

'But he might come out of—!'

Dredd held up a warning finger.

'He took the Long Walk, Morikawa. That's an implicit DNR.'

'Dee En...?'

'Do Not Resuscitate.'

'He came all that way. He saved our lives...' Suddenly Morikawa realised. 'And *you're* gonna turn off the life support! You're gonna do it!'

'Don't think I'm happy about it,' growled Dredd. 'If he dies, then he's a man. If he lives, he is truly the luckiest drokker I've met...' *And if he floats*, thought Morikawa, *he's a witch*.

'And you'd investigate him for mutant powers?'

'No,' said Dredd. 'If he can walk back to the CE, we'll let him.' Without ceremony, Dredd flicked a big red switch marked with three warnings. The lights went off on the healer and LaBrune's breathing slowed.

'Shouldn't we say something?' said Morikawa.

'Go for it,' said Dredd.

Morikawa took a deep breath.

'I'm drokk outta luck,' he mumbled.

'Are you?' asked Dredd. 'You live a life like this Judge, you'll be lucky.'

'You mean him, or you?' asked Morikawa.

The pause went on a little longer than he expected.

'Er... *sir*,' added Morikawa, but Dredd was done talking. He was already walking away, back to duty.

Morikawa watched as the heartbeat monitor slowed. Whatever the reason behind his survival, LaBrune's miraculous luck was finally running out.

Morikawa stood watching LaBrune fade away. Was that gonna be him one day, he wondered. Was that gonna be *Dredd* one day? Dying alone in a hospital, forgotten even by the computers? Taken off life support because someone figured you'd had your shot?

Morikawa looked down at the SJS computer Dredd had left behind. It had clearance to all sorts of places. He picked it up thoughtfully...

'Give me that!' bellowed Dredd, returning.

'Hang on, Dredd,' said Morikawa, with a smile. 'I just wanna look *you* up!'

'That's an order!'

'I'm wondering,' said Morikawa, 'if LaBrune isn't the *second* most-decorated—!'

But Dredd snatched the computer from him.

'This goes back to Timo!' shouted Dredd, marching back down the ward.

Morikawa knew better than to argue. Maybe it was lucky for Dredd if he didn't know. Lucky for himself if he didn't find out. Lucky for someone. Maybe.

'And back to duty!' shouted Dredd from the next ward.

Morikawa kicked the wall monitor resentfully.

The lights dimmed. There was the distinctive sound of a botrunner rebooting, and LaBrune's sleeping body jerked once within the healer.

'Drokk!' hissed Morikawa.

LaBrune's eyes opened.

'Wow,' he said weakly, in a strong Southern accent. 'Where am I?'

Oh man, thought Morikawa.

'Er... Dredd,' he called. 'Dredd?'

SCREAM SYMPHONY

ALEC WORLEY

THE CONDUCTOR-BOT WHISKED the air with his sensor-baton. The glowing keys of the surrounding organ deck pulsed obediently, releasing a chorus of human screams. A bassline of baritone bellows laced with falsetto shrieks plunged through the gothic auditorium of the Carl Heinz Pilchards-in-Tomato-Sauce Clayderman Opera Dome. Vim Del Jarre tugged at the collar of his tuxedo as he watched the conductor-bot through a hole in the stage backdrop.

Vim's latest symphony, 'Mega-City Screams', flitted now through the brisk allegro that heralded the climax of the concert. Pained sobs pulsed like a mighty heartbeat as a tide of wails rose and finally crashed into shivering shrieks. The moan of the single mother pleading for state benefits; the berserker cry of the block warrior blasting round after round into a hated rival; the stark scream of the kneepad salesman diving from the window of his 308th-floor hab, having spent thirty-seven hours on the phone attempting to navigate his tax return. The frustration, the hopelessness, the very impossibility of life in Mega-City One: Vim had embodied every emotional chord, arranging them into a choir of souls crying out as if from within some hellish machine.

As Vim had explained to the interviewer from *Mel-O.D.* magazine, he had spent the last ten years recording the screams of willing volunteers. Countless citizens had passed through his private studio, from juves to eldsters, habwives to heiresses, Umpty addicts to business sharks, a comprehensive confection of citizens. Vim explained how he had encouraged them to talk about themselves, their lives, their frustrations, what it was about life in Mega-City One that made them want to stand up and scream.

Traditional musical instruments—the cello, the piano, the olloflangalliser—no matter how artfully tuned or skilfully played, were too generic, too polished and predictable. Vim wanted to summon the agony of city life, to capture every facet of urban despair, and for that he required an authentic medium, one textured by life itself. The people of Mega-City One would therefore be his orchestra.

Squinting past the footlights, Vim gazed at the darkened audience and felt a familiar shudder. He struggled to suppress the feeling that he had somehow overlooked a crucial flaw in his work, a flaw which, at this very moment, he may be unwittingly parading to the knowing amusement of his peers. Five acts had been too much, hadn't it? He knew he should have stuck with the classical three. He'd overworked the entire symphony, strangled it with his own ambition. The culture bugs that frequented the C.H.PiTS.C. Opera Dome famously delighted in condemning imperfection. They had been known to sit in contemptuous silence at the conclusion of a debut production. Look at what happened to Aldo Dollop, that brilliant librettist whose robo-operas Vim had envied since boyhood. Dollop's career had been reduced to an assembly line of advertising jingles following the yawning silence that concluded his heartbreaking 'Requiem For a Toaster'.

Vim ran shaking fingers through his dandelion hair. The conductor-bot parried and thrust, as if fencing an invisible opponent. On the other hand, Vim wondered, his symphony of screams might contain some grain of brilliance to which he was himself blind. A standing ovation at the Carl Heinz could elevate him to the prized status of 'genius', his ability beyond question forevermore. Vim felt a rush of vertigo at the thought of the glorious gamble he had taken, the momentous result of which would reveal itself within minutes. The conductor-bot slashed and slashed again, summoning wave after rising wave of harmonic roars that converged like an approaching storm.

SOMEONE HAMMERED AT the stage door.

Vim's agent, 'Great White' Willy Wagwent, ignored it, wedging his finger deeper into his ear as he yelled into the payphone. 'Believe me, Morry,' he cried, 'Great White

Willy smells creds in the water on this one. Sign up my boy Vim right now and I'll cut you a special—'

The stage door beside him shuddered again and a voice bellowed from the other side. Willy covered the mouthpiece and bellowed back. 'Fug off, ya muncepacker, I'm on the—'

The door crashed down like a drawbridge, pinning Willy to the floor. He felt an immense weight compress his chest as the unmistakable silhouette of a Mega-City Judge loomed into view like a battleship. 'That's six months for obstruction, punk.' The muscled slab of chin barely moved as it delivered its edict. 'And unless you want six more you'll give me the current whereabouts of Vim Del Jarre.'

'W-why?' Willy gasped, fearing his potential cash-cow may be headed for the slaughterhouse.

The Judge replied with a ferocity that froze Willy's blood. 'Over thirty counts of kidnapping, torture and murder. *That's* why.'

THE CLIMAX OF screams hurtled like a hurricane as Vim paced backstage, preparing himself for the reception to his masterpiece. He wished he could have told that interviewer the whole truth, that although the majority of Vim's volunteer screamers had made exquisite contributions, certain donors had fallen somewhat short of their full potential. As it turned out, hitting the correct register or creating the desired vocal texture was simply a matter of drugging the citizen, tying them to a chair and waking them with a las-scalpel in the larynx. The first citizen to require such encouragement had been a handsome underkex model. His strange staccato shriek so impressed Vim that he employed it as a recurring *leitmotif*: 'the wail of the desirous consumer'. That particular citizen had been good for several variations before finally sagging in front of the microphone. But Vim had hurriedly revived him. For that showstopping aria he had in mind for the second act, Vim required a perfectly shrill *castrato*.

Bludgeons generally produced a wonderful tenor among the males, while various saws, applied in the manner of an overenthusiastic cellist, produced a range of gorgeously gurgling *contraltos* among the females. Vim had exhausted an entire orchestra of flesh and bone, his spent instruments now neatly buried beneath his wine cellar, their screams living on in symphony.

As his sonorous creation plunged through its climax, it occurred to Vim that he had only faintly considered the possibility of capture, as if the sacred pursuit of art would somehow exempt him from arrest. Even now, the thought of spending eternity in an iso-cube seemed little more than fantasy.

Vim ceased pacing and saw—as if somehow summoned into existence by his own idle thoughts—the biggest Judge he had ever seen in his life, marching up the nearby corridor towards him. Vim blinked. The Judge emerged from the corridor and the illuminated exit box above his head poured a pair of white zig-zags down his black visor. The grimacing monster paused and the zig-zags seemed to zero in on Vim.

'You,' he growled, pointing at Vim, 'are coming with me.'

Vim's legs quivered. His symphony was still minutes from closing and he was about to be arrested before hearing his audience respond. He bolted up the nearby stairs. The Judge bellowed after him. Vim's mind raced. If only he could buy himself a few minutes more. As he ran, he pinched the tabs either side of his wristwatch. It seemed the maestro's body needed guarding sooner than expected.

THE CREEP WAS faster than he looked. Dredd rounded a corner and saw Del Jarre slip through a pair of double doors. Smashing these aside, Dredd entered a private lounge, his Lawgiver poised. Corners checked. Empty. A line of tables laden with canapés and shampagne glasses. Curtains bulging in the breeze from an open window.

Dredd went to step forward and the floor tilted under his feet. He veered into one of the tables, spilling a stack of delicacies. He dropped to one knee, resisting the sudden urge to vomit. The shampagne flutes nearby shivered in unison, as Dredd became aware of a faint whistling at the edge of his hearing.

His head reeling, Dredd scanned the room for the source of the noise and saw someone blocking the doorway. A fattie. Female. Blonde pigtails. Major cybernetic augmentation. Her vast torso terminated below the waist in a mechanical repulsor-platform that enabled her to hover a foot off the floor. The entire lower half of her face had been replaced with some kind of white plasteen muzzle that formed an oval speaker in lieu of a mouth. Some maniac had fitted this tub of guts with an acoustic disruptor. The Brits used something similar to disperse loitering juves. The fattie's eyes glittered electric blue beneath a huge Viking helmet bolted to her head. A vast breastplate protected her voluminous belly and the white skirt that fringed the repulsor-platform rippled daintily. She hovered into the lounge as though serving herself on a tray.

Dredd raised his Lawgiver, struggling to take aim. The fattie raised her stubby arms and the wings of her helmet unfolded as if she were about to take flight. The whistle emitting from her muzzle became a piercing scream.

Dredd dropped to his knees, clutching his head in agony. His Lawgiver clattered to the floor. The shampagne flutes simultaneously exploded. The windows behind him flexed and burst. Dredd could feel his ribs vibrating as he watched his Lawgiver shudder out of reach. The air shimmered as his bionic eyes rattled in their socket casings. The fattie was almost on top of him now, concentrating her sonic scream directly at his head until it felt as though his brain were trying to escape through his ears. The fattie's eyes glittered with glee as Dredd's visor cracked. She leaned in. Dredd hoped he had gauged the distance correctly.

Launching himself on his back leg, Dredd drove a staggering right cross straight into the fattie's muzzle. His fist plunged through the speaker, silencing the sonic wail before wedging firmly inside the fattie's mechanised lower jaw. She glared at Dredd, as though she had chomped down on his fist and was refusing to let go.

Dredd struggled to free himself. One of the wings on the fattie's helmet began to flutter uncontrollably as her motor function short-circuited and she began spinning on the spot. Cursing as his legs were flung out from beneath him, Dredd could feel the gears inside the shattered muzzle grinding against his wedged fist. He grabbed a trailing pigtail as the room became a spinning blur. The fattie's eyes flickered, her face suddenly flushed and her ears burst, unspooling tangled grey cords of ear canal.

Her repulsor-platform tipped, snagging on the expensive carpet, wrenching Dredd's fist free and hurling him across the floor. He clambered to his feet. The fattie lay face down on the carpet like a spilled wedding cake. Her arm twitched and her fingers grasped the air, but Dredd had already retrieved his Lawgiver and bounded up the metal ladder outside the open window.

DREDD LURCHED ONTO the roof, feeling blood dripping from his earlobe and sliding warm down one side of his neck. Both ears sang and the cold night breeze did nothing to revive his senses. He could see Del Jarre crouched on one of the panels of decorative plexi-glass that formed the apex of the opera dome's roof. He was peering down at the packed auditorium far below. Dredd staggered towards him, Lawgiver clutched tightly in his hand.

Del Jarre turned, his eyes bright. The creep had gone futsie for sure. Dredd couldn't hear what he was babbling, but he seemed to be pleading for time, gesticulating and jabbing his finger down at the concert below.

Something grabbed Dredd by the ankle. His already precarious sense of balance abandoned him and he fell to the ground. The butt of the Lawgiver slammed into the floor, discharging it, sending a single Standard Execution round through the curved pane of plexi-glass on which Del Jarre perched. The glass didn't shatter, merely cracked in several directions, stranding Del Jarre at its centre.

Dredd rolled onto his back and saw the cybernetic fattie sprawled on the roof behind him, sparks hiccupping from her shattered muzzle. She had evidently risen up the ladder on her repulsor-platform before the machine gave out. Her blazing blue eyes were locked on Dredd, her programming haywire, her bionic fist locked around Dredd's ankle like a manacle.

Del Jarre cried out as another crooked line scribbled across the glass.

'Don't move,' boomed Dredd, his voice sounding tinny and distant to his own ears. He turned and blasted two Armour Piercing rounds into the fattie's wrist. Her fingers spasmed open.

Dredd looked up. He could hear the symphony of screams rising to a crescendo. Del Jarre watched in horror as the climatic notes of his own concerto rattled the glass on which he crouched. Dredd dived towards him, arms outstretched, just as the panel gave way, plunging Del Jarre into the auditorium. Dredd landed on his chest and snatched at air as Del Jarre plummeted, screaming, towards the orchestra and the stage.

*   *   *

THE MEG'S FOREMOST music critic Blusta Kermode shifted in his seat. He was undecided on 'Mega-City Screams'. You couldn't fault Del Jarre for his ambition. His medium was unique, his arrangement technically perfect. And yet the piece lacked a sense of theatre, of soul perhaps. A sense that the creator had invested something more heartfelt than cold intelligence into the creation of his music. What the symphony needed was some kind of final flourish.

As if on cue, a screaming figure plunged down towards the stage. That snow-white shock of hair... It was Del Jarre, diving onstage, apparently enacting a suicidal dénouement—no doubt in witty homage to the great Katarina Kaputnik, who had catapulted her entire orchestra across the city at the climax of 'Biscuit Tin Atrocity'.

Del Jarre's scream, thin and pitiful, perfectly teased out the chords of the closing aria. Kermode gasped despite himself. That aching final note, so evocative of thwarted ego, the futility of perfection. Del Jarre crashed into the organ deck with exquisite timing. Kermode leapt to his feet. 'Magnificent!' he bellowed.

The audience stifled their yawns and looked up from their watches. They saw the Meg's foremost music critic was applauding and instantly followed suite. Bravo! A triumph! A true cry from the heart!

*   *   *

DREDD LOOKED DOWN through the shattered panel from which Del Jarre had fallen. The concert's robot conductor was mindlessly bowing amid a torrent of applause. Judges were trying to restrain blood-splattered concert-goers in the front row from tossing roses on Del Jarre's scattered remains. A ceaseless whine still sang in Dredd's ears. Wouldn't hurt to wait here for a quick medical before continuing his shift.

'All units Sector 177,' his helmet-com crackled. 'Riot in progress at the All-U-Can-Buy in Tucker Jenkins Plaza.'

Dredd holstered his Lawgiver and strode past the twitching remains of Del Jarre's cybernetic bodyguard. The fat lady's malfunctioning voice box slurred a nursery rhyme as her power cells expired.

Dredd snorted. 'Guess the show's over.'

THE GREATER GOOD

MICHAEL CARROLL

I WAS WORKING Control for Sector 72 when I got the call. Justice Department Control provides back-up for the Street Judges, and it's frequently manned by cadets. Not the *little* kids, of course, but from year ten we spend twenty hours a week manning the Control stations. We watch the street cams and provide direct feedback to the Judges. We guide them, watch their backs, and we learn from their actions and decisions: those twenty hours a week are crucial to a cadet's development.

The cadets are overseen by a senior Judge, and a year earlier my supervisor had been Judge Gardino. We had a disagreement on how a particular case should be handled, and Gardino dismissed me. Fifteen years old—ten years as a cadet—and I was out. But Judge Dredd overturned the decision. He told Gardino, *'The moment we put a Judge's life above the safety of the people, we're not fit to govern.'*

After that, I moved up through the ranks pretty quickly. Passed my Year Ten assessments with a perfect score. Two months later, I passed my Year Eleven. Four months after that, I took Year Twelve. Scored ninety-eight per cent. Took it again the next week: one hundred per cent.

The city lost a lot of Judges in 2134—lost a lot of cadets too, when the Academy burned down—so I wasn't *too* surprised when Dredd contacted me: 'Farez? Report to the armoury for your rookie uniform, then meet me in the Lawmaster bay, one hour. Your final assessment.'

Cadets are usually twenty—having trained for fifteen years—before their final assessment. I was sixteen.

My tutor shook my hand and wished me luck, but I could see the *'He's not gonna make it'* look in his eyes. I got the same look from the armourers as they tried to find a uniform and helmet small enough to fit me.

Dredd was waiting in the Lawmaster bay, sitting on his bike right next to a new one. With Dredd, there's no pleasantries. He just gestured to the other bike. 'Let's go, Farez.'

I'd passed Lawmaster Basics the previous week. I would have taken it sooner but I was too small for the bike, and they only come in one size: big and dangerous. We roared out of the Lawmaster bay and onto the streets. The other road users get out of the way when they see a Lawmaster coming, which is good, because the ones who *don't* move aside are either inattentive drivers or they're trying too hard to look innocent. Either way, we pay them special attention.

As we zoomed onto the slipway that would carry us up to Dredd's chosen watchpoint on the Dieffenbach flyover, he called in: 'Control. Dredd and Farez checking in. What do you have for us?'

'All quiet, Dredd. Proceed to the watchpoint and stand by.'

I said, 'Control, run a scan on a green '98 Coopwood Elite, partial regtag 2804 dash 0321, heading south on Fingeroth.'

'Will do. Cause?'

'Rest of the vehicle's tag is obscured by dirt. Violation of Vehicle Maintenance Statute 348a.'

Dredd slowed a little, looked at me as I came up alongside him. 'Good eyes, rookie.'

'Thank you, sir.'

'You're the youngest rookie I've ever assessed. Think I'm going to go easier on you because you're a juve?'

'With respect, Judge Dredd, we're on patrol. Not the appropriate time for irrelevant conversation.'

Dredd's only response was 'Hmph', but when I glanced at him I thought I saw something in his expression. Not a smile, but maybe slightly less of a scowl.

And then the call came in: 'Dredd—proceed to Pauline Fowler Block, apartment 3811. Neighbour reports double homicide. Victims identified as Quintana and Grudfrey Perkins.'

'Dredd responding. ETA three minutes.' Dredd pulled back the throttle and zoomed ahead: I was half a second behind him. 'Farez—it's your show.'

I was familiar with Fowler. Not a nice place. Apartment 3811 was on the thirtieth floor—the closest roadway was on floor twenty. 'Control? Farez. I want an elevator waiting on floor twenty, Judge access only. Run a full scan on the victims. Flag anything suspicious. Send their cit-ID data to our Lawmasters. Get the neighbour's name—run a check for priors.'

'Back-up required, Farez?'

'Unknown at this time. Send a meat-wagon. Stand by.'

By the time Dredd and I exited the elevator on the twentieth floor there was a meat-wagon on the way, and Control had told us everything we needed to know about the victims. The wife, Quintana, had served three years for possession. Should have been two, but she couldn't stay out of trouble in the iso-cube. Husband Grudfrey had been questioned eight times for suspicion of extortion—in each case the victims retracted their statements or identified someone else as the perp. They were not good people. Child Protection Services had been called a couple of times to check on their little girl.

A dozen cits were clustered around the doorway to the Perkins' apartment.

'Still your show, Farez,' Dredd said.

I strode ahead of him. 'Judges coming through!' I yelled. 'Step aside. Any of you who entered the apartment, make yourselves known to Judge Dredd for questioning.'

I stepped into the apartment, took in the scene. On the threadbare carpet were the victims. Grudfrey Perkins. Forty years old. Face down. Single gunshot to the back. Wife Quintana Perkins, same age. Lying face-up. Single shot to the head.

From the hallway, Dredd called, 'You secure the scene, rookie?'

'Secure,' I called back. 'Twin bullet holes in the window, matching holes in the opposite wall. Fresh—still fragments of crystalglass on the floor and the victims. Perp's a sniper.' I stepped over the bodies as I looked out through the cracked window. A straight line between the bullet holes in the wall and the glass showed me where to look. 'Control, send a forensic team to the roof of James Morrow Block. Check the surrounding blocks' securi-cam footage.'

Dredd walked into the room. 'That all you've got?'

'First victim was Grudfrey. First shot spreads cracks radiating from the hole.' I pointed to the crystalglass. 'Cracks from the second hole are blocked by the first. Shows us the order of the shots.'

Back at the wall, I used my boot-knife to dig out the bullets. 'Tiny. Steel. No sign of a propellant. Weapon's a rail-gun. Untraceable.'

Something had been bugging me since I walked into the apartment, and then it hit me. 'Drokk—the kid was *here* when it happened.' Into my radio, I said, 'Control—lock down the building. Victims' kid is missing. Amandine Perkins, female, five years old. Get Child Protection over here and run a floor-by-floor search.'

Dredd asked, 'What makes you think the kid was here?'

'No sign of forced entry. Without a key, the door can only be opened from inside. She saw the shots hit her folks. She ran. The neighbour reported that the door was open—that's how he found the bodies.'

Amandine was found ten minutes later, hiding two floors down in the maintenance room. She was carried up to the apartment by the social worker. He was fifty-five, overweight, greying stubble. 'Name's Nate Stein,' he said to Dredd as he tried to peer past us through the doorway and into the apartment. 'She's in shock, but she'll be okay. So what happened?'

'Sniper,' Dredd said.

'Jovus... Any ideas who?'

'Talk to the rookie,' Dredd said as he stepped back into the apartment.

Stein looked down at me. 'Grud... how old *are* you, kid?'

I ignored him. The little girl was wrapping herself tightly around him, her face pushed deep into the side of his neck. 'You're familiar with the family?'

Stein nodded. 'Yeah. Mommy and Daddy weren't exactly model citizens.' He gently patted the girl's back. Speaking softly, he added, 'This little one should have been taken away *years* ago. I got called out a couple of times on a 272. Mommy was a dust-head—used to get high and take it out on Amandine when she crashed.' Again, he tried to see into the apartment. 'Sniper, huh?'

'Enemies?'

He shrugged. 'No idea. But they weren't popular. No close relatives, either. And little chance of adoption. The Chaos Bug has created *thousands* of orphans—most of them from good homes. So not many people are gonna want to take on the kid of a double-homicide, especially not at this age.'

'This I know,' I said.

He tilted his head to the side a little as he looked at me. 'That what happened to you? The Academy used to get a lot of their recruits that way, right? Parents killed, no relatives, nowhere else to go.'

'Not your business, citizen. You focus on doing the best you can for the girl.'

'Yeah, well, could be that the best is for her to become a cadet too.'

We stepped aside to let the medics carry the bodies out of the apartment, then Dredd returned to the hallway. 'Next step, Farez?'

'We see what the securi-cam footage turns up. Meantime, we resume patrol.'

Stein said, 'Keep me posted. Don't like the idea of someone out there picking citizens off with a rail-gun.' Again, he lowered his voice. 'Even if they *are* complete scum.'

'Right,' I said. 'She'll need clothes, Stein.'

'I can't go into an active crime scene—'

'It's okay if you're with me. Dredd? Take the girl.'

For some reason little kids seem to trust Dredd. Amandine wrapped her arms around his neck and hugged him tightly. Anyone but Dredd, it would have been adorable.

Stein followed me into the apartment. 'Man, those were good shots! Hate to say it, but maybe they got what they deserved.'

He started toward the girl's bedroom, but I stopped him. 'What?' he asked.

His nose made a very satisfying crack when my fist slammed into it.

For a big guy he was fast. He expertly blocked my

second punch, struck out with his own meaty fists—and I dodged to the side, grabbed his arms and planted him face-first into the blood-soaked carpet, pressing down so hard on the back of his head that his muffled screams formed bubbles in the blood.

'You better have a good reason for this, rookie!' Dredd yelled from the doorway. The girl cowered in his arms, crying.

I cuffed Stein and did my best to haul him to his feet—it wasn't easy. 'He's the perp, Dredd—or at the very least he knows him.'

Stein snarled at me, flecks of crimson saliva hitting my visor. 'That's insane!'

'How did you identify the murder weapon as a rail-gun before you saw the crime scene?'

Stein staggered back, his eyes wide. 'You... You *said*...'

'No. I didn't.' I pulled out my radio. 'Control, run a check on Nate Stein, social worker assigned to this case. My guess is he used to be a cadet.' I glared at Stein. 'That right, creep? You were a cadet. You failed. But you've still got a strong sense of loyalty to the city. Thought you could help. Get rid of a couple of bad elements, and rebuild the ranks of the Academy with a new recruit. Everyone wins, right?'

Stein looked down, trembling. 'I... I thought... It's *evolution*. Weed out the bad stuff, keep the good.'

'Stein—how many other cadets have you acquired for the department?'

'T-twelve. But it was for the greater good!'

'*You* don't get to determine what's for the greater good

of the city,' I said. '*We* do. We're the Judges. You're just another perp.'

Stein raised his head, glared at me. 'You? You're a *kid*. A cadet playing at being a rookie! What are you? Fifteen? Sixteen? I made it all the way through the Academy before I flunked my final assessment—that gives me four years more training than you! So maybe you're some kind of freak who's been fast-tracked through the system, but you're *not* a Judge!'

'He is now,' Dredd said. 'Farez, process this creep then report to the Grand Hall for your full eagle badge and helmet.' He passed the girl over to me. 'I'll see you on the streets, Judge Farez.'

Amandine was still crying when I handed her over to Stein's replacements. But that was okay. She was a kid. It's natural for kids to cry.

A few years as a cadet will cure her of that.

THE PACK

ALAN GRANT

I RAN WITH the Pack. What else could I do?

The city was in ruins, and my sector was particularly badly hit. A couple of city blocks came down, demolished by rival Citi-Defs, their smashed-up remains scattered for what seemed like miles around. The sector looked like a warzone—where the war had been irretrievably lost.

Most of the shops had been looted and cleaned out. What little food there was changed hands for a fortune. Rumour had it aid would be coming in from Texas City and Brit-Cit, but I wasn't holding my breath; why should they send aid to us? Besides, I was hungry *now*.

The city blocks still standing were full of rotting corpses, their sweet, sickening stench hanging like a shroud of doom over what little was left. Made me feel like puking all the time. Judges were still out on the streets, but not many—it looked like the Chaos Bug had killed most of them, too. It was every citizen for himself, and life wasn't pretty.

I guess I was lucky. I abandoned my block—Jack Black Welfare—when it became obvious everybody around me was dying. Somehow I managed to escape the Bug— maybe by that point the Bug itself was just weakening and dying out. I found a place to hole up in Magoo's Auto Repair. It was totally burned out and looted, but that was good because it meant nobody had any reason to go there. Not that there were many vehicles left, not around here leastways... and it'd take a lot more than Magoo's robots to fix 'em. They were mostly all gone anyway; the robots, I mean, though Grud alone knows where an unemployed robot without an owner goes. There were still some lying in bits on the auto-shop floor, but there was no electricity to charge 'em up any more so they were totally useless. I ripped the visor off one and wore it to try to keep out the nauseating stink of death. I also armed myself with a plastoid pinch bar, just in case I needed to use a weapon.

Second night I was there, my guts spasming with the need for food, another guy showed up. We talked a bit— he was called Kneepad Jolie, and I guess he looked the way I did: stubbly beard, wild hair, ripped clothes. Guess he used to be some kinda fashion freak, 'cos he still wore a pair of kneepads that used to have goldfish in them. But he said he broke 'em open and ate the goldfish days ago. We were used to being on welfare—spent our whole lives on welfare—so we didn't know how to do much for ourselves. We hardly ever looked each other in the eye, kept our talk to a minimum. I guess we were ashamed. And frightened. And so drokkin' hungry.

That's why we joined the Pack. I'd heard 'em roaming around at night, saw flashes of flame and light through Magoo's broken windows, even heard gunshots once or twice. But I never knew what they were up to. Then one night we were huddled in our blankets when Kneepad said: 'I'm sicka this. We're just gonna die if we stay here. Can't eat rustin' robots. Can't drink lube-oil.'

I couldn't argue with that. 'Mighta been better to be killed by the Bug,' I told him.

'Yeah, but we wasn't,' he said. 'I'm goin' t'see what these folks are doin' out there.'

I didn't want to be on my own again. Ain't good for nobody, bein' on your own, with nothing to think about except dead bodies, and their stench, and now I was goin' to be a corpse too real soon unless something happened. So when we heard the voices we slunk out real careful-like and watched from the shadows.

It was a clear night, fresher than usual 'cos it had just rained. Weather Control used to take care of that, but I guess there wasn't any control no more. It was weird to see stars in the sky, and an ittybitty crescent moon; city lights used to be so bright, you could never see the stars. And the moon always used to have gigantic adverts on it. They were beautiful, I thought, like something off the holovids... only not so real, somehow.

We saw a fatty moving in the dim light, picking his way carefully between lumps of rubble and burned-out cars in what used to be the roadway. Chump needed a bellywheel, really, he was such a lardy gink—but it wouldn't have done him no good 'cos of all the debris. Then there was a flickering light, and the sound of voices.

There was about a dozen of 'em, moving out of the shadows, guys that looked like me an' Kneepad. One of them had a gun, a big old pistol he held up ready to use. The fatty tried to freeze and blend into the night, but he was too big an' too slow. The Pack had seen him.

They descended on him like rad-flies. The fatty pleaded for his life, but guys that are hungry have no mercy. The guy with the gun put a bullet in him, and he fell to the ground, squawkin' and beggin'. Then they were on him, and me and Kneepad saw knives flash in the pale light, and soon the fatty wasn't doin' nothing except lying there.

They ripped and gouged at him, making strange guttural noises like I'd never heard before. The guy with the gun tried to keep some kind of order, shouting at the others, but they paid him no heed. We could hear the sickening sound of fatty flesh tearing as they ripped lumps off him and ran back to the shadows with their booty—arms and legs and lumps of fatty belly. Then quick as they'd come, they disappeared into the night.

Kneepad looked at me and whispered: 'There's one comin' this way. Get that pinch bar ready.'

The guy was carrying half an arm, blood dripping from it like the sauce off a munceburger. I used to love munceburgers. That was when I really realised what the Pack was doin' out there.

As the guy ran past our hidey-hole in the rubble, Kneepad stuck out a foot and tripped him up. I knew what I had to do. I hit him hard with the pinch bar, and heard a crack as it smashed into his ribs. He screeched like somethin' out of a horror vid, but before I could hit him again he'd scuttled away into the darkness.

But he'd left the half-arm behind, lyin' on the ground. Me and Kneepad looked at each other—that was prob'ly the last time we looked into each other's eyes. We both knew what was going to happen. Kneepad scooped up the half-arm—shoulder to elbow, it was—and together we ran back to Magoo's. We went right in the back, into the machine shop, where nobody on the street could ever see us.

We made a fire in silence, using greasy rags and an old blowtorch-igniter that was almost out of charge. Kneepad made a tripod out of old wrenches, and we set the arm on it to cook. It smelled great!

It was evil, eating human flesh for the first time. But we were so hungry, we didn't hesitate to tear into it. It tasted a bit like burned munceburger. We wolfed it down... then brought it right back up again, vomiting all over the place, though after the first couple of retches there was nothing to bring up but bile.

When we felt better, we staggered back to the arm and ripped off another bite. It didn't seem so bad this time. I'd always lived on cheap packaged meals you could buy from the Muckstore with welfare credits, and fatty arm certainly wasn't much worse than them. It was the first food we'd had for near enough a week, and thank Grud it stayed down after that first horrible puke.

I was afraid to go to sleep after that, in case Kneepad had acquired a taste for it and fancied tryin' me, too. But

I saw he was dozin' off, and I figured we'd both had our bellies filled and wouldn't be wanting any more tonight. So I carefully put out our little fire and turned away in disgust from what was left of the fatty's arm. It would serve as breakfast.

In the morning, I took my first dump for a week right at the back end of Magoo's. It wasn't pleasant. But now we knew we could survive, even if it was in the most inhuman way you could imagine.

After that we ran with the Pack. Not every night, 'cos sometimes we were still full from whatever we'd scoffed the night before. Just often enough to keep us alive. Weren't no fatties after that first one, but there was always refugees, alone or in small groups. We were never much in the way of men to begin with—life on welfare makes you feel useless, except when you're watchin' holovids—but we descended from men into animals. Mega-City animals, eating each other just so's we wouldn't starve.

Then one night was were out with the Pack when we stumbled across a skinny woman carryin' a bundle. The guy with he gun—Googleye he called himself, on account of one of his peepers was skew-whiff—put a bullet right in her head. Then the knives were out and flashing in the moonlight.

The bundle she'd been carrying was lying on the ground. It gave a weak little whimper, and one of the guys unwrapped it... and there was a little baby. Skinny little runt, it was. Its little eyes seemed to stare directly into mine, like it was askin' me for food. Googleye lifted his pistol to smash its head in, and suddenly I felt sick.

'Not a baby!' I gasped. 'We can't kill a baby!'

'It's gonna die anyways,' Googleye snarled. 'We might as well have it before it rots.'

I couldn't stand it. Without even thinking, I swung my pinch bar. It hit his wrist, and the pistol fell to the slab. I snatched it up and pointed it at him, waving it at the grim faces that grouped around me. Even Kneepad was glaring at me.

'Not a baby,' I kept saying. 'We can't eat a baby.' The faces moved closer, and a couple of the guys raised their knives. 'Keep back! I swear I'll shoot—an' if I do, we'll be eatin' one of you!'

They inched closer. 'He can't take us all, boys,' Googleye grunted, nursing his broken wrist. 'There's only one bullet in the gun anyhow.'

I wondered what the drokk I was doin'. I was gonna lose my life 'cos of a stinkin' baby that was gonna die anyway. But somehow I felt human again. There were tears in my eyes as I stood my ground, daring them to come any closer.

Suddenly there was a bright light picking us out, and a harsh voice growled: 'You with the gun! Drop it!'

I froze. An instant later, a gunshot roared and took me in the arm. I spun around and fell, almost on top of the baby.

'Stand where you are, all of you!' the voice shouted. But that was like the signal to run, and the Pack began to scatter. More shots rang out, echoing round the slabway. Guys fell, gasping and yelling as they died. Kneepad fell beside me, blood frothing from his mouth before his eyes clouded over and he gave up the ghost.

Then the Judge stood over me, gun pointed right between my eyes. 'Cannibal scum,' he hissed, his finger tightening on the trigger.

I tried to protest. 'No! No, I was protecting the baby! I didn't want to eat it, I was trying to stop them! I swear I never killed anybody!'

He paused for what seemed like all eternity. Then: 'Lie detector says you're telling the truth. Get to your feet.'

I could hardly stand, I was so weak from loss of blood. The Judge scooped up the baby and strapped it to his Lawmaster—nobody had even heard its approach, we were so wrapped up in our own little drama.

'Sector House is this way,' he said gruffly. 'Walk six paces in front of the bike. One wrong move and you're dead.'

AND THAT'S HOW I ended up here, in an iso-cube. Leastways, I get about half a meal a day, some kinda soya gloop, but it fills my belly and that's enough for me. They take us out every dawn to work on the gangs that are cleanin' the streets and movin' the rubble, slowly turning the Big Meg back into someplace fit to live.

'Course, I can't do much, only having one good arm now. But it makes me feel like a human being, doing something useful for the first time in my life.

It's only when I try to sleep at night that the nightmares start, and I see that fatty's arm waving to me in the darkness. Like it's saying goodbye.

PARANOIA

ALAN GRANT

'SOYA-DOUGH AND SYNTHI-DOUGH, *and artificial colouring,*'
I sing to myself, rocking back and forward on my heels as
I crouch in the corner of the room. '*Chemical flavourings
too, and Kreem Goo.*'

It keeps me sane. It has a nice catchy tune—might even
have been a vid-hit. Once.

THE WALLS ARE closing in on me. Worse, so are the corpses.

I figure there are half a dozen in the apartment next
door, same again in the one on the other side. I haven't
heard a squeak out of them for a long time, when they
used to be so noisy I couldn't sleep at night. I still can't
sleep at night... but now it's because of fear.

There are forty floors above my place, and if the Chaos
Bug killed them all, that's another ten thousand or so
dead folk just lying there, festering away, decomposing,

releasing their diseases and their ghosts to haunt the living. Cholera. Dysentery. Ghosts. Far as I know, I'm the only man left alive in Sam Raimi block, and that is a very frightening thought. I remind myself that I don't believe in ghosts, but it seems to be getting harder with every day that passes. At least, I think they're days, but I have no way of knowing, really.

There are Judges out on the streets. Sometimes I hear their sirens blaring, and the crackle of gunshots. Once in a while there's a loud roar as an H-Wagon loops around the block. Sometimes there's a buzzing noise, too, but I can't figure what that might be.

The block still has power, but I'm afraid to turn on the holo-vid to see if there's any news. Rumour used to be that the Judges had a camera fitted into every holo-vid set, so they could secretly monitor the population. I dunno if that's true; the guy next door used to beat his kids sometimes, and nothing ever happened to him. But maybe the Judges had bigger fish to fry, bigger perps to catch, and they didn't have time to come and arrest him.

Sometimes I used to dream of ratting my neighbour up, putting in a call to Judge Pal to say what he was doing to those kids. I could have collected a fifty-cred reward for 'information received regarding a crime'. But I never did it, mainly because like everybody else in the Big Meg, I didn't want the Judges in my life. I mean, there are so many crimes that nobody even knows are a crime that if you rat somebody up, they investigate you too. For all I know, informing itself might be a crime. That's the devious way the Judges' minds work.

Everybody is guilty until proven innocent. Doesn't seem right, but what can you do? The answer is nothing. Nobody could ever do anything in this Gruddamn city except collect your welfare payments, maybe go window shopping, watch the holos, then die. Crime runs rampant, they used to say, but I'm sure it wouldn't if folks had something fulfilling to do with their time. Like what? I dunno. I've never been fulfilled. I don't even know what it might mean.

Now I dream of corpses, tens of thousands of them, millions of them. Corpses and diseases everywhere. But no ghosts. I mean, how can there be ghosts when the dead bodies go to Resyk? All the parts that can be used again are stripped out, all the organs, all the blood. So how can there be ghosts when the bodies don't even exist any more? I don't believe in 'em, but I find myself worrying about them more and more often.

So I sit quietly in my corner and sing my Donut Song, and somehow that keeps the ghosts away, and things don't seem too bad.

I DO KNOW for a one hundred per cent genuine fact that Justice Department used to have spy-in-the-sky cameras absolutely everywhere—tiny flying monitors they used to find out about crime all over the city. Quite often when I went out for my daily walk in the block park, I'd catch a glimpse of one zipping above the heads of the crowds. There could be one sitting outside my window right now, sending back images to Justice Central, and I wouldn't even know until they came and booted in my door. Which is why I keep the shades permanently closed, so I can't tell if it's day or night.

I sometimes hear a loud buzzing noise, but I don't know if it's real or not. They say that perps who get sent to the iso-cubes often go crazy, because they have nothing to look at, nothing to hear, and they start hallucinating stuff. I wonder if maybe that's what's happening to me, because I been cooped up in here for two weeks now—at least, I think it's two weeks, but who knows? Anyhow, the noise isn't always there so I don't worry too much about it.

I suspect the vidphones are still working. But every vidcall is recorded, every 'puter message; with four hundred million citizens, there must have been billions of messages going out every day. The Judges have machines that sift through them all, looking for keywords that would divulge if illegal stuff was being discussed. But of course no citizen ever knew what the keywords were, so I can't call anybody to see what's happening. If I said the wrong thing, first I'd know would be when my door caved in. And then they'd execute me.

See, I'm a looter, and in the Big Meg looting is punishable by death. They announced that on the holo-news when the Chaos Bug first struck. Trying to keep us in our apartments, I guess. They wouldn't listen to no excuses about everybody being dead so they wouldn't need the stuff I'd looted. Judges aren't rational in that respect. Their line is—you do the crime, you die.

'Synthi-dough and soya-dough, and artificial colouring.' It has a nice ring to it. It keeps my mind occupied, so I

don't think of all the bad things. And it drowns out the sound of the buzzing. I'm glad I made it up.

WHEN THE BUG first struck, and they had all these warnings broadcast all over the place, I was sitting at my favourite table in the Café du Sleaze down in the block mall. That was my weekly treat to myself: five creds for a synthi-caf and a Looks-Like-Real-Cream-But-Isn't Kreem-smothered donut, and a one-cred lottery ticket.

That lottery ticket could have been my ticket out. Billion-cred first prize. You could fly to the moon, or a swish resort on some planet. I used to see the big winners on the holo-boards, ordinary folks so excited they'd won that they were close to having heart attacks. But it was never me. It was never most folks. And anyway, the Judges probably made it all up, just to give us some hope.

So I was savouring my donut when everybody else was coughing and sneezing and falling down all over the place. But it didn't seem to affect me. When the guy behind the counter fell down gasping and wheezing, I had a sudden whim. I'd never had a whim before, and now I wish I'd never had that one, either. But with nobody to stop me, I rushed behind the counter, grabbed a huge box of donuts and another of synthi-caff, and hightailed it back to my apartment. Nobody even looked twice at me; they were too busy keeling over or screaming and panicking and yelling things like, *'I gotta get home to the wife and kids!'*

It was only afterwards I realised I'd probably been picked up by the CCTV cams or a spy-in-the-sky. But then I thought, with millions of folks dying, and all the Judges busy collecting corpses and taking them out to dump 'em in the Cursed Earth charnel pits, nobody was going to come looking for a guy who stole some Kreem donuts and synthi-caff. Anyhow, the Judges were falling victim to the bug too, and soon the whole city was dying around me and as far as I knew I was the only guy left alive. The only perp left alive.

'Cos that's what I am: a perp. A perpetrator. Somebody who committed a crime. Just thinking about it gives me a little thrill of excitement, 'cos I never in my life figured I'd be an outlaw. Then again, it sends ripples of fear up and down my spine; it means I'm a marked man. The Judges don't forgive, and they don't forget. One day they'll get me, and I'll pay the ultimate price for my crime.

So I sit in my room, in the dark, with just the faintest light coming in under the door from the hallway, squinting to read the ingredients on the Kreem donut pack. I've never read a book, don't even own a book, but I read those ingredients so many times I know 'em by heart. *'Soya-dough. Synthi-dough. Artificial colouring. Chemical flavourings. Tasting agents. Goo contains culture-made Goo, plus an approximation of Real Kreem.'* I tried to fit all of it into my song, but it's too hard getting the words to rhyme, so I just settled for the short version. I have one donut every time I feel hungry, and a cup of synthi-caff made with cold water, 'cos the hot tap doesn't run any more. Then I sit in my corner and sing my song.

I glance at the door to the hall. Something fat and horrible and buzzing squeezes underneath it and into my apartment. A fly! It sits in the pale strip of light, staring at me. I take off my shoe to squash it. But wait! What if it's one of the Judge cameras, a fly-in-the-sky? It could be sending them my details even as it sits and stares. If I crush it, I'd be destroying Justice Department property, and they'd come down hard on me for that. With my shoe in my hand, I sit there thinking.

Then more of them start to appear, sliding under the door until the dim light near-disappears. Suddenly, I realise what the buzzing noise is. Flies! Billions of 'em, the whole block riddled with 'em. They've feasted on the dead, and now they've come looking for me.

For just a moment I think maybe I'm imagining them, I've finally started having hallucinations. A swarm of them buzzes over and settles on my donut box. One of them brushes against my cheek, and I shudder. It feels fat and slimy and bursting with disease. They're real!

More of them pour in under the door. So I sit very still, pretending I'm not there. I close my mouth and stop singing, but the words keep going round in my head: *'Synthi-dough and soya-dough, and artificial colouring. Chemical flavourings too and Real Goo.'*

I consider my options. I can make a break for it, rush for the door, run outside. And then, no mistake, the Judges will get me. Or I could try to open the windows—but they only open a few inches anyhow, most likely to stop people throwing themselves out and committing suicide. And the spy-in-the-sky cams are out there.

Think I'll take my chances with the flies...

JUDGEMENT CALL

ROBERT MURPHY

HE COULD HEAR him before he could see him. The creak of synthi-leather. The measured step.

Webb had been waiting for Dredd in the Academy locker room for over an hour and now that he could hear him approaching his stomach churned with apprehension. The rookie Judge realised he'd been gripping his half-eagle badge so tightly it had begun to hurt.

One more year and he'd have traded it in for the real thing.

Full eagle.

You almost had to whisper it. He used to fantasise about tracing the raised letters of his own name on the cold metal shield. Now he could feel it all but slipping from his grasp.

Dredd turned the corner and walked past Webb towards a bank of lockers at the end of the room, the steel caps on his boots ringing on the tiled floor. He prised open one of the narrow doors and reached inside. For a moment Webb idly wondered what Dredd might have stored in his locker. Visor wipes? An old but fondly used daystick?

Dredd emerged with an oily rag, nudging the locker closed behind him as he began to polish his Lawgiver. He kept his gaze on the weapon as he walked slowly back towards the seated rookie.

This is it, Webb thought. They must have reviewed the footage by now. They know something happened on that balcony.

Dredd came to a slow stop. He was close enough to smell now—megway fumes and machine oil and somewhere underneath it all a brand of soap you'd think twice about using to clean a hovercab.

Webb thought of at least three ways he could soil his uniform.

'You changed your mind at the last minute,' Dredd declared bluntly. 'Switched from hi-ex to standard execution round. Why?'

Webb knew it would come to this.

IT SHOULD HAVE been a routine zziz bust. A low-level dealer called Insidious Glubb, pushing the stuff for the Tancredy Clan from a squalid apartment in Rosler Block. Dredd had handpicked it to give the three rookies some quality slab-time before they embarked on their final assessment. He figured Glubb might need softening up but he hadn't expected the blinding flash of light and percussive boom of heavy weapons that greeted the first helmet through the door.

'Judge down!' Stearman screamed, her face white with panic. One of the others, Kowoloski, was lying dazed at her feet, his left arm a ragged mess of smoking flesh.

'Let's get some perspective,' Dredd said as he edged around the frame of the door and fired off a round in response. 'No one's made full Judge yet.'

'What's going on?' Webb shouted, his ears still ringing from the assault.

'Intel must have been wrong,' Dredd scowled. 'Looks like Glubb and his friends were expecting someone with designs on their product. Stearman, call in a med-wagon. Webb, toss a hornet cam in there, let's see what we're dealing with.'

Webb fumbled the tiny camera from a loop on his belt, switched it on and lobbed it through the door. A second later he could hear it buzzing the room at speed, relaying grainy images to the retinal display inside his visor.

'Three perps. One down, wounded. Other two reloading.'

'Exits?'

'Looks like a doorway to the rear. Only thing out that way is the balcony overlooking the megway.'

Dredd nodded and raised his weapon. 'I'll draw their fire—you take them down while they're distracted.'

Webb swallowed hard and gripped his Lawgiver tightly. The hornet cam buzzed maddeningly around the ceiling.

'Big mistake, Jays,' croaked a voice inside the room. 'You walked into the wrong war.'

Dredd could tell Glubb was stalling, desperately trying to come up with a plan. The tremor of fear in his voice might as well have been an invitation. With a sudden leap Dredd hurled himself through the splintered door frame and into the room, his Lawgiver blazing. Two neat holes popped open in Glubb's greasy forehead, then the back of his scalp burst apart with a wet crack.

Webb took a deep breath and plunged inside, the acrid smoke catching in his throat. His helmet was slick with sweat and tipped down over his eyes as he lurched against the wall. In the second it took him to push it back he saw the third perp disappear through the door at the back of the room.

'Runner!' he shouted hoarsely.

'Follow him,' Dredd growled, his eye suddenly drawn to a blur of movement and the glint of a blade as the wounded man attempted to take a stab at his leg.

Webb stumbled through the crowded chaos of Glubb's bedroom, past sleeping pods and boxes of junk, and headed instinctively for the sliding door that opened onto the balcony.

It was ominously quiet, the only sound his own laboured breathing and the buzz of the hornet cam as it tracked Webb into the room. A bead of sweat trickled down his forehead. He reached forward with his left hand and began to ease the door open, the dull roar of the megway below filling the room.

Then he heard it.

The scrape of a boot on the rockcrete balcony.

Webb yanked the door open the rest of the way and

staggered out. His right arm trembled as he held his weapon at eye level, searching for a target.

The runner was crouching on the balcony wall, about to jump. Somewhere close by a hoverbike engine whined into life. Webb clocked it over the edge of the balcony as it rose upwards in a blast of hot air. The driver was beckoning furiously with one hand as he manoeuvred the vehicle into position.

One shot is all it takes, Webb told himself. One small cylinder of high explosive and the bike and the perps disappear in a fireball, a mild diversion for the traffic down below. He just had to say the word and the gun would do the rest.

'Hi—'

The runner turned to look at Webb, a faint smirk on his face.

Webb froze. He felt a wave of nausea roll over him.

'Standard execution round,' he stammered.

The runner jumped as he pulled the trigger. The bullet glanced his scalp and sped harmlessly into the sky. There was a muffled thud as he landed awkwardly on the back of the hoverbike, then the high-pitched whine of the engine at full throttle as it peeled up and away.

Webb watched the bright red tail light until it cleared the top of the block and vanished. As he turned to go back inside he heard the tiny metallic clink of the hornet cam dropping to the floor, its power drained. He picked it up ruefully and slipped it into his pocket.

* * *

IT WAS RAINING when Dredd arrived at Justice Central the next morning. His helmet glistened under the harsh strip lights as he strode purposefully towards the surveillance unit. A security door slid open as he approached and then he was inside, the babble of a thousand whispered voices stopping him momentarily in his tracks. Hundreds of Judges and surveillance teks were staring at CCTV monitors, their faces bathed in an eerie green glow. Every time he came here there seemed to be more of them.

It took him a moment to spot Hernandez, hunched over her computer in a gloomy corner.

'What have you got on the Webb shoot?' he asked.

'Ah.' Hernandez smiled, her fingers working the holoscreen. 'The one that got away.' She dragged a grid of camera feeds onto her screen. 'Coverage isn't the best in Rosler Block, I'm afraid. Perps knock the cameras out faster than we can put them up. We caught the hoverbike from the roof, though.'

Dredd studied the blurry image of the man clinging to the back of the vehicle. 'Any ID on the runner?'

'Tick Muldoon. Done some time in the juve cubes. Looks like he's graduated to bigger stuff.'

Dredd stared at the screen and rubbed his chin thoughtfully. 'How about the moment Webb arrived on the balcony? Just before he pulled the trigger.'

Hernandez frowned. 'There's this,' she said, magnifying one of the feeds. 'Playback from the hornet cam synced to Webb's helmet.'

Dredd leaned forward and peered closely at the screen. It showed an aerial view of the balcony with the runner poised on the ledge and Webb with his weapon raised. Hernandez patched in the audio from Webb's comms link and they watched as he took aim, paused and then fired off target.

'His first instinct was hi-ex,' Dredd observed.

'Understandable,' Hernandez nodded. 'Take 'em both down in one shot. Along with a burning vehicle onto a busy megway. Maybe he was erring on the side of caution.'

'Rookies are meant to learn to trust their instincts,' Dredd replied gruffly. 'Pull up his file.'

Hernandez quickly accessed the cadet evaluation records and skimmed through them. 'Jonah Webb, twenty years old. Got a year to go till he makes full eagle, but he's only been in the programme since he was nine.'

'Nine?'

'He's marked down as "Special Intake". Looks like he was part of a recruitment drive from the problem blocks. Mother was a zziz fiend.'

'Which block?'

'Rosler.'

'Give me the boy and I'll show you the Judge,' he muttered. 'Play the clip again.'

Hernandez swept the file off screen and ran the hornet cam feed.

'There's something else there,' he said. 'Something makes him hesitate and change his mind.'

Hernandez slowed down the footage and gazed at the screen.

'Recognition?' she volunteered.

'Worse,' Dredd grunted. 'Compassion.'

*   *   *

WEBB HAD LOST track of how long he'd been sitting in the locker room. He'd been in a daze ever since he got back to the Academy, his mind constantly replaying those few seconds on the balcony.

Of all the people it could have been, it had to be Tick, with a sly grin and a challenge in his eyes.

In that instant, Webb was a young boy again, stick thin and starving, hands clasped over his ears as he shivered on the balcony while his mother did what she had to inside to feed her habit. He remembered the smell of hot munce burgers wafting over on the breeze and Tick's face peering across the divide between their apartments.

'Freshly stolen,' he chuckled. 'Makes 'em all the sweeter.'

Webb had never tasted anything so good.

Once his mother had signed him over to the Jays he didn't have much time to wonder what had become of Tick. But deep down, Webb knew he would see him again.

He could hear footsteps approaching.

Dredd.

Maybe the footage was inconclusive, he told himself. He could admit that he'd made the wrong decision in the heat of the moment. Tell them he needed to put in more hours at the range. Sharpen up his aim.

He knew it wouldn't make a difference. It wasn't just about what Dredd and the others thought. It was about *him* and what it took to be a Judge.

His head was pounding. He looked down at the badge in his hands and was surprised to see that his knuckles were white. Then Dredd was standing over him and asking him a question he could barely hear above the roar of blood in his ears.

Webb stood up and held out the half-eagle badge in the palm of his hand. Somehow, he'd always thought it would be heavier.

Dredd stared at him in silence for a moment and then closed his gauntleted fist around it.

'Your call,' he shrugged, as Webb turned and walked wordlessly away.

COMPORTMENT

JOHN WARE

DREDD'S SPECIAL. YOU don't need me to tell you that, but listen anyway.

First time you see the man and it's awe-inspiring. You find yourself answering a back-up call on some sector-wide cluster-spug and there're helmets all over and someone says, 'Who's senior?' and then you see the man himself. But it's just a moment and then it's gone. If you get a chance to really look at him for more than a second, you'll just see a big old senior Judge, cranky as all hell, and doing his job, just like we all should be, so you get on with doing yours.

But get a chance to work with the man, and you'll see why he's the big deal. I don't mean his history. I'm talking about his character. Back in the Academy, in any discussion group, it would always come down to the given problem being addressed by one of us asking the question, 'What would Dredd do?' We had his training manual, the

Comportment—but seriously: what you want is a chance to watch the man work.

I was working the interrogation cubes in One-Seventeen this one time while the med kids were waiting to see if the new-pattern plasteen knee they'd put into me would hold. You know all about the interrogation cubes, but try working them full time. All the perp sees when they take him into the box is the chair they strap him to and the Judge who grills him. He might see me, too. I'm that shadowy figure looking down into the box from a window, my face half-lit by the console in front of me. I'm the one who contributes helpful input like, 'He's lying.' Of course, that's just a piece of interrogation theatre. Like the lie detector readings are so clear cut. Like they couldn't get an uplift monkey to say 'Lie' every time the wavy line on the screen gets a little wavier.

No. They need me to oversee the whole block of cubes, with all those simultaneous interrogations, and to supply necessary case evidence as the interrogating Judges might require it, and to edit testimonies so that relevant parts are available for instant replay to catch the perp in a lie or to play to his buddy in the cube next door to let him know that the dime has been dropped on him.

It's interesting work. I get to see a lot. I could write my own manual: *Comparative Judicial Procedures*.

I LIKE TO think of it this way: interrogation is judging. See how a Judge works the perp in the box and you'll know how the Judge works the cit on the street. You've got your three basic approaches, like the way we saw things in the Academy: there's your human, your inhuman, and there's Dredd.

I guess we all start out wanting to be Dredd, but after a little while we settle for being human. The human approach—both in policing and interrogating—is all about sympathy. The Judge makes eye contact and uses the perp's first name, maybe even smiles just a little. *I know you, creep. I know all your dirty little urges. I know what you're thinking, so I can second guess you at every turn.* That's what it's all about. We all learn how to do it. It's method acting and kinda fun; and therein lies the danger. Some Judges get a little *too* human. You know what I mean. A lot of the washouts and basket cases and 'transfers' to other duties are Judges who got a little too caught up in the dizzy circus of human experience that is the Meg. Pretty much *everyone* who ever boarded the Titan shuttle suffered from that same lack of necessary objectivity.

So when you think that you're maybe getting somewhat *involved*, or maybe you just never took to the whole human thing, there's the inhuman approach. Do the job. It's the ethos that the Academy's been drilling into cadets since year one. To the cit on the street or the perp in the chair the Judge is an implacable judging machine—an automaton who will put you down or put you away with no consideration for whatever human failings might have led you to where you are.

For some Judges it's an act. They cultivate the toneless mechanical voice, they leave the helmet on at all times.

Notice how so many female judges have that identical retro-dominatrix haircut? All part of the act.

For most it's the reality, though. It's the Judge's default setting. It comes natural and it requires no effort. There's the hitch: a Judge can get stale and not know it or show it until it's too late and then another body is on the belt at Resyk and another badge is mounted on the wall.

Dredd's different. Dredd's special. I've watched him work, and now I know what it is that he never put in the *Comportment*.

Listen and I'll tell you.

AN UP-AND-COMING SCUMBAG in the Sector 117 drugs retail business last year was Pismo Sneely, and it had come to the attention of the Department that this creep might well have been getting his product from one Donald Q. Howsa, who liked to pretend he was some kind of kind of upright citizen.

So Pismo is brought in and I strap him down and tape on the sensors myself, and I don't say a word as I do it. Inhuman, see? Unfeeling. Let this lowlife know that pleas for understanding will fall on deaf ears.

The arresting Judge is Dredd. This is a fairly routine case, but it doesn't look that way when he comes striding in. The man is *angry*.

First time I saw him was by the light of two burning city blocks, with blood and wrecked vehicles and random gunfire all over. Here he is in a quiet room with a guy strapped in a chair, and it's the same expression on his face. You know the face—like it was cast in rockcrete and then dropped down a stairwell. Any Judge would kill for a face that impressive. And that scowl! He's never exactly Mister Sunshine, but put Dredd in front of a lawbreaker and he's snarling and growling like a dog on a chain. It's not an act. The guy hates criminals. They make him mad. That's his secret.

I watched him work on Pismo Sneely, and in no time at all Sneely (three previous convictions) was totally convinced that Dredd's anger was not theatrical, or human, but positively Olympian. This is divine wrath, only barely contained enough to keep Dredd from just pulling Sneely's dirty lawbreaking head clean off before the perp has a chance to spill. And Sneely's spilling straight off, giving up everyone who ever so much as gave him the time of day. Myself, I'm transfixed. I'm marvelling at Dredd's technique and at the same time wondering if the perp is really going to die in there, and should I maybe do something about it. I mean, what do I say to the SJS?

'*Dredd got kind of mad and kind of beat the perp to death but I let it happen because—guys, trust me—it was really something to see.*'

But, naturally, Dredd never lays a glove on the creep. Doesn't have to. His whole manner, his attitude, his comportment, if you will, are plenty scary enough to get Sneely squealing. But seriously: how does Dredd not have ulcers? At his age, do you think they warn him about getting a brain embolism? The man's anger is magnificent not just for its intensity, but for the way he sustains it.

This is long-haul anger. This is something that's with him when he gets out of the sleep machine and it's something that stays with him all the day long. Steady. Dependable. Relentless.

This is how we won the Apocalypse War. I can see that now.

ALL TOO SOON the interrogation's over and Sneely's all wrung out and the case against citizen Donald Howsa is sewn up so tight that if we hear so much as a peep out of his fancy-pants lawyers we can bust them all for obstruction, conspiracy to pervert, and accessory before, during and after.

And that was the whole point. Creeps like Pismo Sneely are barely worth the time it takes to book them. Slime like Howsa we always get in the end anyway. Enough time in the interrogation cube and they're ours. The chance to bust an otherwise respectable law firm like Pardle, Gomez & McFeen, though? That's like the closest thing a tube-grown clone like me (or like Dredd, for that matter) gets to having a birthday.

We're Justice Department: the legislature, judiciary and executive of Mega-City One. We're the Judges. You know: judge, jury and executioner. You'd think that the place in society for solicitors and advocates went out with trial by jury, but no. Just like soap and indoor plumbing didn't do away with fleas and cockroaches, so the Mega-City justice system has somehow yet to eradicate the common shyster and ambulance chaser.

So I beg a favour of Dredd. I tell him I need the exercise. I tell him the truth—I want in on this bust. He throws me a bone and I'm on my way. But there's the truth and there's the whole truth. Sure, I want to take this new knee of mine for a ride. Sure, I want to arrest a bunch of mob lawyers. But what I really want is to play Judge for a day. I'm inspired by what I watched in that interrogation. I want to be Dredd. I want to feel that anger, that pure golden anger.

I've filed all the interrogation records and found someone to fill in for me, and while Dredd's on his way to collar Howsa, I'm down in the bike pool for the first time in weeks, running through the equipment checks and logging on to Control. For a moment it's a sweet feeling, to be back doing some good judging again, and I almost grin, but I suppress it. Remember: What would Dredd do?

Don't get a kick out of the job. Don't enjoy it. Think like a Judge. Think like *the* Judge:

It's a perfect day and the criminals are sullying it. It would be a perfect city, except for the criminals. Those drokking perps. We stamp on them and we stamp on them harder and they always come back. Well, feel my righteous wrath, lawbreakers, because you got me in the mood to do a whole lot more stamping.

By the time I hit traffic I'm in the zone. Someone is going to get well and truly judged.

THE DOOR TO the law office is just like I imagined it, just like they all are. I stare at the words engraved in the gleaming brass-effect plate and I feel my temperature rise: *Pardle, Gomez & McFeen, Attorneys at Law.*

These are the scum who keep filth like Donald Howsa in business and out of the cubes; who keep the Pismo Sneelys of this city peddling their stomm on the streets. My streets.

The fingers of my gun hand are flexing of their own accord.

They'll be sitting right this second in their plush offices, charging their worthless clients fifteen hundred a minute just for a little phonetime and they'll be working on ways to weasel their way out of paying a single cred of those fees in taxes.

My teeth are gritted to keep me from gnashing them. You could break rocks on my chin. I really think that I'm comporting myself to my maximum capacity here.

I open the door before I give in to the urge to shatter it with my boot.

Attorneys at law? This is the eagle of justice on my shoulder, creep. I *am* the Law.

PSIMPLE PSIMON

JONATHAN GREEN

'CONTROL TO ALL units vicinity Charley Rogers Block,' a voice crackled over his helmet com. 'We have multiple leapers. Repeat, mass suicide attempt at Charley Rogers. Judges Hardy and Roach at the scene request assistance. Meat-wagons already en route.'

The grim expression etched on his granite features didn't alter as he swung the Lawmaster off the skedway and onto the intersked, heading for City Bottom. 'Dredd responding.'

THE BODY HITTING the rockcrete in front of him forced Dredd to slam on the brakes, the bike skidding to a halt.

'Drokk!'

He peered up at the vast city block, its designation picked out in letters three storeys high. And there, half a kilometre above him, he saw...

It was little more than a speck to begin with. Then he heard the scream of terror, saw the flailing arms, his eyes zooming in on the plummeting figure. And then he saw the uniform, the helmet, the badge.

He swore again.

The Judge hit the pedway nine seconds later, travelling at a speed of more than fifty metres per second.

'Control—Dredd,' he barked into the com, revving the Lawmaster's engine into life again. 'Have arrived at Charley Rogers. Tell those meat-wagons they're going to need to break out the buckets and spades.'

He couldn't avoid driving over the mess of blood and impact-traumatised tissue covering the pedway as he steered the bike towards the block entrance. Behind him another cit made landfall with a sound like breaking eggs.

It never rains, he thought as he headed for the lifts.

DREDD MADE IT to the top of the block.

'Psi-Judge Mesmer is on his way,' the voice of Control buzzed in his ear again.

A Psi-Judge? Of course. When Judges started jumping, Grand Hall was bound to get jumpy too, especially considering how their numbers had been so drastically depleted since Chaos Day.

'Understood.'

He kicked open the door to the roof, his Lawgiver already in his hand. He took in the scene that greeted him at a practised glance. Lined up on the edge of the roof were a dozen or more cits. At the head of the line was the other attending Judge—Roach. Lined up like that they looked like an Iso-cube execution detail. Only their faces betrayed them, and they all had exactly the same expression: one of abject terror.

There was only one person on the roof who didn't look terrified and that was the juve ten paces away to Dredd's right. He couldn't be more than eighteen. A look of sheer delight twinkled in the boy's eyes as he uttered the words, 'Simon says, jump!'

With a scream of rage and fear, Roach hurled herself into the yawning gulf beyond the top of the building to join her partner as a gory puddle on the pedway below.

Dredd had the juve in his sights in an instant. 'Freeze, creep!'

The boy turned, acknowledging the lawman for the first time. 'You didn't say, "Simon says".'

He'd given the creep a chance. The juve had already killed two Judges now, and Grud alone knew how many others. Zero tolerance. It was the only answer in this situation. It was his judgement call.

'Standard Execution,' Dredd growled, passing sentence. Pulling the trigger in situations like this was instinctual; he didn't have to think about it. It was automatic.

'Don't you want to know why?'

But the perp was still alive, and still talking. Dredd's Lawgiver remained undischarged. The simple act of pulling the trigger suddenly felt like trying to push a fatty uphill without a belly-wheel. Sweat beaded on his brow.

'Aren't you even just a little bit curious?'

'Your confession, creep,' Dredd muttered through gritted teeth. He could feel the perp inside his head, taunting him, mocking his inability to execute his duty, to see justice carried out.

The cits lined up along the edge of the roof remained where they were, whimpering, the wind tugging at their clothes and hair. Not one of them moved a muscle, incapable of doing so.

'I used to be the block idiot, you know,' the juve said. 'Butt of everyone's jokes. You wouldn't believe it now, would you?'

'I'd call what you're doing here pretty stupid, meathead.'

The boy gave a bark of mirthless laughter. 'Do you know what they called me? Simple Simon! They made my life a misery—my family's too—with their constant jibes and the regularly beatings they dished out.'

'So what changed?' Dredd could feel his finger slowly tightening on the trigger. If he kept the creep talking he might weaken the boy's focus enough to break his concentration.

'Chaos Day,' the kid replies. 'Charley Rogers was locked down, but it was too late for us; my family and me. My father was already infected. My whole family succumbed to the bug. I had to watch them all bleed out through their eyes and die.'

'But not you.' Dredd felt the trigger ease back a fraction more.

'Turns out I'm one of the lucky two per cent. No, I didn't die. Instead, I went to bed an imbecile and woke up the following morning a drokking genius. Chaos Day *changed* me.'

'Changed us all.' Another millimetre.

'Ah, but can you do this?' The juve turned his attention from Dredd to the queue of waiting victims again. 'Simon says, jump.'

With a shrill scream of hopeless terror a woman—the next in line—threw herself from the top of the block.

'Not one of them ever had a kind word for me. Not ever!'

'You think you're so special?' Dredd growled, the sweat pouring down inside his helmet now.

'I know I am,' the juve snapped. It was a bitter, desperate sound, like that made by a cornered animal fully expecting to be put down. 'Otherwise how else could I do this?' He turned eyes blazing with the fires of injustice on Dredd, who met the creep's gaze with a flinty stare of his own. 'Shoot yourself in the head.'

The Judge had faced down everything from zombies and alien oppressors to extra-dimensional superfiends. Some upstart psi wasn't going to get the better of him. Not today. Gritting his teeth, Dredd continued to resist.

Simple Simon's stare bore into him, the juve focusing all his rage and hatred upon the Judge. But Dredd saw something else there in those wild eyes now.

Fear.

The creep had never met anyone capable of resisting his powers before. Judge Roach certainly hadn't been able to, nor Hardy, and the ennui-addled residents of Charley Rogers hadn't had a hope.

'What?' the boy gasped, unwittingly giving voice to his surprise, his once indomitable will weakening still further. *'Shoot yourself in the head!'*

Still Dredd resisted.

'How can this be happening? Why won't you do as you're told?'

He heard the crunch of boots on the gravel of the rooftop behind him, and something distracted the boy for a moment. In that instant Dredd felt the force of the juve's willpower loses focus, and the tension in his finger faded. He pulled the trigger, even as the new arrival gasped in horror.

A single round exploded from the Lawgiver barrel and hit the boy square in the centre of his forehead. As it punched out again through the top of his skull, Simple Simon fell to the ground.

Dredd regarded the limp body. 'You didn't say "Simon says".'

'YOU DIDN'T HAVE to shoot him in the head, you know,' Mesmer said as the stretcher bearing the boy was lifted into the med-wagon. The clean-up crews had almost finished hosing down the pedway outside Charley Rogers Block.

'Didn't I?' Dredd muttered, the stony expression on his face unchanging.

'Medics say he'll live,' Mesmer continued, one hand stroking the excessively groomed greying goatee on his chin, 'but that shot of yours took out most of his prefrontal cortex. He's even more of a idiot now than he was before the Chaos Bug unlocked his latent psi-talents and gave him a genius-level IQ.'

'Aim must've been off for some reason.'

Psi-Judge Mesmer gave a weary sigh as Dredd mounted his Lawmaster once again. 'It's a shame you had to lobotomise the lad. Psi-Division could doubtless have learnt a lot from him.'

Dredd fixed his colleague with a cold stare. 'Haven't you heard, Mesmer?' he said, revving the bike's idling engine into life. 'Ignorance is bliss.'

APOLOGY ACCEPTED

ALEC WORLEY

As THE SUN melted into the skyline, Nash Feely tried to ignore what lurked in the shadows that lengthened around him. Sweat soaked through his orange jumpsuit as he laboured atop a pile of rubble, pounding chunks of rockcrete with his sledgehammer, tossing fragments into the battered yellow skipbot below. Nash sang another hymn to the glory of Grud, ignoring the curses and catcalls of his fellow convicts. They had arrived in an H-wagon with blacked-out windows and touched down in this deserted plaza somewhere in the city. The surrounding streets lay empty. The looming city blocks stood still. Nash swore he could hear the crackle of distant gunfire. The two Judges prowling nearby had told them a pedway had collapsed, burying a branch of Pharmville, from which the cons were now charged with retrieving an apparently vital shipment of medical supplies.

'Recover those meds before sundown and the Department will review your sentences,' one of the Judges had said. 'Think about running or giving us any stomm whatsoever and we have clearance to execute.'

None of the cons ventured to ask what had happened to the city while they had been in the cubes. Had the Sovs invaded? The muties revolted? Block war? A collapsed pedway certainly didn't explain the bullet-holes in the walls and the ammo cases that littered the ground, or the faint smell of rotting munce that hit your nose every time the wind changed.

Nash flung a slab of rockcrete the size of a shuggy table into the skipbot as he heard someone holler nearby. A huge bald convict emerged from the rubble clutching armfuls of med cartons. One of the Judges approached.

'I found 'em first!' said the bald con. 'That means more years off my sentence, right?'

By way of reply, the Judge's head exploded.

The other cons scattered, while Nash stumbled down the rubble and crouched in a nearby shop doorway. The remaining Judge had already dived behind a slab of fallen rockcrete. A voice rang out: 'This is *our* block, Judge! And those are *our* meds! You got sixty seconds to walk away!'

The Judge barked into his comm, something about looters. Having demanded back-up, he muttered something into his Lawgiver and returned fire with a single shot. The resulting explosion destroyed an entire storefront, hurling screaming, burning bodies into the street. The Judge withdrew behind the slab as the other looters returned fire. Nash felt shrapnel zip past his ear as he fled down an adjoining street. Behind him, he heard a sudden cry of pain followed by a collective whoop of triumph.

Nash hurtled through empty, unfamiliar streets. There was nothing he could have done to save that poor Judge. Grud knew that, right? Nash found himself on an overzoom strewn with destroyed or abandoned vehicles, and overshadowed by a nearby block. The lights were out and darkness was devouring the streets. Nash shivering at the thought of what seethed in those shadows, an army comprised of his own sins, conjured in punishment for destroying an innocent woman's life.

Nash never knew her first name, only that of her husband, the man he had killed. Xander Boone. Twenty-five years ago, the Boones had lived in a welfare hab up in Rick Astley. Xander was late on a payment, and Nash—fast coming up off his daily boost of muscle-enhancing Roydz—had slapped him across the face. Xander's neck had snapped like a candy stick. Mrs Boone cradled her husband's body, while their little boy fled screaming into the block. When the Judges caught Nash trying to skip town, they jokingly told him he would be safer in the cubes, as they had to caution Mrs Boone for threatening to kill him herself. Her now-catatonic son looked set to spend the rest of his life in a psych-ward. Nice work, creep. That's forty years.

In the few lucid hours Nash had enjoyed during those early months in the cube, he figured all those Roydz may have rewired his brain somehow, maybe rekindled memories of his stern Grud-fearing foster-parents.

Whatever the reason, Nash's dreams became a hell not of flame but of shadow, a nest of living darkness from which his sins emerged bearing bristles and fangs, moist tendrils and sucking mouths, a host of black eyeless, clambering, clutching, whispering things. Every night an army of fresh horrors invaded his dreams, driving him to the brink of madness. Only when Nash sobbed repentant prayers to Grud did his tormentors seem less frenzied in their nightly assaults. He spent most mornings clawing at the walls of his cube, begging for sleep, praying for a chance to make amends for the murder of Xander Boone, and thus banish the monsters forever. Twenty-five years of delirious entreaty finally paid off the morning Nash's cell-hatch hissed open, and two unshaven Judges wearing battered uniforms told him they had a job for him.

Grud had brought Nash into this deserted sector to give him a chance at redemption. But how? Nash cried out to Grud to give him a sign. As he looked up imploringly, he caught sight of the name on the looming city block. His heart soared at the sight of two familiar words: Rick Astley! Hallelujah! The block in which he had murdered Xander Boone and destroyed the lives of the man's wife and child so many years ago. Mrs Boone must still live here. Why else would Grud have brought him here? Nash would become her guardian angel, protecting her from whatever madness had befallen the city. He would prove the depths of his penitence, and devote the rest of his life to rebuilding hers. Then perhaps she could forgive him, and perhaps the things in the shadows would remain there.

'Control, I spotted one of your escaped cons.' The

Judge sounded young. Nash could hear him padding up the narrow stairwell and onto the landing. 'Caught him breaking into maintenance door twelve on the north-west side of Astley.' The Judge paused to catch his breath. 'Am in pursuit.' Whether too tired or too inexperienced, the Judge chose to ignore the foetid pile of garbage bags in the corner of the landing.

Nash burst out from beneath the reeking sacks. He grabbed the lawman's wrist, keeping that Lawgiver at bay, and clamped his hand over the lower half of the Judge's face, hoping to Grud he could suffocate him into unconsciousness. The struggling Judge slammed his booted feet into the wall, shoving them both backwards. The stairwell railing slammed painfully into the small of Nash's back. Momentum threatened to topple the pair over the side and six floors down. The Judge was wriggling free. Before Nash could grab him, the Judge slipped on the railing and fell down the darkened stairwell. Nash turned in time to see the Judge swallowed by the darkness before hearing him hit the ground floor amid a crash of garbage. Silence. Nash choked back a sob. He was a Judge-killer now. That meant spending the rest of his life inside a cube where there would be no escape from the shadows. The darkness in the stairwell seemed to intensify, creeping up the steps towards Nash like a black flood. He bolted up the stairs.

THE AIR WAS busy with flies. Nash had imagined the journey up here countless times, but never like this. Dozens of decaying bodies lay sprawled and stinking the length of the corridor. Bullet-holes dotted the walls. A carpet of congealed blood sucked at the soles of his boots as he dashed through the horror, searching for Mrs Boone's hab. He found it. Someone had sprayed a huge red 'X' on her front door. It was unlocked. Nash pushed it open, disturbing another blizzard of flies. He thought the living room was empty, until he noticed the shrivelled grey-green body slumped on the sofa. A beaker of water stood on the coffee table beside a foil med wrapper bearing the insignia of Justice Department. Nash stepped closer and examined a photo that had slipped from the corpse's rigid brown fingers. A shudder ran through him as he recognised the beaming face of Xander Boone. The man was hoisting his infant son onto his shoulders beside his pretty young wife. Nash fell at the corpse's feet, clutching the hem of its dress in an agony of sorrow.

'I'm sorry,' he cried. 'You can see that, can't you? Please! You have to forgive me!' The corpse creaked as its head fell back, teeth bared as if in silent mocking laughter. Nash sobbed. Grud had abandoned him, perhaps even led him here as punishment. The sun had almost disappeared and the room oozed with shadows. Nash could feel his sins taking shape around him, the nightmares scurrying into his waking hours. He fumbled with the lamp beside the sofa, anything to drive away the shadows.

'Power's out, creep!'

Nash shrieked in fright. Someone stood in the doorway. Another Judge. He had approached in silence, as though he had materialised out of the shadows, and he spoke with a voice that expected obedience. 'You're going back to the cubes.'

Nash howled as he dived low at the Judge, who fired, illuminating the room. Nash felt a burst of pain in his left arm, but it didn't stop him. He drove his shoulder into the Judge's stomach, slamming him against the doorframe. The two men fought as Nash caught the Judge's wrist, slamming it once, twice against the wall, but the Judge refused to drop his weapon. Stars danced before Nash's eyes as the Judge headbutted him, driving his helmet's shield insignia deep into Nash's nose. Spluttering blood, Nash twisted his body with explosive force, wrenching the Judge's arm down over his shoulder and hurling his opponent's body into the glass coffee table, destroying it. Nash kicked away the fallen gun. Still on his back, the Judge produced a huge knife, but Nash was on top of him before he could bring the weapon to bear. He drove punch after punch into the Judge's jaw, willing him to submit, knuckles blazing with pain as he continued his maddened onslaught. Nash became aware of a throbbing pain in his side. The Judge was stabbing him. Consumed with fury, he caught the Judge's wrist, clamping both hands around the man's fist, twisting it until he had the knife aimed down towards the Judge's neck. Nash drove his weight behind the weapon, as the Judge grunted, struggling to hold back the slowly descending blade. The quivering tip found the Judge's corded throat, drawing blood.

'Please, forgive me,' sobbed Nash, as he prepared to drive the blade home.

Another yellow flash illuminated the room and Nash felt something warm spray down his back. He shivered as if with cold, then darkness rushed up and swallowed him before he could scream.

'THANKS FOR THE assist,' growled Dredd as he shoved the dead perp aside. The younger Judge kneeled in the doorway, Lawgiver still aimed and smoking. Dredd had answered the boy's call for back-up and found him at the bottom of the stairwell, lying dazed upon a mountain of garbage bags. Dredd rose to his feet as the younger man removed his helmet and stared intently at the dead perp, saying nothing.

'You know this punk, Boone?' asked Dredd, glancing at his colleague.

Judge Boone answered without looking up. 'Nash Feely. Control ID'd him just after you found me. He's the man who murdered my father. I was six when it happened. Saw the whole thing.'

Dredd regarded the dessicated corpse on the sofa. 'I'm sorry,' he said. 'Chaos Day didn't leave us much time to stand on ceremony.'

Boone retrieved the photo from beside his mother's body. 'After my father...' He paused. 'After he died, Mom went to pieces. Welfare Department put me down for mandatory enrolment in the Academy.'

Dredd grunted. 'I heard Feely rambling when I arrived,' he said. 'Sounded like he came here looking to be forgiven.'

'Forgiven?' said Boone. 'The only kind of forgiveness

my mother would have given him was exactly the kind I just gave him.'

Boone smiled grimly at the glistening bullet-hole in Nash's forehead. 'Apology accepted, creep.'

GOING WHEELY

T. C. EGLINGTON

'IT'S THE SMALL details in life that stick with you, don't you think?' I said.

I wasn't sure if Judge Dredd heard me in all the chaos and the screaming and the catastrophic sound of collapsing blocks. He was punching me in the face with quite a lot of force and it was difficult to get my words out. Not that I blamed him. If anything, I had to admire his unflinching professionalism.

'For instance, I can recall the exact revolting waft you get when you lift a fatty's belly flap up to fit a new wheel.' I spoke louder but he caught me a good one square in the jaw and knocked several front teeth loose before I could elaborate.

'You're going to spend the rest of your life in an iso-cube for this!' he told me.

I was too dazed to respond. I had just committed the direct murder of over one hundred and thirty fatties, as well as sparking a bloodthirsty gang war, and being indirectly responsible for the annihilation of a dozen citi-blocks that would leave thousands dead or injured. Strangely, the only thought going through my mind at that historic moment was, *He seems a lot smaller in real life.* You see, I had always thought of Judge Dredd as a giant amongst men. I couldn't help being taken aback at how normal-sized he was in the flesh. Not only that, I was also pleasantly surprised at how he smelt—a sort of reassuring scent of polished synthi-leather and bike oil. The smell of honest, hard work.

'You smell nice,' I remarked.

There followed an awkward silence. It was broken by the thunderous roar of a collapsing block, echoing with the screams of its unfortunate inhabitants.

A little while later I heard him speaking. 'Control, we've got one for the psycho-cubes. Clifford Spuce. Perp's gone wheely.'

RIGHT UP UNTIL I became the biggest mass murderer of fatties in Mega-City One history, I had an excellent rapport with the morbidly obese. I was the longest-serving wheely salesman at Big Fatz Phat Wheels. I was well liked. Affable. On Sundays I enjoyed a keen interest in historical re-enactments and had won a bronze medal three years running at the annual costume ball—my Ronald Reagan attracted some very favourable comments. Each Christmas I personally organised a fundraiser for Children in Need of Faces. I daresay, if you mentioned the name Clifford Spuce you would hear flattering remarks, or at the very least some mention of my extremely competent salesmanship. The fact that I ended up going on a one-man murderous rampage was as much of a surprise to me as anyone else. But then everyone can have an off day, right?

The trick to being a good wheely salesman is to put on a kind and courteous front at all times, despite any feelings of revulsion you may harbour toward your customers. I had always been extremely good at hiding my own feelings, which was why I was so outstanding at my job. Customers had dropped food on me, groped me, been sick on me, attacked me, and had even tried to eat me. I was always the model of politeness in these situations.

Sure, I had regular appointments with a psych-droid to help me cope with the stresses of work, and sure, they did suggest I might have issues, but I never really held with the psych-droid's evaluation that due to my slim build I had developed an inferiority complex about my size. And all that stuff about resenting my boss because he swindled me out of my shares in the company... I don't know, sometimes you can over-analyse stuff.

It's strange. I never started out the day thinking I was going to have a psychotic breakdown. Mostly I was thinking how I could clinch gold at that year's annual ball for the Historical Re-enactment Society. I had lost out two years running to Margaret Thatcher and I needed to roll out the big guns.

The morning passed without incident, if somewhat trying. It wasn't until the boss's wife came in for a complimentary upgrade that my mood blackened. Marlene was a vast, wobbling mountain of flesh, topped with a wide, doughy face constantly in the process of devouring food. 'My little Cliffy—*scluff scluff!*' she cooed. 'What do you—*glub glub*—think of my new dress?'

'You look resplendent, Mrs F,' I replied tactfully. The frilly white fabric barely hid her gargantuan contours, as if some vast wax effigy had melted into an unflattering mass of bulging flaps, then had a flimsy dish-towel dangled over it. 'If you could just step up onto the scales...?'

Marlene giggled. She always found this funny as the weighing scales were modelled to look like her husband, Jimmy Fatz. The automated Jimmy Fatz gave its verdict: 'Jimmy says you're blubberlicious!'

I winced. I had to listen to that voice a hundred times a day, always accompanied by the same braying laughter all fatties seem to share. *Jimmy says you're blubberlicious!* That translated to, 'You are so massively obese you have your own gravitational system.' It also meant she needed a new Type-3 reinforced titanium wheel—we call them 'diamond disks' in the trade on account of how hard they are.

'I'm going to have to fit you with a new wheel, Mrs F,' I told her.

'Whatever, Cliffy—*glaff sclop sclop!* Jimmy wants me looking my best for our anniversary meal tonight at Mr Creosote's.'

I'm not exactly sure what happened next. It must have been the mention of the anniversary that made me recall Jimmy Fatz offering to buy my shares off me years ago. At the time, I was struggling to cover the legal costs for my father after there had been some overblown incident at the shop that had left seventeen dead. Jimmy had been a regular customer, a convivial man with a good eye for business, and he stepped in to help. He reassured me that he wouldn't change a single thing in the shop, that I could buy back the shares at any time, that he wanted to keep the 'fam' in family business...

Jimmy says you're blubberlicious!

The changes happened slowly. Products were renamed. Jimmy's face started to appear on merchandise. When he altered the name of the shop without consulting me I objected in the strongest terms but, with his lawyer present, he reminded me of the details of the contract I had signed.

Jimmy says you're blubberlicious!

It wasn't Marlene's fault. She just happened to represent everything I hated—she was, after all, a cruel reminder of where the profits were going. It was while changing her belly wheel that the full force of those feelings burst out. I had released the rivets on her old wheel when a huge roll of fat flopped down across my back, engulfing me. Maybe it was the revolting odour that I had come to hate. Maybe it was hearing that 'human floss' joke once too often. Maybe it was the braying laughter. The net result was the same.

A red mist descended. All reason and decorum disappeared as a murderous haze seared my mind. I was partly aware, yes, but it seemed as if I was witnessing the event from a distance. I ripped the plasteen head off the Jimmy Fatz weighing machine with astonishing strength, then I began to pound it down on Marlene's bewildered face, blow upon blow, giggling insanely as she tumbled gracelessly onto her back. I redoubled my assault, savaging her with the fake head, lost in a psychotic delirium.

I came to my senses a while later, covered in blood, numb.

In hindsight, bludgeoning her to death with a replica head of her husband was kind of a weird thing to do, you know? But I felt—and I appreciated the irony of this at the time—as if a great weight had been lifted from my shoulders. Murdering her in cold blood just felt so... *right*. I knew then what I had to do. You see, we have a saying in the Historical Re-enactment Society: in for a penny, in for a pound.

BEFORE THE INCIDENT, Mr Creosote's was the premier eating venue for fatties with creds to burn. They specialised in high-calorie fine dining, delivered with a top-floor view of Mega-City One. I was feeling nervous about my outfit as I stepped out of the lift. Gandhi had seemed a perfect historical figure to dress as beforehand, simple to throw together at such short notice and ideally suited to my build. However, as I entered the restaurant I sensed it wasn't going to command the sort of respect I was hoping for, even with the addition of the antique chainsaw.

A maitre d' greeted me with a quizzical frown. 'Wrong floor, sir?'

The soft burble of chatting voices halted abruptly when I started up the chainsaw. I swung it playfully at the maitre d', who ducked just in time, causing me to decapitate an ice sculpture of an obese swan. 'Deliver me the head of Jimmy Fatz and I won't carve your faces off, you tubs of human effluence!'

Admittedly, as an opener it wasn't the catchiest phrase, but I was still new to this whole game.

A gormless lady with curly red hair blinked at me uncertainly. 'Is this the stripper?' she asked in a disappointed tone. Her comment caused a ripple of laughter. As more eyes turned to my slight figure, the white makeshift shawl I was wearing inadvertently slipped down until it resembled an oversized diaper. The hilarity spread.

'*STOP LAUGHING AT ME!*' I waved my chainsaw threateningly but it spluttered and went out.

The maitre d' regained his footing and accessed the building's security systems. The wave of braying laughter echoed throughout the restaurant, building in volume and intensity. Amid the jeering faces I caught a glimpse of Jimmy Fatz. He was the only one not guffawing. Instead, he wore an expression of dawning horror as he stared at me. It took him a few moments to recognise that the white shawl was, in fact, Marlene's dress. It didn't take long for him to piece together the rest. That was the point the fire alarms started wailing. The noise caused the laughter to falter, then to stop altogether. Red emergency lights flashed on the ceiling.

I stood upon the nearest table. 'I have set fires throughout the building. We are on the top floor and the lifts are disabled. Your only means of escape is the stairway. If you run, you might make it in time... if you're fit enough.'

The maitre d' failed to operate the lifts from his computer terminal. 'Please calmly make your way to the emergency exit at the rear of the premises,' he said in a quavering voice.

'No,' I corrected him. With perfect timing, I managed to get the chainsaw buzzing into life again. 'You all need to *RUN!*'

The effect was instantaneous. I had never really seen a fatty run—you know, really sprint as if their life depended on it. So to see dozens of them suddenly push over their tables and hurtle towards the emergency exit really was a vision to behold. The stampede made the whole floor wobble and sway with the accumulated weight. The fleeing crowd quickly bottlenecked at the only exit. More fatties collided with those already jammed in the small passageway, and there was an ominous shuddering from the stairwell as the repeated shunting rocked the foundations.

Amid the chaos I caught a brief glimpse of Jimmy attempting to escape in the rush of people. I chased after him and, turning the corner, found him trapped in the pile-up of fatties, sandwiched between two identical brothers. I raised the screeching chainsaw.

'You're blubberlicious!' I cackled ecstatically, and immediately thought, *That's it! You nailed it, Clifford!*

Jimmy's eyes filled with abject terror. A cacophonous roar erupted from the building as the corridor and stairway collapsed under the unbearable strain of the massed fatties. My chainsaw arced through the air, missing Jimmy's face by a hair's breadth. He dropped out of sight in an avalanche of rockcrete and human flesh, smashing into the floor below. The whole building shook with the impact and I was momentarily disorientated in the escalating chaos.

It took me several minutes to get back on my feet, angered that my prize had been snatched from me. As the dust settled, I peered through the debris but couldn't catch sight of Jimmy Fatz. Instead, I saw dozens of angry faces looking up at me.

And guns. Lots and lots of guns.

PSYCHOSIS IS A slippery fish.

For a start, if you're in the middle of a one-man killing spree it's hard to tell what's real and what's a vivid hallucination. I could not, in all honesty, tell whether the men with the big guns staring up at me from the room below were real. I knew, for example, that the hole in the floor created from a stampede of fatties attempting to outrun my chainsaw was real—I had definitely done that. The dozens of dead and injured bodies were real—again, that was me. But the gang members huddled around a table piled high with impressive-looking firearms looked too clichéd, too comically gangster-ish to be real.

Two distinct gangs glared up at me—one group covered in a generous mix of scars, the other group emblazoned with blue tattoos. The room itself resembled a warehouse of sorts, consisting mostly of dozens of stacked crates and little else. Many of these had been smashed apart by the falling fatties, revealing their contents: more guns.

The biggest of the scarred group, a bald man who seemed to consist mostly of neck muscles, turned to his counterpart in the opposite gang. 'It's a bust, you drokking scum! You set us up!'

'Smart, Jonesy. Blame it on us first. A bit too quick to be convincing, though,' the leader of the tattooed gang replied. His most outstanding feature was his tattooed eyes. 'He's Wally Squad,' he said to me, pointing at my unusual Gandhi outfit.

'Yes, absolutely,' I replied, grinning.

The bald one waved his gun at me. 'He's working with you, you narcs!'

'Oh yes! Yes, I am!' I gushed.

What I didn't fully appreciate at that moment in time was that Mr Creosote's—Mega-City One's premier fatty restaurant—was a complex money-laundering system for a remarkably violent criminal mob, the Scarredfaces. They traded in illegal, untraceable weapons. It just happened to be bad timing that my urge to hunt and kill my boss, Jimmy Fatz, had interrupted an arms sale with the Blue Tats, a gang equally notorious for their brutal and paranoid nature.

The gunfight was instant and overwhelming as the two gangs turned on each other. The onslaught of bullets and laser blasts filled the room with smoke and chaos and the deafening screech of rapid fire. Bodies fell, blood splattered, bullets ricocheted. Those fatties that had survived the fall from the collapsed floor were now used as human shields in the gang fight. I glimpsed down into the bloody mayhem and, in between the relentless fire of the automatic weapons, spotted my boss drag himself behind a stack of crates. Cackling hysterically, I leaped down and rushed towards him. Foolish, yes, but this was hardly the time to start doing things in half measures.

A resourceful gangster chose that same moment to shoot out the lights, plunging the room into darkness. The intense flashes of gunfire lit up the dark intermittently in a queasy strobe effect. In the first flash I saw my boss scrabbling across several bodies in a bid to escape. In the second flash I saw Jonesy, the scarred, over-necked mob leader, charging at me with a gun in each hand. In the third flash I saw half of Jonesy topple over, dispatched by my trusty chainsaw.

I quickly reviewed my initial impression that I was hallucinating, and ducked behind the nearest crate. The cascade of bullets turned the walls, the floor and the crates into a mess of shattered fragments. People were screaming. I discarded the chainsaw and searched the contents of the box for something a little more substantial. I pulled out a thick column of metal, not realising it was a missile launcher.

'Try eating this, Jimmy Fatz!' I shouted, thinking my murderous sloganeering was definitely improving. I pointed it in the direction I had seen him escape and pulled the trigger. There was a satisfying whoosh as something heavy and streamlined shot out the end of the barrel. The projectile landed in the centre of the stacked crates and, with ear-shattering brilliance, exploded. A gigantic fireball filled the room, knocking everyone to the floor.

Clifford Spuce, I thought to myself, *you are on fine form today.*

It hadn't occurred to me what would happen if you ignited crates full of guns and explosives. At that stage I was really just thinking on my feet. The chain reaction was incredible. The initial, shuddering BOOM! echoed with a series of smaller explosions, separating into a rattling firecracker percussion of gunfire. The floor gave way again, but this time the tremendous force of the explosions was enough to obliterate several storeys, trashing windows and balconies on the south side of the building.

When I returned to consciousness, I was sprawled on my back. The ground sloped off at a steep angle, intersecting with several plush apartments, now littered with bodies, guns and bits of gangsters. I was disorientated, my ears ringing with tinnitus. As I turned my head, I caught a glimpse of Jimmy Fatz several feet away, struggling to free his arm from a sizeable lump of rockcrete. I leapt into action, snatching at a nearby crate of scattered guns. I swung a stuttergun in his general direction and fired several shots blindly. Swiftly, he dislodged his arm, the jerking action causing him to flop onto his belly, which in turn caused his belly-wheel to roll him efficiently down the tilted floor. That was the Type-4 Graphene Dream for you—absolutely impeccable performance. It can take over three tons of weight and not even get close to buckling. Lovely workmanship.

I slid down the floor after him and fired several more shots, incinerating one of the few surviving gangsters.

Jimmy Fatz was quick, I had to give him that. In a few

brief moments he managed to dive behind an upturned sofa, get to his feet and rush down a maintenance corridor. I quickly negotiated the broken slabs of flooring and scattered furniture. By the time I had made it through the double doors he was already most of the way down the corridor, turning a corner. I could hear his belly-wheel squeaking as he ran.

Skree skree skree.

'Listen to me, Clifford, we can sort this out another way,' he called to me breathlessly.

'That right?'

Skree skree skree.

I could hear him frantically rattling door handles in a bid to find an escape route.

'Sure. Name your price. I've got money, shares—anything you want.'

'I want to dance about in your skin. How about that? Can you give me that?'

'Ummmm... Let's discuss options.'

Skree skree krrrrnnnkkk!

I sprinted round the corner and through another set of doors. There he was, trapped at a locked doorway. The explosions had caused windows to shatter, spraying the floor in glass shards, a fragment of which had become firmly stuck in Jimmy Fatz's wheel. He looked at me with the agonised desperation of a trapped animal.

'Listen, Clifford,' he said to me in a strangled falsetto, 'I need to tell you something.'

I strolled up to him leisurely and lifted the gun to his face. 'Oh?'

'I... I'm your father.' He fixed me with an intense expression.

I pushed the gun into the fleshiest part of his cheek.

'Okay, that was a lie,' he admitted feebly. 'But you always felt like a son to me. That counts for something, right?'

I felt an uncharacteristic serenity settle over me. I let the moment of perfection linger. 'You're a big man,' I said in a wonderfully calm, authoritative tone, 'but you've lived a small life. Now it's over.'

Gently, almost tenderly, I pressed the trigger on the stuttergun.

The explosion seemed to rock the entire block, momentous and impressive. A flash blasted through Jimmy's cheek and nose. I realised in a split second that my aim had been knocked off slightly and the entire building had rocked with an explosion. A big one. An ominous trembling shook the depths of the block, then the whole towering structure swayed forwards. I peered out the nearest window and saw the reflection in the glass frontage of the mega-block opposite us. This entire building was collapsing, engulfed in fire.

'Huh,' I murmured to myself. 'How about that?'

WHAT PEOPLE DON'T realise is, I was just a catalyst. Did I set out to kill thousands of people? No. No, I didn't. It was just one of those unfortunate side effects of trying to murder my boss. How could I have possibly known about the Fatalitionists on the twenty-third floor? They interviewed one of them afterwards and, well, I have to say—without being too judgemental here—they came across as crazy. Just out-and-out mad.

The Fatalitionists were a pretty small cult. There were no more than a dozen of them. However, at least half of them happened to be demolition experts with a detailed knowledge of explosives. Their belief system involved lots of religious wibble about 'end times' and 'salvation for the devoted'. Crucially, it also involved an ambitious plan to flatten Mega-City One by strategically collapsing a block that would in turn topple the next block, and so on, spreading a wave of annihilation. It really was colossal bad timing on my part. You see, they had been waiting for some indisputable sign that the end times had begun. Well, I suppose a series of explosions, a gunfight, and giant bodies falling from the sky could be misconstrued as something apocalyptic. But really, you had to be seriously unhinged to begin with.

The building lurched forwards with sickening velocity. I was standing by an open window watching the contents of the block hurtle passed—people, furniture, whole sections of apartments. I saw the maitre d' from the restaurant rush by in a blur, and realised I would be following him in a few brief moments. And I was pleased, I was actually ecstatic. This was the perfect end to the day. I was going to go out in a blaze of glory, my life finally having some meaning, some impact.

And then he laughed...

I turned to see Jimmy Fatz, injured but very much alive, clutching his face and laughing at me. That braying laughter.

'*Hwah hwah! Wooser!*' he said.

The building pitched forward, tossing me through the open window. I tumbled head-first, only to be jerked backwards as my shawl snagged on something. I looked up to see Jimmy lodged in the window frame, a coil of white fabric trapped in between his massive belly and the frame. My stuttergun was gone. The ground rushed up to meet us so rapidly I closed my eyes tightly. There was a colossal grinding crash and I prepared to die.

'OHGRUDNOTYETTTTT!'

Somehow, I was yanked to a painful but safe halt. I tentatively opened my eyes. My trapped shawl had saved me. I dangled several feet above the ground. Surrounding me was the jagged remains of the building scattered in oversized jigsaw pieces. The chain reaction of destruction thundered on as the next block was felled with the force of ours. I peered up at Jimmy, wedged in the window frame. He gurgled incoherently like a big, idiotic cherub.

Hurriedly, I untied the rest of my shawl and fell to the ground. My body was ringing with pain. I stumbled past the bug-smear stains of the dead, my eyes fervently scanning the floor. All about me was chaos and destruction.

'Ha!' I snatched up a gun lying on the ground, a dismembered arm covered in gang scars still clutching hold of it. I rushed back to where Jimmy was trapped. Without tempting fate, I started shooting indiscriminately at him. No more slogans.

That was roughly the point when Judge Dredd turned up. I admit, it wasn't my proudest moment, naked and trying to shoot a gun with a dead arm still attached to it at a stationary target. Dredd knocked me to the ground with one solid punch. Briefly, I caught Jimmy looking down at us, shaking with laughter as he realised what had happened.

Please Grud, I thought.

I lifted the gun but Dredd kicked it from my hand. By accident, it fired a single shot. The bullet ricocheted off a nearby wall, then miraculously ricocheted a second time off Jimmy's belly-wheel—a wheel I had personally attached—and caught him a direct blow to the centre of his forehead. He was finally, perfectly dead. It was a small detail, something too fast for Dredd to even notice, but I would remember that moment for the rest of my life.

'You're under arrest, creep,' Dredd grunted.

I caught a glimpse of myself in his visor and I was smiling so widely it looked positively criminal.

'It's the small details in life...' I began.

ROACHES

CAVAN SCOTT

'SOMEONE HELP ME!'

Decker Hart pounded along the empty zipstrip. He could hear them behind him, scuttling through the trash-filled grime, their jaws snapping relentlessly together.

Klak klak klak!

There were even more now. Stomm! Why hadn't he been more careful? If those things didn't get him, Blatta surely would. Either way, he was a dead man.

Klak klak klak!

Hart tore out of the zip onto the skedway between Price and Goldblum. Grud, the pedway was packed. If there was a breakout here...

Then Hart heard the sound of his salvation. The deep rumble of a powerful engine, Justice Department rubber thundering on rockcrete. A Lawmaster. He'd never been so glad to see a helmet in his life.

'Judge!' he yelled, throwing himself in front of the speeding lawman. 'You gotta help me! You gotta—'

The Lawmaster's brakes squealed as the heavy bike skidded, missing Hart with only inches to spare.

'Jaywalking,' the Judge barked, grizzled jaw thrust forward. 'You just got five months in a cube, creep.'

Grud on a greenie. Did it have to be *him?* 'Whatever! Just lock me up, Dredd!' Hart thrust his wrists forward. 'Get me out of here before they kill me!'

'Who?' Dredd snarled, but Hart didn't have time to answer. On the pedway, a man was convulsing, his shrieking girlfriend flattened against the wall—and he wasn't alone. All around, citizens were going into seizures, ripping at their own inflamed skin. Hart didn't need to watch: he'd witnessed the transformations before. Twitching antennae erupting from shattered skulls, thick ebony shells blossoming from twisted spinal cords. Even as he clambered onto the back of Dredd's Lawmaster, Hart imagined segmented legs clattering on the sidewalk, cheeks ripping as scythe-like mandibles flexed for the very first time.

Klak klak klak!

The difference was he'd never been the prey before. Not until today. Not until one stupid mistake.

'D-don't waste your bullets, Dredd,' Hart stammered as the Judge pulled his Lawgiver. 'Just drive, before they start running. Trust me, these things can move.'

But it was too late. The roaches that had first picked up his scent were already spilling out of the zip, compound eyes driven wild with bloodlust. Dredd fired, standard ammunition ricocheting harmlessly off thick chitinous exoskeletons. Why wasn't old Stoney-Face listening? Forget the freaks on the pedway. These were fully transformed. Ready to kill.

'Hold on,' Dredd commanded, opening the throttle as the roaches leapt towards them. The Lawmaster jolted and raced away from the scuttling horde.

'START TALKING,' DREDD snarled as the Lawmaster powered onto the main megway. They swerved across three lanes, even as the first of the swarm piled onto the slab behind them. 'What *are* those things?'

'They're just people, man. Ordinary people.'

'Don't look ordinary to me.'

'It's in the food, okay? We found these bugs. Big ugly bugs from the Undercity.' Hart could hear the blare of horns, the sickening crunch of metal as cars slammed into each other to avoid the insectoids. 'The boys at the factory did something to them, I don't know, ground 'em up, stuck 'em in the food—*Woah!*'

The Lawmaster lurched again, jumping five lanes at once. 'Need to draw them off the megway,' Dredd grunted, checking the carnage in his rear-view mirror, 'get them away from the traffic.'

He sliced across the path of a truck, making for the next exit. The driver slammed on his brakes, but a collision was the least of his worries. Seconds later the marauding bug-men had knocked the truck off its wheels and were clambering over the skidding wreck. It barely slowed them at all.

'The insect protein's causing the transformations?' Dredd asked, racing towards a covered underzoom. The guy could conduct an interrogation at one hundred miles an hour. Impressive. 'Who did this?'

'I'm no nark, Dredd. You can't ask me no more.' They were in the empty tunnel now, the harsh lighting bathing everything in a cold, grimy nicotine wash.

'Not good enough.' Dredd threw the Lawmaster into an emergency stop, flinging Hart through the air. He hit the road hard, his shoulder wrenched from its socket as he rolled.

'W-what are you *doing*?' Hart screamed, trying to scramble back to his feet. Behind the Judge's impassive figure, roaches had already reached the tunnel entrance. 'They'll kill us!'

'No,' Dredd growled, leaning forward, 'they'll kill *you*. Talk.'

'Oh Jovis,' Hart whimpered, clutching his burning shoulder. 'Okay, okay! It's not just the food. There's this spray, a chemical. It triggers the change.'

'A pheromone?'

'That's it. Blatta uses the bugs as hitmen, yeah? I just spray the mark. Please, Dredd, they're coming...'

'Don Blatta? The gangster?'

'Who else? Anyone who's eaten Blatta's crud bugs out and rips the poor schmuck to pieces...'

'There have been deaths all across the city. Mutilations, like animal attacks.' Dredd's voice was barely audible over the sound of the approaching swarm. *Klak klak klak!* 'Your roaches?'

'They change back after the kill, can't remember a thing.'

'What about you? What did you do to Blatta?'

'For Grud's sake, Dredd, they're right behind you!'

'Tell me.'

'Nothing, I swear!' He was babbling now, eyes fixed on the stampede. 'I was on my way to a mark and tripped, that's all. Got the stuff over me. Please, Dredd, I'll tell you anything, just get me out of here!'

Dredd didn't answer. He just fired his engine, scooping up Hart as he roared past. Pain lanced through Hart's body, but he didn't care, clinging to Dredd like a baby hanging on to its mother.

But Dredd had left it too late. A roach at the front of the pack leapt, landing on the back of the bike. Its front legs scrambled for a purchase, a hooked claw slicing into Hart's chest. Without even slowing, Dredd twisted, pointing his Lawgiver over a battered shoulder-pad and fired, the roach's head disintegrating into a mush of flesh and exo-skeleton. The bug dropped, a leg still attached to the bike, bouncing along the road like a gruesome marionette as Dredd accelerated. The joints finally gave way with a wet pop as they roared out of the tunnel, the dead roach disappearing under the feet of the other insects.

'Y-you taking me to the cubes?' Hart stammered, barely able to think anymore.

'Not yet,' came the reply.

DON BLATTA GLANCED at his watch. What was taking the punk so long? Hart had been a good kid once, someone

Blatta could trust, but he was getting sloppy. This was his last chance. Mess this one up and, well, he'd need taking care of.

Blatta turned a vial of the pheromone over in his fat fingers. Who knew how long they could keep this racket going, how much longer before his chittering killers were noticed? But what if they were? People would be scared, sure, but weren't they always in this town? Scared folk were easier to control and besides, unless someone found out what was in the meat, there was no way to trace the bugs back to the factory. Why would they even look? The Judges didn't care what the dregs of the Big Meg were eating as long as they were being fed. Sure, the crap tasted like stomm but it was as cheap as it was nasty. No one asked questions, which suited him fine.

The sound of a gunshot made Blatta start. His hand went to the shooter in his drawer. What was going on? It sounded like World War Four was breaking out on the factory floor. Worst still, one of those guns sounded familiar. A Lawgiver. Drokk!

Heaving himself across the office, Blatta opened the door and peered out. No one in the corridor. Should he make for the back exit? No, he had to see what was happening. Rushing as fast as his flabby body could manage, Blatta reached the doors just a body smashed through them— 'Three Ladies' Voltullo, or at least what was left of him. The top of Voltullo's head was missing.

The sound of gunfire was deafening now. But that wasn't all.

Klak klak klak!

The roaches? Here?

Raising his gun, Blatta threw himself into the factory, skidding on the floor to land safely behind a workstation. All around, his boys were firing into the far doors, but they weren't shooting at Judges. They were shooting at the mutated bugs streaming through the gap. But what about the Lawgiver?

A flash of yellow and green out of the corner of his rheumy eye answered his question. There, hiding behind a trolleyload of slop. Dredd—and Hart was with him! The idiot had got himself captured. No, wait—it was worse than that. That glint across Hart's bloodstained jacket. The phcromone. That's why the roaches were swarming.

Still, it wasn't every day you had the chance to take out a liability and the law's favourite son with one shot. Perhaps things were looking up. Blatta raised his gun, catching Dredd in his sights.

Screeeeeeee!

Shards of glass rained down as a roach smashed through the window above his head. He twisted, firing off shots indiscriminately as the thing tried to clamber through the narrow window frame. Bullets bounced harmlessly off the creature's glistening shell and Blatta cried out in agony as one found a home in his gut.

With the sound of splintering wood, the frame gave way, the roach tumbling down onto the wounded ganglord. Barbed legs burrowed into white flabby flesh as bile from its frenzied jaws sprayed into Blatta's eyes. Then, there was a sound like thunder and the mutant was thrown from him, gore pumping from a smoking wound in its mutated thorax. Blatta's head snapped around to stare straight into the barrel of Dredd's weapon.

'Armour-piercing. Next one's for you. Give yourself up.'

Not likely. Feeling for his gun Blatta rolled, screaming as pain tore through his belly, and opened fire.

Dredd dropped to the side, throwing himself over Hart's snivelling body and kicked at the trolley. Its wheels squealed as it barrelled forward, Blatta's slugs hammering into the thin metal. When he looked up, the ganglord was gone.

Ignoring the hiss of the mutant roaches that were still trying to fight their way into the factory, Dredd grabbed Hart's good arm and dragged the gibbering perp to where Blatta had been attacked. A lesser Judge would have left Hart to the creatures, citing poetic justice. Another may have seen the amount of dark arterial blood leading up the stairway to the gantry above and given up the chase. Not Dredd. Bleeding out or not, Blatta had to pay.

A roach sprang forwards even as Dredd started hauling Hart up the stairs. The mob had lost the gunfight, overcome by sheer numbers and the insectoids had the run of the place.

'Get up there!' Dredd shouted, pushing Hart ahead, holding off as many of the roaches as he could. How many of these things were there? Thank Grud for belt rations. If the Judges had eaten any of Blatta's laced meat...

Hart had stopped at the top of the stairs, curled up in a ball, convinced that his end had come. Of Blatta there was no sign, the walkway empty save for a line of vats. Insectoid legs clattered on metal as the creatures streamed after them, bucking under the Lawgiver's onslaught. Even as he knocked them back, Dredd felt something crack against the back of his helmet, cold liquid splashing down his neck. Blatta had appeared from behind a vat and was flinging vials at him, smothering the Judge in foul-smelling gunk. It had to be the pheromone.

The mobster gurgled with laughter as the first roach knocked Dredd onto the meshed steel. He jammed his arm beneath the thing's chin, stopping slime-encrusted mandibles from slicing into his face. They had forgotten about Hart, the chemicals coating Dredd's uniform more potent that the perp's stale scent.

He kicked out, feeling his boot connect with solid, writhing bodies. They were all over him, slashing through his tunic, teeth scoring against his helmet. Dredd was only vaguely aware of Blatta staggering back, an arm clamped across his bloodstained gut. The creep was dying, but justice had to be served.

Fighting against impossibly strong legs, Dredd forced his arm up, aiming toward the gangster. No, just a little higher...

'Grenade!'

The explosive round slammed into the vats, rupturing them instantly. Blatta was caught in the deluge of chemicals, slipping on wet, stinking mesh. The effect was instantaneous. Unable to resist, the roaches leapt from Dredd and descended on the screaming crimelord.

Klak klak klak!

* * *

THE THRUM OF three Lawmasters greeted Dredd as he threw Hart out onto the pedway.

'What's the situation, Dredd?' It was Donbavand, a rookie that had found himself in active service sooner than expected after Chaos Day.

'Decker Hart,' Dredd replied curtly. 'Twenty years for conspiracy to murder, handling dangerous chemicals without a licence, and jaywalking. Clean him up and get him on a work team—'

'Dredd, look out!'

A roach leapt through the factory doors. Dredd didn't even flinch. He twisted, dispatching the hissing monstrosity with one final armour-piercing round. Sated by Blatta, the rest of the swarm was already reverting to human form, but there was still work to do.

'What *is* that?' Donbavand asked, crouching down to examine the mutant's twitching vestigial wings.

'Dead,' Dredd growled, stalking over to his Lawmaster. Stowing his gun, he jabbed the bike's comms unit. 'Dredd to Control—Verminator Squad to Blatto Meatorama. Level ten infestation.'

'Roger that, Dredd. Where you headed?'

'To the Undercity. We've got bugs to hunt.'

DEAD MAN TALKING

DAVID BAILLIE

THREE BULLETS PIERCE my chest in quick succession. They rip through my heart and I know that my time on Earth has come to an end. In that moment, that split second before oblivion, I regret every choice, coincidence and accident that brought me here. Brought me into the firing line of Judge Dredd's Lawgiver.

How the hell had it all gone so wrong? I should have been in the office, putting together a report for my latest client—a lady so pretty she made me want to cry. She'd come in two days ago, reckoned her husband wasn't working as much overtime as he said he was. I resisted the urge to tell her that if she gave me half a chance I'd treat her like a princess until the day I died. Instead I said, 'You have a husband with a job? Be smart, don't make a fuss.'

But that hadn't been good enough for her. The broad looked like a million creds—she could find another schmuck with disposable income any day of the week. If he was doing the dirty, she just wanted enough evidence for a decree absolute and an alimony cheque. She left her number on a piece of scented notepaper. Less than a second after she'd left I'd already programmed it into my vone. I knew I wasn't the kinda guy she'd be looking for when this was all over, but it made me smile knowing that for at least the duration of this case I had a beautiful woman on voice-activated speed-dial.

Catching a wayward husband in the act is usually easier than taking Umpty from a juve and I had no reason to think this one would be any different. He worked reception at an establishment called Tanya's Tanning Salon. The Chaos Bug left half the buildings in my sector empty, so all I needed to do was find an abandoned one somewhere nearby with a window on the salon. Then I could hole up with my telephoto lens, flask of synthi-caff, and wait for the money shot of my target and the eponymous Ms Tanya. Or so I thought.

In this line of work it pays to keep your ear to the ground—taking every precaution to minimise surprises is Rule Number One. I pride myself on knowing everything that goes on in my own backyard. You can imagine my surprise then when, instead of a buxom salon bunny, big-time gang boss Azzo Azzopardi appeared in my viewfinder.

Azzopardi usually terrorised Sector 11 but recent events had blurred the boundaries of everyone's stomping grounds. I quickly deactivated my holo-focuser, packed up my stuff, and hoped that none of Azzo's goons had surveillance alarms.

The ping of a hollow-point bullet on the rockcrete just behind my ear told me that they did. 'Drokk!' I cursed into the void and made a run for it.

My legs carried me up the alley by the hottie stand where no one in their right mind ever eats, past old Mr McCririck's Glue Shop and over the wall that leads to... It didn't matter, I didn't make it over the wall, and two enormous goons—pumped on steroids paid for by Azzo Azzopardi—held me down until the boss man could saunter over to inspect the goods.

'What have we here? Why you watch me with your camera?' he said in an exotic, if mystifying, accent. He was a small man, dressed in an impeccable pinstriped suit and very fashionable velour kneepads. 'Why is it impossible to do private business in this city? I do not understand.'

I tried to explain that I was looking for someone else, that I hadn't seen anything, that I had already forgotten everything I had seen and wouldn't be blabbing to no one, but Azzo's over-eager employees had a habit of punching me in the face right before I got to the point of any sentence I was trying to spit out.

'It does not matter,' Mr Azzopardi assured me. I didn't feel very assured.

It was then that I saw the husband I'd actually been paid to spy on, cowering behind a smartly dressed thug the size of a small laundrette. Poor guy—I had no idea what he was caught up in, but I was pretty sure he was only doing it to keep his glamorous young wife in the lifestyle to which she had decided she was accustomed.

She was the reason both of us were in this stomm, then!

Upon being dragged back to Tanya's I was pleasantly surprised to find it was an actual salon and not a torture dungeon covered in plastic sheeting. 'Nice place,' I tried to say but a quick set of knuckles shut me up before I could finish my quip.

'Tell me what you know,' Azzo said with a smile that could kill a kitten.

All I was able to do was cough blood.

'Tough guy, eh? Edward will fix that.' He waved over one of his boys, who I could now see was holding one of those fancy East-Meg Two electric batons that flooded the black market last year. This is where knowing what's going on pays off. You see, I knew these particular weapons of personal destruction had only been sold on in the first place because of an unfortunate design fault. I just didn't know if I would live long enough to exploit it.

I played dead, hoping that it would make Edward complacent with his first swing. He didn't look too bright so I didn't bother closing both eyes. As the baton came down, blue lightning arcing around its circumference, I opened my flask and threw my synthi-caff. It had an even more explosive effect on Edward's nervous system than it would have had on mine. His tongue shot out of his mouth as he spasmed and twitched and his body hit the ground like a sack of munce. I rolled my jacket around my fist and grabbed the baton.

'Okay, here's what happens next,' I said. 'I'm going to leave, you guys are going to go back to whatever you were doing, and we all forget this ever happened. Except for maybe Edward, who's going to need some counselling so that he doesn't freak out whenever he smells fresh synthi-caff.'

No one moved or uttered a word. I wondered for a second if I'd just said all that in my head.

'Are you Judge spy?' Azzopardi asked. 'Wally Squad, maybe? Looking for dirty secrets?'

I wondered what his scam was. Racketeering? Protection? No, I didn't damn well care—I just wanted out of here.

'No! I'm a private detective,' I said. 'Minding my own business. And this is all an accident.'

'There are no accidents,' Azzo said as he turned to my client's probably-not-wayward husband. 'You know this man, don't you? You been telling him about our arrangement?'

The poor guy shook his head deliberately, while the rest of his body shook involuntarily. 'No, Mr Azzo. I ain't never seen him before, I swear to Grud.'

'Lies,' Azzo said as he pulled a gun from beneath brushed velour and pointed it at the whimpering man's forehead.

What did I care? I could make a run for it while he put a bullet in this putz. But then what? Would I just catch the next bullet in that gun as I ran down the street searching for cover? And who was I kidding? Watching this guy tremble I knew I couldn't let him die on my account.

'Fine,' I said, throwing the baton to the ground. 'Leave him alone. I'll come quietly.'

Edward's friend hit me with a punch like a falling skedway and my eyes had to close for a while. When they opened again things had done the opposite of improve.

Azzo smiled. 'Here is what we do,' the boss-man said. 'We make this look like an accident. What's your name, Peeping Tom?'

Through loose teeth, I told him.

'These tanning machines are kind of old. Their settings are all wrong. Sometimes the timer no work. Crispy-fried Peeping Tom. You see?'

I didn't bother nodding. We both knew that I understood.

I tried putting up a fight but the two juggernauts that were packing me into the bronzing booth had seen what'd happened to Edward and were taking no chances. One held me down with little effort while the other strapped me in with even less effort. The last thing I saw before they closed the lid was the gap-toothed grin of Azzo Azzopardi.

'See what you get? Huh? Why you no leave a man to tan himself in peace?'

'Hang on. This is all because you have a secret *tanning habit?* Let me out, you drokking lunatic! I definitely won't tell anyone that! No one cares!' I shouted impotently as the lid dropped.

The lamps came on like a thousand suns. My skin immediately started to prickle and before long I could smell myself cooking. Azzo wasn't kidding when he said the settings on these things were all wrong!

It was then that I remembered who my last speed-dial contact was. Despite the damaged teeth and bruised ribs

I managed to whisper her name just loud enough for my vone to recognise it. A beep confirmed that the call had gone through. When she picked up my heart soared. For almost an entire second. Then I realised that I couldn't actually hear what she was saying through the interference. Of course... These pods would have to be lined with something heavy duty to stop the rads escaping. No way my vone signal was getting through that intact.

Intermittently I could make out a word or two, so I figured she was getting the same kind of reception. I played the odds. 'Judges!' I said loudly enough for my vone to pick up but hopefully not loud enough that Azzo would have one of his man-mountains open the pod and simply shoot me. 'Call the Judges. I'm at Tanya's Salon! '

The vone went dead. It's around that point I passed out—having solar lamps strong enough to turn Antarctic City into a puddle just an inch from your face will do that to you. When I woke up it was dark and there was a rhythmic thumping. The lid opened and I couldn't believe my luck: I was alive, and I'd been saved by a beautiful woman. Although not the one I'd been expecting...

'The tanning pod must have failed. Azzo was right— they are old junk!' I tried to say. But I couldn't. The lamps had cut out too late to save my skin. Literally. My lips had fused together. Nothing I said made any sense through what was left of my deformed mouth.

'Who are you? What the drokk are you doing in my salon?' Tanya asked.

Then a shot echoed and Tanya suddenly had a hole in her chest the size of her chest. I stumbled out of the blisteringly hot pod and, falling to my knees, I saw her: my client. With a gun in her hand and tears on her cheek. She ran over to me.

'You poor man,' she said. Her hand reached out but she couldn't touch me. My heart broke as I realised that what had been a sliver of a dream was now impossible. It was madness to think she'd ever want anything to do a private eye, never mind one with a melted face. She bravely gulped back her horror and told me, 'I picked up your call but all I could make out was that you were at the salon. I came right away. I can't believe she tried to kill you. I knew it was that bitch. I knew I was right all along.'

I tried to tell her how wrong she was. Tell he that she had to get out of here. But all I could do was mumble incoherently through a malformed mouth. The Chaos Bug had made the Judges' response time erratic, but I knew she needed to get out of here quick. If her luck was good she might...

'*Drop your weapon!*' a voice yells from the salon door. A damned Judge. Already. Our call must have been intercepted.

Mascara runs down her cheeks. Her perfect features harden. I can see how this is going to play out and I don't want it to. 'I'm not going to the cubes,' she snarls and lifts her gun.

I look over at the Judge and pray that beginner's luck is an actual thing and she might be able to beat him to the draw. Then I see his badge and I know that isn't going to happen.

Dredd.

'I warned you!' Dredd says as he lets three blasts escape the barrel of his Lawgiver. At that moment I forget all of the asshat mistakes I've made in my life, I forget Azzo Azzopardi and his tanning secrets. All I can think of is this flawless creature before me and how she doesn't deserve to die. Maybe she'll go to the cubes; maybe when she comes out her husband will explain everything and she can be happy. And let's face it—what is my life going to be like with this face?

I leap forward and take all three bullets—and I'm dead before I know if I've saved her.

ONE-WAY TICKET

JONATHAN GREEN

'BIKE CANNONS, full auto!' Dredd growled over the roar of the sked. Screaming traffic noise was immediately drowned out by the chugging boom of the Lawmaster's guns as they opened fire.

One of the mopad's massive front tyres blew with all the force of a detonating Hi-Ex round, the blast lifting the speeding vehicle's cab off the skedway, unbalancing it. As the gang's getaway driver lost control of the thundering juggernaut, the mopad spun across the five-lane highway.

Horns blared as Dredd jinked his bike out of the path of the hurtling vehicle. Behind him, Judge Arnold followed his colleague's line through the resulting traffic chaos, pursued by the blare of car horns and the screech of tyres skidding on rockcrete.

Slowly, inexorably, the mopad began to roll, its metal shell throwing up fat, greasy sparks as it veered across the sked. Twisting his Lawmaster nimbly between two wildly careering automobiles, Dredd brought the bike to a sudden stop in the path of the vehicle as it too slewed to a halt. The cab door was kicked open from inside and two perps struggled to climb free.

'Don't even think it,' Dredd said, his Lawgiver already trained on them.

Knowing there was no way out now, they slowly raised their hands above their heads, resigned to their fate.

'CONTROL—DREDD. GOT two on a holding post on Walker. Catch-wagon and clean-up crew required.'

'Roger that.'

'So what now?' Arnold asked.

Dredd looked at the other man, his granite expression unchanged. The pair from the mopad—one Kostas Wendig and his accomplice Vetch Deichmann—had merely been decoys, hired by person or persons unknown to distract the authorities from the true perpetrators of the Peretti Diamond heist. Lie detectors had proved useless: if a stooge didn't know his employer's identity he couldn't lie about it. 'We follow up our leads.'

A squirt of static alerted them to an incoming data transmission. Dredd glanced at the screen of his bike's onboard computer. 'Getaway vehicle was a rental from We Rent Any Pod in Sector 12. Teks have also come up with something on the weapons used during the robbery.' Dredd turned his attention to his fellow Judge. 'You follow up on the rental. I'm going back to the scene, see what the teks have to say.' He scowled. 'Real perps wouldn't have got away so easily if PSU was still operational.'

'Never thought I'd hear Joe Dredd say he missed the Public Surveillance Unit.'

Even though he couldn't see Dredd's bionic stare through the Judge's visor, Arnold felt its withering intensity nonetheless. 'I didn't.'

With that, Dredd revved the throttle of his Lawmaster and pulled away from the kerb, heading for Peretti's Diamond Emporium at the Bieber Shopperama.

JUDGE THOMAS ARNOLD watched as Dredd's Lawmaster was swallowed by the relentless river of traffic and moments later insinuated himself back into the flow of cars, mopads and bulk haulage transports. Rather than take the overzoom towards Sector 12, Arnold turned onto the skedway that would lead him into the devastation of Sector 7.

The further west he headed, the worse the devastation became—the legacy of Chaos Day. The overzoom was still restricted to two lanes, two years after the event. Pulling off the main sked, Arnold headed down to ground level, into one of the sector's many wastezones. Thousands of square miles of Mega-City One had been left in ruins in the aftermath of Chaos and it might still be weeks, or even months, before the clean-up crews got around to clearing Sector 7.

The broken shell of Gerry Anderson Block rose before him. Despite the top one hundred or more floors having fallen in and crushed those levels that lay below, Anderson was still an imposing edifice. Once home to more than fifty thousand cits, the collapsed ruin had since become their tomb.

This place, this city, Arnold thought as he stared at the ruins of the block. Chaos Day had given the Big Meg a beating such as it had ever known, and in return the city had beaten *him* into submission, again and again, until he had nothing left to give.

All he could think about now, when he thought of the metropolis he had once sworn to protect, was how he wanted *out*. The city he had once fought so hard and for so long to defend—upholding its laws and keeping its streets safe for law-abiding citizens—had turned on him, after all he had done, and taken from him the only things that really mattered.

All that it would take for him to escape the trap of his current existence was a ticket off-world. A one-way ticket.

Arnold pulled up at the edge of the rubble-strewn plaza before Anderson's half-demolished shell and activated his comm. 'Control—Arnold. Taking some personal time.' He hesitated for a moment before continuing. 'Tell Dredd I'll meet him at Gerry Anderson Block in Sector 7 as planned.'

'Roger that.'

Arnold deactivated the comm.

The sudden flash of headlights and the low leopard purr of an anti-grav engine alerted Arnold to the arrival of a sleek, black hover-limo as it set down on the far side of the plaza.

Doors opened and the hired muscle emerged; mobster muscle. Built of slabs of vat-grown genhanced meat and wearing tastelessly expensive suits they couldn't be anything other. The thugs—sporting close-cropped haircuts and with jaws that would give Ol' Stoney-Face a run for his money—surveyed the plaza. It was only when they were happy that Arnold was alone that their boss exited the car. Or at least his telepresence did.

The hovering spherical droid-unit buzzed across the plaza, flanked by the bodyguards, while Arnold stepped over the broken rockcrete. All four met in the middle of the square, keeping a cautionary distance between them.

It was Arnold—impatient for the business he had with the mobsters to be concluded as quickly as possible—who broke the silence that was disturbed only by the hum of the drone's anti-grav propulsion unit.

'Have you got it? Have you got what I asked for?' He looked from one sharp-suited thug to the other and then back again, pointedly keeping his eyes off the hovering droid. Yet it was the droid that answered, using the uplink-distorted voice of crimelord Randall Hopkirk.

'Yes.' The mobster's smug voice was cut through with static. 'The question is, have you got what *I* asked for?'

Arnold put his hand to a pouch on his utility belt and popped it open, extracting a lozenge-shaped piece of dull black metal. 'One data slug containing information on all Justice Department patrols in a five-sector radius, such as they are,' he said, 'in exchange for a one-way ticket off-world.'

'Then it would appear we have a deal,' the drone buzzed.

Arnold hesitated, the data slug gripped tightly between forefinger and thumb. To think that it had come to this.

He turned his attention to the ruins of the block for a moment. What was left of Gerry Anderson was scheduled for demolition, and it was about time too. The place had always seemed to attract trouble.

His brother Benedict had been a resident of the block, along with his wife and kids. Arnold used to visit them when he could grab some personal time every now and again. It was during one of these visits that he had disturbed the tap gang, high on zziz, in the act of beating a body into unconsciousness at the edge of the plaza. The gang had run. It was only then that Arnold had discovered the identity of the poor wretch—Benedict. He was dead.

An uncontrollable rage had come over him. He wasn't some kind of machine like Dredd. Forget the badge and the eagle; in that moment, Arnold had been a man at the mercy of his emotions, and in his rage he had pursued the gang. They hadn't a hope of getting away, of course, and pronouncing judgement he had gunned them down as they fled the scene. All but one.

Just one lowly juve had the sense to surrender. But having obtained the juve's confession, in a moment of madness Arnold had shot him dead. That should have been an end to the matter but, as it turned out, it was only just the beginning.

There had been witnesses to Arnold's act of revenge. Thugs in the employ of Randall Hopkirk had spied the whole thing. Arnold was only made aware of this fact when Hopkirk contacted him and made him a proposition, of the offer-he-couldn't-refuse variety. Hopkirk would keep Arnold's dirty little secret and ensure that Benedict's family were looked after, just so long as the Judge did him one small favour.

Motivated by grief, guilt, and a desire not to see his brother's family made destitute, Arnold capitulated. Hopkirk's not unreasonable request was that Arnold hunt down the local zziz dealer and take him out, a proposal which suited them both. But with Happy Golucky brought to justice it turned out that Hopkirk had just one more small favour to ask—and then another, and another, and another...

It wasn't long before Arnold realised he was in too deep to ever escape the life he had made for himself, not if he didn't want to see what had happened to his brother happen to his sister-in-law and the kids as well.

'So,' buzzed Hopkirk's telepresence, 'do we have a deal?'

Hopkirk's original request had seemed like such a minor matter, clearing one more dealer, along with the filth he peddled, off the streets. Now, here he was, about to make another deal with the devil.

'We do this, and I never have to do anything else for you ever again, you understand?'

'Hand over the slug and Mr Leary here will provide you with everything you need to leave this city and never come back.' The muscle to Arnold's right raised the sleek silver case he was holding in one meaty hand. 'So, Judge Arnold'—there was an edge to Hopkirk's voice that was apparent even through the murmur of static—'do we have a deal?'

*   *   *

'DREDD—CONTROL,' CAME a voice over the comm. 'Message from Arnold. He's taking some personal time but will meet you at Gerry Anderson Block in Sector 7 as planned.'

'As planned?' Dredd growled, one arm outstretched as he pressed the jeweller's face against the fractured glass of a display cabinet. He'd got a new lead on the Peretti heist: turned out the jeweller was in on it from the start. 'That wasn't the plan. Control, you sure it was Arnold that called in.'

'Voiceprint and comm-signal all check out.'

'Gerry Anderson?'

'That's what he said.'

'Didn't Arnold have family in Anderson?'

'Yes, but they were listed among the dead after DoC.'

Dredd's expression darkened. 'Control, catch-wagon to Peretti's—and send an H-wagon to Gerry Anderson. Something's going down.'

The jeweller cuffed, Dredd remounted his Lawmaster and roared away towards the devastation of Sector 7.

'SUCH A SMALL thing,' Judge Arnold said as he handed the lozenge-shaped slug of black metal to the thug the mob boss had referred to as Mr Leary.

Arnold turned his attention from the buzzing drone relaying crimelord Randall Hopkirk's telepresence to the broken plaza outside Gerry Anderson. The night-shrouded ruins of Sector 7 surrounded him, dominated by the skeletal ruin of the abandoned block.

The events of the fateful evening that had led him to this point had seemed so insignificant at first. It was only when he had looked down at the fractured skull of the tap gang's victim and seen that it was his brother that the magnitude of what had happened hit him—and that, as it had turned out, had only been the beginning. Now he was just one more Judge in the pay of the Mob.

WHEN CHAOS DAY had come, Arnold had believed his time had come too, almost as if the Chaos Bug was some form of retribution—divine or otherwise—for what he had done. Whether it was Grud's judgement, the city's, or that of Justice herself, it didn't make any difference. He had committed a crime—numerous crimes, by then—and even if he had been motivated by a sense of loyalty to both his dead brother and Benedict's family, in the eyes of the Law he had to pay.

The Chaos Bug had claimed three hundred and fifty million victims in a matter of days, wiping out eighty-five per cent of the city's population, including those holed up in Gerry Anderson, Benedict's wife and kids among them. After everything he had done to protect them following Benedict's death, the principles he had sacrificed, in the end it had all been for nothing.

He had thought that he, like so many others among Justice Department, would die. He deserved to die. He *hoped* he would die. It seemed only right, somehow. But, against all the odds, he had survived.

Then came Bachmann's attempted coup. As the Grand Hall itself had come under attack from an army of brainwashed simps and Black Ops agents Arnold had thought that surely his time had come at last, that Overdrive, Inc.'s GodCity would bring divine retribution where the Chaos Bug had not. But Bachmann had been defeated— in no small part thanks to Joe Dredd's intervention—and Arnold had lived to fight another day once again.

There was nothing left for him in Mega-City One, least of all justice for all those who'd died when he had not. All that was left for him was to leave this city, and Earth, once and for all.

THE THUG TOOK the data-slug from the Judge with fingers the size of muncedogs and slipped it into a pocket of his tastelessly tailored suit.

'Do you have it, Mr Leary?' Hopkirk's voice crackled from the hovering metal sphere.

'Yeah, boss.'

'Well, that will save you having to recover it from the bloody ruins of his bullet-riddled flesh.'

Arnold's gaze snapped from the droid to the silver case in Mr Leary's hand, the case that supposedly contained everything he needed to start a new life off-world. 'We had a deal,' he rasped.

'Correct, Judge Arnold,' Hopkirk said. Never had Arnold heard the word *'Judge'* pronounced with more cynical disdain and less respect. It was only what he deserved. 'But then I can't risk having a rogue Judge with whom I have had dealings simply leave the planet, now can I?'

Mr Leary raised the hand holding the case again, the lid falling open as he did so to reveal, not a false I.D. and a ticket off-world, but a large-calibre handgun inside a synthi-felt-lined impression. At the same time, the other square-jawed thug pulled a piece from inside his broad-shouldered jacket. Arnold went for his Lawgiver as the thugs opened fire, peppering the plaza with impact marks as they fought to find their aim.

Two against one, with the Judge taken by surprise, his mind elsewhere... This was it. This was when he was going to get what he was owed.

A sudden subsonic thrumming, which Arnold felt in his teeth and bones, told him that he was no longer facing the enemy alone. Half a dozen spotlights came on in a blaze of luminescence that had the thugs shielding their eyes, their target momentarily forgotten. The light would have blinded Arnold too had it not been for his helmet visor.

The instant the H-wagon alerted all those gathered outside Gerry Anderson to its presence above, a familiar gravelly voice boomed across the plaza, amplified by his Lawmaster's loudhailer.

'This is Judge Dredd. Drop your weapons. We have you surrounded.'

'No way, Dredd!' Leary shouted. Randall Hopkirk might have been able to afford the strongest muscle in the sector, but such strength rarely came with a side order of smarts as well.

The two thugs opened fire again, explosive rounds stitching the ground between them and the shadows at the edge of the plaza.

'Your choice, creep,' came Dredd's muted response, and with a deafening boom the Lawmaster's cannons opened up.

Dredd hurled the bike down the side of a mound of rubble, shells tearing up the rockcrete and ripping through the side of the sleek hover-limo parked up nearby. A moment later the cannons chewed through the vat-grown slabs of mobster muscle, transforming Hopkirk's hired guns into bloody lumps of unrecognisable meat.

Arnold heard the brief exchange of fire behind him as he ran for shelter amidst the twisted, reinforced rockcrete ruins of Gerry Anderson, far from the harsh search-beams of the H-wagon.

What was he running from? he wondered. This was what he wanted, wasn't it? An out? But a Judge's training and twenty years' active duty on the streets—twenty of the toughest years Mega-City One had even known—meant that his instincts and finely honed sense of self-preservation took over.

Hearing the waspish hum of anti-gravs Arnold glanced back over his shoulder. The crimelord's surrogate drone-sphere was pursuing him between the broken columns and shattered walls of the block's atrium.

Actinic white light flared in the darkness of the forgotten foyer and a bolt of energy blasted from a laser-probe beneath the sphere. Arnold turned, Lawgiver in hand, and took aim. Lightning fast, the drone fired again as the Judge's finger tightened on the trigger.

Arnold cried out in pain as the searing beam sliced through his uniform and the flesh of his bicep beneath. His own standard round spanged off the shell of the drone, sending it spinning.

'Hi-ex!' Arnold muttered through teeth gritted against the pain.

Gyroscopic stabilisers reasserting themselves, the sphere righted itself and stopped spinning. Another beam of focused light energy burned through the darkness, searing its after-image onto Arnold's retinas, too bright even for his helmet visor.

He cried out again as the beam sliced through the back of the hand holding his gun. Both the Lawgiver and half of Arnold's hand—cut clean across the palm above the ball of his thumb—tumbled to the ground.

The Judge stumbled backwards as the blood began to flow from the stump of his bisected palm. His feet hit a raised step and he fell to the floor at the foot of a flight of stairs that led nowhere.

'This is how it ends for you, Judge!' the crimelord gloated via uplink. 'Turns out you're just as expendable as all the rest. Justice Department will never be able to link Mr Leary and his friend or the data exchange to me, especially once you're dead. After all—I was never here, was I?'

The laser swivelled about its pinion mount, taking aim again. This time it was the incapacitated Judge's head that was in its sights.

Even though he had his left hand clamped over the bloody mess of his right, Arnold couldn't help but laugh.

'The data exchange?' He felt light-headed from shock, but more than that he felt an overwhelming sense of relief; of sins atoned for. Of justice served.

'What?' There was both uncertainty and annoyance in Hopkirk's transmitted tone, but the laser remained inactive.

'You obviously need to pay more peanuts, Hopkirk. Then maybe you could afford monkeys with a few brain cells still intact as well as all that genhanced muscle.'

'What are you talking about?' the crimelord spat, his angry outburst underscored with static.

'That data-slug I handed over to your hired goon was actually a device that activated a trace to your uplink location as soon as your telepresence emerged from the shielding of the hover-limo,' Arnold took great pleasure in explaining. 'It will have transmitted the coordinates of your location to Justice Department. Units will be closing on your position even now. It's over, Hopkirk. You're finished.'

'And so are you!' the Judge heard Hopkirk screech over the whine of the laser powering up to take its final, fatal shot.

Arnold closed his eyes, calm in the knowledge that justice had been served at long last.

'Hi-ex!' came a granite growl from the other side of the darkened foyer followed by the report of a Lawgiver firing.

The droid-sphere exploded, twisted chunks of blackened metal raining down around Arnold, several pieces rattling off his helmet.

*   *   *

'THAT WAS THE plan, was it?' Dredd said, breaking the silence that had descended in the aftermath of the droid's destruction.

'Well, no plan entirely survives contact with the enemy,' Arnold replied, cradling his right hand tight against his chest.

'You realise that you've condemned yourself. That data-transmitter will have given the SJS everything they need to see you sent to Titan.'

'I know.' Arnold laughed, feeling euphoric with relief and blood loss. 'On a one-way ticket.'

Just as he had expected.

TOO HOTTIE TO HANDLE

DAVID BAILLIE

'I CAN'T BELIEVE you've never seen him here. He swings past a couple of times a week, easy. He likes them well done, extra mustard. He's probably one of my most faithful customers!'

Of course Lenny Stark didn't believe a word of it. He'd been eating at Dirty Dan's Hottie Stand—against his better judgement—every Monday now for six weeks, and each of those Mondays the eponymous Dirty Dan had lied about everything from the meat content of the hotties he sold to his latest romantic exploits. Never once had Lenny seen Judge Dredd eating there, which was just as well, because if there was one person in this city that Lenny Stark didn't want to meet on a Monday morning while he was eating at Dirty Dan's Hottie Stand it was Judge drokking Dredd.

While Dan expertly seared the hottie, Lenny peered down and admired his classic watch. It was one of the first generation of the so-called smart watches. Compared to what they had now of course it was about as smart as someone whose diet consisted only of hotties, although it had certainly lasted longer. Lenny tapped the face and it flickered into life. Nine am. Perfect. Everything was going according to plan.

'I always say to him, "To you, Judge, it's free of charge," and he never even responds, just takes his hottie and gives me a chit.'

'A chit?'

'Yeah,' Dirty Dan said, 'like a voucher. I take them into my local sector house and exchange 'em for proper creds.'

'So show me the chits,' Lenny said through a mouthful of hottie, one eye glued to the window across the street as the figures inside went about their early morning rituals.

'I can't,' he said. 'I've cashed 'em all in.' He scratched at his thick black beard. 'After the Chaos thing even the Judges are running low on money. I got a business to run, and it don't make much of a difference if it's got the Eagle of Justice on it, it's still an IOU.'

Lenny finished the last mouthful of hottie. 'Yeah, yeah,' he said playfully. Dan might have been full of stomm but his heart was in the right place, and his hotties, even if they were of questionable nutritional value, were tasty. But more importantly they had given Lenny an excuse to stand here for exactly ten minutes every Monday for the last six weeks.

This was indeed a sweet spot. No fixed cameras covered this patch of road, just the occasional patrolling drone, which could be easily eluded with a well-timed sidestep or by ducking into Dirty Dan's stall under the pretence of admiring his wares.

'Still can't believe your wheels, man,' Dan said, shaking his head, 'What year did you say it was?'

'The best year of them all,' Lenny said with a proud smile. '2015.'

Lenny ran an eye over his car too, taking in its gleaming curves. He'd had to work damned hard to afford it, but it was worth every cred. Sitting in it was like travelling in time, back to the Golden Age of Everything. 2015, the year Stuff was Awesome. Lenny wondered what a 2015 hottie must have tasted like. He shook his head at the galling unfairness of his being alive now.

The surveillance deadspot was something to be grateful for today, though. It was big enough to park the car in, which of course boasted interchangeable plates, thanks to a mechanism he'd installed himself, easily operated from the driver's seat, and his route in and out of the sector was impossible to track as the vehicle changed colour at the flick of a switch. He'd initially been reluctant to coat his pride and joy with nano-paint, but in the end he had to admit that otherwise the car was too recognisable. Anyway, when he wasn't working a job he turned it transparent and let the beautiful twenty-first century chrome shine through.

'Must make all the other guys at Resyk jealous. You never scared someone'll try to pinch her?' Dan's eyes flicked from the car to the hotties he was frying up on the hotplate in front of him, the synthi-onions separating out beneath his spatula.

'Nah,' Lenny said. 'Security at the plant is pretty tight. Has to be.'

He'd almost forgotten that he'd used his Resyk cover story on Dan. He had a dozen or so that he trotted out, and while there were a few others that might have been more suitable, Dirty Dan was never the risky link in this job's chain so he hadn't given it much thought. The only reason he regretted it now was that Dan, being an unusually curious man, had asked lots of questions about Lenny's phantom occupation. Lenny had painstakingly researched everything about that cover story from the interview process to holiday pay (unnervingly thorough and entirely absent, respectively) but didn't especially appreciate being so brainlessly interrupted when he was working.

'Anyone ever get caught stealing stuff? Like body parts, I mean.'

'Hardly ever,' Lenny said as he peered across the street and counted through his windows of opportunity. The first security guard—a heavy-set middle-aged guy, whose trousers would be too tight to allow him to run—unbolted the door. Right on schedule. Lenny watched as the guy's sausage fingers tapped out the sec-code, getting one digit wrong, hit Reset and then repeated, this time correctly.

'Are the bodies naked?' Dan asked.

'Huh?' Lenny had been lost in concentration, watching the security guard return to his post.

'When the stiffs get to you, are they nude already? I mean, is it the Resyk guys that take your clothes off, you know, when yer dead, or is that a separate operation?'

'It's all automated. Robots do everything. There's a human watching most of the time, in case something goes wrong. But it never does.'

'So the robots unbutton and unzip and...'

'Scissors,' Lenny explained. 'They slice everything off, and it all gets dumped down a chute. The fabric is pulped and recycled. Plastics are melted and de-chained into component mini-polymers.' Lenny had to give Dan his due: no one had ever asked so many questions about Resyk ops before. In fact he'd created this cover story specifically to take advantage of people's lack of curiosity when it came to matters of mortality.

'Huh,' Danny murmured thoughtfully as he lined up another hottie, this one for himself since there was no sign of any other customers.

Inside the Savings and Loans the other two security guards looked half asleep as they chatted. Their body language suggested they neither liked each other nor cared what the other was saying.

The street was clear. Not a car in sight. He checked his watch again, the slightly scratched Ion-X glass screen telling him that it was 9.08 am precisely. Perfect.

'Be right back,' Lenny said to Dirty Dan as he binned his hottie wrapper and marched across the road.

Despite being only three floors tall, the Mega-City One Savings and Loans Company building stood tall and proud. So it should, mused Lenny as he marched towards its wall-to-wall glass entrance: it was home to millions of creds thanks to the many high net-worth customers it prided itself on attracting. It was a bank after his own heart, you see—it liked to do things the old-fashioned way. It preferred cold, hard cash, smiling clerks behind well-polished glass, and human security guards. Values that Lenny could really get behind. But right now it was the human security guards he was most grateful for. The fat, sleepy, lazy human security guards.

He wound his way through a couple of dozen well-heeled customers congregated in the reception area, loudly and boastfully comparing their share options and investment portfolios. A second-long glance told him that none of them was as financially comfortable as they let on. The human ape was always lying about which branch he was hanging from, while desperately trying to climb higher up that tree.

'Good morning! How are you? And what can we do for you today, sir?' The clerk smiled at him, her teeth unnaturally white. Her eye shadow matched perfectly the shade of blue in the Savings and Loans Company logo. The booth she occupied was isolated from those around her, offering maximum privacy to the bank's clientele. Perfect.

'I was hoping I could make a withdrawal.' Lenny's tone was as cheerful and sing-song as hers. He slid the note beneath the glass that stood between them, and lowered his gaze as she read it.

This is a bank robbery. I am armed but unless you panic, or attempt to sound an alarm, you will be completely safe. I want you to collect all of the high-denomination cred notes you have in your booth and fill two of the mailsacks that are folded in your top drawer. I know that there is a silent-alarm button beneath the lip of your counter. If I see you even brush against it, you will die.

Until Lenny came along, no one had robbed a bank like this in over a century. The staff weren't trained to deal with it—they were all too busy looking out for drones, AI hacks and cloaking coats. In fact it was the only thing that he had to admit was better now than back in the twenty-first. It was like a tropical island that hadn't seen natural predators in a few generations, and then as soon as some are introduced to the ecosystem: utter carnage. Lenny intended to be that carnage. He glanced down at his watch, straightened the French cuff of his vintage (2015, of course) shirt, cocked his head ten degrees to the left and smiled at the clerk.

'Is everything okay?'

She showed him a terrified smile and he knew in that second that not only was everything okay but that it would remain so. He'd knocked over half a dozen banks like this in the last year and by now he was an expert. He had an instinct for problems, and knew when to cut and run.

Then the clerk's focus shifted slightly. Her pupils flickered. She was looking behind him, over his shoulder. At something. Or some*one*.

'You Stark?' a gruff voice asked from behind him.

Slowly Lenny turned and looked straight into the inscrutable visor of Judge Dredd.

Lenny kept his smile, the same one he'd prepared for the clerk, and hoped that it wouldn't dissolve in a bath of nerves. He did his best to gird himself, even though his guts were threatening to vacate his stomach. He mentally cycled through his options. Right now he had just one.

'That's me, Judge,' he said, as if he were talking to his grade-school teacher.

Dredd grunted, his frame, head and helmet as still as granite. 'That yours?' Dredd's thumb jerked behind him at Lenny's 2015 Classic, currently a vibrant red due to its nano-paint coating.

Lenny looked out. On the other side of the road, through the window, stood Dirty Dan, waving excitedly and grinning like an idiot. 'See?' he mouthed at Lenny. 'I told you... Judge Dredd!'

'Yeah,' said Lenny. 'That's my car. It's a beauty, right?'

Dredd grunted again, the noise merely a confirmation that Lenny had spoken. 'The hottie guy mentioned it last week. Must have been expensive. You work at Resyk, right?'

Lenny's fingers desperately wanted to twitch, his jangling nerves getting the better of the classical bank robber mindset he'd taken great pains to develop. Dirty Dan had blabbed, but that wasn't a disaster on its own. There was indeed a Lenny Stark who worked at Resyk, Lenny had made sure of that. All of his fake IDs had records set up on employment databases for precisely this reason. All that had taken was a few thousand creds in pay-off to the right geeks and keyboard jockeys. But how good was the Stark cover? Had Dredd dug deeper and rumbled him? Searching his peripheral vision Lenny scouted possible exits. Three—the best of which was the main door. Best, that is, if he ignored that fact that Dredd was standing between him and it.

'I inherited it from my cousin. Very sad—he got sick during the big bug thing the other year. Didn't make it. The car's all I got to remember him by.'

'Hope you had it decontaminated,' Dredd said. 'Car's not in your name. Not in anyone's name. The licence plate doesn't belong to any known vehicle.'

Lenny didn't move a muscle. There was a chance he could get out of this. He just had to play the tone right.

'It looks a lot like a vehicle that's supposed to be in Sector 17's Automotives Museum. Went missing four years ago. Don't suppose you know anything about that?'

Lenny pulled his best innocent face and weighed up his three exit options. Ten metres to his left was a fire exit—he knew that the door could be opened with a swift, accurate kick. But before he got there Dredd would likely put a hole in him. To his right was a door, unlocked, that opened onto to a corridor that would take him directly to the Savings and Loans Company's managerial suite. That office had a lockdown protocol, which he could easily activate once inside, but from there his only strategy would be to take a hostage—the antithesis to the kind of bank robber he was. The mental image of dozens of Judges aiming their Lawgivers through gaps in the office blinds filled him with horror. The main door it was, then. But how was he going to get past Dredd?

A dull, rasping sound from the teller position behind him brought Lenny back into the room, his awareness rushing into the moment with a roar. He glanced over his shoulder and saw that the combination of the robbery and the sudden appearance of Dredd had sent the teller into a state of blind panic, leaving her completely unable to think.

The sound had been the two canvas mailsacks, both stuffed full of beautifully crisp creds, as she pushed them through the recess beneath the teller's window onto the customer shelf. The beautiful, terrified clerk had done exactly as he'd asked in his note.

Perfect.

Lenny looked at the bags. Dredd looked at the bags. Then Lenny grabbed one by the drawstrings and hurled it over Dredd's head. It opened at the apex of its trajectory and unleashed its contents across the reception area. The customers gathered there hesitated just long enough to see the huge denominations on offer and then scrambled for the notes. Elbows and knuckles flew, then boots and teeth came into play. Dredd reached down for his Lawgiver, but Lenny was already moving, the other mailsack clamped in his fist.

Dredd's finger was on the gun. Soon he'd have a proper grip, then pull it from its holster, aim and Lenny would be dead. That much he knew. But still he ran, pounding the tiled floor with every ounce of strength he had in his legs. With every step he thanked Grud that he'd decided to have his vintage sneakers refurbed that week, their springy, supportive twenty-first-century soles giving him a magnificent bounce.

Dredd turned, tracking Lenny's arc with a bloodless determination. Then... then he stumbled.

Lenny didn't wait to see exactly what had happened, but it looked like the fight behind the Judge had evolved, its boundaries had bulged, and two or more combatants had accidentally knocked Dredd from his feet.

The Judge landed hard on the floor. Lenny shifted his weight, strafing to the side and then back, so that the mêlée and storm of creds came between him and his potential executioner. When he reached the door it was locked down. He slammed his fingers on the keys he'd watched the overweight security guard press every Monday for the last six weeks, and a heartbeat later Lenny was outside and running.

His Classic was less than a hundred metres away. Lenny aimed his body at it like an arrow. He ignored his only other choice (a side alley—pros: Dredd was old, so Lenny might, just might, be able to outrun him; cons: aside from the fact that Judges had bullets that could shoot round corners, there might be more of the bastards waiting for him) and made straight across the road, giving not a stomm for the cars that were now swerving to avoid him.

Still no sound of a Lawgiver blast. Had he made it?

'Lenny? What's going on, man?' Dirty Dan waved, spatula in his hand and a bewildered expression on his face.

Lenny ignored him and kept running, his pace not letting up for a heartbeat. Then his right foot landed wrong. The hundred-and-twenty-one-year-old rubber sole on his sneaker gave way. Lenny cursed the guy who did the refurb job as he hit the rockcrete slab and tumbled.

He looked behind him. Dredd was standing now, still back in the reception area, taking aim. But there was no way. Was there? What could Dredd see from this distance?

Lenny lifted himself up, kicked off his one useless shoe, and took one of the dozen steps between himself and the rest of his life. In one hand a bag of money, in the other a vintage car key dug so deep into his palm that it was drawing blood.

Something caught his eye. Movement in front of him. A single cred note, fluttering in the wind. Damn it—there was a hole in the bag! Then another note. And then two. It didn't matter; whatever he managed to get away with would do. Along with the cash from his other six heists he could retire, never rob another bank.

Another cred floated into his eyeline. This one tinged red. Lenny's legs gave way and he fell, inches from his beloved car. The last thing he was aware of was the wind whistling through the wet bullet holes in his gut, the mailbag in his hand, and the door of his 2015 Classic fading from view.

THE BODY LAY motionless on the slab.

'Huh,' said Dan. 'He was wrong about my hotties killing him.'

'Hmph,' muttered Dredd as he checked the corpse.

'Free hottie, Judge?'

'You said you know this guy?'

Dan nodded. 'Sure. That's Lenny.'

'Then you're potentially an accomplice, and your offer constitutes an attempted bribe.'

Dirty Dan dropped the hottie he had been preparing, his mouth ajar in disbelief.

'Two years, creep.'

YOU'D BETTER BE GOOD, FOR GOODNESS' SAKE...

JONATHAN GREEN

IT WAS THE night before Christmas, and a lone Lawmaster purred through the snow and darkness of the barely lit skeds of Sector 12. Weather Control was down again—an all-too-familiar state of affairs since Chaos Day—and the resultant chem-blizzard had blanketed the derelict wastezone in a jaundiced marshmallow shroud. Amongst the derelict shells of shattered habs and abandoned factory complexes, the Iso-block stood firm like a sinister rockcrete giant, stern and implacable.

After more than half a century on the streets Dredd could instinctively sense where trouble lay, and the tell-tale coil of smoke twisting lazily between the falling flakes drew his attention, bringing him off the sked and over the broken ground to a bonfire of burnt bodies.

Killing the engine, Dredd dismounted to continue his assessment of the crime scene. Four bodies in total—a street gang, as far as he could tell. He could feel the residual heat coming off the charred remains. No indication of an explosion, no obvious sign of an accelerant or source of ignition, just the lingering stink of sulphur mixed in with the acrid tang of the chem-snow. One for Tek-Div.

He studied the churned-up, half-melted slush, and the scuff of footprints—almost like marks made by hooves—and was about to activate his comm when the scene was abruptly bathed in an incandescent glare as the night was torn apart by the bestial roar of an explosion. A cloud of oily black smoke, shot through with flickering motes of burning material, rose from a ragged hole high in the side of the Iso-block.

'Control—Dredd. Explosion at Iso-Block 309, Sector 12, on the corner of 34th and Peltzer. Proceeding to the scene.'

The cremated remnants of a street gang within three hundred metres of an exploding Iso-block? Dredd didn't believe in coincidences.

DREDD DISMOUNTED AS a second Lawmaster joined him at the foot of the steps leading to the Iso-block entrance. Black smoke was still rising from the ruptured flank of the building several storeys above. He glanced at his colleague. The Judge's head was uncovered and hairless other than for dark, beetling brows and the thin strip of a contrasting grey beard on his chin. His face bore a serene, almost amused, expression, but there was a steely intensity to his gaze nonetheless. A cape flapped behind him, and items of esoteric paraphernalia adorned the uniform beneath, a

Psi-Div badge amongst the ampules of oil, crucifixes and mandrake roots.

'Ah, Dredd,' he said. 'Volk, Psi-Div.'

'What brings an Exorcist Judge here?'

'I was in the area, saw the explosion and thought it my duty to investigate further.'

'You were in the area?'

'Yes, a case of demonic possession at Raymond Tunstall. So many, many cats...'

Any further discussion was brought to an abrupt halt by the distant boom of another explosion that blew out a number of windows.

'This way,' said Dredd, Lawgiver in hand as he climbed the steps, heading inside.

Iso-Block 309 was a juvenile penitentiary, and the juve cubes were in disarray. Their badges granting them access, the two Judges were bathed in the pulsing red glow of emergency lighting and greeted by the ringing of alarms. Indicators on the screens in the block's control room suggested multiple fires breaking out throughout the facility. Worried eyes followed the arrival of Dredd and the Exorcist Judge but their anxious glances were nothing compared to the shocked expression on Judge-Warder Dee's face when he realised who it was that was paying Iso-Block 309 a visit.

Something was clearly wrong—beyond the fact that the juve cubes were on fire. Dredd could see it in the warder's eyes, the agitated glances he kept shooting Volk, and the way he couldn't keep his hands still.

'What's going on?' Dredd demanded.

'I have no idea,' Dee claimed.

'Random fires are breaking out throughout your facility and you're saying you have no idea why?'

'That's exactly what I'm saying,' Dee replied, his tone dangerously defiant.

Dredd checked the lie detector secreted in the palm of his hand. Dee was telling the truth, but pure gut instinct told him that the Judge-Warder knew more that he was prepared to admit.

'Here, let me try,' Volk said, then snapped: 'Look at me!'

Dee obeyed. His anxious eyes met the Psi-Judge's steely gaze and in that moment Volk had him. Two fingers to his temple, Volk pillaged the information he needed from the other's mind.

'He's wearing a device, a talisman, that helped him beat the birdie,' Volk explained while Dee stared back at him, mute, slack-jawed, mesmerised under the influence of the Exorcist Judge's potent powers. 'There's a name.'

'Schwarz,' the Judge-Warder mumbled. 'Pieter Schwarz.'

Another explosion rocked the control room and a fresh warning icon flashed red on the monitor wall.

'That was on the level above,' Dredd said, heading out of the room, Volk close on his heels.

Respirators in place, the two Judges emerged into a smoke-filled corridor, Dredd leading the way. Pausing at the door to an Iso-cube he peered through the narrow rectangle of reinforced, smoke-blackened glass. The obscuring clouds filling the cell shifted, momentarily revealing the carbonised remains of the juve still locked inside, the blackened body contorted in twisted agony.

'Spontaneous human combustion,' Volk said through his respirator, peering into another cell and finding another crisped corpse within.

'Could your demon have done this?' Dredd asked, studying an overcooked body in the next cube.

'No,' the Exorcist Judge replied, his voice suddenly quiet. 'Not *my* demon.'

The crackling spark of ignition drew Dredd's attention to the far end of the corridor, his bionic eyes helping him to see through the smoke and make out the horror awaiting them there.

The beast was huge, its goat-like form resembling the Ancient Greek statues of Pan housed in the Mega-City Museum of Anthropology, its hulking caprine body hunched over to fit within the corridor. The creature was covered in thick matted fur, its muscular body supported by two powerful, backward-jointed, goat-hooved legs. The demon stood at the entrance to another cell. This time the door was open, the cube's occupant already in the monster's clutches. The beast held the fear-frozen juve off the ground in one clawed hand, setting the wretched youth alight with a click of its fingers.

A pair of twisting horns scraped against a light-fitting as the monster turned its misshapen head to face them, a cruel intelligence flashing in its inhuman eyes. It ran the tip of a thick grey tongue over chisel-like teeth as an eerily high-pitched giggle rose from within its broad barrel chest.

'Naughty or nice. Slice and dice,' the demon jabbered, letting the burning body of the juve drop to the floor.

Dredd opened fire, six standard execution rounds finding their target in quick succession. Where the bullets hit, puffs of black smoke burst from the monster's body rather than blood. The goat-beast didn't even flinch or give a bleat of pain.

The demon's baleful glare fixed on Dredd. *'Naughty!'* the creature hissed, fists bunching.

'Let me,' Volk said, stepping forward, fingers to his temple.

The Exorcist Judge stretched out his other hand towards the demon and a crackling burst of visible psi-power leapt from his fingertips, zigzagging through the air to strike the monster. The beast recoiled instantly, its shaggy form bathed in ethereal fire. Giving voice to a shrill scream of pain the demon staggered back as Volk prepared another telekinetic assault.

Hissing, its inhuman eyes glowing with furious balefire, the goat-demon's body dissolved into smoke, which then vanished through a grill in the floor.

Dredd looked at Volk, who was sweating and panting for breath. Projecting the psi-lightning had clearly taken its toll. But it didn't take a psi to read the question uppermost in Dredd's mind.

'Our foe is a Krampus,' Volk explained, 'an entity that pre-dates Christianity by several centuries. During the Middle Ages it became associated with the Father Christmas myth, as an anti-Santa. Where one gives, the other takes away. Where Father Christmas rewards, the Krampus punishes. It originated in the Alpine regions of Europe.'

'I don't care where it's from,' Dredd growled, 'only how we stop it. To do that we need to know where it's gone.'

Putting his fingers to his temple once more, Volk closed his eyes, concentrating hard. 'Sub-Level 4.'

The sound of shuffling footsteps behind them alerted Dredd to Dee's presence. Drooling and clearly still dazed from Volk's psychic probing, Dee must have followed them there from the control room, robbed of the ability to make effective decisions himself.

'What happens in Sub-Level 4?' Dredd demanded.

'Tell us!' Volk commanded, turning his formidable powers on the Judge-Warder again.

Dee's face was as expressionless as a sleepwalker's. 'Experiments.'

'Experiments? Into what?' Dredd persisted.

'Modifying children's behaviour.'

'Sanctioned by Justice Department?'

The Judge-Warder couldn't lie. 'No.'

'Why am I not surprised?' Dredd growled. 'Pieter Schwarz anything to do with these experiments?'

'Yes.'

'Why him?'

'His family were émigrés from Euro-Cit.' Dee's voice was an emotionless monotone. 'They died during Chaos Day. Pieter was one of a number of children taken into the care of the state as an orphan.'

'What did these experiments of yours involve exactly?' Volk asked, exerting his will upon the Judge-Warder even more forcefully than before. Dee visibly weakened before the mental assault.

'We were trying to... alter brain patterns... alpha-wave interruption... The child was sedated... W-we...'

Overwhelmed, Dee's body went limp and he fell to the floor, unconscious. Volk allowed the tension in his own body to ease. 'It's quite clear that whatever form Dee's behaviour modification experiments took, they managed to awaken the boy's latent psychic potential.'

'Then how does the Christmas demon fit into all this?'

'Schwarz must have manifested it, whether he was conscious of the fact or not.'

'You mean he could have dreamed this demon into being?'

'Well, it answers the question what do you give a wrongly incarcerated juve who has nothing for Christmas.'

Dredd looked from the Judge-Warder, blacked out on the floor, to Volk. 'Els are out of action,' he said, 'so we're going to have to take the stairs. But first, I want you to do something for me.'

THEY FOUND THE Krampus waiting for them in a lab on Sub-Level 4, deep in the bowels of the Iso-block. Its filthy black form was in stark contrast to the sterilised, snow-white surfaces of the laboratory.

It the centre of the room, tucked up tight in a hospital bed, and hooked up to all manner of machines, was a child, barely eight years old. The only signs there were that the boy was even alive was the steady bleeping of sensory output monitors and the agitated movement of his eyes behind their closed lids.

The bestial entity was advancing on the child, taloned hands outstretched, the floor tiles charring and cracking beneath its heavy, smoking hooves. The rank animal musk of the creature merged with that of smouldering brimstone and antiseptic cleaning agents in the recycled sterile air of the lab.

Sensing the presence of the Judges, the demon turned, lips curled back from wolfish fangs, and a guttural growl escaped its throat. The monster snorted, flexing strong taloned fingers and lowering its heavily horned head. There would be no fleeing to fight another day this time.

With great pounding footfalls the beast charged. Dredd opened fire. The creature recoiled as each round hit home, viscous black ichor spurting from their points of entry rather than curls of mist as before. The beast's charge faltered and it gave voice to a braying scream of pain, its eyes blood-red with rage.

'Holy bullets, creep!' Dredd declared as the goat-demon came at him again.

As the two Judges had made their way down into the depths of the Iso-block, Dredd had emptied the standard execution rounds from his Lawgiver while Volk had dipped each of them in holy water and blessed them.

'*Naughty!*' bellowed the Krampus.

'You're on my list now, pal,' Dredd said and fired his last round.

The bullet hit the demon square in the centre of its skull, between its curling horns. The beast went down, its eyes rolling back into its head, the thick grey tongue lolling from between yellowed fangs. It slid to a halt at Dredd's feet.

Thick, sulphurous smoke began to rise from the demon's body in great billowing clouds as its unnatural flesh dissolved. Soon all that was left of the monster was a puddle of oily black sludge on the floor of the lab.

The sedated child slept on.

'ANOTHER CASE CLOSED,' said Volk as the two Judges exited the still-burning Iso-block, the comatose child carried in Dredd's arms.

'For you maybe,' Dredd replied, 'but I still need to determine how an orphan in the care of Justice Department came to be a part of Dee's experiment into behaviour modification. There will be a trail, I just need to trace it back to the source of the corruption.'

'I'll take the boy back to Psi-Div,' Volk said. 'The department could use a new recruit of his calibre. If he could summon a Krampus whilst asleep, imagine what he could accomplish fully conscious and having been trained to focus his powers.'

Dredd scowled. 'I'd rather not.'

Emergency crews had arrived and were dousing the fires. Dredd and Volk mounted their Lawmasters, the Exorcist Judge laying the child across the seat in front of him. An antique watch suspended from his uniform chimed the hour.

'Midnight,' Volk said. 'The witching hour. Happy Christmas, Dredd.'

'You sure about that?'

Gunning the throttle of his bike Dredd pulled away from the Iso-block, back into the sector's wastezones.

Volk watched as the tail-lights of Dredd's Lawmaster vanished into the night. It had stopped snowing. It looked like it wasn't going to be a white Christmas, after all. Perhaps Weather Control was back online.

The trail Dredd planned on following would go cold sooner or later, Volk was certain of it. In fact, he would make sure of it, just as he had made sure that Dee wouldn't give the game away and reveal the Exorcist Judge's part in the conspiracy either. Volk had collected the child, as planned, and in due course it would be time to put the next part of the scheme into operation.

Yes, thought Volk, as he steered his bike away from Iso-Block 309, heading into the midnight clear, this Christmas was going to be a very happy Christmas indeed...

BACK-UP REQUIRED

ROBERT MURPHY

DREDD LEANED BACK, opened up the throttle and the Lawmaster surged forward with a guttural roar. He could feel the engine straining as it gathered speed but he barely glanced at the blue-lit displays flickering with data. The tek boys could spend hours analysing the numbers but it only took Dredd one long ride to work out what minor adjustments might be needed to achieve maximum performance.

He'd driven further than he'd intended on the night patrol, lost for a moment in the intuitive process of breaking in the new bike, and the Meg-Way now skirted miles of Chaos Bug-ravaged blocks that had been all but abandoned. Resyk teams had done their best to clear the bodies but the stench of death still hung heavily in the air.

A sudden crackle of static on the comms link caught Dredd's attention.

'Say again?' he ordered, listening intently to the long hiss of feedback inside the helmet.

'Back-up required,' a faint voice replied. 'Mexler Block.'

Dredd weaved towards the edge of the Meg-Way and sped down the ramp. He peered up at the vast blocks, scanning the names emblazoned on the sides.

Something about the request made him uneasy. Mexler was a limbo block, yet to be classified fit for rehabitation and stranded in a sector where Justice Department had been unable to restore an official presence. What would a lone street Judge be doing out there? He reached instinctively for the Lawgiver in its holster, resting a gloved hand on the grip.

'Identify yourself,' he ordered.

For a moment there was only the steady rumble of rockcrete under the wheels of the bike. Then a barely audible voice emerged from the static.

'Carfax.'

Dredd's eyes narrowed. *Carfax*. The name had a familiar but unhappy ring to it yet he couldn't quite recall why.

The towering shape of Mexler loomed up ahead, the few illuminated letters on its side that still worked casting a weak red glow. He swerved off the main road and slowed down as he approached the entrance to the block, slipping his Lawgiver out of its holster. He scanned the building, noting the tiny handful of upper-level apartments that had lights on, their residents too weak or too stubborn to seek refuge elsewhere.

The plaza in front of the block was deserted and strewn with rubbish, the ground-level arcade of fast-food outlets and cred-loan stores haphazardly boarded up. On the far side of the plaza the west stand of the Mex Packers stadium rose fifty storeys high, the hazard tape fluttering between the ground-level arches the only hint of the unspeakable horrors that had occurred inside.

Dredd eased the Lawmaster through the detritus, its headlights picking out munce wrappers mingled with blood-stained rags, a cloud of purple flies rising lazily off a sticky crimson patch on the ground.

Too recent for a Bug casualty, Dredd thought.

Too fresh.

He whipped the Lawgiver up into a firing position before he even heard the whine of the bullet that shot past his helmet and exploded in a spray of rockcrete chips behind him.

Dredd fired a single shot back in the direction of the shooter and gunned the engine, spinning the rear wheel in a wide arc. He heard another blast of gunfire from the arches under the stadium and then the distinctive boom of a Lawgiver in response. He caught a glimpse of Justice Department colours in the muzzle flash of the friendly weapon and he sped towards it, the tyres of the bike churning up clouds of acrid black smoke.

'Carfax, do you copy?' Dredd shouted over the roar of the engine.

'I'm inside,' a voice replied on the comms link. 'Residents' entrance. Will cover you.'

Two powerful shots rang out from within the entrance hall followed by the thud of each bullet punching through distant walls. Dredd veered towards the entrance as the crackle of small-arms fire erupted around him, bullets ringing as they clipped the frame of the bike. Then he heard the split-second explosive ignition of a rocket being fired, whipping his head round in time to see the smoke trail from the warhead as it whooshed out of the shadows.

He gripped the right brake lever and nudged the bike into a slide, the warhead skimming past in a shimmering wave of heat and smoke. The Lawmaster bucked and screamed as Dredd tried to control the momentum of the skid, his kneepad scraping the ground as he guided it towards the entrance to the block. The warhead shattered the glass front of an empty pet-piercing salon and detonated with a boom that reverberated in his chest. Debris rained down on him as he brought the bike to a shuddering halt on its side.

He hauled himself out from under the bike and ducked into the entrance hall, his ears still ringing from the sound of the explosion. The floor was strewn with things the looters had discarded, a pathetic sprawl of clothes, broken tech and personal trinkets. Something fragile crunched under Dredd's boot as he strode towards the nearest pillar, one of a dozen that anchored the huge block to the ground, and propped against it he found the lone, injured Judge.

'Armour-piercing rounds?' he grunted.

'All I've got left,' the Judge replied, extending a gauntleted hand. Dredd gave it a cursory shake, unable to suppress a grimace of disapproval as he glimpsed scuffed boots and greying hair that had to be an inch over regulation inside a battered helmet.

He remembered Carfax now.

Their paths had crossed just once before, during one of the Department's periodic drives to explore alternative methods of administering the Law. Carfax had advocated a softer approach, urging Judges to get to know the cits in their sector and make their presence felt in a less intimidating way.

'What happened?' Dredd asked bluntly.

'Came across suspects with intent to loot,' Carfax replied, his breathing laboured. 'Thought they were juves looking to boost vidscreens for a quick cred. Chose to engage them verbally.'

Dredd stared at him in silence for a moment. 'Why?'

'I recognised one of them,' Carfax replied, holding his gaze. 'This was my patch before the Bug. Kid had lost his folks in a Meg-Way smash.'

Dredd rubbed his chin. Start empathising with every cit with a sob story and you get block soft, he thought, your ability to judge dispassionately compromised forever.

'We were doing good work here, Dredd,' Carfax protested. 'Getting through to them.' He spat on the ground, flecks of red foam lingering on his lips. 'When I got up close I could see they weren't local. Lot of ink from rival blocks.' He winced as he shifted his weight against the pillar. 'They were on me in seconds. Didn't even see the blade. But I knew enough to hit full auto and fight my way to cover.'

Dredd glanced at the smear of blood on the pillar where Carfax had been leaning. 'So what are we dealing with?'

'Seven, eight perps. My guess, a more sophisticated group with richer pickings in mind. Probably using local knowledge to pinpoint zziz labs that have been left standing empty.'

'The creep you recognised?'

Carfax stared at Dredd for a moment, his expression changing from defiance to weariness. 'His name is Rikki.'

A sudden burst of gunfire strafed the ceiling, showering them with dust. Carfax flinched and pressed himself closer to the pillar. Dredd could hear the crunch of rapid footsteps as the gang slipped out of the shadows of the stadium and advanced towards the block.

'Better ammo up,' he warned, tossing a spare clip from his belt to the wounded Judge.

'They need access to the upper levels,' Carfax explained through gritted teeth. 'There was a lab on seven.'

A starburst of white light flared in his eyes and his stomach churned. He felt his limbs go weak and then Dredd was beside him, hauling him back to his feet.

'Control, need a med-wagon at Mexler,' Dredd ordered.

'Gonna be a wait on that,' a voice replied on the comms link.

'Might as well make it a meat-wagon by the time it gets here,' Carfax grimaced.

'Odds are against us as it stands,' Dredd agreed. 'They're going to fan out, look to hit us from all sides. Hi-Ex might take some out of the equation, a ricochet might take one behind cover...'

'That's assuming they haven't already lit the whole place up with the heavy stuff,' Carfax interjected.

Dredd glanced out at the plaza. He could see figures shifting in the shadows, more now. Two perps with bright blue hair were manhandling a long metal barrel into position on a tripod.

The new Lawmaster, lying flat on its side by the entrance, gleamed in the neon red glow of the giant Mexler sign.

'Got to draw them in closer,' Dredd murmured. 'Offer them a target.' He gave his Lawgiver a cursory check, brought the weapon up into a firing position and prepared to step out into the hallway. Then he felt something hold him back.

'Wait,' Carfax urged, his bloody fingers clenched tightly around Dredd's arm. 'Let me talk to him.'

Dredd turned slowly to face him, then offered a barely perceptible nod. Carfax forced himself into a standing position, his left hand cradling his wounded side.

'Rikki!' he shouted. 'I'm not going to lie to you—I'm in bad shape. Blood's pourin' outta me like munce soup. Only hope is a med-wagon, 'cept they probably got a dozen eldsters to defrib before they can make it out to this stommhole.'

Out on the plaza somebody snickered. Dredd could see them start to break cover, the street fighters among them making quick, zig-zag runs, their bodies hunched over.

'Even if we wanted to fight, we ain't got the metal,' Carfax drawled. 'I feel like that kid who got jumped by the Vargas Blockers. What was his name? Six Finger?'

Dredd watched them sliding forward on their bellies and elbows, converging on the entrance. They were like rad-rats swarming on fresh carrion, emboldened by the pain in Carfax's voice. The perps with the mounted machine-gun hauled it brazenly forward.

'Six Digit,' a voice called out, closer than he'd expected.

'That's it.' Carfax chuckled, then gagged and spat a bloody wad onto the floor. 'Remember when his mama called us in? Everyone standing around that big red mess thinking, *"You sure it's him?"'*

Dredd tapped the side of his helmet. 'Lawmaster to voice control,' he said softly and a blue panel began to glow beneath the damaged windscreen.

'Why did you come out here, Carfax?' he asked.

Carfax slid the ammo clip into his weapon, a smile of resignation crossing his lips. 'Could ask you the same thing,' he replied. 'Wanted to see if there was anything left to believe in.'

They heard the crunch of broken glass just outside the entrance.

'Bike cannon, full auto!' Dredd roared and the plaza erupted in a fury of deafening gunfire and piercing screams.

Then Dredd strode out through the smoke and started to shoot.

THE MECHANIC WAS waiting for him in the vehicle bay, a mug of steaming synthi-caff in one hand. Dredd cruised to a halt, flipped the kickstand out with the heel of his boot and dismounted.

'All yours,' he grunted. 'Rear wheel's out of balance. Fuel injection needs tuning.'

The mechanic slowly surveyed the Lawmaster with its cracked windshield and dented bodywork, running a thumb along the jagged groove that marked the path of a bullet.

'Shoot your way out of trouble?' he asked gruffly, bending down to study the scorch marks around the cannon barrels.

'Talked our way out,' Dredd said over his shoulder as he walked away.

The mechanic shook his head, grabbed the bike by the handlebars and heaved it towards the workshop.

A CELEBRATION

MICHAEL CARROLL

As HE STRODE through the Grand Hall of Justice, Dredd squared his shoulders and mentally prepared himself. His presence at the gathering wasn't required, but Judge Morphy had told him that it was *expected*. 'Sometimes it's important to remind the cits that Judges are people too.'

The sounds of casual laughter grew as Dredd neared the annex. He activated his helmet radio. 'Dredd here. Anything for me, Control?'

'Nothing pressing, Dredd. Schedule has you down for twenty at the post-grad celebration.' A slight pause. '*Your* post-grad celebration. Your brother and most of your yearmates are already there.'

'Acknowledged, Control.'

Morphy was waiting for him at the door to the mid-sized room. 'Some of these folks haven't seen their kids much in the past fifteen years and might never see them again, Joe.

So just shake a few hands. If you can't be friendly, at least be *polite*. Understood?'

Dredd nodded. On the far side of the room, directly beneath the 'Class of 2079' banner, his brother Rico chatted with Judge Gibson and two eldsters.

Gibson saw him and beckoned him over. 'Joe, meet my mom and dad.'

Mrs Gibson looked from Dredd to Rico and back. 'Oh, you're twins!'

'Clones,' Dredd corrected.

Gibson's father said, 'Our boy here says you two are top of the class. Highest scores ever, is that right?'

'That's right, sir,' Rico said. 'Not that your own son is a slouch.' He playfully punched Judge Gibson in the arm. 'He was right behind us in the rankings.'

Gibson nodded. 'Yeah, there's no shame losing the top spot to *these* guys.' He held up his left hand, index finger and thumb less than a centimetre apart. 'It was *this* close.'

'Incorrect,' Dredd said. 'You ranked twenty-eighth overall.' The pause that followed was filled with Gibson gritting his teeth, Rico rolling his eyes, and Gibson's parents looking away.

Rico leaned closer to Dredd and muttered, 'Nice. Go bother someone else, Little Joe.'

Dredd considered the situation as he turned away. What was the point of Gibson lying to his parents? It was obvious that they were already proud of him.

Nearby, Judge Ellard was talking to an elderly woman. Ellard glanced at Dredd and gave him a nod. 'Joe, this is my grandmother. It's a double celebration—Gramma's seventy-four years old *today*.'

Dredd didn't quite know what to do with that. People get older if they don't die. That wasn't exactly new information.

Ellard prompted, 'It's customary to wish her a happy birthday.'

The old woman said, 'You should take off your helmet, you know. Otherwise when you go back outside you won't feel the benefit.'

'Helmet's for protection, not warmth,' Dredd said. 'Removing it is an unnecessary risk.'

'I remember when there were *real* police officers,' the woman said. 'Nothing wrong with Judges, but back then, there wasn't all this *instant justice* you lot are so proud of. We had proper judges and lawyers and *trials*. No matter what you did, you had a chance of getting away with it.'

'Times have changed,' Dredd said, 'and that's *why*.'

'I mean, back in the forties my friend Hester Zuppardi killed her husband with rat-poison and everyone *knew* she did it, but she got away with it because she could afford the best lawyers.'

Dredd stared down at her. 'There's no statute of limitations on *murder*, citizen. Failure to report makes you an accessory after the fact.' He unclipped a set of handcuffs from his utility belt.

Ellard pulled Dredd aside. 'Joe, Gramma's been telling that story for *years*—it never happened. I checked. Zuppardi's husband died of a sudden aneurysm. There were *rumours* that he was poisoned, but no evidence. It never even went to trial. Gramma's just embellishing the story to make her own life seem more interesting. Old people *do* that, sometimes.'

'Lying to a Judge. Six months.'

A deep voice from behind Dredd said, 'Let it go, Joe.' He turned to see Judge Morphy wearing that fixed stare he'd always used to keep the cadets in line.

'She broke the law,' Dredd said. 'We don't make exceptions for family members.'

'But we *are* expected to demonstrate compassion.'

Dredd nodded. 'Understood.' He turned back to Ellard's grandmother. 'You're on a *warning*, citizen. Any more unsubstantiated reports of a crime, you'll do time in the cubes. Don't care *how* old you are.'

He started to move toward the door, then looked back at Ellard's now-trembling grandmother. 'Happy birthday, citizen,' Dredd said. Then added, 'Stay out of trouble.'

Aware that everyone in the room—Judges and citizens alike—was now staring at him, Dredd realised that something more was required. 'That goes for *all* of you.'

He strode out of the room, satisfied that he'd done his part. 'Control. Dredd here. Back on duty. What have you got for me?'

THE DINNER PARTY

DAVID BAILLIE

'I'LL PUSH THIS knife through his throat if you don't get me a hovcopter,' the Rev screamed through the panic-room intercom. 'Guaranteed safe passage!'

'Damn it,' Rhodes said, kicking the door. 'Dredd's gonna kill us!'

'Kill *you*, maybe,' Farnby adjusted her helmet and smiled. 'I'm not the one that can't kick down a drokking door.'

LESS THAN AN hour ago it had been going perfectly. All three members of the Sector 31 D.S.C. arrived on time and cooed, as expected, at Sammy Mallet's luxurious penthouse apartment.

'Is this one of those with the fancy Fast Exit Fire Escape system?' Lavazzatori asked.

'Fast Exit?' Desdimona asked. He seemed a lot less sure

of himself than the other two. Or maybe just less full of stomm.

'Sure,' Sammy said, escorting them out onto his balcony, 'I'd go down it every morning, but the block Judge said he'd bust anyone using it for non-emergency purposes.'

'It's like a slide from an aqua funpark.' Lavazzatori stroked the curve of the carbon-fibre chute. 'I've read the specs. It spirals around the inside wall of the block. Carries you and your family safely to the ground floor in about thirty seconds. State of the art. And pricey, too.'

'Yes,' the Rev said, straightening out his vestments, 'you seem to have done rather well for yourself, Mr Mallet. I look forward to hearing your story.'

The robo-servant buzzed pleasingly as it carefully placed the entrées before each guest.

'Why don't we begin in the time-honoured D.S.C. way?' Sammy Mallet said as he turned to his left and offered Harry Lavazzatori an upturned palm. 'Visitors first.'

Lavazzatori was a thick-set man in a suit that he probably figured everyone thought was more expensive than it was. His hair was scraped back off his forehead, and it gleamed even in these gentle lights.

'Where to begin?' he said, cramming a lemon and kale munce cube into his mouth. 'I avoided the Mob growing up, didn't want no part of it—even though I got a couple of uncles could have set me up very nicely, you know? I always wanted to succeed under my own steam. Be my own man. So instead I went into construction and tried my best to stay clean. No matter how tough that is in this city.'

'Here comes the twist,' the Rev announced with glee as he wiped the munce grease from his plate with a fat thumb and then sucked on it.

'But when reality comes calling, you can't just hide behind the door and pretend you're not in. A new block I was building was going way over budget. The accountants said we were gonna have to pull the plug. So I... cut some corners. One of my suppliers had a bunch of cheap rockcrete. Now, I knew it maybe wasn't as safe as it should be. I knew the law would frown on it if they ever found out... But I had to choose between that, or all the guys I had working for me being out on the street. They had families to feed and bills to pay, you know?

'In the end it didn't make no difference, anyhow. Statue of Justice toppled, took down my whole block with it a week before our completion date. Of course, that didn't stop Dredd from sniffing around.'

At the mention of that name Sammy Mallet's eyebrows lifted. 'Dredd?'

'Sure,' the Rev said, his voice booming out, 'no matter what we tell our wives and mistresses, this ain't the Day of Chaos Survivor's Club.' He drummed his fat digits on the table percussively, like dramatic punctuation. 'Apart from anything else D.O.C.S.C. is too cumbersome an acronym!'

Lavazzatori dabbed his mouth with a napkin and continued. 'I don't need to tell you guys, but the day Dredd showed up was the most terrifying of my life. He just stood there in my office like he was made of stone, saying as little as possible, waiting for me to trip myself up. He knew something was off, but he couldn't prove nothing. Luckily, my accountant got snuffed by the Chaos Bug so we managed to pin it all on him. What can I say? I put on a good innocent face when I need to. Probably genetic!'

Sammy laughed. 'That's some tale.' He snapped his fingers and the little robot butler reappeared, cleared away the plates and simultaneously produced the next course from its cylindrical torso.

'Is this *real* duck?' Desdimona asked. Sammy smiled and nodded, and you could tell he was pleased that they were all impressed.

'The Chaos Bug saved my skin too,' Desmond Desdimona said, inhaling the exquisite aroma of his meal. 'Dredd was pretty preoccupied for months afterwards. He delegated *my* case onto a younger Judge, who just kinda... gave up, I suppose!' Desdimona took a bite of the duck and sighed. 'He was just a kid, this other Judge. Believed everything I said. Which was just as well, since I maintain that I was, and indeed am, innocent.'

'Come now,' the Rev said, his mouth full of succulent dark meat. 'Pull the other one, it has insurance claims on it.'

'That's my business,' Desdimona said. 'Insurance. Life insurance, mostly. My parent company was holding a promotional sale—I would have been a fool not to take advantage. And the timing was just, well...'

'He knocked down his wife,' the Rev said as he guzzled down another glass of wine, 'a couple of days after pumping up her premiums. He's been telling us ever since that it was an accident.'

'It *was*!' Desdimona's voice became shrill. Then his features softened. 'Although... I admit that my vision was maybe a little impaired by the synthi-whisky I'd been drinking that afternoon. You know, the good stuff they don't let 'em import from Cal-Hab.' A cold chuckle filled the room.

'You'll have to give me the name of your synthi-Scotch guy!' Mallet said.

Desdimona, more than happy to oblige, scribbled a name on a slip of paper and passed it across the table. 'Tell him I sent you.'

'So what's *your* story, Reverend?'

The Rev put down his glass, of course now empty, and offered Sammy a toothy grin. 'I've been a minister at the Undivided Church of Grud now for coming on thirty-four years. I've seen it all—The Apocalypse War, Necropolis, Judgement Day. During every one of those I counselled my flock through the horrors, I was there for them in their time of need, I mended each and every one of their various crises of faith. My job description, if you will, is to keep as many of the faithful as *faithful* as possible, regardless of what's happening in the world.'

'The Undivided Church, unless you ain't heard of them,' Lavazzatori piped up, 'only opens its doors to those with enough creds to be truly worthy of Grud's love.'

'We're all sinners, my child,' the Rev said, 'but some are certainly of a higher net worth than the others.

'At the end of every service I perform there is a collection, a silver bowl passed from parishioner to parishioner, into which they are invited to drop as many creds as they can afford to part with. I then deliver that money to the armed security van that shows up at my church once a week, and in return I receive a salary that, while healthy, is perhaps unrepresentative of my effort.

'What the Undivided Church of Grud *doesn't* know is I figured out very early on in my ministry that no one seemed to notice if I retained a little for myself from that silver bowl. To help with my numerous... expenses, you understand.'

'How come they never noticed?'

The Rev laughed, his jowls wobbling as he shook his head. 'The Church's cash turnover is gargantuan. Why would they be concerned about the minor indiscretions of a single place of worship? That was until one of my flock began to wonder how I could afford a bigger car than him, better suits than him. I'm sure you can see where this is going.'

Everyone around the table nodded as the butler tidied away the plates and refilled glasses.

'Edward Seasalt, a diminutive man, with a bulbous head and a ravishing wife. He let me know in no uncertain terms that unless I shared some of my spoils with him he would go straight to Church top brass and expose me.'

'What did you do?' Sammy asked, his eyes wide with anticipation.

At that moment the robotic waiter sputtered and beeped, making the Rev start. He looked at the droid for a moment and something about its spasm seemed to sober him up.

'Seasalt. What did you do with him?' Sammy asked again.

'Why nothing,' the Rev said, folding his napkin and placing it on the table.

'Nothing?'

'That's not what what you said last—' Desdimona began, then gasped and grabbed his shin.

'He simply disappeared,' the Rev said. 'Probably the Chaos Bug thing, as you've all mentioned. Now what about dessert and then we can get to *your* story, Mr Mallet. I can't wait to hear what you have to say for yourself.'

Desserts appeared and they were unsurprisingly decadent. The sudden shift in tone had escaped none of them, though, and the conversation had all but evaporated.

'So,' said the Rev, 'are you on your own up here? Only a single member of the Sector 77 D.S.C.?'

'We're not so lucky on this side of the city,' Mallet replied. 'Even after recent events, I'm the only guy I know who managed to give Dredd the slip. It's why I'm so keen to meet others!'

'Indeed,' said the Rev, leaving a long enough silence that Mallet had no option but to start talking.

'I suppose you could say that I'm the most unequivocal criminal here. You guys all have stories, reasons for what you did. I just wanted creds—and I wanted them fast. I tried a few rackets before I found my forte. Counterfeit tech—no money in it. Smuggling—too risky. Robbery— only a fool would even attempt that these days, right?'

The members of the Sector 31 D.S.C. all regarded him in complete silence.

'So I became a blackmailer. It was a lot easier than I

thought it would be, actually. My first mark was a politician. I hung around the red-light district, and followed the guy with the sharpest suit. Figured out who he was and then buzzed him a message. If he wanted his wife to remain unaware of his extracurriculars then it'd cost him.

'I picked up a few gigs that way before getting bored. Some of these perverts weren't as scared of their wives as I'd hoped. So I shifted up a gear. I called a hitguy, told him I had a job for him. I met him at the back of a quiet hottie bar, where no one was listening, and instead I offered him heaps of creds if he'd give me his client list.'

'Jovis!' Lavazzatori exclaimed. 'And did he?'

'No,' Mallet said. 'And neither did the next hitman I called. But the third guy did. And so it started. People are *terrified* of the Judges. That's where the big money is. As soon as word was on the street that I was in the market for info, I couldn't move for tips and targets. I had cash flow like you wouldn't believe. And it was easy work; all I had to do was promise to keep my mouth shut.'

The Rev's eyes narrowed. 'I see.'

'I don't,' Desdimona said. 'What's going on?'

The Rev stood up, his chair tumbling behind him. 'The little robot has a microphone in it. I heard it broadcast some feedback earlier. Mallet's looking for new marks. This is a drokking scam.'

Lavazzatori cracked his knuckles. 'Bastard! You reckon you can pull this stunt on us and walk outta here in one piece, you got another think coming!'

The Rev picked up the robot and tried to prise it open.

'You have this all wrong,' Mallet said, his voice wavering. 'I'm not trying to blackmail you.'

The Rev bounced the robot against the wall, but it stayed resolutely intact.

'Business started grinding to a halt after Chaos Day. No one really cared about keeping secrets after they'd watched their neighbours and families die screaming. People re-prioritised. I thought it was gonna be a temporary thing but it's amazing what proximity to so much death and destruction does to people.'

'I don't care! Whatever your story is—' the Rev's face was now puce—'you can shove it up your—'

But Sammy Mallet continued. 'My apartment was already wired for sound. Vid-cams in every corner and behind every mirror. It made sense. Dredd was chasing down one of my targets for fraud, and wondered where the hole in his company finances came from. Where the money had gone. A hell of a lot of money. It didn't take him long to track me down.'

Lavazzatori stood up too. 'Dredd?'

And that's when Rhodes kicked down the door.

Or tried to.

He howled in pain as his knee gave way, the door swinging half-open on its hinges.

'What the drokk are you doing, Rhodes?' screamed Farnby as she tried to push past his crumpled body. 'Get out of my way!'

Inside the room, panic erupted. 'You stomm-guzzler,' the Rev bellowed. 'You ratted us out!'

'It's my Judge!' screamed Desdimona, his voice a falsetto.

'That's the kid I gave the slip! He's after me! What do we do? What do we *do*?'

Lavazzatori ran for the balcony. 'I know what I'm doing! Fast Exit, right?'

Desdimona raced after him, and before anyone could say anything else, the safety cover had been ripped off the fire-exit chute and both men had disappeared.

The Rev followed, but when he got there he looked glumly down into the entrance to the tube and frowned.

'You'll get stuck halfway down,' Mallet said, his voice full of defeat. 'If you make it that far. Just give up, man. You're not getting away from them.'

'Maybe not,' said the Rev as he slid a wicked-looking knife out from inside his belt. The blade glinted. 'But neither are you.'

'DAMN IT,' RHODES said when they finally got into the apartment. 'He's gone.'

'That guy that knew you? What's the story?' Farnby prowled through the living room, Lawgiver poised.

'Desmond Desdimona, forty-four-year-old insurance salesman who, six months ago, killed his wife. Due to his line of work he knew exactly how to hide the evidence. Got the car cleaned and fixed up before even Dredd got to see it. It was my first rookie case and I've been looking forward to nailing him since—'

'Yeah, yeah,' Farnby said. 'Less of the soliloquies and more judging and you'll have half a chance of catching your perp.'

'Fewer,' an electronic voice came from somewhere within the apartment.

'Huh?' Farnby spun around, trying to locate the speaker.

'Fewer soliloquies. Not less.'

Rhodes found it first, tapped the door with the knuckle of his gauntlet. 'Panic room.'

'You better believe it,' the voice replied. 'I got your rat in here, and a knife to his throat. Now, boy, let's you and I talk about getting me a hovchopper!'

DESMOND DESDIMONA STIFLED a howl as he hurtled down the twisting tube. It wasn't exactly built for comfort, and it didn't help that Lavazzatori's feet kept hitting him on the head. 'Will you stop that?'

'Not my fault. You shoulda let me go first!' Lavazzatori's final syllable gushed out of him as he slammed onto solid pedway. He gasped, his eyes jammed shut as he writhed on the ground. 'Jovis! You'd think they'd at least put something soft down. My back!'

'Uh... Harry?' Desdimona's voice whined.

Lavazzatori opened his eyes and saw Dredd. Even closer, the barrel of his Lawgiver.

'Yeah,' Dredd said, 'figured they might mess this one up.'

DREDD RADIOED CONTROL, alerting them to the two perps he'd cuffed to the holding post at the foot of the block, and rode the speedy elevator up to the 333nd floor.

While it was frustrating having to bring so many rookie Judges up to speed so quickly, Chaos Day hadn't left them with any alternative. Simulated training exercises were now a luxury the Justice Department could no longer afford, and controlled environment operations such as this one were the order of the day. He glanced at the elevator info screen. Barely floor 200. He wondered if he'd always been this impatient.

'WHAT ARE WE going to do?' Rhodes stuttered.

'What indeed,' Dredd remarked as he stepped over the threshold, his eyes fixed on the panic-room door.

Rhodes adopted something akin to composure. 'We have to evaluate how important the asset is. Mallet...'

Dredd nodded. 'Go on.'

'Well... This sting has been running for three weeks, it's netted forty-three perps so far, all of whom claim to have gotten one over on you, sir. There can't be many more left—and even if there is, the other chapters of this D.S.C. are bound to start thinking something's fishy.'

'Agreed.'

'We don't have much to lose by storming the room,' Rhodes said hesitantly.

'I can hear you, you know,' the Rev called out.

'You left the intercom on?' Farnby asked, incredulous.

Rhodes' head fell.

'Farnby—plant a charge,' Dredd ordered as he took the regulation five steps back. 'Should be enough to take down those doors.'

'I'll kill him, I swear!' the Rev's crackled voice rang out.

Farnby hit the timer, and three high-pitched beeps later the room was filled with dust and debris. The doors of the panic room landed with a clatter.

'I didn't touch him,' the Rev called out, his face wet with blood from the blast, his hands raised above his head.

Sammy Mallet coughed. 'He was gonna, though! The knife was right at my throat! That's attempted murder! And what's with blowing up the room? My life doesn't matter any more?'

Dredd waved his hand to clear the air. 'I told you when we started this, Mallet—too many people died because of your scams.' He lifted his Lawgiver and put a bullet in Mallet's forehead. 'It was only ever a *suspended* death sentence.'

The Rev let out a whimper then, and peered through the swirling dust. 'I'm sorry, I'm sorry—I only ever took a few creds. It's no big deal!'

'We might not have got you to confess to Seasalt's murder, but I *know* it was you. Luckily we have an opening in our Simulated Training Exercises programme. Congratulations, you start today.'

Dredd picked up the Rev's knife and handed it to Farnby. 'Good work.'

He turned then and glared at Rhodes. 'Call Control, request a new door for the apartment and a clean-up crew. Set up the next D.S.C. sting. Sector 77 chapter's next.'

Dredd walked away, and Rhodes let out a breath he wasn't even aware he'd been holding on to. Dredd stopped, looked at the door.

'And this time, get it right.'

HUNTING WITH MISSILES

KARL STOCK

CLAY ENJOYS IT when they don't see it coming until the bitter end. That moment when their face FILLS the frame in the drone camera, the final terrified flinch. Death is rocketing towards you and there's nothing you can do, you poor bastard. Life has outrun you. A pinboard collage of those faces hangs above his desk, his most satisfying kills. Men, women, young, old... they're all fair game.

'That's us here, ya bam,' rasps Erchie, his faithful ghillie droid, turning off the truck's engine. Erchie's an import from the rich game country of CalHab. Clay isn't a technician. He leaves the positioning of the mobile missile battery to the robot, which absolves him of all the boring calculations and lets him get on with remote-flying the missiles. Somewhere in the wastelands is always a safe bet. Had PSU still been on its feet, this game would be nigh-on impossible.

'I shall take my position,' Clay mutters to himself,

climbing from the passenger side of the truck cab into the concealed snug from which he flies his missiles.

'Gaun yersel',' replies the deliciously guttural henchdroid, 'uh've goat aw day.' So brutishly authentic, programmed with the language of violence. It stirs his loins to hear such pure, dangerous efficiency.

Of course, there are purist Hunters Clubbers out there who think assassinating targets with Jericho SP6 cruise missiles is overkill. Some are lobbying to have him thrown out. *'But you can knock out a whole city block if you position them right!'* they whine at every meeting. *'What sort of test is it? A bullet or a las-beam, that's all you need. Whites of the eyes or it doesn't count!'*

These cretins talk about meeting their victims' gaze, but they've never seen the faces he has right at the end. Yes, it's a simple job to take out a lone target with an intercontinental ballistic missile if you're willing to dish out some collateral damage. But what greater craft can there be than to wipe out a single person in the heart of a city of fifty million and leave everyone around them unscathed?

Besides, not many people have the family wealth or the Grudgiven Ivy League brilliance to import multiple items of heavy ordnance from South Am on a regular basis and keep them hidden until they're needed. For Clay Bossman III, his method is a status symbol as much as a signature technique. Each missiles costs one and three quarter mill. The mobile battery is Robot War guerrilla surplus, a fully reconditioned classic Foord hovertruck with six retractable launchers hidden in the rear. A former Space Marine in

Sector 44 agreed to retool the launchers for contemporary ordnance, all questions answered in cold cash.

It's a beautifully bespoke machine of death. They're all jealous of him, pure and simple. The politics of envy.

Butterflies of excitement well in Clay's stomach. He's blown people out of the cab of a cruising mopad and obliterated them from a deserted sked while they've been on an evening run, but today will see him attempt his first truly fast-moving target. His remote drone cameras have reached their target high above Aubrey Plaza Plaza, and right on schedule his prey emerges.

Every morning at a quarter to ten, Cannula Drip takes to the skies for a training flight, showing off some of the skills that have made her Mega-City's foremost rhythmic batgliding display artist. She lives in a lux-apt high above the floor of the city, but word of her flights has spread all the way to City Bottom. Morning walks to the block mart or the benefit line are timed to include detours through viewing galleries, the better to let Drip's aerial grace and precision brighten the day of all who see her.

'She's there!' exclaims Clay, rolling the joystick array on the arm of his bucket seat into position and snapping down the encephalovisor. He prefers to steer with a combination of mental and physical ability.

'You gonnae talk 'er doon or whit? Shoot then, ya fanny.'

The crumbling blocks and shot-down flyovers of the wastelands sear past at a hundred kilometres per hour, wretched people just visible scavenging amidst the ruins. On occasion they make for good target practice, but not when a genuine prize is in sight. Ahead rise the grey and rust-brown spires of the Mega-City, still breathing. Still alive. This is where his skill as a rocketeer comes in. You don't just want to hit your target with the missile you're flying, you want to miss everything else. Thickly congested air: hov-buses, overskeds, flyovers, flyunders, skysurfers. Keep them safe. To destroy any one of them would be a betrayal of his talent.

He meets Cannula Drip in freefall through Le Grande Canyon, the darkened hundred-foot gap between a boulevard of blocks so tightly packed for the best part of a mile that updraft howls through it like a storm. Batgliders and skysurfers know it well. Hit the air just right, kill the power and you can defy gravity for short but wondrous seconds.

It's perfect for Clay. A clear view. No one else around, target slowed almost to a stop, bouncing on the air currents. He'll take that. A kill is a kill is...

Gone.

At the moment of impact. Vanished.

But where...?

A drone-cam picks her up. Behind the missile Drip falls away at speed, retracted wings snatching her from him. She raises her arms and the foils snap out once more – and something else.

'Jetpack!' hisses Clay.

'She's a f—in' cheat,' barks Erchie, censor circuit cutting out the profanity. If there's anything that spoils killing people it's bad language, Clay believes.

He taps his thumb once, twice, three more times, each time the launcher alongside him barking out as another missile is fired. There's no room to turn Tube One in the Canyon and Drip is already doubling back at speed. Reinforcements are required.

The ambush occurs at the last minute, as Tube One leaves the Canyon. He catches a single glimpse, just before the feed goes dead: Judge on the walkway, Lawgiver raised, muzzle flash reporting... and the line is cut.

One missile gone. Time is of the essence now.

'That's the polis come,' grates Erchie. 'Only a shite-fer-brains sticks aroond noo.'

He ignores the robot. Cannula Drip is the best in the world at what she does, and he demands the right to kill her. He's worked rather hard to get to this stage in his career, quite frankly.

Tubes Two and Three engage her amidst the traffic. She's trying to gain altitude, to put some distance between herself and the grids of cars below. That isn't what Clay would do. He would hide in the traffic, put others in the way, see if they might take a rocket for him. Drip has flown well, but with her act of feeble altruism Clay knows she'll be better off dead.

The H-Wagon blindsides him just before he reaches cruising altitude, the laser taking out Three instantly. But Two soars free, and as it clears the hovercar lanes Clay hammers down on the throttle. Open up, burn that fuel, faster than any jetpack. He's so close he can see the creases on her glider's leathers...

Too late. Lased from behind by the H-Wagon. The drone eye watches as Drip wheels away from the debris, heading for cruising altitude...

'Ur ye stupit? Let's get oot ay here!'

'Not yet.' Drip circles gracefully on the current, jetpack shutting off, settling into an angled descent back around Plaza, when...

BOOM!

Number Four flies out from behind the hov-bus that was sheltering it. Perfect impact, dead centre. Limbs sprayed here and there.

'*Yes!*' Clay punches the roof with delight. 'We did it!' It's the kill which puts him over Fat 'John' Fontana's record of forty-three Assassinations by Heavy Ordnance and one closer to Arnie Drzzk's total of fifty-six Kills by Remote Means Only. The specialist records held by true artists of the game.

'Mibbes no,' butts in Erchie with a surly bleep. 'Look.'

He looks. The drone is in descent, capturing Drip's remains for later viewing enjoyment as they flap and plummet to the ground. The morning light twinkles on metallic surfaces. His mouth curls, first in anger that someone could take his achievement from him, and then dawning fear.

'Robot.'

The voice cracks like sledgehammer on stone all around the Foord. 'You in there. This is Justice Department. You've had your fun, now stand down.'

Judge Dredd. Unmistakeable. It's a trap.

'Aww balls,' clanks Erchie, leaning forward to observe something above them through the windshield. 'H-Wagons. Ye've been decoyed. They must've had a trace on yir signal.'

Clay can hear engines around them. How many he doesn't know.

'F— this. Yir on yir own.' The robot slumps forward, reformatting to protect its complicity in dozens of murders.

The Club. It's the Club, he knows it. Hoggurt, the old fool: he's grassed. Sniper's rifles and strangulations, a bitter old relic of the past.

'You hear me? Step outside or suffer the consequences, creep. We're due some words with you.'

The record. It's all gone now but the record. Two missiles left. He can still beat Fontana at least, they'll remember him for that. He pulls the joystick and the battery lurches round...

'Suit yourself. Vape it.'

...and he catches sight of his face reflected in the control screen, wearing a terrified flinch he knows so well...

MIRACLE ON 34TH AND PELTZER

JONATHAN GREEN

'TWAS THE NIGHT before Christmas, and all through Mega-City One, the perps were stirring, especially in the vicinity of the Ebenezer Bieber Shoporama in Sector 12...

Several klicks away, beyond the ravaged waste zones that were the grim legacy of Chaos Day, a shipment of Christmas treemeat was coming in over the West Wall from a Munce Company plantation out in the Cursed Earth. In a nod to the festive season, and at the recommendation of the company's marketing department, the strato-transporter was being pulled by a team of robo-reindeer.

Elsewhere, members of the Die Laughing Eldster Euthanasia Glee Club were enjoying a final sing-song and stand-up comedy routine by Noel Ding-a-Ling, aboard the *Ho-Ho-Ho Polar Express*. Ding-a-Ling was an entertainer so used to dying on stage that he had taken the decision to do it properly, in front of a paying audience, one last time on that cold Christmas Eve. He fully intended to go out with a bang when the hoverbus reached its final destination/crash-site, in an uninhabited region close to the North Pole.

And at the corner of 34th and Peltzer on City Bottom, at St Jude's Mission for Lost Causes—on the opposite side of the sked from the ominous edifice of Iso-Block 309—Bob Kringle walked through the empty, unmanned kitchens, lamenting the fact that he had so little to offer the homeless and hungry that Christmas. As those poor souls who depended on his charity gathered outside the mission, he offered up a final, desperate prayer to Grud that He might, in His beneficence, find a way to provide for those in need, particularly at this time of year.

While aboard a strato-station suspended high above the city, the leader of a gang of frock-coated, skull-masked hijackers declared, 'Weather Control is ours!'

'WHAT DO YOU want?' Tek-Judge Abel hissed, teeth gritted against the pain of the gunshot wound. Blood as dark as mulled wine ran through the fingers of the hand clamped to his side.

'Our demands are simple,' the hijacker said, crouching down before the Tek-Judge. Abel was shaking now, as shock took hold of his body. 'We simply want a white Christmas.'

'A white Christmas? Then why lay siege to Weather Control? I thought you must be from Total War, or some other pro-dem group.'

'We have been forced to take drastic action because when we went through the appropriate channels our demands were summarily dismissed,' the skull-face spat.

'But...' Abel gasped.

'During the Enceladus crisis, Simon Callow Block, like so many others, suffered power outages. My friends and I, as well as other like-minded citizens, gathered in the block library to keep warm and wait for the end. To pass the time before what we thought was the inevitable came, we shared readings of classic stories from the library's online copies of Dickens' classics.

'One we all particularly enjoyed was *A Christmas Carol*. And then the crisis was averted and the sudden ice age came to an end. Remembering how reading Dickens' *Christmas Carol* had made us feel, the joy and hope it had placed in our hearts, following years of misery in the aftermath of Chaos Day, we felt that the people of Mega-City One deserved a traditional Christmas to raise their spirits, just like the Christmases of yesteryear. And so we petitioned the authorities for a white Christmas.'

'But your request was duly turned down,' the Tek-Judge said weakly.

'As far as the rulers of this city are concerned, there is no such thing as the season of goodwill, so now we are taking matters into our own hands.'

'STANDARD EXECUTION,' DREDD barked, and fired.

Halfway across the plaza, the skyboard-riding Santa lurched as the Lawgiver round hit him in the back.

While the board continued to skim over the heads of the screaming shoppers, Santa's legs gave way and he tumbled over the side. The powerboard slowed to a halt and the perp was left hanging by his billycord, stolen purses and shopping bags scattering across the rockcrete beneath him, spilling their contents over the concourse.

Dredd activated his helmet-comm. 'Control—scratch that Sector 12 tap-gang and send a meat wagon to Bieber Shoporama.'

'Wilco.'

Revving the throttle of his Lawmaster, Dredd prepared to resume his patrol when his radio burst into life again. 'All units alert! Receiving reports that a group calling themselves the Ghosts of Christmas Past have laid siege to Weather Control and taken the crew hostage.'

Dredd looked at the perp still dangling from his now deactivated skyboard.

'Dredd responding,' he said, dismounting his bike and sprinting across the plaza.

'Brother Cratchit,' the leader of the hijackers said, addressing the skull-masked terrorist now seated at the controls of the weather station, *let it snow, let it snow, let it snow!*'

'Very good, Brother Scrooge.'

'Are you insane?' Abel spluttered from between bloodied teeth. 'Do you have any idea what you're even doing?'

'Brother Cratchit here is junior block janitor,' Scrooge replied, almost boastfully. 'If he can operate Callow's central heating systems and keep the cleaning meks in order, then he can create a gentle snowfall over Mega-City. Isn't that right, Brother Cratchit?'

'That's right, Brother Scrooge,' the other man replied, and started prodding buttons on the vast console in front of him with enthusiasm.

Outside the hovering weather station, atmospheric agitators crackled, cloud-seeding particles were scattered into the stratosphere, and vast turbo fans began to blow. The weird science that helped Justice Department regulate the weather over the metropolis worked its magic and great white clouds began massing.

As the nimbostratus gathered, so the swirling air currents began to whirl with ever-increasing force, and it started to snow.

'It's a total whiteout out there!' the pilot of the Munce Company treemeat transporter shouted in panic as the hover-vehicle was buffeted by powerful gale-force blizzard winds.

Turning his gaze from the violent snowstorm visible beyond the windshield of the cockpit, he looked to the digitised displays of the guidance systems, but the screens were dead.

'Sensors are down,' his co-pilot explained, her face pale. 'Must have frozen up. We're flying blind!'

As pilot and co-pilot initiated emergency landing protocols, the robo-reindeer—harnessed to the transporter by their steel-rod reins—galloped on through the snowstorm, their noses blinking red like running lights, and inane grins fixed on their garishly painted faces.

ABOARD THE *HO-HO-HO Polar Express*, Noel Ding-a-ling couldn't quite believe what was happening. He was having the gig of his life. He had the passengers in hysterics. In fact, two old dears had already pulled their Christmas crackers, as it were, dying from a stroke and a heart attack respectively, brought on by his joke about the Judge and the Brussel sprout.

Putting a hand over his mike while the busload of suicidal geriatrics continued to fall about—and in some cases pass out—laughing, he turned to the droid that was plugged into the driver's seat. 'Any chance you could drop me off somewhere?' he asked peering out of the bus at the blizzard that seemed to have blown up from nowhere. 'I've changed my mind.'

'Where do you get your material?' the droid said in a deadpan monotone. 'That is the best gag I have heard since you boarded the bus. "Any chance you could drop me off." That is hilarious. Of course I cannot drop you off. This is the *Ho-Ho-Ho Polar Express*.'

Noel Ding-a-ling's four-letter response was drowned out by the hull-buckling roar of an unexpected impact as the hoverbus collided with the treemeat transporter. For a moment, both vehicles were swallowed by a rapidly expanding ball of roiling tangerine-orange flame and greasy soot-black smoke. And then, as the explosion receded, the hoverbus began to fall towards the city below, while the transporter rocketed skyward.

HIGH ABOVE, AT the heart of the blizzard, Dredd recoiled, throwing his hands up into front of his face, as the burning transporter hurtled past him, what was left of its team of robo-reindeer trailing flames.

'What the drokk was that?' he growled, steadying himself on the powerboard. 'Dredd to Control,' he said into his comm. 'Aerial collision over Sector 12. Expect multiple fatalities. Notify traffic, med-teams and clean-up crews.'

Dredd continued to ride through the blizzard, ignoring the freezing chill of the wind and shielding his helmet visor against the worst of the snow spatter with a gloved hand. As he reached the eye of the storm, the winds abruptly abated, and looking down Dredd could see Weather Control below. He didn't waste any time; he headed straight for the strato-station.

As he approached, he could see two hijackers standing guard at the docking port where the terrorists had breached the facility, their hover vehicle berthed beside it. He took them out with a double-tap shot and both perps toppled towards City Bottom in silence.

Moments later, Dredd was on board, taking out one hijacker after another, often before they were even aware that they were under attack. As quickly as the Ghosts of Christmas Past had taken the weather station, Dredd had made his way to the control deck.

'Drop your weapons!' he commanded as he burst through the door.

Three skull-faced gunmen turned to face him. The first took aim. Dredd fired. The hijacker was thrown back into the room, hitting the deck, where he remained motionless.

'Brother Marley!' cried out the one who called himself Brother Scrooge.

'Marley was dead to begin with,' Abel growled. 'You're all ghosts now.'

As the two remaining hijackers hosed the entrance to the control room with bullets, Dredd returned fire. First Cratchit, then Scrooge, fell back against the console, the controls awash with their blood.

His finger still locked on the trigger of his gun, a final stray bullet from Scrooge hit a bank of computers on the other side of the room. There was an explosion of sparks and the fairy lights of the control panel winked out.

Beyond the perimeter of the strato-station, the snowstorm abated as quickly as it had arisen.

AT ST JUDE'S Mission, Kringle gazed out across the snow-blanketed street in open-mouthed shock, as did the hungry and homeless who had queued up outside, taking in the devastation that the hoverbus crash had inflicted. Iso-Block 309 was in ruins.

Crossing himself, Kringle offered up a prayer of thanks to Grud that the bus hadn't landed on his side of the street.

A second detonation, far overhead, had them all looking to the sky again, as the last flakes of snow drifted to the ground. And then it came, like a vengeful comet, plunging through the parting clouds—the wreckage of a Munce Company strato-transporter, pulled by a team of blazing reindeer. It promptly hit the sked with another apocalyptic explosion. Kringle and the lost causes that had been drawn to the mission dived for cover, throwing hands over heads as wreckage rained down around them.

Something landed with a soft thump in the snow in front of Kringle, and sat there crackling quietly to itself as steam rose from its crisped skin. It looked like a perfectly cooked joint of meat.

Casting his eyes heavenward in disbelief, Kringle watched as roast treemeat and sizzling sausage-fruit rained down on the street, landing in the snow drifts. On this night of all nights his prayers had been answered.

Perhaps it *was* going to be a happy Christmas, after all.

In no time, an orderly line had formed along the street with Kringle at its head, dishing out the tasty treemeat to the hungry who had gathered there.

Feeling a firm hand upon his shoulder, Kringle turned with a start, and found himself looking up at the firm jaw and hard-set features of a Judge, a skyboard held in one hand.

'That treemeat is the property of the Munce Company. Theft is a serious offence.'

'But I was only—'

'As is handling stolen goods.'

'—trying to help those in need!' Kringle protested.

Dredd looked down the line of lost causes. 'And all of you creeps witnessed the crime and didn't report it?'

'I wasn't trying to pass blame!' Kringle felt sick. What had seemed like a Grudsend had quickly become yet another stick with which to beat the downtrodden.

'That's got to be a couple of months' cube time each at least,' Dredd said, ignoring the man's pathetic pleas.

None in the queue dared say anything, in case their words were taken the wrong way too.

'Consider yourselves all under arrest.' Dredd's gaze drifted to the ruins of the Iso-Block on the other side of the junction. 'But in light of the city's current situation, I am commuting everyone's sentence to hard labour.'

Kringle stared at the Judge in confusion.

'You will be set to work rebuilding Iso-Block 309. As such, bed and board will be provided by the City.'

Tears gathered at the corners of Bob Kringle's eyes as the enormity of the Judge's pronouncement sank in. 'Thank you, sir. Thank you, and... Happy Christmas!'

Dredd looked down at the weeping man, his mouth set in an unrelenting scowl. 'Save it for someone who cares, punk.'

APARTMENT 1027C

STUART ORFORD

She clutched Bear tight to her chest and the soft toy happily spoke its sole refrain. Panicking, she clapped a small hand over Bear's mouth in a failed attempt to keep him quiet. As the toy finished, she turned his head round and wagged a small finger at it in admonishment. Bear accepted the rebuke in apologetic silence.

It was a tight squeeze in the cupboard. Daddy had thrust her in here, amongst his things, before grabbing his funny Citi-Def hat and gun, his face a mask of horror. In the past she'd giggled at him when he'd worn it as it kept slipping down over his eyes 'cause it was too big. Now, though, she'd nodded silently as he pushed her back deep in the cupboard's shadows, promising her that she'd be safe and he'd be back soon.

Soon had been a long time ago.

The countless chirruping laser burps that had accompanied Daddy's leaving had long since fallen silent, their passing marked with screams that had sent shivers down her spine. They hadn't been the last, though. Every now and again a plaintive scream would echo from somewhere in the block, making her jump and clutch at Bear for comfort.

The bad men were still out there. She knew that. Out there and stalking through the block doing bad things just like they had done to Mommy. Why Mr Mitson had bad men visiting him she didn't know; he was always nice to her, but she wouldn't be friends with him anymore.

Her belly rumbled painfully. She turned Bear's head round. 'Are you hungry, Bear?' she whispered.

Bear didn't look overly hungry. His tummy was big and round, comically stretching what he was wearing to near bursting.

'I bet you are,' she declared.

Bear nodded once, happy to please.

'I am too.' She grinned and let go of his head.

She gently pushed at the cupboard door, opening up a crack through which she peered out into the apartment. Deep shadows lurked in corners where Mommy's reading light didn't reach. She peered around and let loose a small gasp as she saw the apartment door was open, haloed by the flickering of the corridor light that Mommy had complained to Block Maintenance about last week.

Looking to see if any of the bad men were lurking to jump on her, she strained her eyes so hard that they began to hurt. None were there. She pushed the cupboard door open, holding out Bear and turning him round so that he could get a good view before pulling him quickly back.

'Anyone there, Bear?'

The soft toy shook his head slowly, impelled by tiny fingers.

'Are you sure?'

A nod.

Trembling, she crept out. The kitchen was on the other side of the huge sofa that hugged the Tri-D in a semi-circle. Bear held tight within one fist, she tiptoed across the room. Getting to the edge of the sofa, she took a quick look to check nothing was hiding behind its mountain of cushions. The space was empty except for her usual collection of toys spread out across the floor. She made a grab for her bumblebot torch and sent a beam of light across the floor emblazoned by the shadow of the bumblebot logo.

The kitchen lights were out and she could only see the barest outlines of the cupboards. She waved the bumblebot torch into the kitchen, lighting the interior and sending the bumblebot logo dancing across shiny plastic doors. The kitchen looked empty and, with a quick kiss for luck on Bear's head, she made a dash for it. Grabbing her steps, she opened the fridge door to be bathed in a wash of cold air and soft light. It took five attempts to sit Bear down on the side, the soft toy refusing to settle into position, toppling either onto his face or back. Annoyed, she wagged another finger at him before beginning to dig through the fridge. Hands full of food, she dumped it all on the work surface by Bear and began sorting into two piles.

'Here you go, Bear,' she murmured, pushing the smaller of the two piles in front of the toy before starting on her own. She munched away, enjoying the weird mix of flavours that she'd assembled, belly filling up quickly. Satisfied, she raided Bear's untouched pile, stuffing it into various pockets.

Reaching for Bear, she knocked him off the surface as a scream echoed into the apartment. The voice warbled for a moment, tailing off into nothing. She stood, frozen to the spot, and listened, Bear forgotten on the floor. Another scream followed, making her jump and scuttle into a corner. She sat down quickly and hugged her knees, rocking.

'Bear?'

She spotted him lying in a heap in plain view of the archway to the living room. In a flash she was across the floor, protectively scooping up the soft toy, fear of the bad men forgotten. Her eyes searched the living room but it remained empty. The cupboard looked inviting but she remembered something her Mommy had said that if she ever got lost, that she must find a Judge.

'What we need to do is find a Judge, Bear. They will be able to help.'

Bear agreed.

Opening a few drawers created a set of steps up to the kitchen surface. Mommy had told her off about this, saying it was dangerous and not to be done, but in this instance it was the only way. Getting to the surface, she crawled along to the window and pulled up the blind. She was sure that there would be a Judge outside. Judges stop bad men, that's what Mommy and Daddy always said. A Judge had given her Bear last year when they had gone on a special visit to Justice Central. He had been very nice, kneeling down to introduce her to Bear whilst Mommy and Daddy had talked to another Judge. He'd let her try his helmet on, although it had wobbled on her head just like Daddy's funny hat.

Outside the block a shimmering curtain of dim light crackled, obscuring the other blocks and the sky. On the ground, a wave of people erupted into view, charging towards the curtain. On the other side she thought she could see figures waving their arms but couldn't be sure. The first people reached the curtain and erupted into flames, their fellows behind desperately trying to stop but the momentum and weight of the surge behind pushing them on to their doom.

She fell back in shock, thumping her head against the wall, mouth wide open in a scream that never came. Slowly, she regained control but her head hurt really badly. Scooting to the edge of the counter, she dropped over the side.

'My head hurts, Bear,' she murmured. 'What do we do now?'

Bear's paw pointed to the Tri-D.

'It's not time to watch shows, Bear.'

Bear shook his head and pointed once more.

'Of course! Judge Pal's *Report-a-Perp Show*,' she chirped in delight. 'He'll help.'

She dashed over to the Tri-D and punched the on switch. The machine remained quiet. She punched it again and then kicked it when nothing worked.

'It's not working,' she exclaimed in anger, giving the set another kick.

Bear pointed to the apartment door.

'Into the block? You sure?'

He nodded.

'Okay. I suppose there's got to be some Judges stopping the bad men.'

Holding the soft toy tight, she inched her way around the back of the sofa and towards the door. A nasty smell was coming from the corridor outside, like synthi-eggs gone off. Pocketing the bumblebot torch, she grabbed her nose in disgust. Even so, she could *taste* the smell, getting stronger as she neared the door. Bear was thrust quickly round to get a view of the corridor beyond.

'Well?'

Bear shook his head, small gloved paw making wafting motions in front of his face.

'That bad?' She hesitated, unsure if this was the right path to take but Bear reassured her with a hug.

She stepped around the door and into a nightmare. The corridor was littered with bodies in grotesque poses and states. Some were charred beyond recognition, bodies haloed in circles of black soot, while the rotting remnants of others were collapsing in on themselves. Here and there, some lay frozen in terror, eyes bulging wide. Those left were marked by dark red holes in their chests, the insides mercifully hidden in the flickering light.

A large hat, emblazoned with the Citi-Def logo, sat forlornly on the floor one door down. Daddy's funny hat. She ran towards it, jumping over a smouldering body that could only have been old Mrs Gunnarson from across the hall, her robo-terrier partly melted on her chest.

Then she saw them. Daddy was lying face down over

Mommy's lap as she sat on the floor, back to the wall where she had originally fell as they'd come back from their trip out to the Billy Carter Mezzanine Park. A short time ago and a lifetime away she'd skipped down the hall, Daddy chasing after her, pretending to be a big monster. As they'd reached their door, Mommy had screamed and briefly she'd seen the bad men; a gaunt one had clasped Mommy round the throat, his other clawed hand poised delicately in front of her chest. Daddy had bundled her into the apartment and the cupboard as Mommy continued to scream.

Mommy's head was lolling at an angle, hair covering her face but not the hole in her chest.

She dragged her eyes away. Tentatively, with much encouragement from Bear, she let go of her nose and pushed Mommy's hair back. Mommy's eyes were shut and her face looked peaceful. She planted a kiss on Mommy's brow and let the hair fall back.

She tiptoed round Mommy's legs and peered down at Daddy. His face was set in an angry glare like he often gave her when she'd done something really naughty. She attempted to smooth out the frown and the grimace, deft fingers fruitlessly pushing at rigid skin. Giving up, tears started to trickle down her cheeks and sobs welled up in her chest.

Bear gave her a hug. *You must be strong*, he seemed to say.

The door to Mr Mitson's apartment had been partly ripped off the hinges and left hanging precariously in the frame. From within came a glow that looked like his Tri-D set had been left on. She edged into the apartment on her knees. The room inside was chilly, like a fridge door had been left open. Mr Mitson's sofa had been pushed up against one wall where no one could sit on it, leaving the centre of the room empty. In its place sat a small black ball covered in white domes that glowed with the same weird light as the curtain outside.

Her head began to ache once more, a constant annoying buzz. She stuck a finger in one ear and wiggled it around in an effort to try and dislodge the noise.

Stay still.

She jumped backwards with a yelp and spun on the spot to see where the lady was who had spoken.

Don't be scared, I'm a Judge. Where are you?

The room was empty, the lady's gentle voice seeming to come from within.

'I'm Alice. I live in 1027c, but I'm next door in Mr Mitson's. There were bad men. They killed Mommy and Daddy,' she replied cautiously.

Find somewhere to hide and keep the bear with you. I'm on the way.

Alice looked around and climbed up the back of the sofa, rolling over the other side into a hill of cushions. As the sofa was curved it left a small space between it and the wall. She slipped into the spot, pulling cushions over her in a soft cascade. Once buried, Alice hunkered down further, arranging the cushions to give her and Bear a view of the room.

She shivered, cold despite her coat. It felt like the room was getting chillier, small puffs of condensed air accompanying each breath. A faint swish pricked her ears. Was it just an odd block noise like Mommy and Daddy used to say when she couldn't get to sleep, or had the bad men come back? There it was again... this time louder. An outline, a suggestion of a shape, tall, imposing and dark glided into the room.

She knew at once... a bad man had come. Alice squeezed Bear tighter than she had ever done before, his small form almost bent double in her arms.

The bad man moved with a soft purpose into the room... then stopped. The outline of his dark helm, embellished with bat-like wings, turned towards the sofa. The helm tilted slightly and the bad man took a step forwards towards her hiding spot.

Please go away, please go away, please go away.

The helm straightened and a dark arm reached out as the bad man took another step forward, his outline eclipsing the glow from the funny ball and sending her into darkness.

Please go away, please go away, please go away.

'There it is!' A man's voice, full of authority.

'Judge Fear is here! I can sense him!' The lady's voice.

She felt rather than saw the bad man turn in front of her, his movement allowing the ball's glow to return.

'Andersssson!' A voice, sibilant and dreadful. The bad man's shadow of an arm flicked out.

'Mantrap!' the lady yelled.

In the glow of the ball she saw two Judges—a blonde lady, clutching at her leg, and a solid-chinned man.

'Gaze into the face of Fear!' proclaimed the bad man,

lunging forward to grab hold of the man-Judge's helmet, his own dark helm opening wide. The urge to scream filled Alice but Bear's softness enveloped her in soothing warmth.

The Judge's muscles bunched and, in her mind, she saw a single tremor ripple through his body. Then his steel returned.

'Gaze into the fist of Dredd!' roared the Judge, his fist smashing through the bad man's helm and out of the back, showering her hiding space with chunks of dark metal. The bad man reared up, stumbling back a step, long, clawed fingers clutching at the ruined helmet.

'Incendaries, Dredd! They'll work on this beauty!' yelled the lady-Judge, her Lawgiver uttering a sharp retort.

A blaze of light erupted; at its heart the bad man. 'Foolsss! You cannot kill what does not live!' he mocked, voice dripping evil. The bad man collapsed to his knees, his body enveloped with fire. From out of his head a ghostly bubble seeped, the transparent image of the menacingly winged dark helm within.

'His spirit form's escaping!' gasped the lady-Judge.

'Forget it! The shield's all that matters!' commanded the man-Judge, his own Lawgiver spitting a shot that cracked the funny glowing ball into countless fragments. 'This is Dredd! Shield is down! Hit the Billy Carter Block with everything you've got!'

The cold broke and the apartment's lights flickered back into life. Alice stood up, cushions falling from her shoulders, Bear still held protectively in front. The man-Judge whipped round, Lawgiver raised. She squeaked in fright.

'Stomm! Got a juve here, Anderson.'

'Hey kiddo,' called the lady-Judge. 'You must be, Alice, right?' She nodded. 'Don't worry about him'—she motioned towards the man—'he looks mean but is a real softie. Aren't you, Dredd?'

The Judge harrumphed.

'Come over here.' She turned to her companion. 'Help me get this off, will you?'

Alice climbed over the sofa and walked slowly towards them. She could see that the lady-Judge had some weird thing attached to her leg, wicked-looking metal teeth stuck deep into her boot.

'I see you have Judge Bear. Has he been protecting you?' Alice nodded.

'Good. I'm Judge Anderson and this is Judge Dredd. Thank you for being a brave girl and helping out.'

'You're welcome,' she replied automatically.

'Judge Bear?' queried Dredd.

'Yes... ouch!' exclaimed Anderson as Dredd prised the strange metal thing off her leg. 'It was an initiative started sometime back in Psi-Division as way of monitoring children with high latent psi-abilities that had potential to be Judges.'

'Hold still, will you? Grud knows what you may catch from that thing.' Dredd pulled out a small pen-like device from his belt pouch. 'And they thought dressing up a toy bear in a Judge's uniform was the best way to go?' He stabbed Anderson in the leg with the pen.

'Double ouch! Anyone ever told you that your bedside manner leaves much to be desired?' She didn't wait for a reply. 'The bear was my idea but it's more than that. It monitors and projects a cushioning psi-field, just in case they manifest.'

And you can hear me quite clearly, can't you, Alice?

Alice nodded.

'I need to call her in, Dredd. The Dark Judges and her parents, the stress, has unlocked her abilities.'

'Do it as we go.'

'Right, Alice, a nice Judge from where I work is going to come and pick you up and take you somewhere safe. Is that okay?' asked Anderson.

'Can I keep Bear?'

'Of course you can, kiddo,' she answered, smiling and ruffling Alice's hair. 'Brave girl,' said Anderson, limping past Dredd.

'Yeah.' Dredd headed towards the door. At the threshold, he stopped and looked back. 'See you on the streets.'

NO ACT OF KINDNESS

STEVE FRAME

THE FULL STOP wasn't like other bars. The place was always full of writers and actors and other long-hairs. This one night, the writers and actors and other long-hairs didn't see the squad of Judges that had encircled their building, waiting with the patience of predators. Judges that didn't know why citizen Abraham Skootum had to be brought in. Judges that didn't care why.

'Come on, guys, I'm just Joe Cit. I don't know nothing about stories.' Abe's gaze skittered around the semi-circle of drunks and poets that had him trapped at the the bar: alone, isolated and afraid. No hint of mercy in their faces. One tall figure, looking like a hairball a dinosaur had coughed up, spoke for them all.

'Too bad, Abe. It's talk or walk night. You know the rules. Tell us a tale or take a hike.'

Abe cringed at his sentence. 'Please, guys...' He looked to the cadaverous hairball. 'Gastang, tell them. I'm not like you. I scrape the tanks down at Bunce's Munce. What's to tell about that?'

Gastang stepped up, took hold of Abe's shoulders, and held him at arms' length. Past the explosion of facial hair, dark brown eyes danced with life and good humour. 'Everybody has a tale to tell. *Everybody*. So tell it.' He gave Abe a little shake before retreating.

A moat of silence separated Abe from his audience. A glass slid towards him and the warm scent of the good stuff rose up in welcome. 'For the telling,' said a low voice. The glass rattled on the bar as Abe tried to pick it up. His head was filled with a wash of white noise. Say something. Open your mouth. Speak.

He opened his mouth and a tiny choking sound came out. Slippery glass beneath his fingers clicked a tattoo against his teeth as he tried to drink. The white noise deafened him. Say something. Anything. *Talk!*

'I really hate the jays.'

There were murmurs of assent at this. Heads nodded. 'Damn straight, Abe.'

'When I was little, I fell off my hoverboard and I was banged up pretty good and bleeding all over and crying fit to burst and this Judge comes along and busts me for causing a disturbance and damaging city property. I mean, two weeks in a juve cube?' Abe looked round, expecting to see smirks and yawns. None. Not one.

Gastang spoke into the quiet. 'That's a righteous anger, Abe.'

'They've been on my case my whole life.' The white noise faded as the words leapt from him. 'Then Little Abbie came along, just six months before Necropolis. What a time to pick to come into the world. Only she wanted to come out all wrong. So I have to get Evie into our old Foord and high-tail it to the hospital and Evie's bleeding now and 'cause I'm speeding, a Judge pulls us over. And it's Dredd.'

'Oh man,' came from the circle of listeners. 'Tough break.'

'And I can't speak. I can't get a word out, I'm petrified. And Dredd is going like, "You got a mental condition, citizen?" And I'm going bug-eyed and he spies Evie. He goes, "Drokk," and then, "Follow me," and he's off. Sirens, lights, the whole ten yards. At the hospital, he gets us fast-tracked through, no waiting. After, he writes me up for a ticket and a psych evaluation.'

'Miserable bastard,' someone at the back said.

'The doc said Evie would have bled out if it had been a few more minutes.' Faces blurred into crystal shards as he cuffed at his eyes. 'I guess Dredd saved them both.'

People shifted in their seats. Throats were cleared. Outside, the Judges waited.

Abe didn't see his circle of listeners now. 'During the Big Nec, I kicked in our apartment door, busted up our living room. Made it look like the place had been wrecked, you know? I thought it might help. Me and Evie and Little Abbie, we holed up in the bedroom. I even pulled a dead body—old Mr Evans from next door, he'd hung himself—along the corridor, put it in front of our apartment. It smelled something awful. I guess we just waited to see if we would die. Or be killed. Only it never happened and

I thought maybe we could get through it. We had a little radio but all I heard was the Sisters telling everyone they were gonna die. That's when I heard about them four. The Dark Judges.'

He stopped to take a sip, setting the glass down with a solid thunk. 'I figured there was only four of them and it's a big city. Odds were, they were nowhere near us. I was wrong.

'You'd think it would be the dead of night they would come. It was about lunchtime. Evie was feeding Little Abbie and it was real quiet. I heard these shuffling footsteps come into our apartment and a voice, whispering to itself. And...' He glanced at Gastang. 'Singing. Little snatches of something. Crazy. And I knew it was him... Death. I could feel it. Like there was a sick kind of radiation pulsing off him. We could all feel it, and Little Abbie started to squirm, and I heard the footsteps stop. He was listening.'

Abe stared at the floor, his hands, the wall, anywhere but the people facing him. 'I was so scared. I knew Little Abbie was going to give us away. I wanted so bad to live just then. Grud help me for thinking what I thought next. I looked at Evie and her eyes were like plates because she knew. She knew what I was going to do. She clutched Little Abbie to her and shook her head at me but I still crept towards them.' He stopped to swallow. 'One life instead of three. Then the door started to bend inwards, like there was a strong wind behind it, then it split like the cheap plastic it was and he was standing there and he's hissing something about judging us.' Abe looked up but his audience seemed very far from him. 'I guess Death saved Little Abbie that day.'

Gastang licked at paper-dry lips. 'What... ah... what happened next, Abe?'

The solitary man on the stool looked puzzled. 'I don't know. I mean, I do know but I'm not sure.'

'Just tell it then,' Gastang said.

'He came into the bedroom. He said, *"The woman and child firsst. Women, who alwaysss bring new life, new sssinners."* I remember him saying that and I felt something inside me. It was like I was filling up with... iron. Molten iron. Pressed under the weight of the world I stood in his way and said no. Not these two. Not today. Not ever. Then Death stretched out his hand and says, *"I just reach out my hand and sssqueeze."* His fingernails poked into me. I've still got the circle of marks on my chest. But that was as far as his hand went in. I looked down at it and he looked down at it. Then he pulled his hand back a bit and poked at me again. Only this time, I grabbed his hand and I squeezed back. I remember the flesh slid off the bone like cooked meat. I remember the bones cracking like sticks and this rank smell. He jerked away. He hissed something about returning with his brothers. "No you won't," I said to him. Then he was gone.'

Abe looked to his audience. 'Grud on a Mo-pad,' a voice said.

'And that was it?' Gastang asked.

Abe shrugged. 'I reported it to our block Judge. When we finally got one back.'

Gastang shifted in his chair and chewed at his beard. 'What did he say.'

'Threatened to throw me in a kook-cube.'

'Damned jays never cut a guy a break.'

'You got that right.' Craning round, Abe checked the clock behind the bar. 'Uh, listen, guys, I gotta go. Evie will have my hide if I'm late. Sorry I can't...'

'Sure, Abe, go safe. Helluva story.'

OUTSIDE THE FULL Stop, Abe walked no more than ten paces before dark shapes fleeted out of the shadows to surround him.

'Abraham Scootum, you're detained under the emergency powers directive. You can come quietly or not. Makes no difference to me.'

Senior Judge Beria wondered who this shabby little punk was and why the Chief Judge was so interested in him, why he had to freeze his ass off out here while that Wally Squad freak in there coaxed his story out of him. The shabby little punk was giving him some eyeball. Beria drew his daystick.

'Good choice, citizen. Gives me a chance to warm up.'

'No. No you won't,' the punk said. The words struck Beria like a lead sap. Numbness spread through his skull. His daystick clattered on the pedwalk, too heavy to hold.

Abe never heard the whistle of the daystick from the Judge behind him as it cut an arc through the night air.

* * *

'THAT HIM? HE doesn't look like much.'

Tek-Judge Rodd glanced round as Dredd spoke before turning back to the monitor. On the screen, Abraham Scootum sat in a holding cell, staring at nothing. 'That he doesn't, but everything else checks out. If he's lying, he's better than our detectors. Psi-Div says he's been around the Dark Judges. There's the wounds—five incisions around his heart with no trace of a scar. Minute traces of decayed tissue, though. Snatch squad says he faced down Beria with a word or two.'

Dredd grunted. 'So what have you got?'

'There's some radiation off him.'

'He's a mutant?'

'Nope. His DNA checks out clean. He's got zip psi-potential too. The radiation, it's exotic stuff, but not dangerous. How he did it?' Rodd shrugged. 'No idea. This is something we haven't seen before.'

'Good to see Tek-Div living up to its budget appropriations.'

'Anything I come up with would be pure speculation.'

'So speculate.'

'I think he's changing reality. To suit his own narrative. It's a very localised effect but...' Rodd trailed off under Dredd's silent appraisal. 'Here,' he said, holding out a cup of synthi-caff, steam rising from the watery brown liquid.

'I never asked for one.'

'Not for you. For him. Build empathy, establish trust. Dredd, just go with it, okay? Whatever it is he's doing, he's doing it now. No one's been able to stay in that room longer than a minute since he came round.'

Dredd grunted again but took the proffered cup.

'Be careful in there,' Rodd murmured.

HE FELT IT as soon as the small, mousy man looked at him. As if the air in the interrogation cube was at a higher pressure; a pervasive energy pushing against him, pushing him away. It took an effort of will to face him, to just place the cup in front of him. Gripping the table to anchor himself, his jaw creaked with the force needed to speak.

'Abraham Scootum.'

'Every Judge I meet tonight seems to want to tell me my name.'

Cold anger burned through the old Judge as sweat soaked his uniform. His body trembled, muscles clenching tight, keeping him facing this punk. Not walking away. 'Watch the lip.'

'You people grind us down every chance you get. You hate us.'

Dredd spat his reply. 'It's a view. Wrong. But it's a view.' What he said next took more effort than he thought imaginable. 'I need your help.' The pressure on him eased a fraction, no more. He took whatever opening was offered. 'Only one person has done anything close to what you did. I know how *I* did it. I need to know how *you* did it.'

'Why should I help you?'

It was building again, like a wave pushed up on a hidden reef. Standing straight needed just about everything he had. Dredd knew he only had seconds left. He took the biggest lever he had to the man. 'I saved your wife. Your child. You owe me. Now talk.'

The Judge towered over him, a grim black monolith. Abe sighed and drew the cooling cup of synthi-caff towards him. Drokkers always had an angle on you. Freakin' always.

'What do you want to know?'

YOU SHOULDA BEEN THERE

MICHAEL CARROLL

BY HIS OWN proud admission, Presley Butcher hadn't learned much in his thirty-seven years, but he *did* know that it was every right-thinking citizen's duty to get in the way of the Judges. An unwritten rule that everyone understood.

You don't have to do anything actually *criminal*, of course—only a spugwit ties their own shoelaces together—but slow them down when you can. It made sense, in a kind of karma way, even though the concept of karma was another thing about which Presley Butcher didn't know much.

You slow down a Judge, even just by a second or two, then that might mean whoever the Judge is chasing gets away. So then later on, that cit repays their luck by slowing down another Judge, and the cit *that* Judge is chasing gets away too. A chain of ordinary citizens helping each other out, even though they might never meet. It was kinda beautiful, in a way. Poetic. And somewhere down the road, just when you've got a Judge bearing down on *you*, maybe it all pays off and you become the next link in that chain.

On the morning of September 1st, 2082, opportunity knocked for Presley Butcher and he metaphorically squared his shoulders, set his jaw and stood up to open that door. As he drove his ancient but beloved Brit-Cit Leyline Mini Driver along the west side of Sector Thirteen's 151st Avenue—a neighbourhood nicknamed 'The Boulevard of Broken Teeth' by many of the locals who liked to think that they were tough—he spotted a Judge coming up fast behind, Lawmaster lights flashing and siren wailing. Standard protocol was to immediately pull in to the side to give the Judge enough room to pass—the rest of the traffic on that cracked-asphalt street was already doing just that—but Butcher grinned to himself and kept a firm grip on the wheel. 'Drokk you, Judge. Not movin'.'

He *would* move, of course. He knew that even as he was denying it. But he held his nerve, and held the wheel, for as long as he could. The Judge was less than twenty metres away by the time Butcher' survival instinct overrode his arrogance and took control.

The huge Lawmaster roared by and he could see the Judge—young, tall, slender build but with wide shoulders—scowling as he passed.

Butcher gave a short, quiet snort as he watched the oversized motorbike rumble away through the morning traffic. 'Showed *him*.'

In O'McDonald's Bar that night he regaled his friends

with the exciting details of his adventure. 'Dredd, his name was. Saw his badge when I replayed the Vehi-cam later. He comes up behind me and he's all'—Butcher mimed a Judge riding a Lawmaster, clenched fists out in front of him as he rocked from side to side on his barstool—'weavin' around, tryna get past and I'm like, no way, drokker. You don't own *these* streets. He moves to the left, but I see this comin' and I block him again. Dredd starts to goes right, but I see that too. Drokker's gettin' worried now, because he, like, suddenly realises where he is, right? Like, until now, he's got his mind on his destination, not on his route. But you can see it in his eyes that he's thinking, "Stomm... this is the *Boulevard* and I'm here without back-up!"'

'Wait, you seen that in his *eyes*?' Jannie Scrumly asked. 'Didn't he have his, like, his *hemlet* on?'

'*Hel*met,' Old Eddie Gaul corrected. Eddie got twitchy when people mispronounced simple words. One time he punched his brother Neville in the throat for saying 'edumacation,' but in Eddie's defence Neville had been saying it that way for the past forty-four years and still thought it was funny, so everyone agreed that Neville had got off lightly.

Butcher continued, 'I mean, I saw it in his *expression*. His body-language, y'know? He kinda tensed up, then looked around. Seen Judges do that before, in the Boulevard. We all seen that, right?'

A few heads nodded, and Butcher took that as encouragement to carry on. Most of them knew the truth: they'd been there. A Judge walks past you on the street, and later this is transformed into a story about how the drokker was going to run a stop-and-search—and you were *carrying*; that would have been bad—but you managed to stare him down, persuaded him to move on by sheer force of will. Or you see a pair of jays threatening a perp with their daysticks, and this later becomes a story about how the poor drokker was chased down by an entire squad who caved in his skull so hard his eye popped out, and he wasn't even guilty of anything. They just picked him because the Judges have kill-quotas. Everyone knows that.

Butcher was half-way through telling the story for the second time—unprompted, but no one had moved away yet, so that meant they were still interested—when Monty Chesterton interrupted him.

'Yeah, one time I was over at Keller's just, y'know, hanging in a booth near the corner, and this Judge walks right in and this guy comes up to him and he gives him this baggie, right, and he says to him that he got it from that guy and he points over in my kinda direction and the Judge looks right at me and says, "Creep with the hair?" and I near browned my keks. Swear to Grud and Jovus and all their little holy fairies, I thought I was a dead man.' Monty nodded, mostly to himself, and took another sip of his beer. 'That was when I cut my hair, see? You didn't know me then, but I useta have the full double-mohawk and mullet combo, orange with alternating white and red tips. Did it because it made me stand out. Heh. Learned my lesson right there and then. Don't stand out. You wanna make it *hard* for the Judges to remember you, not easy. Am I right?' Another sip, and then as he was smacking his lips he looked up and saw that everyone was staring at him. 'What?'

'We *know*,' Eddie Gaul said. 'You've told us that same drokkin' story eighty million times.'

'I'm just *sayin*'.'

'Time you *stopped* sayin', then.' Eddie turned back to Butcher. 'Go on, Pres.'

'Right,' Butcher said. He looked down at his empty glass for a second, but the mood had been shattered. Monty's story was lame, they all knew that. But it was no less lame than anyone else's. 'Ah, drokk it...'

Jannie asked, 'What's wrong?'

'How the hell did we end up like *this*?' Presley Butcher asked. 'We're all so drokkin' scared of the Judges that we inflate the smallest non-events into great big conflicts. Monty here's been coasting on that "Judge looked in my direction" story for *years*. That's all that happened. The Judge *looked* in his direction. Nothing else. And we're all the same, every one of us. Okay, sure, some people around here really *have* gone up against the Jays, but the rest of us... They got us so... so... *cowed* that we make up a bunch of crap just so that we can persuade ourselves that we've still got some control over our lives.' He looked around the bar, at the frowning faces of his friends. 'You wanna know the truth about this morning? The *actual* truth, not the story? I'm driving along, Judge Dredd is coming up behind me, I hesitate for a bit, then I pull over just like everyone else. Take a guess at how long I really hesitated. Never mind everything I just told you about me moving left and right and anticipating his movements so I can slow him down. None of that happened. Go on. Take a guess how long I waited before my nerve snapped.'

No one responded. Most of them were looking away. They knew what was coming.

'Four seconds, *that's* how long. That Judge barely even noticed, just rode on past.' Presley Butcher put down his glass, and stared at it. 'We tell ourselves that we're tough guys, that our little neighbourhood here is one of the last free strongholds in the city, that they've not beaten *us*. But we're not fooling anyone. The Judges have taken damn near everything from us. About the only thing we got left is our freedom to lie about how important we are.' Even as he was speaking, he knew that nothing was going to be the same again. This cluster of friends would shun him, and he couldn't blame them for that. It was another unwritten rule of life in Mega-City One: don't confront people with the cold, unfiltered reality of their lives. You're only allowed to burst your own bubble, not someone else's.

Eddie Gaul, still not looking Presley in the eye, said, 'Maybe you oughta *go*, Pres. Get on home, get some sleep.'

Butcher nodded. He appreciated Eddie's kindness, even though he knew they would never talk about it. This was a way to save face. He wouldn't be able to pretend that this rant hadn't happened, but he could paper over it a little. Tomorrow, maybe in a couple of days, he'd come back and make lame jokes along the lines of, 'What the hell was *in* that drink?' Then he'd stick to the background for a while, try to blend in long enough for the ache to fade from the sore thumb he'd made of himself. A good six months would do it. By then, enough other people would have accumulated enough dumb things that his 'weird brain-fart' would seem fairly tame by comparison.

He slid down from the stool, and as he was shrugging himself into his jacket the bar's door crashed open.

All of the patrons' voices faded to silence as the Judge's silhouette filled the doorway.

Butcher knew, somehow, that this was the same Judge from earlier that morning. And that he was here for one reason only.

Judge Dredd crossed the room, heading straight towards Butcher. No one got in his way. No one tried to slow him down. 'Presley Rowell Butcher. On the charge of deliberately obstructing an officer of the law in pursuit of his duties, two years.'

Butcher turned around, hands behind his back, and Dredd cuffed him, then steered him out of the bar.

Three full minutes passed before anyone else moved.

'MAN, YOU SHOULDA *been* there,' Athena Dittmar told her little brother Judson a couple of days later. 'I swear, I thought we were all dead. He kicks the door open, puts a coupla rounds in the ceiling as a warning. My friend Tammy? She got shrapnel in her face from the ricochet. Right in her *face*, swear to Grud, and the drokker doesn't even care. Blood streaming down her face from all those cuts, he didn't even look at her. But he looks at *me*. Right *at* me, like he's sizing me up. So what I did was, see, I stared *back*. That's what you've gotta *do*, Judson. Let them see that you're not scared of them. You look them in the eye and you make them think, hell, *this* one's gonna be trouble. They're not worth it. 'Cause they're all cowards, the Judges, deep down. Body-armour, helmets, gloves. Means they're scared of getting hurt, right? But he saw me giving him the cold-eye, and he backed down. Picked on some other poor drokker instead, took him away on a jumped-up traffic violation.'

Judson Dittmar nodded throughout his sister's tale. He was fourteen already, old enough to have heard a lot of stories like this. Even if Athena was embellishing a little—which he knew she was, because she'd been home the night the Judge had raided the bar—the *essence* of the story was true. That's what was important. These tales served to remind the ordinary people that they lived or died at the whim of monsters.

In school the following day, Judson did his duty and repeated the story to his friends. For impact, his rendition of the tale placed himself at the centre of the action, even though it had happened in a bar. 'They don't mind that I'm underage,' he explained. 'The owner knows my folks, so they let me in, long as I don't talk about it, so you can't tell anyone, got it? I'm never gonna forget that night. I mean, I was sitting *next* to the guy the Judge killed. Shot him in the *face*, just for lookin' at him funny.' Judson brandished his spotless shirt sleeve as evidence. 'Had to put this through the machine, like, *three times* to get the blood out. You can kinda see some of it still there.'

Judson swore his friends to a silence he hoped they

wouldn't keep, and boosted his own reputation in the process.

His friend Chelsey Boulting revised the tale a little when he related the story to his younger cousins. They were horrified at the senseless, brutal actions of the Judge, but mightily impressed with the manner in which Chelsey had courageously put himself in the line of fire, saving the life of the Judge's young and attractive female victim, who then rewarded Chelsey with more than just thanks and an appreciative handshake.

Although Chelsey—and everyone else in the Boulevard of Broken Teeth—died in 2134 when the entire neighbourhood was crushed by a collapsing City Block, for the rest of their lives his cousins proudly related the story of the time he had fought the law, and the law had backed down.

This is an excerpt from Michael Carroll's new novella, *Fallen Angel*, out now...

ABOUT THE CONTRIBUTORS

David Baillie is a Scottish writer and artist who works in comics, film and television. As well as various strips for *2000 AD* and the *Megazine*, he also created and wrote the series *Red Thorn* for Vertigo/DC. He lives in London with his darling wife, mischievous daughter and a multitude of unforgiving deadlines.

David Bishop is an award-winning screenwriter, dramatist and the author of 20 published novels. A former editor of *2000 AD*, he has written TV dramas broadcast on BBC1 and plays for Radio 4. His novels have featured Doctor Who, Judge Dredd, Freddy Krueger and Nikolai Dante, while his non-fiction books *Thrill-Power Overload: The First Forty Years of 2000 AD* and *Endeavour: The Complete Inspector Morse* are considered definitive works on their subjects. Having written nearly 50 issues of *The Phantom* for Egmont's *Fantomen* comic, he is co-creating original graphic novel *Dani's Toys* with Northern Irish artist Ruairi Coleman. David was awarded a Robert Louis Stevenson Fellowship in 2017 to write a historical mystery set, and won the Pitch Perfect competition at Bloody Scotland 2018 with that project. The resulting novel, *City of Vengeance*, will be published by Pan Macmillan in 2021, the first in a series featuring Renaissance Florence sleuth Cesare Aldo.

Michael Carroll is the author of over forty books, including the award-winning *New Heroes* series of Young Adult superhero novels and the best-selling cult graphic novel *Judge Dredd: Every Empire Falls*. He currently writes *Proteus Vex* and *Judge Dredd* for *2000 AD* and the *Judge Dredd Megazine*. Other works include *Jennifer Blood* for Dynamite Entertainment, *Razorjack* for Titan Books (co-written with artist John Higgins), and the *Rico Dredd* trilogy for Abaddon Books, for whom he has also created the acclaimed *JUDGES* series which explores the genesis of the world of Judge Dredd.

Dr **Jonathan Clements** is the author of many books on East Asian history, including biographies of Marco Polo, Admiral Togo, Khubilai Khan and *A Brief History of the Samurai*. His books are available in over a dozen languages, including Chinese editions of his biographies of the First Emperor and Empress Wu. He is the co-author of *The Dorama Encyclopedia: A Guide to Japanese Television Drama Since 1953* and *The Anime Encyclopedia: A Century of Japanese Animation* (both for Stone Bridge

Press). His book *Anime: A History* (British Film Institute) received a 2014 CHOICE recommendation as one of the year's outstanding academic titles, and was nominated for the Society of Animation Studies' McLaren-Lambart Award for best scholarly book. He was a Visiting Professor at Xi'an Jiaotong University, China from 2013-19.

T. C. Eglington is a house writer for *2000 AD* and the *Judge Dredd Megazine*, on strips including *Judge Dredd*, *Tales from Mega-City One*, *Tharg's Future Shocks*, *Tharg's Time Twisters*, *Tharg's 3rillers*, *Past Imperfect*, *Outlier*, *Thistlebone* and *Blunt*.

Taking part in the *2000 AD* forum monthly writing competition led **Stephen Frame** to think he could actually write. His latest work, a short story about the big, bad wolf working as a private eye in 1930s Los Angeles, appears in the Michael Terrance Publishing short story anthology, *When You Read This I Will Be Dead*. He is currently working on a contemporary urban fantasy novel. Possibly he will finish this before the heat death of the universe.

Alan Grant started his career in comics as an editor at DC Thomson in 1967, moving to London in 1970 to work for IPC, where he edited 2000 AD from 1978 to 1980. His British comics work has included *Judge Dredd*, *Robo-Hunter*, *Strontium Dog*, *Bad City Blue* and *Mazeworld* for *2000 AD*, as well as *Tarzan*, *Star-Lord*, *Toxic!* and *Eagle*. He is the co-creator of cult character The Bogie

Man, and has worked for US publishers including Marvel, Epic (on *The Last American*, with John Wagner and Mike McMahon), Dark Horse and DC Comics (especially on *Batman*). He is the owner of the publishing company Bad Press Ltd.

More recently, Grant has written two children's books published by Curly Tale Books (*Sammy the Rainbow Snail* and *The Quite big Rock*), both illustrated by his daughter Shalla Gray, and adapted Mark Hamilton's *NeoThink* trilogy into graphic novel format. He's currently writing a book aimed at rebellious teenagers.

Jonathan Green is a writer of speculative fiction, with more than seventy books to his name. He has written everything from *Fighting Fantasy* gamebooks to *Doctor Who* novels, by way of *Sonic the Hedgehog*, *Teenage Mutant Ninja Turtles*, *Judge Dredd*, *Robin of Sherwood*, and *Frostgrave*. He is the creator of the *Pax Britannia* steampunk series for Abaddon Books, and the author of the award-winning, and critically-acclaimed, *YOU ARE THE HERO—A History of Fighting Fantasy Gamebooks*. He also edits and compiles short story anthologies. To find out more about his current projects visit www.jonathangreenauthor.com and follow him on Twitter @jonathangreen..

Jonathan Morris is one of the most prolific and popular writers in the world of *Doctor Who*, having written five novels for BBC Books, innumerable audio adventures for Big Finish and BBC Audio and dozens of comic strips and articles for *Doctor Who Magazine*. He's also written and script edited for TV and radio, and has just finished his first original SF novel.

Robert Murphy started writing for small press comics and has since written several stories for *2000 AD*, including three series of *Tharg's 3Rillers*. He also works as a TV producer, specialising in arts and history programmes.

Stuart Orford writes just for the fun of it and he blames it all on *2000 AD*, Tolkien and Pratchett. Without them, his keyboard would still have the letters on them. By day, he remains a mild-mannered web manager. By night, he becomes a less than mild-mannered writer with grand illusions of getting rid of the day job. With one competition win published in *Judge Dredd Megazine*, one novel on Amazon and other tales in the works, he's getting there and still having fun doing it.

Gordon Rennie is one of *2000 AD* and the *Megazine*'s most prolific creators, with co-creative credits for *Caballistics, Inc.*, *Glimmer Rats*, *Missionary Man*, *Necronauts*, *Storming Heaven*, *Rain Dogs* and *Witchworld*. He has also written *Daily Star* Dredd strips, *Judge Dredd*, *Harke and Burr*, *Mean Machine*, *Past Imperfect*, *Pulp Sci-Fi*, *Rogue Trooper*, *Satanus*, *Terror Tales*, *Tharg the Mighty* and *Vector 13* and *Absalom*. Outside the Galaxy's Greatest Comic, Rennie has written for anthologies *Heavy Metal* and *Warhammer Monthly*, as well as *Species*, *Starship Troopers* and *White Trash*.

One-time *Doctor Who* and *Torchwood* script editor **Gary Russell** began what he laughingly calls "his career" as an actor before editing *Doctor Who Magazine* for Marvel UK, co-creating the audio production company Big Finish and writing over 35 books on subjects as not-very-far ranging as *Doctor Who*, *Frasier*, *The Simpsons* and a series of *New York Times* bestselling *The Art of The Lord of the Rings* movie tie-ins. He temporarily relocated to Australia to write and produce *Prisoner Zero*, an animated adventure series for the ABC/Netflix and since his return to the UK has been overseeing animated reimaginings of old 1960s missing *Doctor Who* stories for BBC Studios and wrirting children's television scripts for Beano Film & TV. He's also written a number of comics, games and First Day cover pamphlets for Royal Mail stamps. No, seriously...

Author and comic book writer **Cavan Scott** is a UK number one bestseller who has written for such popular worlds as *Star Wars*, *Doctor Who*, *Star Trek*, *Vikings*, *Warhammer 40,000* and Sherlock Holmes. He is the author of *Star Wars Dooku: Jedi Lost*, *Judge Dredd: Alternative Facts*, *The Patchwork Devil*, and *Cry of the Innocents*, and is part of Lucasfilm's Project Luminous publishing initiative. He has written comics for IDW, Dark Horse, Vertigo, Titan, Legendary, *2000 AD*, and *The Beano*.

A former magazine editor, Cavan lives in Bristol with his wife and daughters. His lifelong passions include classic scary movies, folklore, audio drama, the music of David Bowie, and walking. He owns far too many action figures. Discover more about his work at www.cavanscott.com.

Simon Spurrier makes stuff up for a living.

Comics credits range from *2000 AD* to *Suicide Squad*, via creator-owned projects like *Cry Havoc*, *Coda* and Eisner-nominated *The Spire*. He's currently writing *Hellblazer* for DC and *Alienated* for Boom! Studios.

He's worked as an art director behind the camera, published several prose novels, and now writes for US Television.

He lives by the seaside, tweets at @sispurrier, and strongly believes it goes 1) scone 2) jam 3) cream.

Karl Stock has written *Tharg's Future Shocks* for *2000 AD*, Dredd prose fiction for the *Judge Dredd Megazine* and strips for Rebellion specials including *The Vigilant* and *Cor! & Buster*, as well as interviews and features about comics for the *Judge Dredd Megazine*, *Tripwire*, *Comic Heroes* and more. He is the co-author of the 40th anniversary edition of *Thrill-Power Overload*, *2000 AD*'s official history, and lives in Scotland.

James Swallow is a BAFTA nominated *New York Times*, *Sunday Times* and Amazon #1 bestselling writer of over fifty books, including the Marc Dane action thrillers *Nomad*, *Exile*, *Ghost* and *Shadow*, the *Sundowners* steampunk western series, and fiction from the worlds of *Doctor Who*, *24*, *Warhammer 40,000*, *Halo*, *Stargate*, *Blake's 7* and more. His other credits feature scripts for videogames and audio dramas, including the *Deus Ex* series, *The Division 2*, *Ghost Recon Wildlands* and *Disney Infinity: Star Wars*.

He is the author of three *2000 AD* novels—*Eclipse* and *Whiteout*, featuring Judge Dredd, and *Blood Relative*, featuring Rogue Trooper—and the Judge Dredd audio dramas *Dreddline*, *Jihad*, *Grud is Dead*, *Blood Will Tell* and *Double Zero*.

Find him online at www.jswallow.com or on Twitter at @jmswallow.

John Ware was runner-up in a competition to be published in the *Judge Dredd Megazine* with his story 'Comportment,' after Robert Murphy's 'Judgement Call.'

Alec Worley is an award-lacking author from South London. He writes comics, prose and audio dramas with swords, fangs and lasers in them. He's probably best known for his work on *2000 AD* (*Judge Anderson* and *Durham Red*) and Games Workshop's *Warhammer* universes. He doesn't own a cat and he's not on Twitter, but you can go have a poke around on his website: alecworley.com.

COPYRIGHT

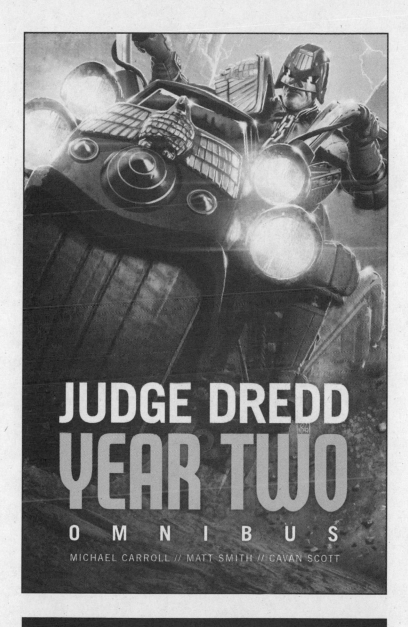

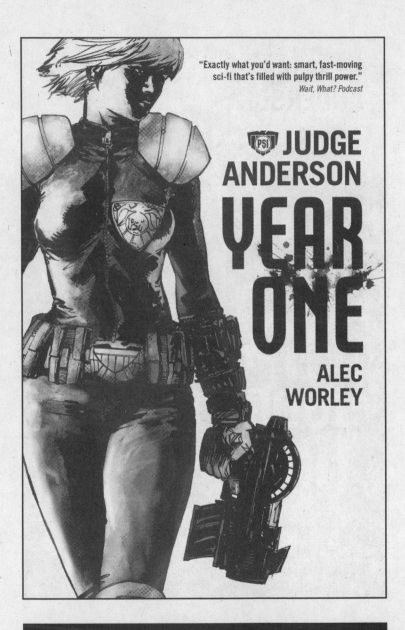

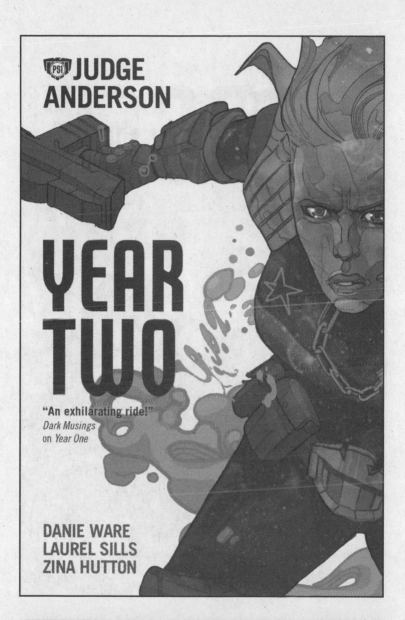

THE GENESIS OF THE WORLD OF JUDGE DREDD®

JUDGES

VOLUME ONE

THE AVALANCHE • LONE WOLF
WHEN THE LIGHT LAY STILL

MICHAEL CARROLL • CHARLES J ESKEW • GEORGE MANN
EDITED BY MICHAEL CARROLL

THE GENESIS OF THE WORLD OF JUDGE DREDD®

JUDGES

VOLUME TWO

GOLGOTHA • PSYCHE • THE PATRIOTS

MICHAEL CARROLL • MAURA MCHUGH • JOSEPH ELLIOTT-COLEMAN

EDITED BY MICHAEL CARROLL

WWW.ABADDONBOOKS.COM

Follow us on Twitter! www.twitter.com/rebellionpub

THE FALL OF
DEADWORLD
O M N I B U S

MATTHEW SMITH

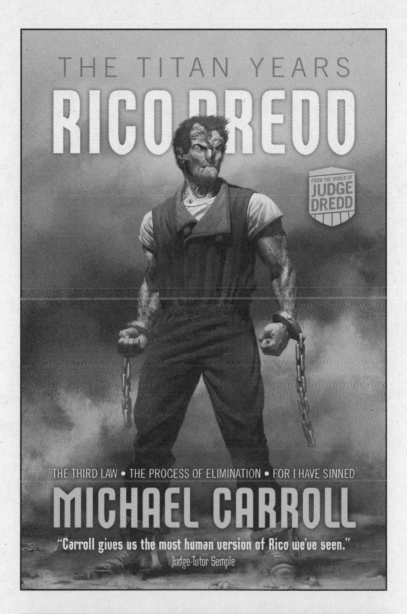